# INFESTATION

Insect shapes. Millions of them . . . cascading down off the walls of the burned-out cavern, spilling out into the open air, dropping to the ground and surging forward.

She couldn't move.

This was the worst part of the nightmare, the feeling of unendurable helplessness as those glittering little monsters poured across the rubble toward her. Her last optical image before the camera was wrenched apart by bright-alloyed jaws was of the Great Annihilator hanging low above the fire-swept horizon.

Then she felt them opening up the body of her strider, breaking it apart with the ugly sound of shredding metal.

*Other AvoNova Books in*
*the* **WARSTRIDER** *Series by*
*William H. Keith, Jr.*

WARSTRIDER
WARSTRIDER: JACKERS
WARSTRIDER: NETLINK
WARSTRIDER: REBELLION
WARSTRIDER: SYMBIONTS

# WARSTRIDER

## BATTLEMIND

### WILLIAM H. KEITH, JR.

AVON BOOKS • NEW YORK

WARSTRIDER: BATTLEMIND is an original publication of Avon Books. This work has never before appeared in book form. This work is a novel. Any similarity to actual persons or events is purely coincidental.

AVON BOOKS
A division of
The Hearst Corporation
1350 Avenue of the Americas
New York, New York 10019

Copyright © 1996 by William H. Keith, Jr.
Cover art by Dorian Vallejo
Published by arrangement with the author
Library of Congress Catalog Card Number: 96-96031
ISBN: 0-380-77969-2

First AvoNova Printing: August 1996

AVONOVA TRADEMARK REG. U.S. PAT. OFF. AND IN OTHER COUNTRIES, MARCA REGISTRADA, HECHO EN U.S.A.

Printed in the U.S.A.

RA  10  9  8  7  6  5  4  3  2  1

# Prologue

The associative known as Sholai was the first to notice the infalling Web.

One moment, there was only empty space, ablaze with thick-scattered stars and the hazy light-river of the Great Circle, with Tovan and Doval agleam like bright, close-set eyes, with Lakah'vnyu showing a slender crescent embracing the night glow of the vast Gr'tak cities. The next moment *it* was there, dropping out of nothingness, a slim, egg-smooth complexity of organic forms, colored an impenetrable and light-drinking black.

Sholai, for this cycle at least, was nine-in-one, two greaters, three lessers, two receivers, one deeper, and an artificial, the union of nine giving its associative a shared intelligence level of well over two thousand. It was currently patrolling a sector of space along the outskirts of the Doval–Tovan system's primary ice belt, maintaining the old watch for comets or asteroids perturbed by the system's dim, distant third member, bodies of a type that more than once in the Associative's long, difficult history had bombarded the homeworld of Lakah'vnyu, in many cases wiping it nearly clean of life, in other, more recent catastrophes causing damage enough to blast newly risen civilizations back into unjoined barbarism. This was why Sholai's motion detectors were set at full spread and receptivity, watching, waiting for anything on an orbital path that might eventually pose a threat to the Family.

Indeed, the ancient threat posed by the system's numerous cometfalls was the primary driving force that had taken the Family into space in the first place, a step that had led, after

1

another thousand circuits of Lakah'vnyu about Doval–Tovan, to the stars. Since the Gr'tak had finally achieved the age-old dream of spaceflight three hundred generations before, civilization had not fallen once, and all within the multiple collectives felt more secure knowing that even if a ten-kilometer chunk of ice did make it past Sholai and its share-companions, the Family was now firmly grounded not in one coastal swamp, but in a thousand.

The Family would survive. . . .

The target Sholai was tracking now was disturbing, however. It was certain that the object had not been there a moment before . . . and its surface was reflecting radar and laser energies in such a way as to suggest a smooth and sculpted outer surface, like polished ice, rather than the broken and rubble-strewn surface of a typical comet. The target was almost certainly artificial.

In size, the thing rivaled the largest of the Gr'tak space colonies, nearly eight *eli* long and massing well over three million *g'shah*. Something that large should have registered on Sholai's instrumentation long before it had actually noted the thing's presence, no matter how black it was. As Sholai considered this paradox, it arrived at the only conclusion possible, that the thing really had appeared out of nowhere . . . or, rather, that it had appeared out of someplace other than the normal continuum of time and three-dimensional space.

Sholai's people had never developed a means of traveling faster than the speed of light—a velocity that appeared to be an absolute limiting factor in space travel. The fact that voyages to the stars required centuries at half of that speed, however, meant little to a species possessing immortality.

The Lakah'vnyud Cooperative of Sciences had long speculated about the possibility of circumventing the speed of light. Neither Sholai nor any of the associatives its individuals maintained membership in had ever explored the Science Cooperative's discussions, but it was aware that the concept was at least theoretically possible . . . as it was aware of the theoretical possibility that there were other intelligences elsewhere in the universe. Sholai's artificial engaged the library memory. Columns of text scrolled down the display screen in the pitch-verbalization script of the Family's principal scientific language.

No . . . this object, whatever it was, was like nothing ever encountered or manufactured by the Family. Sholai had its artificial transmit a full report on everything noted so far. At this distance from Lakah'vnyu, the signal would take two hours to get there.

The object, meanwhile, was doing a most uncometlike thing. It was accelerating, *hard*, boosting at an incredible three hundred gravities toward the inner system. Sholai fired its thrusters, seeking to bring its ship into an intercept orbit, but in seconds the stranger had passed sunward of it, still accelerating, moving too fast now to catch.

Still transmitting, Sholai turned its ship and decelerated to kill its momentum and drop it into a sunward vector, trying to follow the stranger anyway. The alien spacecraft— that *had* to be what it was—had passed twelve thousand *eli* distant, yet the magnetic fields that seemed to be a by-product of its propulsion system had registered hundreds of *gan*. And now, something strange was happening to the alien ship. . . .

# Chapter 1

*Humankind has suffered a long and sometimes humiliating chain of displacements throughout the course of history. It is, perhaps, to his credit that he has continued pressing out, seeking to explore the universe about him, despite these repeated blows to his pride. In the sixteenth century, the Copernican Revolution started things rolling with the demonstration that Earth was not the center of the universe. In the early twentieth century, Shapley showed that Earth's solar system was not even located—as had been assumed from the more or less even distribution of the Milky Way across the sky—at the center of the Galaxy, but was instead positioned off in the suburbs, some 25,000 light years from the core.*

*Contact with non-human intelligences—the Naga, in particular, in their original, if mistakenly presumed, guise as "xenophobes" bent on destroying Man— completed the toppling of humanity from its pedestal of arrogance. There were creatures—things—abroad in this our Galaxy capable of eradicating Mankind completely . . . and of not even being aware that they had done so.*

—*The Human Perspective*
PROFESSOR DWIGHT EVERETT MARTIN
C.E. 2566

The Great Annihilator dominated a sky crowded with suns and light. It hung suspended within the cavern of stars and thronging nebulae, an immense, ragged-rimmed pancake of incandescent gas, a tight-packed spiral of star stuff grinding into ultimate and utter destruction as it whirled in toward the intensely hot, dazzling core of light at the center.

*It doesn't* look *black*, Captain Kara Hagan thought with a wry flash of irreverence. But, of course, the black hole itself, squirreled away at the center of that sweeping, in-spiraling accretion disk, was invisible at this distance of some hundreds of light years, lost in the glare spilling from the annihilation of suns. So vast was the scale of that accretion disk that its outer arms appeared motionless; and even toward the center, where friction and radiation drove the temperature of the in-falling mass into blue-white fury more dazzling than a lightning stroke, Kara could only just make out the lazy drift of vast clots of gas and dust and starcore debris. Like searchlights, actinic, blue-white beams cast ghostly pillars of hazy radiance light years out from the black hole's poles. The energies represented by those ghostly beams, Kara knew, were awesome. An analysis of their light would indicate the unmistakable 511-keV signature of positronic annihilation, the telltale gamma-ray deathscream of anti-electrons shrieking into oblivion as they plowed through an electron sea.

Elsewhere, Heaven was cold, unwinking flame. Stars thronged in unnumbered hosts across a vast and gently curving wall shot through with twisted filaments of gas and knotted, tangled nebulae—a vast cavern walled with stars and ringed by multihued clouds of molecular gas. Within, space itself seemed to glow with the harsh illumination of ionizing radiations that would have reduced any unprotected and merely human body to a charred cinder in the blink of an eye. Kara, however, was well protected at the moment, her body the egg-smooth, night-black ovoid of one of the new Naga-grown warstriders in its space-traversing mode, hurtling through the void at the Galactic center.

*It would be so easy to lose all sense of scale here*, she thought. Galactic surveys made from afar indicated that this cavern at the Galaxy's heart measured a thousand light years across . . . but there was no way the human eye or mind could comprehend such distances. That wall of glowing suns, that band of red and blue and silver-tinged nebulae could be a few kilometers distant, so far as her senses were concerned.

There were times when human senses, even augmented by sophisticated electronics and bioprostheses, were laughably inadequate.

She couldn't see them, but scattered out to either side across a crescent five hundred kilometers across, forty-seven other Mark XC Black Falcon warstriders were pacing her, matched perfectly to her course and speed. Designated as First Company, the Black Phantoms, of the First Battalion, First Confederation Rangers, they were organized into four squadrons of twelve, the first under Kara's direct command, the other three commanded by lieutenants. Deployed as a reconnaissance patrol, they were moving swiftly and in near-invisible stealth, the nanotechnic outer layers of their hulls set to absorb every photon of radiation, whether at radio, radar, visible light, or gamma-ray wavelengths, rather than allowing even a flicker of reflection to give them away. Commo chatter had been subdued since they'd entered this region, not so much from fear of the enemy overhearing—

the new commo modes made eavesdropping impossible—as because of the oppressive scale of the space they were traversing.

"*My God in heaven*," she heard someone say over the tactical link. Her comm control program identified the speaker as Sergeant Deke Kemperer, in Second Squadron.

"I'm registering enough rads out there to fry us all in a microsec or two," Warstrider Valda Harrison added. "I hope to hell these magshields hold. . . ."

"Zero out that talk," Kara said, a little more harshly than she intended. In the midst of such splendor, such immensity, it would be easy to become overawed and lose any sense of purpose or focus. "Let's keep our minds on the job."

"It's not like the machine bastards can hear us," Lieutenant Pellam Hochstader said. The tall, bearded lieutenant was Second Squadron's commander. "We *do* have secure commo freaks here."

"I wonder what this empty part was like," Third Squadron's Lieutenant Ran Ferris added thoughtfully, "when it was all full of stars?"

"Poetry later, Ran," she said, but she knew he'd caught the warmth in her mental voice. "Right now, we're here to kill things."

"If we can find the gokkers," Kemperer added.

The immediate absence of any opposition added to the void's oppressiveness . . . and the haunting mystery that permeated it. The emptiness was explained easily enough, of course. There were multiple black holes here at the Galaxy's center, burrowed away at the very center of the thronging beeswarm of stars that formed the core of the Milky Way. Hanging in the far distance, some three hundred light years away, was the object long known to Earth-based astronomers as Sagittarius West, centered on the fierce and tiny pinprick of Sagittarius West*, the precise gravitational center of the Galaxy's great spiral, a compact accumulation of some millions of solar masses at the heart of a sweeping spiral of violently heated gas. Much closer at hand, a few light days away at most, was a smaller but stranger denizen of the zoo of strange objects at the Galactic Core, the fifteen-solar-mass black hole known since the late twentieth century as the Great Annihilator. Those two massive and enigmatic objects, Sag West* and the Annihilator, had long before swept this innermost core of the Galaxy's central bulge clean of most stars and gas.

The cavern was not quite empty, however. Periodically—every ten million years or so—in-falls of gas from the molecular cloud ringing the Core spiraled in to the cavern's heart and coalesced in a dazzling spray of new star formation, a short-lived starburst, relatively speaking, as the infant stars were then drawn on to fiery and tortured deaths in one or another of the Core singularities. Evidence of past starburst periods was still visible as ghost remnants of exploded stars, and by the handful of thinly scattered survivors of the hungry singularities isolated by distance.

Here, too, were worlds, those clots and crumbs of matter at the Galactic Core too small to accumulate mass enough for a star. Some were gas giants, others rocky or icy bodies ranging from earth-sized worlds down to sand and gravel, all barren and radiation-seared. Many had been transformed into cometlike objects with long, silvery tails as the radiations of this place blasted atmosphere or subliming water vapor into space.

And there were worlds—or things—stranger still: a neutron star flung from the Core eons past at incredible speed, made visible by its wake through the dense plasma of the Core, a tail one hundred light years long; great arcs of plasma that looped and plunged through heaven, some reaching thousands of light years out beyond the Galactic poles and delineating the Galaxy's magnetic fields of force; the tattered remnants of ancient explosions that must have given the entire Galaxy a quasar's brilliance.

Against so vast and yawning a chasm, against such arresting cosmic splendor, it seemed incredible that Intelligence could manifest itself in any visible way. Even on worlds like Earth, where the megopoli sprawled inland from the coasts for hundreds of kilometers and the sky-els stretched from the equator far into space, it was possible to look down from orbit and be hard-pressed to see any sign that Man had left his mark on the face of the planet at all. Here, the scale was vaster by many orders of magnitude, and yet Kara could see definite hints of . . . *order* . . . and of artifacts vast on a superhuman scale. Most of the stars remaining within the Core cavern were stragglers, randomly adrift, and yet *some* . . .

Kara, frankly, was having trouble ordering and processing all that she was seeing. The scale of this place, immense beyond human comprehension, had left her a little dazed and feeling very small. The very large in the natural order of things she could accept, even appreciate, but the artificial nature of some of what she was seeing was stunning, even crippling when it was suddenly revealed to any mind programmed through human scales and values.

With an effort of will, through the link established by her personal Naga fragment, she could shift her center of awareness to any surface of the vehicle or receive visual input from a full three-sixty in three dimensions. Looking astern, she could see the slender, gleaming silver thread of the Gate the reconnaissance force had just come through. As straight as a laser beam, it stretched like a razor's slash across more than one thousand kilometers, a two-kilometer-thick cylinder containing the mass of hundreds of suns, packed to densities approaching those of a neutron star, then set to rotating about its long axis at relativistic speeds. The process warped the spacetime matrix in its vicinity, opening countless hyperdimensional pathways. Kara and the others of the Phantoms had followed one of those paths to reach this place, located some twenty-five thousand light years from the worlds known to Man. The largest structures devised by human engineering were the sky-els that connected the surfaces of most human-inhabited planets with their synchorbitals, but the tallest of those, though considerably longer than the Stargate, were insubstantial wisps of gossamer in comparison to that space-rending colossus.

Yet even the Stargate paled by comparison with the scale of some of the engineering evident in this alien place. Here, entire stars were being moved, herded from place to place like immense, grazing animals, the process evident in their regimentation, in the geometrical perfection of their alignments with one another. She could see stars arrayed in circles, in polygons, in precisely ordered clusters, as though they'd been penned awaiting some deferred judgment.

And the Great Annihilator—with only a minute fraction of the mass of the black hole at True Center, yet the focus of inconceivable and inexplicable energies and phenomena—was itself ringed by an artificial construct, a structure of some kind just barely glimpsed at this distance, a ring of pinpoint lights and nearly indiscernible supporting structures in a rigid and geometrical array.

Strangest was one particular string of stars describing a great, gently arcing curve reminiscent of the twist in the shell of a nautilus or the curve of a galaxy's spiral arms. Kara counted forty-three stars in that one line, each precisely and evenly spaced from its neighbors, the whole vast array stretched across the sky from the zenith and terminating at the radiant core of the Great Annihilator. Those few close enough to Kara's location to show a tiny disk revealed, on optical magnification, that one side had been induced to flare with the blue-white intensity of a nova, while the opposite hemisphere seemed darkened and blotched by comparison. As nearly as she could tell from this distance, someone, some*thing* had somehow manipulated those stars, exciting them to blow off vast and continuous flares on only one side—in effect transforming them into titanic guided missiles moving ponderously and unstoppably through space. And as for their destination . . .

Kara had the distinct and thoroughly uncomfortable feeling that the Web intelligence was deliberately guiding those stars, nudging them one by one and in perfectly regimented order into the maw of the Great Annihilator. It was chilling. The builders of this place, the machine intelligence known to humanity only as the Web, had built a ring around one of the black holes at the Galaxy's heart and now were steadily feeding it suns.

*My God*, she thought, watching through full-extended sensors. *These things toss stars around the way we would throw a ball. Star miners, star drivers, star destroyers . . . and we're challenging them for control of the Galaxy. . . .*

So immense were the energies marshaled there that it was hard to tell what was the result of intelligent planning, and what might be the workings of natural forces, of physics on a galactic scale. Those vast arcs of plasma showed a regularity that might well suggest deliberate manipulation . . . or simply reflect the order stamped by intense magnetic fields on clouds of charged particles.

The Web, it was now known, was an extremely old machine civilization, one that presumably had arisen as the product of organic intelligence in the very dawn of the Galaxy's existence, though whether as tools of that intelligence or as the next step in its evolution was still unknown. For some billions of years, the machines, a lifeform of their own now in every way that mattered, had been quietly building here at the heart of the Galaxy, wielding forces that humanity could only wonder at. The scope of their engineering prowess was staggering.

Perhaps most unsettling of all was the knowledge of the sheer, inhuman *patience* the Web must possess. It was using gravity and the ability to transform stars into rocket-powered projectiles to herd dozens of suns across hundreds of light years—a process that must have taken untold millennia to begin with and would take many more to complete. The scale of what Kara was seeing here, the ring around the Annihilator's accretion disk, the mass of the rotating Stargate, all spoke of a civilization that thought in terms of millions of years, of eons rather than of decades.

What kind of mind could think in such terms?

And how could it be outthought and defeated?

Kara was still trying to assimilate, to comprehend what that kind of power meant. There was so much Man yet had to learn about the Web and about what the Web was trying to accomplish, both here at the Galactic Core and beyond, in the quieter backwaters of the Galaxy's far-flung spiral arms. It was possible, though not certain yet, that the Web had created the huge spinning constructs called the Stargates. Two were known, the first locked between the mutually orbiting white dwarfs that were all that remained of the star called Nova Aquila, a second here at the Galactic Core.

And there were hints of others, she knew, scattered across the length and breadth of the entire Galaxy.

*But that's Daren's worry,* she thought, thinking briefly of her half-brother back at Nova Aquila. *And Dev's. . . .*

The thought of Devis Cameron, of what he had become,

sent a shudder through her consciousness. He, of all humanity, had been the first to see this place . . . in a way. She'd studied the records returned to human space by the probe he'd sent through the Nova Aquila Gate. But it was so hard to think of him as . . . *human.* She swiftly turned her thoughts to more immediate matters.

The other warstriders continued their high-velocity sprint across the void, though there was no way to tell by looking at the stars or nebulae about them that they were moving at all. An hour ago, they'd entered a carefully mapped and plotted hyperdimensional pathway opening close by the blurred silver surface of the Nova Aquila Stargate; a timeless instant later, they'd emerged here, hurtling at high speed into the void of the Core. Though they possessed plasma thrusters for maneuvering, their primary drives grasped local magnetic fields, intensifying them, manipulating them to provide both velocity and changes in course.

A world expanded from pinpoint to dusky sphere ahead. It was a barren and radiation-scorched place, utterly and forever lifeless—at least insofar as life could be defined as collections of organic chemicals. From space, the surface appeared to be a mottled patchwork of black rock and pale white-and-tan salts, its face peppered with craters and slashed time and time again by literally world-wracking collisions. As Kara drew closer, it became apparent that here, too, the machine rulers of this realm had stamped their imprint in the lifeless chaos of rock and desert. The surveys of this place, based on data gleaned by robotic probes, had designated the world as Core D9837.

She hit the first traces of air, a thin haze of vapor about the burned-over world. There was scant atmosphere here—mostly carbon dioxide and a scattering of other heavy gases—but her entry speed was so high that her strider struck flame as it stooped toward the world, scratching a white contrail across its deep blue-violet, light-tortured sky.

To left and right, above and below, the other striders of the reconnaissance company hit atmosphere as well, but Kara was scarcely aware of them as she rode her strider down the long, flaming shaft of incandescence, sensing through her biolink with the machine's AI the searing buffeting she was taking during the approach. Fire stood frozen in the sky overhead, looped in titanic streamers, arcs, delicate filigree traceries of energy, and in the spiraled magnificence of the Great Annihilator. Below, the face of a planet nearly as large as New America or Earth lay in rad-seared desolation, its surface curiously worked and reworked by processes unimaginable into vast, sprawling, and subtly alien geometries, shapes worked out in near–right angles, glowing strips of light, and convoluted mechanisms arranged in patterns not easily retained by merely human memory.

The contrails of her comrades appeared, glowing gently, though the light here was uncertain. Core D9837 orbited no sun but was an orphan, a mote adrift with other crumbs left over from the rubble of an extravagantly wasteful Creation. The only light was the soft and ruddy glow from the background stars, highlighted here and there by the sharper brilliance of blue-white flares or hotter suns, or by the softer arc-light glow of the Annihilator's polar jets.

The other forty-seven warstriders of the Phantoms rode their own craft toward landing, burning off excess speed in glowing friction with the atmosphere. Operating now strictly according to programmed instructions loaded into their striders' AIs, the warcraft descended in gradually flattening trajectories, steering by powerful magnetic fields interacting with the magnetic fields of this world and this alien, flame-ridden sky. Part of their mission was survey mapping; strider AIs processed streams of data as they overflew a strangely shaped and ordered topology, a gray terrain that should have consisted of stark, raw deserts, barren canyons, heat-weathered mesas—and probably once had been just that—but which at some point in the remote past had been extensively reworked.

It almost looked as though some child giant had used this world as clay, sculpting bizarrely twisted and alien forms from naked rock and leaving them to bake beneath that searing sky. Kara could see walls, towers, domes, and less readily namable structures, linked together by a subtle architecture that obeyed no human laws of perspective or design. Towers speared the heavens, ebon-black or mercury-silver in color, with angles oddly distorted from geometries used by Man. A deep, convoluted, and black-shadowed canyon reaching for fully a thousand kilometers across the planet's face had been turned into an elaborate trench lined with machine hardware, spanned by glittering bridges and floored by forests of antennae and mechanisms of unknown and unknowable purpose.

At an altitude of less than a kilometer, Kara pulled her nose up, spilling energy freely in a burst of high-intensity magnetics, supplementing her rugged deceleration with the whining shriek of plasma jets. The new setup and link with the Mark XC striders permitted accelerations and decelerations unheard of in human-occupied flyers, with the thrust limited only by the tolerances of the machine's drives and hull strength, though the visual cues unfolding on the viewscreen in her head took some real getting used to.

So far, there'd been no response from the defenders of this alien place. Past the trench now, still descending, she led her company toward the landing site chosen from space just moments ago, an open patch of gray plain partly surrounded by spiked, bristling towers each half a kilometer tall or more. Surface-penetrating radar and IR traces gave indications of a labyrinthine tangle of structures hidden beneath the surface.

"There's the LZ, gang," she called over the tactical frequency. "Let's take 'em on in."

"Roger that, boss," Lieutenant Hochstader replied. "Looks like we caught the gokkers napping."

"Don't count on that, Lieutenant," she replied. "They know we're here."

"I wonder," Warstrider Miles Pritchard said. "I get the feeling that maybe they know, but they just don't *care*."

That was a frightening thought . . . beings so advanced, or so different, that human beings had little or no impact on their plans. But then, Core D9837 seemed to be a very minor part of their operation in this place, a debris pile with no significance to their vaster strategies and goals.

"Maybe they don't care," Sergeant Willis Daniels, her top sergeant, added. "*Yet*."

"Well, we can damn well give them something to care about, Will," Kara said. Extending her craft's flight surfaces, she flared out above the selected landing zone, her warstrider's outer hull, a Naga-grown composite, changing both shape and texture as surface-mobile modules unfolded.

Normally in a landing op like this one, she would have loosed clouds of nano converters to change the soil to a charged surface, but the ground here already bore current associated with the surrounding alien structures. Magnetics engaged, slowing Kara's strider to a gentle hover meters above the ground. Legs extended, insectlike, black, gleaming, and chitinous, with tools and sensors extruding to taste the alien air. Carefully, she pivoted through a complete three-sixty, scanning for some response from the foe.

The scout force had not known what to expect on this run; that was one reason the operation, code-named Core Peek, had been organized. So far, humans had managed to snatch only the briefest and most unsatisfactory of glimpses of Web activities at the Galactic Core. Only one manned vessel had ever come through the Nova Aquila Gate to this place, and that had been destroyed seconds after its arrival. Many succeeding attempts had been made by sophisticated robot probes, all with Naga cores deliberately downloaded with misleading information, in the hope that Web intelligence about the location of Humanity's worlds could be confused. Operation Shell Game, that effort had been named; presumably, it had worked, since the Web had not launched another effort against the worlds of the Shichiju in the past two years.

But at the same time, Humanity had learned little about the Web. Some of those probes had been spotted and destroyed instantly, while others had survived for a long time before being detected and hunted down. The planners of this mission had suspected that Model XC striders, slipping through the Gate at high speed and with full stealth nanoflage engaged, might get all the way to Core D9837 without being spotted. Their entry into atmosphere, however, could not have gone unnoticed. Webbers were known to see into the infrared.

Her view of her surroundings, relayed through her strider's external sensors and unfolding directly in her mind, was overlaid by smaller windows, one showing systems status displays, another showing a map of her surroundings, complete with the blue-pinpointed positions of her comrades and the locations of unknowns—potential enemies—in red. And there *were* unknowns out there, hundreds of them, with more appearing on her screen every moment. The shadows beyond the unit's LZ literally crawled with . . . *things*, though at this range all that could be said about them was that they were metallic, that they possessed powerful, self-contained magnetic fields, and that they were moving.

They were, in fact, beginning to converge on the landing force.

"On alert, people," she snapped. "We've got company!"

"I've got bogies at three-five," Daniels called. "Comin' in fast! Don't know what they are. I can't get a hard fix and I've never seen—"

And then the machine army struck.

# Chapter 2

*The DalRiss taught us that intelligence could evolve in surprising ways, yet remain fundamentally the same as that possessed by humans. They were alien, but we could, at the very least, understand their point of view.*

*The Naga taught us that it was possible to look at the universe in ways fundamentally different from the typical human worldview. They were difficult to understand but ultimately comprehensible, once we grasped the alien nature of their perceptions.*

*The Web taught us to redefine the very nature of our understanding of what intelligence is.*

—*Report given before the*
*Imperial Xenosophontology Institute,*
*Kyoto, Nihon*
Dr. Daren Cameron
C.E. 2572

"Hit them!" Kara yelled over the tactical commo link. "*Hit them!*"

She triggered a bolt of blue-white lightning, sending the charge lancing across a kilometer of open ground and into a close-packed cluster of fast-moving, robotic shapes. Chunks of metal flew, spinning lazily. Other warstriders joined in as the Phantoms dropped into a broad, double circle nearly ten kilometers across, each member of the recon force several hundred meters from his or her neighbor, weapons and sensors facing outward. Lightnings flared around the circle, punctuated by the shrill hiss and thunder of volleyed rockets. The attack was developing on all sides with a speed that Kara could scarcely credit.

"Overwatch," she called, opening the command frequency. "This is Spearpoint. Are you getting this?"

"Looking right over your shoulder, Captain," a woman's voice answered in her mind. "We've got a good feed on all of you. Give us ten minutes down there, if you can!"

"We'll try to last that long," Kara replied, the sarcasm giving an edge to her voice. A sudden rush developed on her front, and she swung her particle cannon to cover it, triggering a thundering barrage of manmade lightnings that illuminated the darkling surface of the world in savagely strobing, actinic flashes. Continuing to fire the CP gun, she flashed a mental command to her AI, unfolding the high-velocity rotary cannon from her flank and putting it into action with a buzzsaw shriek. Hypersonic slugs of depleted uranium shredded the hardest metals and composites, flinging metallic debris high into the sky.

As fast as she could smash them, though, more crowded in from behind. She had the impression that those underground tunnels must be pouring new machines onto the surface faster than the Phantoms could destroy them.

"There's too many of them," Hochstader warned. She could see him on the magnified image on her screen. His strider, opposite Kara's on the perimeter and ten kilometers away, was unfolding like a black-petaled flower, revealing the deadly armory encased within. "They'll overrun us in seconds!"

"Steady, Pel," she replied over their private channel. "Focus on the job."

They kept firing.

*Machines . . .*

The word was laughably inadequate. The devices gathering in the shadows of the eerie and nightmare-grown towers around them were mechanisms, yes, grown from metal or plastic or polymer-ceramic composites, but the sheer diversity of shapes and sizes and obvious function defied any rational attempt to catalogue or identify. As the first of the Web devices sprinted toward the human line, her overwhelming impression was of a bizarre and wildly varied zoo of insects—glittering, faceted shapes with jointed bodies and spiky or whiplash antennae. Some bristled like porcupines, some were crisply angular, while others were smooth and naked as eggs. Most were small, some literally the size of insects, others the size of Kara's head, with a sprinkling of a few genuine monsters as big as her warstrider or bigger. Many had legs, ranging in number from two to uncountable ripplings on long, flat things like centipedes, but others levitated on powerful magnetic fields or flew by other means the human team could not identify.

So far, human military and sophontology experts alike had had no luck at all classifying the Web combat machines, or figuring out what they were after. Confederation military slang simply called them "kickers," after the Nihongo word *kikai*, "machine."

They seemed to use nanotechnology as did Man, literally growing individual components molecule by molecule. That gave them a high degree of flexibility in their design; a combat machine might fly in space or walk or slither along on glittering, metallic tentacles, or it might do all three . . . or it might change its own form in order to meet changes in its environment.

Warstrider technology, Kara reflected as she continued sniping at the lead elements of the Web assault before they could move in closer, had borrowed that philosophy from the Web, and from the Naga before them, with combat machines that could change shape and form, color and weaponry to meet changing battle conditions . . . but the Web machines were still the undisputed masters of that technique. Machines seemed purpose-grown within seconds of a perceived need; existing machines demonstrated a weirdly shifting polymorphism, as though they were able to somehow digest and regrow the substance of their bodies into new shapes on the spot.

Some of those shapes were bizarre almost beyond belief. To her right, what looked like a small sea of quicksilver was flowing over the uneven ground toward the company's perimeter. It looked like an animated puddle of liquid mercury, its surface a metallic silver and very bright, the whole rippling along the ground in a huge, fast-spreading sheet. At first, she wasn't even sure it represented a threat. It looked odd, certainly, but there were no weapons, no indication that the thing was attacking.

Then, with devastating suddenness, the pool of quicksilver exploded in great filaments of gleaming metal, rising up high into the air, then arcing down. Warstriders Kearny and Pritchard were caught in the net flung across their machines. Both opened fire, lasers and particle beams sliding across and through the apparently liquid but coherent metal in explosive puffs of vapor . . . but the liquid reformed and scattered more looping arcs. Where it touched the Naga-hulls of the warstriders, hull metal detonated in fiery bursts and fuming clouds of oily black smoke, the deadly touch dissolving ceramplast and nanoflage surfacing in white flame.

Kara's sensors were picking up powerful, shifting magnetic fields ahead, the fields animating the liquid metal. Blue lightning played across the surface, and then a bolt of blue-white fire lanced through the protesting atmosphere, striking Kearny's strider with a devastating concussion and a splatter of melted hull metal. Kara pivoted her own machine to the right, opening fire with every weapon in her strider's arsenal, slamming a shrieking swarm of M-310 missiles into the thickest part of the quicksilver pool, stabbing and slashing with lasers, particle beams, and rapid-fire cannon. Explosions ripped through the liquid metal, scattering it in gleaming splatters. Kearny's strider was down, unmoving; Kara's cockpit readout indicated null function, systems down. Pritchard's strider was still fighting, some of its weapons obviously knocked off-line, but the lasers and one rapid-fire cannon still in action, blazing away as the tentacles of silver lashed and sparked in dazzling displays of energy.

Kearny was gone . . . and Dandridge and Fontaine as well, their striders no longer registering as active on her tactical display. More kickers were appearing on her tactical display every second; the damned things appeared to be surging up from underground. Others were descending from space, drawn to this barren world from elsewhere within the Galactic Core.

"Let's tighten up the perimeter, people," she called. The circle was already shrinking though, as the remaining striders shifted position to better support one another. She could hear others in the company calling to one another over the tactical links.

*"They're almost to the perimeter over here! Someone give me a hand!"*

*"Jordy, watch it! On your right at zero-one-five!"*

*"I've got more on sector three."*

*"Kuso! They're coming up out of the ground!"*

*"This whole planet is some kind of goddamned factory!"*

*"Hold on, Cyn! I'm on it!"*

*"I'm hit! I'm hit! Kuso! There's too gokking many of them!"*

Kara's AI rasped warning . . . too late. Something struck her strider, a savage, jolting blow that gouged a kilogram or two of Naga-hull from her dorsal-left surface and left her hivel cannon a useless, partially disemboweled wreck. She didn't feel pain as such with the blow—the bioelectronic linkage between her brain and the strider's artificial intelligence was not designed to transmit pain—but the shock was jarring nonetheless, both physically and emotionally. It staggered her, rocking her back on legs and magnetics both. As warning lights cascaded across the viewscreen opened in her mind, she decided that the ability of individual Web machines to repair themselves would be pretty damned useful; her hivel cannon was dead, and with it three important sub-circuit networks in her fire control array. The Naga segments that composed part of her hull and working systems had a limited self-repair capability, including regrowing damaged electronic circuits, but this was beyond their scope.

More high-velocity missiles shrieked through the thin, hot atmosphere, glowing brightly with friction as they snapped overhead, but her AI had already noted that they would miss and did not alert her to the threat. She eased off on her magnetics and flexed her legs, gentling closer to the ground as she continued firing at the advancing enemy. With a thought, she unfolded her starboard-side missile launcher and loosed a hissing volley of M-310 missiles into the lightning-flecked gloom in the distance.

An instant later, a laser speared her, the five-megawatt beam sinking into the black heat sink of her external nano.

Five megawatts striking a target for one second yields the same energy as the detonation of a kilogram of TNT. Kara's external nano could handle about three quarters of that inflow, shunting it into her primary storage cells, but the rest had to go somewhere. The explosion was as thunderous, as concussive as the earlier slug strike had been, and she lost nearly one square meter of her nanoflage as her hull erupted in white-hot fury.

The Web machine that had fired at her was a hulking, black and brown monstrosity of ill-fitted angles, parts, and legs, only a little smaller than her warstrider, its hull built around the length of the weapon that appeared from its size to be its entire reason for existence. Less than a hundred meters away, it crouched, readying a second shot; Kara triggered a bolt from her CP cannon first and felt an intense and savage satisfaction as the blast carved a man-sized chunk of metal and ceramics off the enemy device and scattered it on the thin, hot winds as droplets of condensing vapor.

"Is this supposed to be proving something?" Sergeant Kemperer yelled. She glanced at the magnified image of his strider, off to her left. Part of his machine's hull was glowing dull red, and the surface had taken on a pocked appearance from multiple hits by high-velocity slugs and high-energy beams.

"Just keep taking them down, Deke," Lieutenant Hoch

stader told him. "Don't let them organize and don't let them break through the line, or we've had it." His voice sounded remarkably calm against the shriek and thunder of battle. Naga-grown symbiotic implants—like the cephlinks of decades before—conferred a kind of electronic telepathy on those who were jacked into the network, a communications channel secure from the thunder and crash outside the striders' black hulls.

Kara called up a long-range situation map, shrinking the ten-kilometer circle of the Phantoms to a tiny green oval, surrounded by a seething ocean of red. She'd hoped to identify some one arc of the defensive perimeter that was not under massive assault, allowing her to pull back striders from one area and plug them into another if things became desperate. There was no such arc, however. If she wanted to pick up reserves, she would have to do it by shrinking the perimeter, and the volume of firepower from the surrounding enemy forces was a good reason not to do that. If that incoming fire became any more concentrated than it already was, targeting a smaller area . . .

The Webbers, she noted, were showing nothing even remotely like combat tactics. The patterns on her display indicated something more akin to the blind, chemical reaction of antibodies to an invading bacterium. The more defenders the human force burned down, the more appeared behind the first ones to continue the assault.

Still, Kara had the impression that their attack, fierce and unrelenting as it was, was more for show than anything of substance. It might even be a diversion of a sort, an attempt at a primitive kind of combat tactics. As she fought, she could see a vast army of Web machines off on the horizon some fifteen kilometers away, building . . . *something*, a towering black metal something in the distance, as literally millions of individual, quasi-living parts leaped and skittered and flew and flowed into one another, their bodies dissolving, reforming themselves before her eyes.

It looked like a pyramid, growing higher moment by moment, five-sided on a pentagonal base, encased in something like translucent black plastic, though fire directed at it by her strider and those of her companions bounced and flared as harmlessly from that surface as might hurled rocks from a starship's hull.

"Pel?" she called. "This is Kara."

"Yeah, boss."

"Throw a high-mag scan on that pyramid coming up in my sector. What do you think?"

"It's big...."

"I can *see* that."

"Sorry. I couldn't resist."

She could feel the warmth of Hochstader's grin. He was a big, gentle, easygoing man, popular with his troops, and with a sharp tactical sense that Kara had come to rely on since he'd joined the Phantoms the year before. He possessed a quiet reserve that the most intense firefight couldn't penetrate.

"It looks like they're using their mutability against us," he continued, more seriously. "You see what they're doing under high mag?"

"Yeah. Looks like the little ones are melting together, or reorganizing themselves, somehow, to make the big one."

"What do you want to bet they've analyzed our firepower and energy output and are building one big combat machine that we can't scratch but could swat the lot of us like insects?"

"I'm not taking those odds. I think that's what it is ... a really big warstrider. Overwatch? Are you copying this?"

"Roger that, Spearpoint. And we concur with Lieutenant Hochstader's analysis. Are you ready to pull out?"

She hesitated, weighing her options. They couldn't stay here much longer.

"Overwatch, we still don't have what we came for. We want to shove these things hard enough to find out what makes them break, and so far they've been doing all the shoving. Give us another couple of minutes."

"Copy that. We'll be standing by, Spearpoint, if you want to abort."

"Rog."

The pyramid was moving forward now, its form apparently stabilized. Kara stroked the thing at radar wavelengths, measuring. Nearly half a kilometer high, it appeared to be levitating on tightly reined-in magnetic fields stronger than those found flickering at the heart of a sun. Its base, all but lost in deep shadow, was not flat but appeared to bulge downward, again in a five-sided figure, making the object an immense and lopsided decahedron, its glossy surface mostly black but picked out here and there with pale yellow bands and surfaces. The surfaces appeared smooth; she saw nothing like antennae or weapons marring those vast expanses . . . nor was there any indication that it was a command unit of some kind.

It came closer, bulking higher until it blotted out most of the ragged spiral of the Great Annihilator high in the sky. Lightning played about the base; one bolt reached out and connected with Warstrider Harrison's damaged Falcon, the play of energy briefly illuminating the entire battlefield with the radiance of many suns. By this time, all of the surviving warstriders were firing at the advancing, floating mountain but with no success that Kara could detect. So far as she could tell, volley upon volley of missiles, of laser beams, of charged particle bolts, of hard-driven streams of high-velocity deplur rounds could not even scratch that terrifying and apocalyptic vision of destruction.

Lightning flared once more from the pyramid's base. Excess charge bled through air and seared the ground beneath; the primary beam shrilled thunder as it passed low above Kara's warstrider, and for a horrifying moment she thought her machine had been hit . . . but the bolt passed on across the perimeter and briefly caressed Miles Pritchard's machine.

She could hear him screaming as his machine exploded in blue flame and molten Naga-matrix.

"Pritch!"

The screaming cut off sharply as the link failed. With a jolt, Kara realized that fully half of the recon company's warstriders were down, unresponsive . . . and the smaller Web machines were spilling into the perimeter now through gaping holes in the defensive line.

Not much time left. Maybe, though, they could still test the Web's resilience. "Heads up, everybody!" she called over the general channel. "I'm taking that gokker with a Heller!"

"Negative on that, Spearpoint," Overwatch called. "You're too close—"

"Gok that," Kara snapped. "If it's a choice between letting that monster step on me, and taking a bite out of him as I go down, then it's chow time!"

She was initiating the launch sequence as she spoke, keying in mental code phrases that unlocked her Falcon's two CTN-20 Hellbrand missiles. Her dorsal surface split in two, the launcher unfolding as protective panels blossomed open. Another command overrode the fail-safe mechanism; each Hellbrand carried a seven-kiloton tactical nuclear warhead, pocket microyield thermonukes with a blast radius of at least ten kilometers, and they were programmed not to detonate within fifteen kilometers of their launch point. Kara, however, was in no mood to be fussily particular.

"Nuke!" she yelled, with much the same fervor of a golfer shouting "fore." She gave the mental launch command, and the CTN-20 *whooshed* from its half-buried launch tube, yellow flame stabbing from its aft venturi, trailing white smoke as it arced toward the huge target just a few kilometers away. A heartbeat later, she sent the second missile arrowing after the first.

The first missile was swatted down by a bolt of lightning, but the range was so close that the pyramid didn't have time to shift aim to the second high-velocity target. It streaked in low, striking the pyramid just beneath its base.

An intense, dazzling, blinding pinpoint of radiance expanded in an instant to engulf the pyramid; seconds later, the sound hit, and with it the shock wave of a blast equivalent to seven thousand tons of conventional high explosives.

"Hunker down, everyone!" Kara yelled into the inferno, but it was uncertain whether anyone even heard her. The roar, deafening, cataclysmic, blotted out everything else. The light, so dazzling at first, turned dark as a hot wind shrieked inward toward the sudden vacuum that marked ground zero, swirling dust and smoke and furiously burning gasses in and up and out, the whole rising in a filthy gray pillar of boiling ash.

Kara could no longer see the cloud. That flash had burned out most of her optical sensors, and the searing wind lashing across her warstrider now kept her plastered against the heaving, buckling ground. She felt the wind stripping the last of her nanoflage from her hull. Then two of her four legs were ripped away, and her magnetics lost their grip on the magfield within the alien world's surface. It was like being caught in a hurricane, and as the roar peaked in a thunderous crescendo, her Falcon was smashed back across the ground.

There'd been little hope for any of the human-jacked striders on the surface of Core D9837. That had been known from the beginning, the results already factored into the plan of battle. They were here to get information, data on the Web that was already being relayed back to intelligence personnel waiting with the Unified Fleet on the other side of the Nova Aquila Stargate.

Kara disliked suicide missions as a matter of principle, but this was one she'd been forced to accept. The human alliance needed this data, and this was the only way of obtaining it.

She surveyed the almost solid block of red warning discretes illuminating the lower right corner of her visual display. Her Falcon was very nearly dead, its AI partly burned out, her cerebral link with its electronics faltering.

Maybe . . . maybe the best thing to do now would be to simply switch off.

# Chapter 3

*What is life? The old standby definitions, handed
down from the dawn of modern biology, can no longer
be said to provide even an approximately correct or
comprehensive answer. Life metabolizes, taking in fuel
and giving off waste while producing energy. The
same can be said of fire. Life seeks to reproduce itself.
Again, fire spreads . . . and the DNA and RNA molecules that are the basis for terrestrial life replicate as
a part of life's dance, without themselves being life.*

*Perhaps most disturbing to those seeking to define
life is the evidence presented by such nonhuman species as the Web, creatures that undoubtedly perform
all of the functions generally associated with life processes, including reshaping their environment, meta-
bolizing raw materials, eliminating waste products,
and reproducing themselves. The fact that all of these
functions are performed by machines assembled
through nanotechnic processes similar to those
evolved by human industry should not prejudice us to
the fact that the Web is alive.*

*It is simply a very different kind of life, one that we
still have trouble even beginning to understand.*

—*The Dance of Life*
Professor Ellery Hawkins
C.E. 2572

Kara wasn't ready to quit just yet, however. The magnetic
field embedded in the planet's surface was faltering, some

of its circuitry disrupted, perhaps, by the detonation of the nuke. She could barely edge along, the ventral surface of her battered strider scraping and bumping across the smoking, burned-over ground. Her strider's legs were gone. She still had some auxiliary manipulators folded up inside their storage compartments, though, and as that thundering, howling wind died away somewhat, she was able to deploy them, first to hold herself in place, then to drag her battered machine slowly across the ground.

The heat and radiation weren't bad, considering; the ambient ionizing radiation of the Galactic Core was actually stronger by far than that released by a single micronuke, though with her energy-drinking nanoflage gone, the full brunt of protecting her warstrider's more delicate contents now rested on its magnetic shields.

Using the strider's Naga components to build new lenses and shove them into place, she managed to bring a suite of optical sensors back on line. The view she got was bleary, dark, and unsteady, but it showed her the classic mushroom cloud towering above the battlefield, looming high in a sky gone black, masked by windswept dust.

Astonishingly, the alien pyramid was still there, though it no longer floated in the air. Judging from the glowing cavern ripped into its side and base, it might well be crippled. Her electronic sensors were down and she couldn't detect the play of magnetics within the alien structure, but it was resting on the ground, canted at a thirty-degree angle, as though the forces holding it aloft had abruptly snapped off and dumped it there. The play of deadly lightning had ceased as well, and as Kara watched its form emerging from the roiling pillar of the mushroom's base, she dared to believe that she might have actually killed the thing.

The nuke's expanding blast wave had pulverized the pyramid's smaller cousins as well, sweeping most from the ground like clots of dust scattered by the descent of a broom and leaving the larger ones wrecked and half-melted. She scanned her tactical display. *Kuso!* Seventeen warstriders left operational, out of the original company of forty-eight.

"Ran!" she called over the tactical channel. His strider

was still operational, thank God, the only one of her three
lieutenants. She tried to stifle a small stab of relief; she had
special and quite close feelings for Ran Ferris . . . but ones
that she kept tightly reined in when they were on duty. Even
the hint of favoritism—especially sexual favoritism—could
destroy the best of military units. "Ran, do you copy?"

"Right here, Captain," he replied.

"Let's pull in the perimeter. Everyone who's left, pull in
tight for mutual defense."

"Affirmative," Ran said. "Will! Cyn! Are you on-line?"

"Here, Lieutenant," Sergeant Cynthia Gonzales replied.

"Me too," Sergeant Willis Daniels added.

"You heard the Captain. Let's get 'em rounded up."

Together, the officers and NCOs began herding the dazed,
surviving warstriders across the flame-scoured plain, gathering them at a wreckage-strewn depression in the earth not
far from where they'd originally touched down. The surface
of the battlefield might have been swept clean by nuclear
fire, but the Webbers had been emerging from underground
as well as descending from the sky, and Kara had every
reason to believe that more would be appearing at any moment.

Kara reached the depression and surveyed the blasted
landscape. The other surviving striders began appearing
now, dragging their way through the rubble or floating just
above it in awkward dips and lurches. A quick scan of the
display showing the company's readiness figures gave her
the bad news. Only six of the warstriders possessed all of
their weapons intact, and two—Ed Furillo's and Angel
Shannon's—were completely unarmed, with all weapons
burned away or sealed uselessly inside faulty hull panels.

Her tactical display showed something else as well. There
was movement in the shadows of the towers around the LZ,
and in the sky high above the spreading cap of the mushroom. The Webbers were emerging once again onto the fire-
savaged surface of this world.

"Maybe those of us who can should fire our Sabers,"
Cynthia suggested. "Targets of opportunity . . . while we
still can."

"Negative on that," Kara told her. "This is recon, not search-and-destroy. We'll wait and use them if we have to, and only in self-defense."

She caught the other woman's mental shrug, and a hint of disagreement. "As you say, Captain."

"Captain Hagan!" Will called. "Check the pyramid!"

Pivoting, she focused her damaged sensors on the ruin of the artificial mountain. The gaping hole in its side and bottom appeared to be closing, the edges softening and blurring as the countless small machines that had made up its bulk in the first place rearranged themselves. She could see individual pieces flowing down the canted surfaces or dripping off the rim of the base to the ground below. Was it repairing itself . . . or dissolving back into its component parts? She couldn't tell, but it was uncomfortably clear that the nuclear strike had not solved their problem.

It had only postponed it.

She stared for a long moment at that huge and enigmatic structure. Looking into the hole in the thing's side was like staring into a cavern, a mysterious black place filled with unknown horror. The horror was made worse by the knowledge that she'd gambled, and lost. Her decision to use nukes had been a bad one; the enemy had been slowed, but not stopped . . . and the price she'd paid had been half of the company, and probably the success of the operation as well.

"Ran?"

"Yeah?"

"You've got command. Hold the perimeter."

"Now wait a minute, Kar. . . ."

"We need more data. We still don't know how they're coordinating, how they're working together. Maybe I can get close enough to find out."

"That's not necessary, Captain," the voice of Overwatch said.

"I think it is."

"Kara, you can't go in there!" Ran told her. "Not alone!"

"Who's going to stop me?"

Ran's strider unfurled one gleaming manipulator, jointed

and oil-shiny. She watched the glitter of several imaging lenses as they scanned her.

"What are you going to do, Ran?" she asked quietly. "Dismantle me?"

The appendage hesitated, then gave an eloquent mechanical imitation of a shrug. "Damn it, Kar," he said, using a private channel now. "What is it? You're feeling guilty about the nuke?"

"Negative," she snapped. She knew she was lying, and she knew Ran heard the lie in her voice. "Take over. Hold until relieved."

False bravado, that. And useless. *Wasteful.* But she was out of answers and she had to do *something* . . . something besides wait for the enemy to overwhelm the last of the warstriders huddled together on Core D9837 and bring the operation to its final and inevitable conclusion. She pushed past Ran without another word, making her way toward the distant, towering pyramid.

She was afraid.

She had liked it better fighting the Empire . . . not that those days were over, by any means.

Since the dawn of Man's emergence as a spacefaring species—since the end of the twentieth century, in fact, when the old United States and the Russian Commonwealth had turned their backs on the high ground of space—Mankind's destiny, both on Old Earth and off, had been directed by Dai Nihon, the empire of Greater Japan. Through control of orbital industrial facilities and, ultimately, the secrets of faster-than-light travel and the quantum power tap, they'd spread that empire to the stars, building the Shichiju, an empire of over eighty colonized worlds and hundreds of research, mining, and military outposts scattered across a sphere of space over a hundred light years across.

Thirty years earlier, an unlikely union of diverse worlds and states scattered along the Shichiju's periphery had declared independence and, after a short, bitter war, united as the Confederation, with its capital at New America. The peace that followed had been fragile and uncertain. Imperial Japan and its Hegemony far outnumbered the newly independent worlds, and no one was betting that they would keep their newfound independence for long.

The immediate threat of renewed war had ended, though, when Dev Cameron—or his downloaded personality, at any rate—had returned unexpectedly to human space after a twenty-five-year absence with a portion of the DalRiss exploratory fleet, bringing warning of the strange civilization that appeared to be energetically transforming the Core of the Galaxy.

The Web. For the first time, it was clear that *Man* was at risk . . . not just some one faction or political group. For survival, Confederation and Empire had allied with one another, joining their fleets and their efforts in an imperfect military union. A battle had been fought at Nova Aquila as the Web came through the Stargate from the Core; victory had been won, though not so much by the efforts of the Unified Fleet as by the intervention of the Overmind, a still poorly understood phenomenon arising out of the combined interaction of billions of interlinked minds working through the human computer network. Since that battle, Confederation and Imperium had maintained their uneasy truce, studying the Web and preparing for its next emergence.

For two years, now, the Unified Fleet had maintained its watch at Nova Aquila. A science team aboard the *Carl Friedrich Gauss* continued to study what little data had been gleaned thus far, both about the Web and the Nova Aquila Stargate. Teleoperated probes were sent through, both for information gathering and as a part of Shell Game, the attempt to plant disinformation about the human worlds for the Web to pick up.

And there'd been raids like this one, both Confederation and Imperial.

She looked again at her warning discretes. Her strider would never make it into space again anyway; any attempt by her to get off this barren world would be doomed to failure.

So she might as well make the sacrifice of her strider count for something.

Her progress across the open ground had been slow. Her magnetics were generating scarcely enough lift against the faltering local magfields to hold her aloft, much less to propel her forward. She was compelled to drag herself along with her manipulators, and that made for slow going.

The pyramid was less than five hundred meters away now, towering upward above her and canted slightly forward, as though it might at any moment topple over and crush her beneath its immense weight. From this range, the surface appeared to be crawling, writhing with a pseudolife of its own. The crater blasted into the thing's side was definitely smaller now, as though the machines making up the pyramid's bulk were realigning themselves to fill it in. She could make out movement inside and the blue flicker of something that might be artificial lightnings at the very edge of her resolution.

"If you can get a little closer, Captain," the voice of Overwatch told her, "we might be able to get a look at what's going on in there."

"That was the idea," she said. It was good to know Overwatch was supporting her decision now. Well, through the telemetry, they could see the same readouts that she could. They knew she was never going to get this strider off-world again.

*"Watch it! Watch it! They're breaking through!"*

*"Lieutenant Ferris! We need support over—"*

*"C'mon, people! Tighten up! Watch your fronts!"*

*"I've got kickers! Kickers breaking through sector one!"*

*"Valda! Where are you?"*

*"Valda's bought it—"*

In the distance, she could hear the shouts, the screams, the firm commands and harsh emotions. It sounded as though battle had just been joined back at the perimeter. She wasn't tuned into their tactical frequency now, but she was hearing their voices from someone's commo console back at the command center. She was tempted to open the tactical channel again, to find out what was happening, to find out if Ran was still okay . . . but she suppressed it. The rest of the Phantoms were on their own now.

As was she.

She saw a scuttling of shapes ahead and froze in position, panning left to right with her particle cannon. The shapes— long-legged and as gracefully sleek in their movements as spiders—were visible for but an instant, and then they were gone, lost in the rubble. She was close to a spill of debris from a building knocked flat by the nuke. Reaching out to some of the twisted metal-alloy ribs that had formed the structure's foundations, she hauled herself along more quickly, moving hand-over-hand like a monkey swinging through the trees.

The enemy kickers ignored her. Possibly, she thought, she'd been spared this long because she was only a single machine. She was beginning to get the idea that the Web did not fully understand the concept of individuals carrying out operations apart from the activities of *other* individuals.

An interesting datum, that, and possibly one that would prove useful.

A laser flared, the beam striking her hull from the left and boiling away a few hundred grams of the now-dead Naga shell. The Web, it seemed, was taking an interest in her again. Possibly she'd moved too close to the pyramid, which bulked high above her like a vast and overhanging cliff of polished rock. The laser fired again, missing her by centimeters. Pivoting, she returned fire with her particle cannon, the electrical discharge snapping across the blackened rubble of the fallen building with the dazzle of an arc-welder's torch.

The cavern, shrunken now somewhat, was still immense, a vast hollowing of the cliff above her head, the interior aglow with soft, blue light. She tried to make out the shapes there, tried to make sense of them, but there was nothing for her mind to grasp hold of. All she could really see was . . . *movement.*

Insect-shapes. Millions of them, many as small as her hand, some as large as a personal flitter, a few bigger than a house. They were cascading down off the walls of the burned-out cavern, spilling out into the open air, dropping to the ground and surging forward. Laser fire sniped and hissed around her; she hit the ground heavily, her strider rolling to port, as her manipulators were burned away in the sudden onslaught.

She couldn't move.

That was the worst part of the nightmare, the feeling of

unendurable helplessness as those glittering little monsters poured across the rubble toward her, a swarm as unstoppable as the incoming New American tides at Columbiarise. She could hear the gnaw and chink as they began disassembling her warstrider, feel the machine rocking heavily as they rolled it further onto its side, sense the stripping of the last of her surface armor. . . .

She gave the mental command to abort, but all systems were shutting down now in a cascade failure, nothing responding, her senses switching off one by one. Her last optical image before the camera was wrenched apart by bright-alloyed jaws was of the Great Annihilator, hanging low above the fire-swept horizon.

Then she felt them opening up the body of her strider, breaking it apart with the ugly sound of shredding metal. . . .

# Chapter 4

*One of the great enlightenments arising from the past few centuries of technic revolution is the knowledge that it doesn't matter whether our sensory input is passed along a few centimeters of optic or audial nerve tissue, or is being beamed across thousands of kilometers of empty space. Late in the twentieth century, a private commercial venture placed a small, primitive, and simpleminded robotic device on the surface of Earth's moon; for a fee, attendees at an entertainment center on Earth could teleoperate the device, steering it across the face of the moon as onboard cameras relayed views of what lay ahead.*

*In this way, thousands of people, youngsters and adults, shared in the thrill of exploring the moon in person . . . while never leaving their seats in that en-*

*tertainment center on Earth. This, arguably, was the
first of a long chain of experiments in large-scale
teleoperational presence.*

> —*The Physics of Mind*
> DR. ELLEN CHANTAY
> C.E. 2413

Kara blinked into darkness. She was lying on a couch,
molded to conform to the curves of her body; the air was
close and stale, and tasted of her own sweat. There was no
light save the gleam of console readouts near her head,
winking pinpoints of green, red, and amber.

Fear continued to claw at her mind, raw and savage and
demanding. She was being *disassembled. . . .*

Then, with a sound of broken vacuum, the lid to her cof-
fin-sized chamber swung open. Four technicians in blue and
gray jumpsuits were there, bending over her, removing the
oxygen mask from her face, unclipping the electronic leads
that attached to the metallic plates showing in her head,
hands, and forearm.

"Captain?" one of the figures, wearing sergeant's chev-
rons on her jumpsuit sleeve, said. "Captain Hagan? How
do you feel?"

Catatonia beckoned, warm and inviting. Her sense of self
shifted uncertainly; she had to think for a moment about
who she was, what she was doing. . . .

"Like I just got stepped on." Her voice cracked. Her
mouth was very dry. For a handful of seconds, her inner
compass spun blindly, and she didn't recognize this place.
"Where . . . ?"

Comtech Sergeant Ellen Gillespie was used to the mud-
dle-headed confusion of striderjacks emerging from their
pods. "It's okay, Captain. You're back. And safe. You're
aboard the *Carl Friedrich Gauss*, at Nova Aquila, on the
war deck. The link held long enough to pull you back."

The link. She swallowed, trying to clear her mind. It was
always a bit confusing after a long-range teleoperational
link, but this one had been a lot worse. She'd been *there. . . .*

With an effort of will, she dissolved the link endpoint

contacts, letting her Companion transform them once more into unadorned skin.

Her Companion, a one-kilo Naga fragment living inside her body in close symbiosis with her nervous system, could nanotechnically reform skin, bone, and muscle tissue into contact endpoints for machine interface—a vast improvement over the older cephlink design with its permanently grown implants in brain and skin. Called ''morphing'' after an ancient computer technique for manipulating images on a computer, the technique had redefined how many humans thought of their bodies . . . and how they used them. Several of the technicians bending over her now had cosmetic morphs—delicately reworked ears for one, a decorative set of scales and ridges above golden cat's eyes for another.

Kara felt confused, lost in a spinning disorientation. She remembered, now, having climbed into this life-support pod several hours before. Indeed, she'd never forgotten . . . quite. But jacking a warstrider required intense concentration and a complete elimination of outside distractions. During the past few hours, her body had been isolated from her brain, kept alive by the pod's life support systems and *Gauss*'s primary medical AI while her brain had jacked her warstrider by remote control.

The military high command was still calling teleoperated warstriders the Great Experiment. She wondered how many of the Fleet's senior officers had tried this experiment for themselves. She closed her eyes, trying for a moment to blank out the confused tumble of images, to remind herself that *this* was real, that *that* had been a kind of waking dream.

From where she was lying, she could see part of a large viewscreen set into one curving bulkhead of the wardeck. Her dream—her nightmare, rather—was still being played out there. She could see the floating pyramid aloft once more, see rippling, glittering movement on the ground in the distance that must be hordes of Web machines. The image was being transmitted by one of the survivors of her company, still holding the perimeter back on Core D9837. Briefly, she closed her eyes, trying to reconcile conflicting emotions—her happiness at being away from there . . . and her anger and disappointment at having been ripped away from her people before the mission was complete.

When she opened her eyes again, another figure, this one in white and wearing a major's rank tabs, was leaning over her pod. "Captain? How are we feeling?" he asked.

She didn't care for the man's multiple personality address, but she accepted his examination of her face, including the pupils of both eyes.

"A little woozy, sir," she told him.

The insignia on his jumper identified him as a senior psych department officer, a psychtech. "Give me a contact," he told her in a brusque, professional manner. "Left temporal, please."

She focused her thoughts, and a patch of her skin just above and in front of her left ear hardened to the shiny slickness of polished gold, then extruded itself as a slender filament. The psychtech reached out with his right forefinger and touched her link tendril as it twisted slightly in the air in front of her face. The tip of his finger was changing too, enveloping the tip of her contact. At the touch, she felt something like the flash of a strobe light go off just behind her eyes, then savored the faintly erotic rippling of data cascading at electronic speed from her Companion's memory stacks as it uploaded at the psychtech's coded request. She caught a bit of peripheral information in the backflow; the psychtech's name was Peter Jamal, he was from Liberty, and he was worried about what might have happened to these people "in there." His daughter's birthday was in two weeks, and he was disgruntled about having to miss it.

"What's your name?" His voice sounded inside her head, bypassing her ears and speaking aloud in her head.

Recognition—and memory—were flooding back, banishing the vertigo and disorientation. "I'm okay," she told him.

"Let's have your name," the voice insisted.

She nodded, knowing Jamal needed to check her responses. "Kara Hagan," she said. "*Captain* Kara Hagan, Confederation Military Command, First Company, First Battalion, First Confederation Rangers."

"Who are your parents?"

"General Victor Hagan. Senator Katya Alessandro."

"What was your mission?"

"To teleoperate a Mark XC Black Falcon through the Nova Aquila Stargate to the Galactic Core," she recited, rattling off her mission statement from memory. "To attempt a landing on a rogue planet, Core D9837, to test Web responses and defenses, and to check out I2C teleoperational protocols and capabilities at intragalactic ranges."

The psychtech grinned at her as the direct electronic link between them was broken. "I think you came through okay, Captain."

She pulled in her contact, feeling the tendril melt back into her scalp. "How . . . how about the others? We were taking some pretty heavy subjective casualties."

The grin faded. "About what we expected. Nineteen seem unaffected, so far. Including you." He nodded toward the viewscreen, where particle cannon blasts flared in silent, blue-white fury. "Nine more are still on the other side, though they'll be pulling out soon, I imagine. The others . . ." He shrugged.

She sighed. "Give me the bill, Major."

"Twelve are in various stages of withdrawal or link psychosis. Two are brain dead. Feedback through the I2C relay. The other six . . . well, we're trying to revive them. It doesn't look good, though. We're working on downloading their personalities, but they may be headed for permanent citizenship in a ViRworld now. I really can't say anything more definite than that."

Kara bit her lip. "Who were the two?"

The psychtech's eyes unfocused as he consulted some inner list downloaded through his biolink. "Warstrider Miles Pritchard," he said after a moment. "And Lieutenant Pellam Hochstader."

Damn . . . *damn*! She squeezed her eyes shut, working to channel the pain that threatened her self control off into a harmless circling.

She hadn't known Hochstader that well; he was a good and reliable officer, but he'd only been with the unit about a year, and his quiet reserve had kept him a bit aloof from the other Phantoms, Kara included. Pritch, though, she'd known rather longer, and more personally. He'd been a friend and an occasional drinking and ViRsim buddy for a couple of years now, despite the difference in their rank—a social barrier that was far less imposing in the free-spirited Confederation than it was within the Imperial military. She knew she would miss his quiet humor . . . and the steadying effect he'd had on the rawer members of First Company.

She could still remember his screams as his warstrider had melted around him.

That, she reminded herself, remained one of the risks associated with I2C teleoperations. It could well be that combat would *never* be safe, despite the new advances in teleoperated warcraft.

Two years earlier, the possibility of renewed war between the Confederation and the Shichiju had been averted—or at least deferred—when a disguised Kara had led a raid against an Imperial research facility on Kasei, the world in the Sol system once known as Mars. Her prize had been a brand new advance in the Imperium's study of quantum physics, Instantaneous Interstellar Communications, or I2C, for short.

The technology still seemed wondrous, even magical. Create two electrons, or any other pair of quons—particles small enough to fall into the Alice-in-Wonderland weirdness of quantum physics—in a single event. The electron pair will be identical in that elusive quality of electronness called "spin," even though it has no more to do with rotation than a charm quark has to do with the rules of subatomic etiquette. Separate the two electrons, then subject one to an event that reverses its spin.

The other electron will change its spin as well, instantly . . . *even if the two are separated by a distance of many light years*.

It was as if the two electrons were somehow one and the same electron, a direct manifestation of one of the kinkier aspects of quantum theory. The effect, counter-intuitive and downright magical though it seemed, had been predicted since the mid-twentieth century and even demonstrated in early laboratory experiments, but at that time there'd been no practical way to exploit the phenomenon. Almost six centuries later, however, Imperial researchers had discovered how to trap each half of a paired quon in nanotechnic quantum electron cages, keying them to detectors that could read spin without affecting it, within the parameters set by Heisenberg's Uncertainty Principle. This meant two computers could be linked together so that one could read the changes in an array of thousands of electron cages; each change, each flipped electron, could represent one bit of data in the age-old binary data structure of yes/no, on/off, spin-up/spin-down. When a particular sequence of electron spins was imposed on one array—the transmitter—the paired array registered the same sequence, light years away.

In practical terms, this meant that communications could be set up between two computer systems that were absolutely secure—untappable, untraceable, and unjammable, even across vast interstellar distances.

This, in turn, meant a titanic stride forward in military science. The ground military combat machines known as warstriders, and their spacefaring kin, warflyers, had long been operated by an on-board pilot who was linked— "jacked in," in military parlance—to the machine's operating systems and AI in such a way that the machine actually became his body, responding to the slightest thought while the organic body, cocooned in a life-support pod, was temporarily cut out of the brain's control network. Throughout the warstrider era, military systems designers had dreamed of being able to have the pilots direct their electronic charges from a distance, teleoperating them into combat from a place of safety. After all, what did it matter if the imaging lenses feeding the pilot a view of his surroundings were half a meter away . . . or many kilometers? The control and sensory feedback systems all remained the same.

But the modern battlefield was a poor place for experiments in remote control. Half at least of any conflict in modern warfare was waged in unseen dimensions, an electronic battle fought between opposing computers on a plane and at speeds almost completely beyond the human ken; communications, *any* communications, could be intercepted and jammed. Control codes, *any* control codes, could be jammed or broken, countermanded, and even hijacked.

Any, that is, except signals propagated through quantum pairing. With I2C, not only could unit COs keep track of events on a battlefield light years away, but the striderjacks piloting a company of warstriders could teleoperate them from a distance . . . even when that distance was measured in thousands of light years. It meant that at planetary distances there was zero time delay due to speed-of-light limitations, that warstriders could be jacked from thousands of light years away, that the striders could be subjected to stresses that would have killed human pilots physically riding them. During the passage from the Stargate to Core D9837, the striders in Kara's company had been boosting at over two hundred Gs—an acceleration no human could survive—and the high-radiation background of the Galactic Core itself made direct exploration of that hellish environment impossible, even with heavy shielding.

It was a remarkable achievement, a military dream come true.

Unfortunately, the dream so far had not succeeded in making warstrider military operations *safe* for the pilots. They might be well out of range of the enemy's energy beams, but there were other, more insidious dangers in combat. Dangers affecting the *mind.* . . .

Carefully, and with Jamal giving an assist, Kara sat up, then swung her legs out of the opened conmod. The pilot deck was a broad, low-ceilinged, brightly lit room occupied by dozens of coffin-shaped conmods identical to hers. Most of them, she saw, were already open and empty, their occupants moved elsewhere after their warstriders on distant Core D9837 had been junked. But a handful were clearly still occupied, their covers sealed tight, and with small galaxies of lights winking at the console life-function readouts mounted on their sides.

The conning modules were the life-support pods of her comrades in the Phantoms, the warstriders still fighting for their lives in the Galactic Core.

As she rose unsteadily to her feet, someone shouted on the other side of the room, an alarm sounded, and med techs rushed to gather beside one of the occupied modules just as the cluster of console lights began shifting from green to amber and red.

The top of the coffin cracked open, then slid aside, revealing a still, jumpsuited form inside. Kara couldn't see who it was, but from the location she knew it was someone in First Squadron.

The figure sat up—a sharp, abrupt movement—and screamed, shrill, harsh, and ragged with stark terror. It was Willis Daniels, her First Squadron senior sergeant. The med techs were struggling to hold him down while one of them pressed a hypogun's muzzle against his throat.

Kara started toward the cluster of men and women, but the major reached out and stopped her, a hand closing on her elbow. "You can't help, Captain."

She pulled away. "He's one of my people, damn it."

By the time she reached the tableau of techs and the struggling striderjack, the anesthetic was taking effect and Will was slumping back into his conmod. His eyes were still wide, however, staring at some horror invisible to the others present. His hands were balled into tight, white-knuckled fists, and his face and uniform were drenched with sweat. Kara caught an acrid whiff of urine and the frantic tic of a muscle at the corner of his eye.

One of the techs looked up and met her eyes, then shook his head slightly. "T-P," he said. "A bad one."

T-P. Transference psychosis. It was the part of the down side of long-range teleoperations through FTL links. A warstrider, a *good* warstrider, was good precisely because he could so identify with the machine he was jacking that it literally became his body, responding to his slightest thought. The trouble with such close identification, though, was that when the machine was destroyed, it was impossible to convince the jacker's brain that he was safe, perhaps light years from the slashed wreckage of his strider.

With direct feeds to the striderjack's brain, there literally was no way for the mind—specifically the subconscious mind—to remind itself that it wasn't housed inside the strider itself—not with millions of years of evolution determining how the incoming sensory perceptions were interpreted. In the old days, when the pilot was actually inside a warstrider as it was being pounded to scrap, the pilot might manage to escape, he might die, or he could suffer serious mental trauma from the shock of feeling his "body" torn apart. Now, even though his organic body was safe, there was actually a greater danger of mental injury than there'd been in the bad old days of direct combat.

It was nothing so simple as the old cliché of being frightened to death by too realistic a dream; despite advances in psychodynamics, the human brain was still in many ways a mysterious and poorly understood entity, and it was capable of throwing astonishing inner defenses into place against what it perceived as dire and immediate threats. With the physical, traumatic death of the striderjack no longer a possible outcome of battle, it turned out that the chief dangers in combat were insanity, catatonic withdrawal, or any of a fair-sized constellation of stress-induced symptomatologies.

Stunned, hurting inside, Kara turned away, nearly bumping into Major Jamal, who'd followed her across from her conmod.

"I wonder," she told him quietly, "if we're doing anybody any favors with the teleoperational stuff." She nodded toward the nearest of the empty pods. "My people are still getting killed in there. Or worse."

"You know," he said a little sadly, "people used to argue that the machine gun would make war too horrible to exist. Same for nuclear weapons. Now here we have a new technology that's supposed to save lives, and we're still losing them."

It seemed a strange sentiment for a military man . . . though perhaps it could be expected of a psychtech. Even so, Kara had to agree, and nodded. "Maybe there's no way around it," she added. "Just new and different ways of killing people."

She wanted to say something more, something to the effect that at least teleoperation seemed to be cutting down on casualty percentages—two dead out of forty-eight was not bad, after all—but that really wasn't the point. There was still what she had come to think of as the suicide-mission factor to consider. Two years ago, something like Operation Core Peek—sending a couple of companies on a strictly one-way sneak-and-peek into the Web's no-trespass zone at the Galactic Core—would have been unthinkable. If for no other reason than that, some way would have had to have been found to get the information out, the op would never have gone down unless the people who'd gone in had a fair chance of coming back again. Now, though, with warstrider pilots able to operate their craft from the theoretical safety of a command base ship, the politicos and brass were a lot likelier to draw up op plans for lamebrained missions that didn't have a chance of success, missions where *survivability* didn't need to be considered. As a result the pilots were certain to be subjected to even more combat stress than they'd faced before.

Case in point. Hochstader and Pritchard would still be alive if they hadn't been sent in on Core Peek, an operation where the mission parameters stressed that the warstriders would return to the Stargate and Nova Aquila if practicable . . . but which everyone actually involved in the planning had known would be a suicide mission. If traumatic deaths were down, the ratio of psychological injuries was certainly higher. How many in her company, she wondered, would spend the rest of their existence in the make-believe of ViRworlds?

At the thought, she felt a swift chill of fear. *Ran . . .*

Ran Ferris's con module was one of the very last that remained sealed. She glanced up at the viewscreen, ignoring the tangled and wildly shifting nightmare shapes and images flickering across it to concentrate on the columns of text winking on and off down the screen's right-hand side. That image, she saw, was coming from Number Ten—Ran's Black Falcon. He was one of four striders still in the fight; as she watched, med techs were gathering around two more of the high-tech coffins, and Jamal quietly excused himself to go attend another newly revived pilot. She glanced around the war deck, spotted the conmod for Number Ten, and hurried over. It was still sealed, of course, but med techs and engineers were already gathering around it.

On the screen on the nearby bulkhead, the pyramid loomed colossal. Blue lightning flashed, stabbing, exploding. . . .

The image shivered, then abruptly shifted to a different view, from a different strider. An alarm sounded, and the lights on Ran's console began shifting from green to amber to red. One of the techs touched a control, and the top of the module hissed open, revealing Ran's body inside, his face taut, pale, and drawn behind his breathing mask. His eyes opened, the pupils black and enormous, still staring into some horror invisible to the rest of them. As the room lights hit them, the pupils closed down to pinpoints, and he blinked.

*His autonomous systems are back on line*, she thought. *Thank God. . . .*

"They're breaking through!" Ran's shout drowned out the alarm and echoed through the war deck compartment. "Stop them! Stop—"

He blinked again, suddenly aware that he was no longer inside his warstrider. Several technicians reached down to hold him; Kara brushed past them and laid one hand on his shoulder. "It's okay, Ran!" she told him, urgently, and gently. "It's okay! You're back. It's over."

He struggled for a moment, then relaxed, opening his eyes and fixing his gaze on Kara. "You're . . . okay?" he asked, his voice hoarse.

"Fine. How do you feel?"

"Don't ask. Kuso, that's the best argument I can think of for immortality. I *hate* getting killed!"

"The worst part is coming back to do it all over again," Kara said, nodding agreement. "Can you sit up yet?"

"I think so."

As she helped him get up and out of the conmod, she wondered if Core Peek had been worth the price they'd paid for too damned little in the way of solid intel.

"I wonder if it was worth it?" Ran asked, staring up at the image on the viewscreen and echoing her own dark thoughts. He seemed to sense her mood and reached out to put his arm around her shoulder. Normally, she discouraged such PDAs—public displays of affection, as they were known in the military—but she was tired and unhappy, and she needed that fleeting brush of human contact.

"Damned if I know, Ran," she said, letting him squeeze her close. "Damned if I'll *ever* know."

# Chapter 5

*Anyone not convinced that genuine differences in thought processes, in worldview, in concepts such as self, duty, or society, exist between the members of different intelligent species—the products, remember, of separate and distinct evolutions, biologies, and histories—is invited to consider those differences as they are manifest between different cultures within the same species—Man. Japanese of traditional backgrounds perceive themselves quite differently in many fundamental respects than do, say, Hispanics, Europeans, or Americans. They are more in tune with their social surroundings, less tolerant of difference, more willing to sacrifice personal comfort or freedom for the good of society. It has been suggested that their talent for working together toward common goals is responsible for their remarkable success in the twenty-first century, when theirs became the dominant culture on Earth.*

—*Rising Sun's Glory*
DARLENE HU
C.E. 2530

Admiral Isoru Hideshi was completely naked, as were the other five—three men, two women—sharing the shuttle pod's small passenger compartment for the passage across open space to Tenno Kyuden. The six of them were strapped into six of the twelve couches filling the pod's claustrophobic cabin. Acceleration provided their only sensation of weight.

His nudity bothered him scarcely at all; it was a small loss of *men*—the word could mean either face or mask— that was more than compensated for by the rich symbolism of the act. By shedding their clothing, Hideshi and his fellow passengers were acting out a kind of play, symbolically leaving material possessions behind as they took passage to the very Gates of Heaven.

And, of course, their nudity made it easier for the security personnel, who were examining them even now with a ruthless, near-microscopic scrutiny through the array of sensors embedded in the surrounding bulkheads and in the seats to which they were strapped.

Impassively, Hideshi watched the Great Wheel unfold before him on the vessel's viewall. *Tenno Kyuden*—the Imperial Palace—was far more splendid, more spectacular than any holo, even than any ViRsimulation could possibly render it.

In some ways, the Palace reminded him of one of those immense, glittering, crystal-heavy chandeliers that some Western cultures affected in ballrooms or fancy dining halls. It had begun as a simple wheel attached at its hub to the jackstraw-tangled complex of the Singapore Synchorbital station, but in the past few centuries, construction had been unceasing as more and more modules and apartments and Imperial functionary habitats had been added. Now the structure was wider than the largest *ryu* dragonship and far more massive. Its rotation provided varying levels of spin gravity for the habitats within, the precise acceleration of a given level depending on how far it was from the hub, where it was essentially zero.

The Wheel's hub was attached to a tangle of zero-gravity structures that zigzagged out along the orbital. The entire complex was positioned at the synchorbit slot above Earth's Singapore Sky-el, the slender elevator tower that connected the island of Palau Linggae on the equator, located just south of Singapore, with that spot in orbit some 36,000 kilometers directly overhead where orbital period precisely matched Earth's twenty-four-hour rotation.

Moments before, the pod had left the main sky-el receiving bay and was drifting now across open space toward the Wheel's hub.

"Pod *Swan's Flight*, this is Palace of Heaven Approach Control," a voice said softly inside his head, speaking through his cephlink. "Passenger One. Verify, please, your identity."

Hideshi gave a single sharp, precisely military nod. "*Hai*. Rear Admiral Isoru Hideshi, of the Imperial carrier *Soraryu*. I open myself to your inspection."

He could feel the cold fingers of a security observer aboard the Palace probing his cephlink, then pushing through the nanotechnically grown circuitry to his personal RAM, opening files, extracting data, examining, comparing. . . .

Such stringent security safeguards were necessary, of course, and Isoru accepted them without reservation. His career, no, his entire life had been dedicated to the Empire and to the ideal of the god-Emperor, and the Emperor's safety was of paramount importance. The shuttle was one of a small fleet of service and orbital transport vehicles kept at Singapore Synchorbital for the sole purpose of carrying visitors to and from the Imperial Palace. Passengers aboard those shuttles, as well as on the handful of tube shuttles that connected the hub of the Great Wheel with the rest of the Synchorbital, could be meticulously scrutinized during their approach. Any deviation from the expected, any suspicious shadow picked up within his body by the X-ray and infrasound scanners, any change in the arrays of data stacked within his personal RAM, and he would be immediately apprehended by the army of security personnel waiting within the Palace. If the threat were deemed serious enough, he would be cut down before docking by one of the remote lasers mounted in the bulkheads . . . or if the threat were more serious still, the pod could be detonated long before it was close enough to be a threat to the Palace or the person of the god-Emperor.

Hideshi cast a wary eye on his naked companions. One

of the men was Captain Shigeru Ushiba, his chief aide, but the other four were strangers to him. He hoped he wasn't about to be vaporized because one of them was detected carrying a bomb in his or her abdominal cavity.

Evidently, he was not. "Thank you, Admiral," the voice said in his mind. "You and your companions are clear to approach the Palace of Heaven."

The pod slowed as the Great Wheel expanded to fill the viewall, then grew larger still, until he could make out individual windows and lights gleaming in the vast structure's shadowed recesses. Riding a magnetic beam, the pod was drawn smoothly toward a brightly lit docking collar mounted on a non-rotating portion of the hub. Pod melded with collar in a barely felt surge of deceleration that dwindled almost immediately to the endless fall of weightlessness, and in the soundless flurry of nanotechnics welding the two seamlessly together. In another moment, a pinpoint hole appeared in one of the pod's bulkheads, widening swiftly as the hull material dissolved.

As the last of the bulkhead evaporated, a line of armored Imperial Marines on the far side snapped to attention—a difficult parade-ground maneuver for men lightly anchored by magnetic boots in the hub's microgravity environment—and a brightly robed Shinto priest gestured benediction. Six acrobatic *annaigakari*, passenger handlers trained in maneuvering themselves and others in microgravity, swam into the pod's cabin and began unlocking the safety restraints—yet another security measure. The red-coveralled handlers carried the passengers one by one into the receiving bay's interior, where they were scanned once again by low-intensity, broad-fanned lasers that measured and patterned every square centimeter of their skin.

Most of the new security precautions, Hideshi mused as the blue beam hummed and drew its glowing line slowly across his body, had been introduced within the last two years. There'd been a time, before that damnable Confederation raid on Kasei in 2569, when Tenno Kyuden had been just another orbital facility, and security precautions had been limited to palming your ident and downloading your business into an AI-monitored computer at a manned checkpoint.

Kasei—the terraformed world once known as Mars—was the site of an important research facility. Confederation raiders had penetrated the security of the Pavonis Mons Synchorbital and compromised the entire planetary tracking and defense network long enough for Confederation warstriders to land near the research station at Noctis Labyrinthus Bay and hijack its most important secret, a prototype of the new interstellar communications system. The TJK, Imperial Security, discovered that the saboteurs who'd penetrated the Planetary Defense Network had done so through the agency of Naga *isoro*, parasites. The Naga fragments used so extensively in the Confederation could actually rework skin, muscle, and bone to completely change a person's looks. Both by centuries-old tradition and by Imperial law, *gaijin*—foreigners—weren't even permitted to set foot on Kasei or its synchorbital, yet the enemy agents had disguised themselves so effectively as Nihonjin that they'd slipped through the place's security barriers completely undetected. As a result, the Empire's new and highly secret faster-than-light communications system had been stolen from under the Fleet's nose, along with the best chance the Empire had possessed to crush once and for all the rebellious outer provinces and return them to their proper place within the circle of Empire and Hegemony.

No wonder Imperial Security had become just a trifle paranoid about the Tenno Kyuden in the two years since the Kasei outrage. The elaborate scanning and screening procedures were designed to sniff out gaijin wearing Nihonjin *men*; if the enemy were able to slip, say, a small fission device aboard Tenno Kyuden, hidden in the belly of what *seemed* to be an honest Nihonjin businessman, the blow to the Empire would be incalculable. Worse even than the loss of the Imperial Military Command Staff, which maintained its offices here, would be the loss of face to the entire Empire, especially if the Emperor himself were killed or wounded.

Yes, a little nudity and discomfort could be tolerated in the face of such stakes as these.

The scanning laser snapped off, and a door dematerialized. A Palace attendant floated through, managing to bow almost double from the waist as she extended a transparent package containing a folded, pale gray garment. "*Dozo*," she said. "Please accept this small token, O-Shoshosan."

"*Hai*," he replied curtly. "*Domo arigato*."

The garment began as a bulky, one-piece jumper with the consistency of paper, but by the time he pulled the trim tabs snug at either hip, the nanotechnics within the weave had tailored it into a snug-fitting Imperial Navy uniform, full dress, space-black in color, complete with boots and the appropriate ribbons and awards on his breast. Ushiba entered, carrying two small personal computers, one of which he handed to his commanding officer.

"Thank you, Shigeru," Hideshi said. "I'm glad the prohibition against personal weapons does not extend to these, *ne*?"

"*Hai*, Shoshosan," his aide replied with a smile and a bow. "Though, as you frequently remind me, information is the deadliest weapon of all."

The admiral chuckled. "Best not to speak of weapons here, Taisasan," he said. "The bulkheads here have ears, quite literally. We don't want to make our hosts nervous, do we?"

"No, Shoshosan."

Hideshi raised his voice slightly. "We are ready to attend the Lord Munimori, at his convenience, of course."

Two more *annaigakari* floated into the room, bowed, then turned to lead the way to Munimori's office suite. Since both Hideshi and his aide had long experience in space, the *annaigakari* didn't offer to carry them like so many parcels, and the admiral was grateful for the small concession to his pride.

They boarded an elevator pod that carried them swiftly and soundlessly from the hub to the outermost station ring, where spin gravity was maintained at a constant one G. The landscape was mingled green parkland, gardens, and the close-clustered buildings of densely structured cities, many done in traditional architectural styles that brought to mind parts of Kyoto or Osaka, all beneath a sky of slatted mirrors, admitting sunlight from outside. This corridor, with a permanent population of over 800,000—all in government or military service—was known with good reason as the Circle of Heaven. It was a place now more space colony than space station, a miniature world where spin-gravity gave the feeling of walking on a full-sized world, but where the horizons were sharply constrained and seemed to curve up and out of sight where one's gaze followed the arc of the Great Wheel.

Hideshi felt lost . . . as though he'd just been dumped on the surface of a strange world. Before either he or his aide could lose face, however, a captain with the aiguillettes of the Imperial Staff met them at the elevator terminus; a ten-minute trip in a maglev transport whisked them soundlessly around the ring's curve to Munimori's private residence. The place was low and modern, an understated bit of Imperial Minimalist architecture built into the side of a hill overlooking the Circle of Heaven. At the door to the atrium, they removed their boots, handing them over to a house servant with a stiff bow. "The general is waiting for you, honored sirs," the servant—a young, nude, pale-skinned genie—said with a deeper, answering bow. "Please, if you would follow me."

They were led through several traditionally furnished rooms. The last was a paper-walled anteroom dominated by a perfectly matched pair of *inochi-zo*, the lovingly crafted, silently writhing life-sculptures that embodied—depending on the genetics of their design—purest and unending agony or purest and unending bliss. The eyes of the pain-*inochi-zo* followed them in silent pleading as they walked through the low doorway and into Munimori's private sanctum; those of the pleasure statue were closed and unheeding.

Stepping through the opposite doorway, they entered a formal garden, a peacefully contemplative bit of Zen artistry, the simplicity of rocks, moss, and gravel calling to mind mountains, forest, and sea—a world in miniature echoing the larger world of curved horizons beyond the vine-covered wall. Fleet Admiral Munimori was there, clad in a light, silk robe. The slave announced the guests, bowed low, and vanished.

"*Konichiwa, O-Gensuisama,*" Hideshi said, bowing. Ushiba bowed as well but remained silent, as was proper. "We have come at your order."

"Thank you, Admiral," Munimori replied. He was an extremely large man, nearly as broad in girth as a sumo wrestler and just as stockily muscular. He was holding a small scroll open as he sat cross-legged on a reed tatami. "It was good of you to come."

"I am honored at the invitation, Gensuisama."

"Please, be seated. I will summon tea."

Hideshi bowed thanks and acceptance.

"And how are things at New America, Shoshosan?"

"As chaotic as ever, my Lord Admiral. The Confederates continue to show an astonishing inability to work together toward a common goal."

"So."

"Their command structure is disorganized, and the individual fleet components cannot even work with one another, much less with the Imperial Fleet. Last week there was an ugly incident in Jefferson, New America's capital, between the crew members of a destroyer from Liberty and a cruiser from New America. I gather that several men ended up in a local hospital, and a spaceport bar was reduced to splintered furniture and shattered crockery."

In quiet, measured tones, Hideshi continued delivering his verbal report, relying on his RAM for most of the details and only once falling back on his computer, which maintained a data link with the main computer aboard *Soraryu*, docked at the Synchorbital. Unnervingly, Munimori continued to study the scroll, which appeared to be a collection of haiku by the twenty-second-century poet Hagiwara. Occasionally, the fleet admiral's eyes would flicker toward Hideshi as he spoke, but outside of the occasional noncommittal grunt or "so," he said nothing. That was deliberate, of course; if any part of Operation Shoki went wrong, Munimori would save both *men* and peace of mind knowing that he'd neither publicly praised nor officially condemned the idea.

A nude, female servant appeared, a genie with long, silver-blond hair and downcast eyes, bearing tea on an antique lacquered tray. For a time, business was interrupted by polite and soft-spoken pleasantries. It was not the ritual of the full tea ceremony, of course, but there were the civilized amenities to observe.

"Our agents report everywhere the same," Hideshi concluded. "Confederation society and technology are changing rapidly, and the pace of that change is accelerating. Our Fleet sociologists believe that within seventy years, if things continue at this pace, the biotechnical gulf between the Frontier and the Imperial core worlds will have become uncrossable. This poses a grave danger to the future security of the Empire."

"This is so." Munimori was silent for a time. He appeared to be in thought, and Hideshi elected to remain silent as well, rather than risk interrupting him. His report was nearly complete in any case.

"Often," Munimori said after another long pause, "the old ways, the conservative ways, are best. Too often, people rush forward blindly, embracing new ways, new technologies, new . . . things before those things are fully understood. *Ne*?"

"*Hai*, Gensuisama."

"I do not trust those who embrace this so-called new biotechnology. The introduction of alien parasites into one's own being . . . this lessens that which is human."

"Operation Shoki," Hideshi said carefully, "will ensure that humanity remains human, Gensuisama. All is in readiness."

"How do you like your new command, Admiral?"

"I was . . . most honored to receive this command, Gensuisama. *Soraryu* is an excellent ship, with a good crew. The squadron is well-trained and responsive. I have no doubts about their abilities."

"That is good." Without another word, Munimori picked up the scroll of haiku and began reading from it again. Seconds later, Hideshi felt a presence at his elbow; a servant had appeared, called silently by Munimori's cephlink. The interview was over.

Hideshi was somewhat troubled as he left the admiral's quarters. No specific orders had been given, but within the framework of custom and *haragei*, a word poorly translated as visceral communication—speaking without words—Munimori had told him precisely what he wanted done. Execute Operation Shoki.

It would be war.

He felt a pounding excitement in his breast. With luck, Isoru Hideshi might earn for himself a place in the ViR-history documentaries as the man who reconquered the Confederation for the Empire.

And after that, Man would be united again . . . united and ready to face these strange, new *gaijin* from beyond the constellation of the Swan.

United beneath the flag of the Empire.

# Chapter 6

*There are more things in heaven and earth, Horatio, than are dreamt of in your philosophy.*

—*Hamlet,* act I, scene v
WILLIAM SHAKESPEARE
C.E. 1600–1601

Only typically human arrogance could leap so brazenly to the conclusion that the worlds of Man had been singled out somehow by the Web for destruction or assimilation into the Web's matrix. That implied that the Web was particularly concerned about human activities, either at the Core or out in the Galaxy's spiral arms, and that was simply not the case.

There were, at the time, some twelve to fifteen *million* intelligent species scattered throughout the Galaxy humans called the Milky Way . . . the uncertainty of the figure being due both to the difficulty of providing an exact definition for that slippery word "intelligence," and to the impossibility of drawing a precise boundary for the Galaxy. Of those millions of species, some—a few percent of the total, perhaps—were engaged in actively exploring the universe about them, sending ships or probes to other stars, colonizing the nearer star systems, investigating strange or unusual phenomena, building empires based on commerce, information, or military conquest.

With so much traffic crisscrossing the Galaxy, it was inevitable that many of those exploring minds should encounter the Web. Sooner or later, any outward-questing people would decide to investigate the peculiar phenomena emanating from the Galaxy's Core. Too, it was inevitable for any spacefaring culture to eventually stumble across one of the huge, spinning structures, thread-slender in proportion to width but massing as much as a giant planet, that were positioned at the gravitational balance points of thousands of post-nova white-dwarf pairs scattered across the Galaxy.

At the time of the battle on Core D9837, for instance, the Djenna were preparing their own penetration of the Galaxy's central regions. A warrior species, quadrupeds descended from six-limbed carnivore stock, the conquerors of two hundred worlds, they'd encountered a stargate caught between two orbiting white dwarfs a few light centuries from their home cluster. Analysis of the flight paths of alien vessels moving toward and away from the gate structure suggested that one path in particular might lead to the aliens' home system. Eager to discover another *chu*-enemy with which to engage in honorable war and hero-naming—the Yath, lamentably, were now extinct—the Djenna prepared their warfleet to deliver the necessary First Challenge.

Some ten thousand light years to antispinward of the

Djenna homeworlds, the Xaxerg!k readied their four-hundred-twelfth attempt to pass through another enigmatic, whirling cylinder recently discovered a few sevens of light years from their homeworld. Descended from scavengers, these armor-plated creatures—reminiscent of Terra's annelids but far larger—had a dozen-odd senses that were distant analogues of smell or taste, employed in distinguishing among subtle variations in soil chemistries. Stolid and somewhat unimaginative, the Xaxerg!k were possessed of a tremendously stubborn persistence. Their first 411 probes had gone through their stargate and vanished, never returning; patiently, they readied number 412, not necessarily expecting success but unable to conceive of a new strategy that might produce better results.

On the other side of the Galaxy, opposite the Xaxerg!k in relation to the Core, the Seiliag had already encountered the Web some hundreds of years earlier, when living machines had descended from the green-yellow skies of that species' world and begun disassembling their cities. The Seiliag, evolved from arboreal cephalopods dwelling throughout the planet's littoral regions, had the knack for growing metal-crystal cities in the treetops of their coastal *garthech* forests that were themselves living beings drawing chlorine from the $Cl_2N_2$ atmosphere and excreting metallic salts. For reasons unknown, the Web creatures had relished the crystalline city-beings, dismantling them and hauling the shards skyward. The Seiliag had never left their world and had no effective means of fighting back. For the past three hundred of their world's long years, they'd withdrawn further and further into the dwindling *garthech* forests, waging a desperate guerrilla war against the invaders. For their part, the Web machines never seemed to be entirely aware that they were fighting a war at all . . . but any attack on them or their operations brought swift and certain retaliation.

Five thousand light years rimward from the embattled world of the Seiliag, the *#* were nearing extinction at last. Warm-blooded, trisexual amphibians with a static culture, an introspective turn of mind, and a love of arithmetic poem cycles, they possessed little in the way of technology and had no interest in exploring the universe. They had not encountered the Web directly and were unaware of the existence of any other intelligences in the universe around them. Twenty-three hundred years earlier, however, the Web had detonated two close-orbiting F-class stars less than two light years from the *#* system. The *#* sun, an old, stable K4 star, put out relatively little ionizing radiation, and the mutation rate on the system's sole inhabited world was low. Life on that world, including the *#* themselves, was not well adapted to the significantly higher radiation levels generated by the storm of charged particles that swept through the system a few years after the two neighboring stars brightened to a dazzling, day-visible brilliance. Among those *#* that did not sicken and die from direct exposure, many died of starvation as the many-legged fungi-arthropod symbionts that were the amphibians' primary food source grew scarce, and more and more *#* egg mats rotted in the birthing pools, failing to yield even a single wriggler . . . or worse by far, hatching monsters. The radiation storm was past now, and rad levels were falling everywhere, but the balance had tipped against the *#*, their gene pool already so depleted and nonviable mutations so common that the worldwide *#* population, never robust, was plummeting. The fact that three sexes were necessary for procreation instead of the more usual two only complicated things, making successful matings rare and sealing the amphibians' doom.

And eighty-five hundred light years further rimward, quite close now to the worlds known to Man, the refugee fleet of the Gr'tak continued on a quest that had already lasted through nearly four thousand years.

Humanity was destined never to meet any of the first four of those disparate peoples—Djenna, Xaxerg!k, Seiliag, and *#*. All would be extinct long before humans would have a chance to reach their parts of the Galaxy. In the case of the Djenna that was, perhaps, just as well; the immense warrior quadrupeds held a peculiar reverence for bloodshed and warfare that could have led only to grief for one, and more likely both, species, had they and the humans met. It was a pity that humans would not be able to exchange thoughts and philosophical points of view with the other three, though. The Xaxerg!k had much to teach about persistence and patience, the Seiliag about symbiotic relationships and the essential ecological unity of Life, the *#* about inner peace and the beauty of mathematics; and all three species could have learned much in turn, had they been able to communicate with humans.

The Gr'tak refugees, however, were nearing human space, drawn on by the steady pulse of microwave and modulated radio transmissions that they'd first picked up over six hundred light years out from Sol and the Imperial Shichiju. Their fleet numbered some ten thousand ships, ranging in size from the small single-seater patrol vessels like that piloted by Sholai, to immense structures that had begun as space stations orbiting lost Lakah'vnyu but had been given drives and been transformed into spacefaring arks when the Enemy had fallen upon them from the depths of space.

Sholai was still alive . . . or, rather, the *pattern* of Sholai still lived, though of the individual components in this cycle—three greaters, two lessers, one receiver, two deepers, and an artificial—only the artificial was the same as the one that had recorded those original events in the Gr'tak system nearly four thousand years before.

By addressing its artificial, Sholai could relive that first arrival of the alien craft, second by second, as it had happened so long before.

It saw again the alien's transformation as it unfolded, the smooth surface splitting along invisible seams, then everting in spiky arrays of probes and what was almost certainly weaponry. A pause, as though lightning-fast series of calculations were being made, and then the vessel split in half, the one ship becoming two, each a mirror image of the other. Traveling on slightly diverging vectors now, the two intruder vessels began slipping apart from one another. Sholai had boosted to maximum acceleration but had been unable to catch the intruder.

Hours later, one of the alien vessels began decelerating, killing its now fantastic velocity as it flashed down toward the world of Lakah'vnyu. Sholai could draw on the memories of other associatives to see that part of the story; it hurt, hurt with the deep wrench of traumatic dissociation, to see again that cloud-swirled crescent of oceans and mountains, plains and swamp, with enormous areas of its night side generating vast and roughly geometrical patterns of light. The probe seemed to take no notice of the Gr'tak city complexes . . . nor did it acknowledge the veritable cacophony of radio and laser-borne informational traffic.

Still decelerating, the probe flashed inward past the broad, circling belt of space communities orbiting Lakah'vnyu. Seconds later it struck the planet's upper atmosphere, momentarily vanishing in a blaze of blue-white radiance, then arrowing down toward the nightside on a dazzling streamer of white flame. Explosion—a detonation brighter than the initial fireball—and now the probe descended not as one huge vessel but as a vast and unstoppable swarm of smaller craft.

The Gr'tak were a peaceful people, with a unified civilization built from the beginning as a cooperative multiassociative. They possessed formidable weaponry, but their weapons were designed to shatter or deflect the comets and asteroids that periodically threatened their home world.

In any case, the Gr'tak had no experience with hostile strangers, not when their own polysymbiotic culture emphasized cooperation over competition. Aware, now, of the strangers' arrival, their first thought was to attempt communication.

When their collectives began dying, disintegrating in savage blasts of fusion heat, they were quick enough to learn. By then, however, it was far too late.

The second probe, following its own course, missed Lakah'vnyu by a considerable margin. Still accelerating it plunged toward Doval and Tovan, the double stars that warmed the world of the Gr'tak. Minutes later, shedding heat from its outer hull by means of magnetic fields powerful enough to rival and even surpass those of a star, it hurtled deeper and deeper into Doval's photosphere, vanishing in a shock wave lost against the sheer, raw fury of the sun's radiance.

It was several of Lakah'vnyu's rotational periods before the ship surfaced again, having completed its assigned operations deep within the star's core. Lakah'vnyu's primary was a twin star, both members white in color and fairly evenly matched in temperature and mass. The emergent vessel hung above the surface of Doval for a time, almost as though tasting the flow of protons comprising its photosphere . . . then moved to Tovan to vanish once again. By that time, the entire surface of Lakah'vnyu was locked in a deadly embrace with what were now clearly perceived as invaders. The Gr'tak knew of machine intelligence; indeed, most of the population utilized at least one artificial as a working part of each collective individual, and the concept of artificial intelligence was anything but foreign to them. The invader, however, appeared to be *all* machine, with no trace of its organic forebears. Shortly before it was eradicated in a savage fusion detonation, the Lakah'vnyud Cooperative of Sciences determined that the invader might well represent an intelligence so old that any organic component had been discarded ages before.

Fighting continued, but the fight was already a lost cause. The initial swarm of machines had embedded themselves in earth or sea, burrowing deep, applying fusion fires to transmute native rock into needed elements and metallic alloys, excreting bizarre and twisted shapes of metal alloy and polymer. Machines attacked by local forces, or even simply approached by Gr'tak representatives, were vigorously defended by further hordes of hunter-killer robots, jointed-legged things all glittering in shiny metallic casings, powered by pocket fusion plants and mounting powerful lasers and particle beams as weapons. The larger units, carefully protected, burrowed deeper and deeper into the planet's crust, excavating vast caverns and filling them with gleaming machinery of increasing complexity.

Before long, more machines were appearing on the surface, larger and more powerful than those of the first wave. Nuclear detonations continued to wrack the surface of the world, obliterating Associative cities, but the invaders seemed immune to heat and radiation alike, stalking through the shattered, smoking rubble beneath black and flame-shot skies, burning down not only the fleeing Gr'tak, but all life, ruthlessly, indiscriminately, almost as though the invaders couldn't tell the difference between an associative and a lesser.

The Gr'tak defense, such as it was, began crumbling. The first refugees were already streaming off-world, crowding into the orbital habitats, where anxious associatives were trying desperately to reconfigure themselves into new composites that might be able to provide workable responses to this sudden and devastating threat. Many colonies were already accelerating clear of the planet; no associative wanted to abandon Family . . . but in many cases life-support assets were already stretched perilously thin, and all cooperatives agreed that it would be better to save a few than to gamble for the lives of a few more . . . and risk losing all.

Five days after Sholai spotted the incoming Web probe, Doval exploded. The quick-gathering storm of radiation sleeting through the inner system was enough to convince those colonies that had elected to stay put to abandon their old orbits and begin accelerating at full drive.

More of the invader machines, meanwhile, were materializing on the outskirts of the system, raising terror among the crowded inhabitants of the now mobile colonies . . . though it appeared that they bothered with Gr'tak ships only when those ships attacked them first. The colonies were unarmed and did not seem to be on the invaders' agenda. Whether that was because the invaders possessed some sense of morality or fair play, or because they were for the most part unconcerned with the Gr'tak save as a source of raw materials, was unknown.

The exploding sun grew brighter, and still brighter, as the world of the Gr'tak drowned in a sea of radiation. On the surface, the last of the defenders died as temperatures soared and seas boiled. The invaders continued their enigmatic building tasks among strangely shaped towers and unfathomable machinery. The planet's atmosphere, flash-heated to incandescence, was stripped away, but the invaders were no more bothered by vacuum than by hard radiation.

Days later, Tovan exploded as well. By that time, though, all organic life on the surface of Lakah'vnyu had been extinguished, and the last of the mobile colonies, those that had not lingered so long that they'd been caught in the expanding shock wave of the nova, were now well beyond the limits of the system.

Aboard the largest of the refugee orbital colonies, the Great Council of Associatives shared their memories and pondered what course to take next. Clearly, they couldn't remain here . . . but they had no particular place to go, either. The Gr'tak had begun probing to other nearby star systems a century before, but the species's concept of community and mutual association discouraged colonization. In any case, the race had never learned the secret of traveling faster than light, and a colony voyage was a daunting prospect involving centuries. Outside of automated laboratories and research stations, there was no world to offer them refuge.

Besides, there was still the Enemy to consider.

The invaders, whatever they were, clearly were uninterested in organic forms, ignoring them entirely unless they were provoked. Union with another Associative, a large and powerful Associative, would be necessary if organic life in the Galaxy was to protect itself from the machine enemy.

Clearly, there was but a single alternative. The Gr'tak survivors would become nomads, traveling until such an Associative could be found. The Council had carefully considered the possible courses; other novae—exploding stars—had been observed in the heavens for millennia, and it had been noted that the vast majority always seemed to appear within the borders of the constellation of the *di'taak*. In most respects, one direction was very much like another in the absence of any clear sign of interstellar intelligence . . . but if the novae were an indication that these star-destroyers were traveling in a definite direction, plying their deadly trade, then there was really only one possible choice of course. Eight days after the destruction of their world, the Gr'tak nomad fleet had set off, holding to a course bearing on the constellation of the *eba* tree, on the opposite pole of the Heavenly Sphere from the *di'taak*.

Sholai possessed in its stored memories the lives and histories of over fifty previous Sholais, all the same mind, though bodies had died and been replaced time after time. In four millennia, the Fleet had trekked across over eighteen hundred light years. During that time, they'd more than once found worlds similar to Lakah'vnyu, worlds where they might have stopped and set about recreating their lost civilization. But for the Gr'tak, however, the proper way to solve problems was to add additional segments to the whole, bringing to bear new points of view and intuition to look at the problem in a different way. This approach was mirror image to Gr'tak biology, with its interlocking group minds arising from multiple but interconnected individuals. The entire race had been faced by a terrifying, an overwhelming new problem in the form of the invaders that had destroyed their suns and world; with most of the Gr'tak dead—only a few eighties of eighties of eighties had survived aboard the Fleet—the survivors had been hard-pressed to salvage even a fraction of the race's total knowledge. So many, many, many irreplaceable artificials lost, with all their lore. . . .

The Gr'tak, what was left of them, at any rate, had to find another Grand Associative, a *whole* and unbroken Associative, with which they could join and mingle data.

That mingling was part tradition, part cold necessity. Gr'tak philosophy was given form by the Great Circle, composed of myriad stars of every color and brightness, the one composed of the many. Most Gr'tak had trouble even imagining solving any problem without the active collaboration and participation of a number of associatives.

Unfortunately, the Galaxy was extremely large. Theory predicted that intelligence should be fairly common, arising as a natural product of basic physics and chemistry on worlds of as many as one out of every thousand suns. If theory was accurate, four million stars or more across the Great Wheel possessed worlds blessed with intelligent life . . . but finding even one required searching as many as a thousand barren systems, a search that could take a very long time indeed.

Still, they'd tried, stopping at numerous stars as they moved outward from their former home, with the deadly, pearl-gleam light of their suns' funeral pyre fading behind them. On several, they found the crumbling remnants of civilizations long dead, and once they found a world populated by mossy, many-legged things that made tools from stone but were stubbornly and belligerently uncommunicative.

In any case, the Gr'tak knew that only a culture as advanced as their own would provide the answers they needed. They continued searching.

At long last, though, they'd encountered the faint, nonrandom crackle and buzz of modulated RF signals, a definite beacon shining in radio light against the misty backdrop of the Great Wheel, signals that spoke of Life . . . and Mind. The discovery had been purely random; had the Fleet continued on its original course, they might easily have skimmed through the outer fringes of that signal as it expanded at lightspeed across interstellar space and never even noticed it, or the message it carried.

Now, long after the detection of that first signal, space glowed ahead of the Fleet, rich in the muted colors of radio and microwave wavelengths. They were deep inside the volume of expanding radio noise now, a volume encompassing some thousands of stars; directly ahead, the innermost core of that radio shell beckoned, a cluster of discrete radio sources bearing the unmistakable imprint of technic civilization. Samplings were analyzed, ordered, tasted. The Gr'tak knew a quickening excitement. There was a richness of experience here that suggested Associatives on a grand scale.

The nearest star centered on its own glob of radio noise now hung scant light hours ahead of the hard-decelerating Fleet. . . .

# Chapter 7

*The Xenophobes—or the Naga, as humans eventually called them, after an ancient Terran serpent deity of wealth, peace, and fertility—were terribly hard to understand precisely because they were so different. Composed of countless trillions of individual cells, each massing one or two kilograms at most, a planetary Naga was like a single titanic brain, with the cells serving as interlinking neurons. They occupied the crust of the planet they'd infested, tunneling vast chambers underground, converting rock through a kind of natural nanotechnology into organic, living material. Active Naga eventually tunneled through to the surface of their world, manipulated magnetic fields in order to launch bits of themselves to the stars, then settled down into a kind of contemplative senescence . . . almost as though they were waiting for something.*

*Their view of the universe was strangely twisted from the human; for them, the universe was an endless sea of rock with a central emptiness, a world literally inside-out from what humans perceived. Nonetheless, with contact came communication, and with communication, slowly, came a halting but growing understanding.*

—*The Naga: A Study in Xenophobia*
PROFESSOR DEREK K. BROWN
C.E. 2554

The CRS *Carl Friedrich Gauss* had not been designed as a luxury liner, nor as a warship. She mounted lasers and particle beam weapons, but the bow lasers had been installed as sweepers, computer-controlled weapons for disintegrating the bits of dust and cosmic flotsam that might endanger the vessel during high-speed maneuvers. Despite the fact that she was a converted passenger ship, her lines were not particularly elegant; her central spine, just under half a kilometer from blunt prow to massive aft thruster nacelles and made cumbersome by its clutter of blisters, nacelles, and strap-on slush-H tanks, was girdled by a broad ring mounted on a rotation cuff a quarter of the way back from the bow. When she was in free fall, her plasma drives silent, as now, the ring's stately rotation provided spin gravity. During acceleration, the ring section's decks, with nanotechnic tiles that reshaped themselves beneath the crew's and passengers' feet, adjusted the deck's angle to compensate for the change in acceleration vector.

As a research ship, *Gauss* would have been comfortable enough, if a bit spartan. With the addition of the Phantoms, however, space was at an absolute premium. The Phantoms' striderjacks were not the only guests aboard. The company had brought with it eighty-five other officers and enlisted personnel, ranging from mechanics and weapons technicians to General Vic Hagan himself, and his tactical staff.

Her father, Kara knew, had not really chosen *Gauss* as his temporary headquarters just because Kara and the Phantoms had been transferred aboard. *Gauss*, at the moment, was the center of all research into the Web, and he'd wanted to stay on top of the data Kara and her people were bringing in, as it arrived and was digested.

The conference room was on Deck One in the *Gauss*'s ring section, with gravity provided by the ring's slow spin. The broad, curved viewall screen showed no sign of that rotation, however, since the image was being piped through from a camera mounted in *Gauss*'s stationary prow.

The room had been empty when Kara was ushered in by a Confed marine guard in full dress. The viewall showed the Nova Aquila Stargate, needle-slender at this distance, its silvery length reflecting the light of the two white dwarf stars that circled one another at a distance of some 800,000 kilometers, the Stargate balanced at their center of gravity. Each star emitted a stream of scarlet flame that spiraled around half an orbit to vanish into the ends of the Gate like silken streamers at the end of a twirled baton. The scientists and technicians studying the Web and associated phenomena believed they were channeling star stuff into the Gate and across the Galaxy to some other site . . . but where that site might be, and why they were mining the stars of plasma stripped from their atmospheres; was still unknown.

Several other ships of the Unified Fleet were visible onscreen as well. *Shinryu*, the big ryu-class flagship of the Imperial Navy contingent. *Constitution* and *Reliant*, a pair of cruisers with the Confed squadron. *Karyu* was the Confederation flag, by far the largest vessel of the entire Confederation fleet. Originally an Imperial ryu carrier, she'd been captured twenty-seven years before at the Second Battle of Herakles. Kara's father had often joked that he'd named his daughter after the huge battle prize.

Also visible were a half dozen of the big, rough-surfaced starfish shapes that were living DalRiss cityships, each kilometers across, vaster by far than even the largest of the human-built ships.

The Unified Fleet had been parked here, orbiting the double star–Stargate trio at the hopefully safe remove of nearly one astronomical unit, where they could keep a watchful eye on the enigmatic Stargate. The fleet's actual eyes were much closer in, of course—robot flyers teleoperated by pilots maintaining I2C links from both the *Karyu* and the *Shinryu*. If Web machines emerged through the Gate's invisible portals, the fleet would know about it instantly, rather than in the seven to eight minutes it would take for news of the arrival to crawl out from the Gate by more conventional means.

The door hissed open at her back. "Kara!" a familiar voice said. "I'm so sorry to keep you waiting!"

She turned, smiling. Her father, General Victor Hagan, advanced toward her with outstretched arms. He, too, was in full dress uniform, the two-toned grays of the Confederation Navy. Normally, he would have been stationed aboard *Karyu* with the Unified Fleet's Confederation Military Command Staff, but he'd been crowded in with the other guests aboard the research ship for almost a month, now . . . and he still always managed to present the crisp perfection in dress and bearing of the professional military officer. Kara wasn't sure how he managed it. He must, she decided wryly, grow himself a new uniform every couple of hours to keep it looking that sharp.

She also suspected he donned fresh-grown grays each time he was going to meet with her, for whatever reason. *He can be sentimental that way, sometimes*, Kara thought with a secret smile.

"Hi, Dad," she said, returning his hug. "You didn't keep me waiting at all."

He pushed her back and held her at arm's length for a moment, studying her face. "You're okay?"

"Clean bill of health. No static."

He let her go and glanced around the empty room. "I told Daren you were back," he said, glancing around. "I was expecting him to be here."

Kara shrugged, unconcerned. "The day my brother can be anywhere on time. . . ."

"He has been busy," Vic said. He looked at Kara a moment longer, then grinned with evident relief. "Damn, I'm so glad you're back. Back and. . . ." He broke off, embarrassed.

"And still sane?" Kara said, filling in the blank. "Or as sane as I ever was, at least."

"The casualty figures haven't exactly been encouraging," Vic said.

"No, they haven't," Kara agreed. She cocked her head to the side. "You know, Dad, it seems sometimes that the high brass has declared open season on striderjacks like us. Each mission they dream up is hairier than the last one. We're going to lose more good people if they keep sending us into hellholes like the Core."

"How was it?" Vic asked. "How was it *really*?"

Kara suppressed a shudder, crossing her arms, her hands

clasping her elbows close to her sides. "Well, you'll get my report when I write the thing and download it. I just came up from the intelligence debrief on the war deck, so I haven't exactly had time for the routine scutwork."

"I'm not looking for your report," he told her. "I wouldn't normally get to see it anyway, unless I asked for it special. And then, well, it looks bad."

She nodded. Having a general for a father, especially one as high-ranking and as powerfully connected as *the* Victor Hagan, could be a real problem, especially when she was trying to carve out her own career as a Confed military officer. The fact that her mother was Senator Katya Alessandro of the Confederation Senate made it even worse. There was always the assumption—unspoken, of course, but very real—that she'd gotten her rank because of her family connections.

Vic spread his hands. "But I *do* want to know what you saw in there," he continued. "I'll be briefed, certainly, and I'll get to see both the recordings you made and the conclusions from your regular debriefing, but it helps me a lot to have an eyewitness run-down. I'd appreciate hearing . . . well, your impressions. Of the Web. Of what we're up against."

Kara shrugged. "I don't know what I could say that you don't know already. I'm really not sure what we learned today that we haven't known since the battle here two years ago." She paused, frowning. "There *was* one thing I wanted to make special mention of. There were times when I was moving around on the planet alone . . . and Web machines were moving around too, in easy range, but they ignored me. Didn't even look at me, as near as I could tell."

"That's interesting."

"I thought so. I don't know what it means, but it seems like a, well, a weakness, maybe. Something we can exploit. I got the distinct impression that they are so wedded to the idea of lots and lots of parts working together as a whole, they tend to neglect individuals. They may not even think of individuals the way we do. Maybe that means they tend to overlook them."

"That seems a little farfetched."

"Oh, I don't know. It's like you might overlook a couple of scraps of metal lying on the landing deck where you *know* damned well you parked your flitter. The pieces could be a very important part of your flitter's magdrive train, but you tend to see the flitter's absence, not the pieces' presence."

"Interesting analogy," Vic said.

Kara reached out one slim hand, holding it above a contact plate on the table. "May I?"

"Of course."

At her mental command, a patch of skin centered on the heel of her palm hardened into a peripheral contact plate, and she brought it down onto the black translucence of the table's receiver pad. She felt the thrill of a solid link, gave a second command, and waited as her download trickled through to the AI controlling this compartment's electronics.

There was a flicker in the air above the table, and then the image coalesced, showing the surface of Core D9837, and the ragged, double-beamed spiral of the Great Annihilator in the sky. In several brief scenes and uneven leaps, she took him through a sketch of the battle, with special attention lavished on the huge, floating pyramid.

"I'm sure you've already seen this," she told him.

"I was following the op realtime," he told her. "Through the data you were relaying to Ops." The bald words could not—quite—mask the emotion behind them. He'd been worried. Well, so had she.

"This pyramid thing," she said, pointing at the holographic image. "It's new. Or, at least, it's something we haven't run across before. I don't remember seeing anything quite like this at Nova Aquila. It might be primarily a spacecraft design, but I had the impression it was just as comfortable on a planetary surface . . . or floating above it, rather."

"We haven't really seen how they fight *on* a planet," Vic said, eyes narrowing as he considered the image. "In fact, I think our assumption has been all along that they tend to operate mostly in space."

"Not entirely true," Kara reminded him. "We've seen them entering and leaving stars."

"Yes. And when they have that kind of technology, it

makes you wonder what they could possibly want something as paltry as a planet for.''

"Raw materials, most likely," Kara replied.

"Maybe." He pointed into the image, indicating the distant black and silver towers. "Of course, if this architecture is theirs, it suggests they do still use planets for habitation."

She shook her head. "I never got close to those, but my impression is they weren't inhabited so much as *used*."

"Ruins of some other race that used to live there?"

She frowned. "I don't think so. Core D9837 is a rogue, remember. Its star, if it even ever had one, must have been swallowed up by a black hole a good many millions of years ago." That, at least, was the prevailing theory of the planetologists aboard *Gauss*, who'd suggested that the barren world's high velocity through the Core was the result of its being ejected when its star perished. "And the environment. Kuso! I don't see how any organic life form could have ever lived in there. Organic molecules would break down . . ." She snapped her fingers. "Like that."

"The current theory," Vic said, "is that the Web's creators evolved on the fringes of the Galactic Core, where the radiation levels weren't so high. They moved into the Core to tap the more freely available energies in there, and along the way they learned how to download their minds into machine bodies."

She shrugged. "Sounds plausible, I suppose."

"Which leaves us still wondering what people who mine stars use planets for."

"Kuso, Dad, we don't know anything about them. These people don't just mine stars. They herd them into great, gokking chorus lines and drop them into giant black holes! As far as I can tell, planets are nothing more than inconveniences to them."

"It certainly seems unlikely that machines that live in space, if live is the right word, would have any use for buildings," Vic pointed out.

Kara nodded. "My guess was that those structures might be the upper works of factories or other underground facilities, maybe built that way to shield them against the ambient radiation. I know that as we kept killing their combat machines, more kept appearing from underground, like we were up against an inexhaustible supply. Maybe they use planets, and the raw materials they offer, as sites for manufacturing their machines.'' She paused. ''There's also the Naga to think about. The fact that they seemed to have been designed to convert planets into more convenient concentrations of raw material for the Web.''

''True,'' Vic said quietly. ''Though we obviously still don't know all there is to know about that.''

''We'd damn well better find out.''

Two years ago, shortly before the Battle of Nova Aquila, Dev Cameron's probing of the Web concentration at the Galactic Core had demonstrated that the long-mysterious Naga were originally, long, long ago, biomachine constructs controlled by the Web. Humanity had first encountered the Naga almost a century before, when they'd attacked human structures—cities, sky-els, anything with high concentrations of pure metal—on several worlds within the Shichiju. For years, humans had called them Xenophobes and waged a desperate and relentless war of extermination against creatures that, in fact, had been only marginally aware of humans and were inherently unable even to conceive of intelligent beings other than *Self*. In 2541, however, after numerous failures and the loss of millions of lives, Dev Cameron had finally managed to establish communications with them.

What had followed had changed the course both of history and of human technology. It was discovered that the Naga were chemists extraordinaire, that they acted in some ways like extremely complex serially linked computers, and that they could analyze and pattern any material, including human tissue, and even nanotechnically alter it to improve its function. At Mu Herculis, during the Confederation Rebellion, Dev Cameron had accidentally entered into a symbiotic relationship with a planetary Naga, initiating an exchange that had ultimately led to a far better understanding of those creatures.

Symbiosis with the Naga had eventually become commonplace, and it was becoming more so all the time. Twenty-five years ago, most human-machine interfaces had been carried out through cephlinks, electronic devices nanotechnically grown inside the human brain. With the help of the alien DalRiss and their mastery of biological processes at a molecular level, a single cell from a planetary Naga that had had contact with humans could be trained to enter a human body, where it served as an organic neural cephlink ... and far more. The result was a symbiont like Kara herself, with a Naga Companion riding her central nervous system that could facilitate her union with machines and with other humans. Xenosymbiotic biotech, it was called, and some hundreds of millions of humans—most of them in the Confederation—had already received Companions and become what many claimed was a new and more advanced type of human.

The one big mystery remaining, of course, had been something the Naga themselves had never been able to clarify, and that was where the creatures had come from in the first place. The discovery of the Web—and the first probing of the Web's stronghold at the Galactic Core—had demonstrated that the Naga had originally been life forms created by the Web intelligence. Though there still were no solid answers, the best guess of the researchers working on the problem was that the Nagas had been designed as advance scouts of a sort, creatures scattered abroad beyond the Galaxy's central Core to begin converting worlds into immense factories, steadily converting raw material into ... something else. Worlds where a Naga had at last grown so vast that it had broken through to the surface—a world Naga was equivalent in mass to a small moon and numbered hundreds of trillions of cells—were eerily transformed, the surface features molded into bizarre towers, domes, and weirdly sculpted, vaguely organic shapes.

The buildings Kara had seen on Core D9837 had been like distant echoes of the organic-looking architecture grown by mature planetary Naga. It seemed to verify that the Naga were following some very old, embedded programming, orders passed down to them by the Web eons before but that had somehow become garbled along the way. The Naga did not remember the Web, but—more interesting—the Web seemed to recognize Naga, although as a kind of cancer, cells that no longer responded properly to direction or control. In effect, the Naga were continuing to follow their original programming that required them to spread across the Galaxy, preparing planets for the arrival of the Web . . . but some accident long before had cut them off from Web control and turned them loose on their own. For a long time—some estimates said eight billion years—they'd been slowly spreading across the Galaxy, drawn to worlds of a particular mass and magnetic moment, and colonizing them.

It was a chilling thought that literally billions of worlds across the entire Galaxy might already be infested with wild Nagas, while only a handful had been contacted and domesticated by humans. "Domestication" was a relatively simple process, involving no more than allowing cells from a Naga that had had peaceful contact with humans to exchange data with the uncontacted Naga, but the sheer scale of the alien infestation was staggering.

Vic, Kara noticed, had taken a seat at the table and was now leaning back, his eyes closed, a look of concentration on his face. She remained silent, waiting, until he opened his eyes again.

"Well, *that's* weird," he said.

"What is?"

"An oddball effect with Shell Game." He frowned. "Dr. Norris just called up from Bay Seven. I don't quite know what to make of it."

"So what's the problem?"

"They've just recovered one of the Shell Game probes. You know, the ones we've been sending through the Stargate to pass disinformation to the Web." She nodded, and he went on. "We program a certain percentage of them to go through, take a quick look around, and come back. The Web nails some, of course, but most of them have been able to return. We'd never have been able to plan for Core Peek without that reconnaissance data. That's how we identified all of those rogue planets and bodies in there, including D9837."

"So, they recovered a probe? What's so weird about that?"

He looked at her steadily. "If I'm understanding what Norris is trying to say, the probe they just picked up is one scheduled for launch in . . .'' He closed his eyes, concentrating on some inner pulldown data feed from his Companion. ''Another five hours from now.''

Kara's eyes widened. ''You mean—''

''I'm afraid so. Somehow, the damned thing came back to us over five hours before we launched it. It looks like the physics boys were right. The Stargate is also a gate through *time*.''

# Chapter 8

*Progress in physics has always moved from the intuitive toward the abstract.*

—MAX BORN
Professor of Theoretical Physics
University of Göttingen
mid-twentieth century C.E.

Kara was excited. ''Time travel! Let's get down there and have a look at this!''

''Daughter of mine,'' Vic said in his best lecturing tone, ''you've been in the military long enough to know that generals do *not* jump and run at every report from the ranks. Besides, we're supposed to meet Daren. Damn it, where is he?''

She chuckled. ''You know Daren. Tell you what. I'll bounce down and have a look. Give you a report later, okay?''

''Sounds good to me. I'd just as soon get a briefing later anyway. When physicists like Norris start throwing data-intensive words around, it gives me a headache. *Especially* when they tack the word 'quantum' on at the beginning.''

Kara laughed. "I know what you mean. Sometimes I think physics took a distinct wrong turn. Somewhere between Clerk Maxwell and Albert Einstein."

"Einstein I don't mind so much," Vic said. "It's Heisenberg that worries me. If the guy had just been able to make up his mind . . ."

Ten minutes later, Kara walked into the hangar bay, watching her step as she crossed an open space cluttered with crates and expendables containers, cables, power feeds, and the low, black-and-yellow shapes of K30 cargo haulers weaving in and around the larger, hulking shapes of tele-operated heavy loaders and military equipment. Spotlights glared from the upper reaches of the gantries and crisscrossing support struts that masked most of the overhead. The noise—a clangor of metal-on-metal, the bark of shouted orders, the hiss of a laser arc welder—joined in ear-pounding cacophony.

Bay Seven was located in the spin-gravity portion of the ship. Someone dropped a heavy tool kit to the metal deck grating from a height of several meters, and the clash nearly made her jump and whirl; somehow, she controlled the reflex and kept walking, searching for Dr. Norris and Lieutenant Coburn. They were supposed to be in here, preparing the next Shell Game probe for its flight into the unknown, and downloading its memory when it returned.

She found them at last in one corner of the cluttered bay, working together at an out-of-the-way table secluded somewhat from the rest of the activity by a wall of supply crates and empty missile transport canisters.

Cal Norris was a slight man with wispy gray hair, the slightly enlarged eyeballs of a man who'd undergone a Companion reshaping to correct extreme myopia, and a wry sense of humor. Lieutenant Tanya Coburn was a pretty, red-headed warstrider officer who'd been part of Kara's own Phantoms, but who'd been reassigned to the *Carl Friedrich Gauss*'s science department in order to provide them with her expertise in handling teleoperated recon probes.

"There you two are," Kara told them. "What's all this about time travel? You have the brass all worked up."

Norris looked up and quirked a grin at her. "They're

getting nervous, are they? Can't say I blame them.'' He nodded toward the inert probe on the table in front of them. ''This thing is getting *me* damned nervous.''

''Oh, don't mind the Doc,'' Tanya said. ''He's as excited about this as a kid on Armstrong Day.''

The sleek object on the table was a Mark VII reconnaissance drone, a tiny, jet-black manta-shaped craft two meters long, with a small anticollision strobe on its back, and the alphanumerics AE356 painted in dark gray on the trailing edges of the manta's wings aft. Normally, the craft was teleoperated. On this mission, however, the on-board AI had carried out the necessary navigational routines.

''So what happened?''

''*That* happened,'' Norris said, waving one arm at a cargo trailer parked by a stack of empty missile crates five meters away. Resting on the cart was another Mark VII, an exact duplicate of the probe in front of her. Without taking even one step closer, Kara could read the ID on its side, AE356.

''Maybe you should see this, Captain,'' Tanya said. She led her over to a viewwall on the nearby bulkhead and palmed the interface. The screen lit up an instant later, showing the familiar camera view of the Stargate. It looked like it was being shot from a remote flyer operating somewhere within a few thousand kilometers of the Stargate's surface. In the center of the screen she could see a tiny, blinking red light.

After holding on the view for a moment, the scene zoomed in closer. Kara could just make out an elongated shape there, something black, with a shiny hull, and what looked like an oval port or sensor lens on the front. The flashing light was a standard anticollision strobe mounted on the object's dorsal surface.

''That was about half an hour ago,'' Tanya said. ''Our sentry probes picked up its AI transmission, requesting clearance to return to the *Gauss*. The only problem was, we didn't have any probes out at the time.''

''We're not scheduled to launch AE356 until sixteen hundred hours this afternoon,'' Norris said irritably.

''What did it have to say for itself?'' Kara asked.

Norris shook his head, scowling. ''According to it, it was launched from the *Gauss* at sixteen hundred hours today. It entered the Stargate at seventeen-fifty and some odd seconds. Twenty-one point three one seconds, to be precise. It performed its scheduled reconnaissance of the Galactic Core, in particular watching for any activity that might be the result of your raid in there this morning. It noted some activity, but nothing that could be considered threatening."

"No buildup for a counter-raid through the Gate," Tanya said, elaborating.

"That's good."

"It was pursued by a number of Web machines," Norris continued. "Its AI was able to elude them and it returned through the Stargate, entering at twenty-thirty-two hours, zero-three minutes, twelve seconds."

Kara blinked. "That was half an hour ago? That probe over there . . . is nine hours and some older than this one?"

"They are the same probe," Norris said, nodding, "but manifested nine hours apart in the temporal dimension."

"And how do you explain that?"

"Well, it's been known since the late twentieth century that devices such as that should open gates in time as well as space. The equations allow space and time to be more or less interchangeable. Rotate an object this way, and the change in perspective can be manifested as a change in referent time instead."

"Whoosh!" Kara passed her hand rapidly above her head, from front to back. "I'm afraid you just overshot, Doctor."

"We know that spatial translation through a Stargate depends on approaching the gate along a certain, mathematically calculated path. Yes?"

"Fine so far." The precise path for the Phantoms' transit to the Galactic Core had been very carefully downloaded to her RAM, and she'd been warned in no uncertain terms that if she deviated at all from that path, her strider would be lost.

"Changes in the approach path can change your exit point," Norris continued. "That much is obvious. It turns out that certain changes in your approach can be expressed not as a change in space, or not in space only, but in time as well. We've known this, from the math, but this is the first time we've seen any evidence that this sort of thing happens in the real world." He grinned ruefully, shaking his head. "This is really going to gok up the whole idea of causality, I'm afraid."

Kara saw what he was getting at. She patted the probe on the table. "Like for instance . . . what happens if you decide not to send old AE356 here through the Gate? Is that what you mean?"

"That's exactly what I mean. Physics has always tried to erect barriers to prevent any flow of information across time. We've always been aware that the math, and especially the weirder aspects of quantum mechanics, have allowed for time travel. But we've tried to jigger things so that in practical terms, at any rate, it's impossible to violate causality, to have the cause happen *after* the effect."

"I'm curious about something," Kara said. She rested her hand lightly on the casing of the probe that had not been launched yet. "For the sake of argument, this is Probe One, okay?"

Tanya and Norris both nodded.

Kara walked the five meters across to the second probe, where it rested in its cradle. "And this is Probe Two."

"Fine," Norris said. "What does that prove?"

Kara leaned closer, studying the alphanumerics printed on the second probe's flank. "Doctor, come over here with me. You're my witness. Tanya? Go to Probe One. Take a look at the letters on the starboard side aft."

"Okay."

"Use your cutter, the one on the table there. See if you can make a mark on the letter 'E.'"

"I think I see what you're after," Norris said. He leaned over next to her, fixing his gaze on the gray letters. "Go ahead, Tanya."

Across the room, Tanya picked up a small laser cutter, the size of a pen, and brought the tip close to Probe One's side. As Kara and Norris watched, a black line drew itself slowly across the back of the E, between the middle and top horizontal arms.

"Oh . . . my . . . God . . ." Norris said quietly, almost reverently.

Kara walked over to Probe One, where Tanya was standing with a quizzical expression. "What happened?"

Kara pointed at the mark on the back of the E. A wisp of smoke was still curling from the blackened streak charred into the gray paint. "That happened," she said. "Over there, while we watched. You went from left to right, didn't you?"

Tanya's eyes widened. "You saw it?"

Kara nodded. "These two probes *are* the same."

"It makes no sense," Norris said, shaking his head. "I mean, even if Probe Two *is* Probe One, several hours later in the future, what we do to one shouldn't affect the other." He stopped, then blinked several times. "Should it?"

"Hell, how should I know, Doctor?" Kara said. "I'm just a striderjack, remember? But you know, they say that paired electrons, the ones in quantum couplings, used in the I2C? They say that in a way those aren't really two different electrons, but the same one. That's why when something changes the spin of one, the spin of the other changes the same way, even when it's light years away. It doesn't make sense, not the way we look at the universe. But it happens, and the laws of quantum mechanics say it has to be that way."

Norris pursed his lips, started to say something, reconsidered, then reconsidered again. "Still can't buy it. I mean, okay. We have proof that Probe Two is really Probe One, just a few hours older, but sent back through time, somehow, to a time before it was launched. Right?" The two women nodded agreement. "Okay. So what if we decide, hell, no. We're not going to launch the damned thing at all. What happens then? Probe Two disappears because we didn't launch it in the first place?"

"Maybe we should try," Tanya said, one eyebrow arched. "I'd like to know what happens."

Kara shook her head. "I think we'd better run this one the way the orders are written. Later, when not as much is riding on it, maybe then we can play. For now, I'd say you should get the probe . . . Probe One, I mean, ready to go." She looked across at Probe Two curiously. "And on time."

Tanya laughed. "If this gets routine, we could save a hell of a lot of money on recon probes. Just get one ready, recover it before we send it out, download the intel, then forget the whole thing. We have our data without risking the probe!"

"Somehow," Kara said, "there's got to be some kind of a law in the universe that says you can't do this." She thought of her father's comment earlier and grinned. "I'm starting to get a headache."

Minutes later, she returned to the conference room on Deck One. Her father was still there, as was Daren Cameron. The younger man sat on the table with one knee up and the other leg dangling.

Daren was a dark-haired man in his late twenties, stocky bordering on pudgy, wearing a sharply tailored civilian skinsuit with elaborate shoulder halfcloaks. A doctor of xenobiology from the University of Jefferson on New America—he'd taken the full doctorate download by the time he was seventeen—he was Kara's half-brother, the son of Katya Alessandro and Devis Cameron. And *there* was a strangely twisted love triangle, Kara thought, if ever there was one.

"Hey, Sis! How was the Galactic Core?"

"Hot."

"Yeah, it's been hot on Dante, too." Dante—DM-58° 5564 II—was a world in the Shichiju, home of the Dantean Communes, a species of communal organisms that Daren had been studying for some time now. Their particular mystery was whether or not they could be classified as sapient; certainly, their intelligence was of a radically different order from human or DalRiss, enough so that communications with them might be forever impossible.

"I meant hot as in radioactive," Kara said, faintly exasperated. Daren, frequently, couldn't see beyond the limits of his own rather narrow field of vision, and he was self-centered enough that he could rarely empathize with the problems of others. Assigned to the *Gauss* as part of the xenobiology team studying the Web, he'd nevertheless continued with his own work as well, researching the question of Commune intelligence.

"Ah." Daren shrugged. "So, did you military types find anything useful in there?"

Kara bristled. She sometimes had the impression that Daren didn't think much of the military, or of its ability to gather data or solve problems. "We picked up a thing or two," she said. "I'll be uploading to the milnet later." She turned to Vic. "You were right, Dad, about what Dr. Norris had. It was weird. I think I'm going to want to file a report on that, too." She cocked her head. "Unless it's classified?"

"Oh, it'll be classified. Lately they've been classifying how many times the senior staff has to go use the head. But with I2C, there's no chance of an intercept. You're right, of course. ConMilCom ought to know about this."

"Know about what?" Daren asked.

"Classified, brother dear," Kara told him sweetly. "Not for civilian download."

"Your mother was worried about you, Kara," Vic said, as though stepping in to head off a confrontation. "I passed the word to her that you were okay as soon as I knew, but I imagine she'd like to hear from you herself."

Kara brightened. "I was planning on paying her a visit. I'm off on a twenty-four as soon as I finish my reports."

"ViRcom?"

"Hubot, actually. I figured since they've put the system in for surface leave, I might as well use it."

Teleoperated hubots, humanoid robots ridden by the operator's linked-in mind the way a striderjack rode a warstrider, had long been popular on Earth and some other worlds of the Shichiju, a means of visiting other places and conducting face-to-face business on the planet without actually leaving home. The robot's electronic senses provided a full range of sensory input, giving the rider the feeling of actually being there, and concessions on Earth and elsewhere had long rented travel time to popular historical sites and tourist playgrounds.

With the development of I2C for other than strictly military applications, hubotravel, as it was becoming known, was growing more popular than ever.

Vic nodded. "Well, have a good time. Give your mom my best, and tell her how much I miss her."

"Yeah," Daren smirked. "And don't do anything that'll make you rust."

"You should know," she told him. Since hubotraveling had become available to researchers with the Fleet, he'd been using them to visit the wet, hothouse world of Dante. She teased him sometimes about turning into a rusted, tin-man statue on the beach next to some Commune hive.

It was five more hours before Kara could get off duty and make the trip down to *Gauss*'s communications lounge. As she stepped into the large, softly lit chamber, filled with the white ceramic commods that always reminded her of coffins or modern-era sarcophagi, she saw that most of the pods were occupied. *Gauss* boasted a crew of several hundred, and the comm modules provided access not only to conversations with loved ones back home, but to entertainment as well.

Selecting one of the empty pods, she climbed inside, snuggled back into the padded seat that adjusted itself to fit her contours, and let the cover hiss quietly shut. Her Companion had already begun growing endpoints, which quested sightlessly toward the pod's link contacts.

For several centuries, now, the standard means of interpersonal communications had been the ViRcom, virtual reality communications. Through cephlinks—and more recently through Naga symbionts—two or more people could climb into separate comm modules and meet in a virtual world run by the AI communications software moderating the exchange. For each person in the link-up it was like stepping into another world, one where you could interact on several levels with the others. The system had soon gone far beyond mere communications, of course, and begun serving both as an entertainment system and as a means of doing business. Virtual dramas, sex fantasies, games, and adventure role-playing were all accessed through the commods. Nowadays most people carried one or more analogues resident in their personal software, versions of themselves in different dress or personae, as well as AI-driven secretaries that could field incoming communications and handle day-to-day routine business without bothering the original, or primary, personality.

Once, the limitations of the speed of light had hampered direct conversations across distances of more than a few light seconds. The advent of I2C had changed that, however. During the last two years, I2C technology had begun revolutionizing all forms of long-range communication. Linking together the various business and government computer networks employed by the worlds throughout the far-flung

Shichiju and Confederation systems had been the first big step, but other forms of personal communication had swiftly followed, including both standard ViRcommunications and the use of hubots.

"Communications," a voice said in Kara's ear. "Please upload any necessary clearances at this time."

She'd been granted a twenty-four-hour pass—all of the members of her company had been promised a twenty-four after Core Peek—and the clearance number would reserve for her more than the usual one- or two-hour session inside the pod. A menu unfolded itself in her mind, and she quickly checked off the appropriate boxes . . . standard communications, ship-to-New America, no game-play, no special software prostheses, with hubot transference at the far end through the Be There agency in downtown Jefferson. The monitoring AI took only milliseconds to grant her request and open the necessary I2C channels.

With the last of her choices complete, the menu in her head vanished as she gave the Go command, and she was plunged into a static-fired darkness. In a sense, at least, her mind hurtled twelve hundred light years, instantly.

The Imperials who'd developed I2C had tried hard to keep it secret, of course; had they been successful, they would have won an immediate and overwhelming military advantage over the tiny, scattered forces of the Confederation. The Confederation's freewheeling, free-market approach to all technology, however, had guaranteed that I2C would find a much broader application, one that was very quickly transforming every aspect of human life almost as completely as the revolution in xenosymbiotic biotech.

Until the advent of I2C, for example, hubotraveling had been limited to the surface of one world or, at best, to orbit. Now, hubots could be ridden anywhere from anywhere, so long as the appropriate I2C electronics and computers were in place.

The static cleared. She opened her eyes . . . expecting to see the interior of a hubot rental agency. What she saw instead was the looming, dark violet sky of Core D9837, the pale, ragged spiral of the Great Annihilator, the thrust and gleam of the alien buildings on the horizon.

Kara screamed . . .

# Chapter 9

*An entire world can reside comfortably within the spaciousness offered by a few geloyabytes of computer memory. Run either by an outside controller or by a dedicated AI, that world can be as richly detailed as necessary, both through data provided from outside sources, and through the mechanics of chaos theory.*

*It has been suggested, in fact, that more humans will one day live in imaginary, virtual worlds than might at that time inhabit so-called reality.*

—*Worlds Without End*
JENNIFER WARD-HARDING
C.E. 2570

. . . and immediately, with some effort, brought herself back under control. This had to be illusion, a ViRcom illusion of some sort. *Had* to be. She was standing on the broad, open, radiation-baked plain where her company had made its last stand hours before. The ground underfoot was charred by the nuke she'd set off, crunching like broken glass beneath her boot as she took a hesitant step forward. She felt a hot wind on her cheek, and a prickling sensation on her skin, that might have represented the ambient background radiation. No, if she were *really* standing in this place without any protection whatsoever, she would have been dead before the nerve endings of her body had time to react.

Instead, this was some sort of elaborate ViRdrama, one almost certainly drawn from the information she herself had gleaned from Core D9837. The question, though, was not so much how she'd gotten to this virtual place as who had intercepted her en route from Nova Aquila to New America.

Her first thought, in fact, was that the Web must have done this; it was impossible to stand on that plain and look up at the black-hole accretion disk hanging in the sky and not feel—despite the impossibility of her survival in that place—that she'd been physically dragged here.

*And you know that can't be, Kara*, she told herself fiercely. *You haven't* really *gone anywhere, no matter what it might feel like.*

She closed her eyes for a moment, reminding herself consciously that her body was still lying in the life-support commod capsule back aboard the *Gauss*, that her mind—most simply defined as a kind of complex, multilayered program running on the organic computer she called her brain—had not really left her body. These images she was seeing, the sounds she was hearing, the sensation of crunching gravel underfoot and heat caressing her skin, all were being played inside her brain through her symbiotic interface. It could as easily be the fictional display of an AI running an entertainment ViRdrama, or the setting for a ViRcom meeting with someone.

She opened her eyes. A tall, slender figure was approaching her from the shadows of the nearest of the alien structures. Though she could see it only in silhouette at first, the movements were too much those of a human for it to be one of the Web machines. She stood her ground, watching as it drew closer.

Then the figure walked into the brighter circle of light around Kara, and she gave a small, involuntary gasp. She recognized the lean features, the Confederation Navy uniform, the erect bearing and manner . . . and she knew who had intercepted her, even if she didn't understand the actual mechanics.

The figure was Dev Cameron's.

Involuntarily, she shuddered. Though she'd worked with him before, she still hadn't completely reconciled herself to the existence of this . . . *being*, a technological ghost, the ghost, in fact, of the man who once had been her mother's lover, who was her half-brother's father. During the last battle between the rebel Confederation and the Imperium, twenty-seven years before, Dev Cameron had been physically aboard a DalRiss cityship, helping to direct an assault against Imperial naval forces. His mind, however, had been dispersed across a vast network of Naga–DalRiss computers and communications nets, a program resident in the entire, interlinked network rather than on any one, limited node.

When the DalRiss ship housing Cameron's body had been destroyed, his body had been destroyed as well. Somehow, though, the mind had lived on, resident within the complex and interwoven communications links connecting the nodes of the rest of the DalRiss fleet, a high-tech ghost.

"Hello, Kara," Dev said, and his smile was most unghostlike, precisely the same as the one she'd seen in holographs of the man made before his "death." "I'm glad you came through Core Peek okay."

"What do you want with me?" she demanded. "Why did you . . ." She hesitated, searching for the right word. "Why did you *abduct* me?"

Dev shook his head. "I'm sorry, Kara, if I startled you. But I needed to speak with you, and I needed to do it away from others who might be listening in. I'm currently resident in the data banks at Jefferson University, with access to New America's planetary communications center, so when I felt your transmission coming through, I thought I would snag the opportunity to waylay you, as it were, and have a brief talk. Do you mind?"

*Yes, damn it, I do mind,* she thought. *I mind the arrogant presumption, I mind being mentally kidnapped, and I mind being scared half to death.*

"I2C links are supposed to be untappable. How the gok were you *able* to 'waylay' me? Sir."

"Please, I'm not a *sir.*" Dev's face twisted as he spoke, though whether the expression represented wry amusement or displeasure, Kara couldn't tell. She was beginning to realize that one reason she disliked having to deal with this . . . this *ghost* was the fact that in so many ways it was no longer human.

Kara didn't mind working with nonhumans, with *genuine* nonhumans, that is, the DalRiss and the Naga. They were strange, they thought in strange ways, and it was sometimes hard to understand them, even when the AI-directed translation programs interfacing with them were apparently operating perfectly. Words and concepts like devotion, duty, mercy were quite different for the DalRiss than for most human cultures and were nonexistent for the Naga, who "thought" in many ways more like complex computers working in parallel than like humans. But they were *alien*. You expected that.

Dev Cameron, though, had once been human . . . and the image he was projecting for her benefit now, that of a tall, young, gray-eyed, smiling human male, supported that idea. For over twenty-five years, however, he had existed as a complex software program operating within the confines of an alien symbiotic computer communications network. The world that network defined was a very large one, but she couldn't understand just what it was he was experiencing. The Dev-ghost had tried to explain it to her once . . . "like swimming in an alien sea," he'd said—but that told her very little. Once, Kara had downloaded herself into an Imperial computer network while engaging in a covert operation, and the sensory symbology being used there had been that of an underwater world. That had been alien in itself, and yet it had been designed by humans. An *alien* sea must be quite different, but Kara couldn't understand what that difference might be.

More than that, though, was the knowledge that the thing that Dev Cameron had become no longer thought like a human. Whether that was because his mind had changed over the past few decades, or simply because he'd experienced things no human had ever experienced before, she wasn't sure. She did know that speaking with him, on any level and on almost any subject, frightened her.

It was an emotion that she did not at all like.

She was aware that Dev had been patiently waiting there as conflicting emotions had chased one another through her thoughts. It struck her that a moment or two for her, a human, was actually a lot longer for Dev—who no longer relied on chemical reactions in the neuronal relay race that made up a given thought. She was pretty sure that he thought a lot faster than ordinary humans, though how much faster that might be she had no way of knowing.

"Okay," she said at last, when it became obvious that he wasn't going to answer her. "What *should* I call you?"

"How about Dev? That's my name."

*That* was *your name*, she thought, but she didn't verbalize it. "Okay," she said. "Dev. How did you manage to kidnap me?"

"I'd hardly call it kidnapping, Kara. It's not like I'm holding you for ransom, after all." He smiled, obviously trying to turn it into a joke.

"Gok it, answer my question!"

Dev looked startled, as though he was genuinely surprised at her anger. Suddenly he reminded her of Daren; both Camerons seemed to share an inability to . . . to empathize, to feel what someone else was feeling.

"You're right, of course," he said finally. "The I2C *is* untappable, but I didn't need to tap it. The main Confederation linksite for New America is at the University of Jefferson; incoming I2C communications are downloaded here and then retransmitted to the rest of the planet by normal electronic feeds. As soon as the carrier signal alerting Be There to your arrival was retransmitted from the university, I knew you were coming and, well, sidetracked you."

"Okay. That's how. Now why?"

He hesitated, as though considering how much to tell her . . . though his electronic thought processes were substantially faster than hers and any hesitation must be purely for show. Possibly, she thought, he did it to reassure her that he was still human. Too much of that kind of thinking was entirely too twisty for Kara's peace of mind. It was better to accept everything at face value, rather than try to interpret each glance, expression, and nuance.

"I saw the reports you transmitted a few hours ago," he told her. "Both about Operation Core Peek, and the wayward probe on the *Gauss*."

"What!—that stuff's classified! Level Blue!" It wasn't that she distrusted the Dev-ghost. Hell, his intervention with the newly awakened human Overmind had won the Battle of Nova Aquila and probably saved all of humankind.

Her problem with Dev, she was pretty sure, arose from the fact that she couldn't *read* him, couldn't understand his motives or what he was thinking or why he was performing a particular action. If his thoughts really were significantly faster than hers, if he really had instant access to immense volumes of information, then holding a conversation with him was like talking with a smug and self-assured super genius; there was always the feeling that he was condescending to speak with you . . . and that he was speaking with you at all only for obscure and probably insulting reasons of his own.

"I have the appropriate security clearance," Dev said. His tone had taken on a slightly acid edge, as though he were lecturing a child. Or an overly officious bureaucrat. "Perhaps you should see it."

She was about to agree . . . but then she realized the futility of demanding to see anything in a virtual environment which he controlled. In any case, Dev's official clearance had to be a lot higher than hers. He'd been a senior officer within the Confederation almost thirty years ago, before his . . . death. It stood to reason that he would have access to stuff a mere striderjack captain didn't even know existed.

"Forget it," she said. "Obviously, you've already seen it. Why the intercept?"

"Frankly, I needed to talk to you about the time-travel aspects of the Stargate," he said. "But I'd rather our allies not be aware of this stuff."

Kara frowned. "The Impies, you mean?"

"Imperials, yes. They would be extremely upset about our gaining a technology like time travel."

"We don't have time travel," Kara said. "We have a probe that appears to have doubled back on itself, but that doesn't mean we're about to be able to change history, or anything like that."

"Doesn't it?"

She brushed aside the question. "Are you saying the Imperials are spying on us at the Gate?"

"Of course they are. They have considerable interest in the Web, and in Web technology. And many feel like they're at a disadvantage with us when it comes to *obutsu*."

The word was Nihongo for *filth*. In this context, it referred to the aversion most Imperials had to incorporating alien *isoro*—parasites—into their bodies as symbiotic communications systems. There were a few Japanese who'd embraced the new biotechnology . . . but not many, and official Imperial policy tended to be extremely conservative.

"The great danger," Dev continued, "is that some factions within the Imperial goverment may be on the verge of moving against the Confederation anyway. They fear that a divided Mankind will be at a disadvantage when facing alien threats like the Web . . . and I have to admit I see their point. They want very badly to bring us back into the fold.

"More than that, though, they fear what we on the Frontier are becoming. You may have noticed that there's been a major propaganda offensive throughout both the Shichiju and the Confederation, taking an antibiotechnic stance, and urging human unity as the way to defeat the Web."

She nodded. "I experienced a ViRdocumentary a few weeks ago," she said. "Um . . . *Staying Human*, I think, was the title."

"Produced by Hegemecom, one of the Imperial media mouthpieces. It advocated competing with the Web on human terms, rather than trying to adopt the enemy's own tactics in order to fight the Web on its terms."

"I didn't think of it as propaganda," Kara said. "It all seemed to be pretty much open and honest to me. The straight hont."

He grinned. "Propaganda is the spreading of any information, true or false, to further one's own cause. The best propaganda is always the truth . . . slanted so that it doesn't *look* slanted."

"Maybe. Most of it was looking at the old question about what being human really is. The question's always fascinated me."

"And me," he said, the grin turning wry. "For obvious reasons."

She cocked her head to one side. "I suppose I shouldn't ask," she said, "but I can't help wondering. *Are* you human? Still?"

He raised an eyebrow. "That's a rather personal question,

don't you think?'' He laughed, turning it into a jest. ''And all I can honestly say in answer is . . . I still *feel* human. I exist in an electronic world as 'real', whatever that means, as what you experience in a ViRsim. Maybe more so. I perceive myself as human. Sometimes I think of myself as the universe's first virtual human, but even so I tend to define humanity by what's going on—'' He stopped and tapped the side of his head with his forefinger. ''Up here.''

''I don't mean to pry.''

''Not prying just to ask.'' He looked thoughtful, and once again Kara had to remind herself that every expression he made, every seemingly casual gesture or look, was done deliberately and for specific effect. Like propaganda. ''Are the people who download themselves into virtual worlds still human?''

That stung. She thought of Willis Daniels and the others, patterned and downloaded that afternoon, because the trauma of the battle on Core D9837 had made them dissociate from both their physical brains and their Naga Companions. She wouldn't know for several days yet whether they would become communicative again; the hope, of course, was that they could wear imaginary bodies in a virtual world until a way could be found of rejoining them with their real bodies. This was a brand-new aspect of psychomedicine, however, and one that still had a rather low success rate. They, like so many others recently, might be condemned to spend the rest of their lives in a virtual world.

''They're human,'' she said quietly. If they weren't, then those people were as dead as Miles Pritchard and Pel Hochstader, and the patterned minds stored now in *Gauss*'s databases nothing more than a cruel hoax. Straightening, she faced the image of Dev. ''Just what is it you want from me?''

''You're going to visit your mother.''

''Yes.'' She felt her guards going up again. Her mother, she knew, still had strong feelings for Dev, and she didn't want her hurt.

''I want you to tell her all about that probe. And I want you to suggest that the *Gauss* begin initiating experiments in using the Nova Aquila Gate . . . as a *time* gate.''

She gaped at him. ''You're serious!''

"We're discussing the survival of the human species," he told her bluntly. "That's not something I would joke about."

Dev had given the problem a lot of thought and was by now convinced that he was right. "We have no direct proof, of course," he told Kara, "but the Stargates were almost certainly constructed by the Web. You've demonstrated that anyone can use them, however. If we're to win this thing, we're going to have to use them against their creators."

"There's been speculation that the, um, predecessors of the Web . . . an advanced organic species that created the machine intelligence that later became the Web . . . that they built the Gates."

"Or built the first ones and passed the process on to their high-tech offspring. Yes. You know, when the DalRiss explorer fleet first came here, we found evidence that this star system had been inhabited when their sun went nova. It's circumstantial evidence, but that kind of cold-blooded genocide points rather strongly to the Web, a machine intelligence that doesn't care about or perhaps doesn't even recognize organic life."

"'Or just plain hates the stuff," Kara put in.

"Possibly."

"The Stargates are constructed of degenerate matter," Kara said thoughtfully, "like in a neutron star. A spoonful of the stuff weighs thousands of tons. We think that the Web deliberately seeks out double stars and triggers novae to create the conditions for forging the things. But we don't *know*."

"One of the things we should establish is whether or not the Web is building new Gates. There's been some evidence that they're building something at Alya." Alya A and B were the home suns of the DalRiss, which the Web had detonated in a twin nova two years before. "But we have no hard data. And the Imperials aren't eager to scout aggressively."

"They're afraid we might stir them up," Kara said. "They've not been real thrilled about the Core Peek operations, for just that reason." She cocked her head to one side. "We've known that devices like the Gate might allow travel in time. According to Dr. Norris, back aboard the *Gauss*, the theory has been in place since the twentieth century."

Dev nodded, pleased that Kara seemed to be dropping her reserve and allowing the distance between them to close, that she was listening to him and to what he had to say. He knew she didn't like him, and he hadn't been sure that he was going to be able to communicate with her on any meaningful level.

"By my estimate," he told her, "the Stargate at Nova Aquila contains roughly the mass of a super-Jovian gas giant, compressed to near–neutron star densities." He opened a new window in her mind, filling it rapidly with scrolling equations and with a detailed, three-dimensional diagram of a Stargate.

"In Einsteinian spacetime," he continued, as animated pathways drew themselves in red and blue, "and under certain conditions, spacelike translations and timelike translations can be viewed as different aspects of the same thing. Time and space are two different aspects of the same thing. We've known all along that the paths leading into a Stargate could be spacelike, timelike, or both. It turns out that vectors leading into the Gate more or less along its axis of rotation tend to translate as vector changes in time."

"Hold it," she said. "Let me look at this. Dr. Norris was trying to tell me about this earlier, and it zipped right past me. I want to *understand* it."

"Certainly." Dev had long ago grown used to the fact that humans—*real* humans, as he thought of them, people still in their physical bodies—thought far more slowly than he did. Existing now as patterns of electrical charges riding the circuits of computers, both human-made electronic and DalRiss-grown Naga-organic, his own mental processes were far faster and more efficient than those of any purely human, organic brain. Holding conversations with humans was becoming more and more tedious for him, much like communications across distances of several light minutes or hours had been like before I2C had eliminated the problem of speed-of-light time lag.

His attention shifted to the three-D diagram of the Stargate. *That* stirred memories, and not all of them pleasant.

Twenty-seven years before, he'd been aboard a DalRiss living starship at the Second Battle of Herakles, linked in through a Naga communications net that was dispersed throughout the DalRiss-human fleet. The DalRiss ship housing his body had been destroyed. Somehow, though, his mind had survived.

Or had it? Dev considered the question sometimes, especially when he was in a lonely frame of mind. If what had survived was only a copy of his original mind, right down to the memories and the slightest emotion, then the original Dev Cameron had died in that battle, and what lingered was a copy with memories too numerous and too sharp.

After his "death"—he still didn't know how else to think of the destruction of his physical body—he'd found both refuge and purpose by remaining with the DalRiss cityships whose Naga computer nodes had been serving as a distributed network for his linked mind at the time. For the next twenty-five years, he'd accompanied a DalRiss fleet at their request, exploring out from the space known to humans and DalRiss, following the curve of the galactic arm spinward toward the constellation men called Aquila.

At Nova Aquila they'd discovered the Stargate, a one-thousand-kilometer long needle rotating at the gravitational balance point of two closely orbiting white dwarf suns that, eighteen hundred years previously, had gone nova. The light from that cosmic explosion had reached Earth twelve hundred years later, shining brilliantly in the night skies of Earth in the year 1918.

Theory made it clear enough what the Stargate must be. Tippler and others, as far back as the twentieth century, had suggested that degenerate matter formed into such a cylinder and set rotating at velocities approaching that of light would open pathways within the savagely twisted spacetime within which the cylinder was embedded . . . pathways through space, and stranger by far, pathways through time.

For a moment, he turned his attention from the diagram to the glorious background of stars at the Galactic center, the pearly smear of encircling nebulae, the warm gleam of a far-off supernova, the icy smudges of countless ice worlds turned comet by the radiance of the nearer suns. The Great Annihilator looked much the same as it had looked to him two years before, when he'd become the first human to penetrate the core's secrets.

Well . . . the first human *mind*, at any rate, and it had not been his, not exactly. He gave a small, internal grimace at the memory, a piece of his personal history that still pained him when he thought about it.

Faced with the need to find out who had built the Stargate, and where those builders were coming from, Dev and his DalRiss hosts had prepared a probe. Constructed almost entirely of Naga cells packed into the form of a small ship only a few meters long and given DalRiss control and propulsion systems, the vessel had possessed storage capacity enough to hold a copy of Dev's downloaded mind, a duplicate possessing all of Dev's intelligence and many of his memories, that could occupy the Naga probe as observer and pilot.

This Dev duplicate had piloted the Naga craft through the Stargate, following the departing path marked out by the uncommunicative alien vessels. It had emerged close beside an identical Stargate at the Galactic Core, some hundreds of astronomical units from the Great Annihilator itself.

The probe had been almost instantly discovered and attacked. The Dev-duplicate had been able only to record its brief memories of that place and launch the remnants of the probe back through the Core Stargate before being destroyed. Those memories had been reintegrated into the waiting Dev-original's mind; he now "remembered" the events on the other side, just as though they'd happened to him.

In a way, they had. Part of those memories included the Dev-duplicate's anger and sense of betrayal at what had happened. So far as it was concerned, it had been the Dev-original, so perfect was its duplication. Those memories had raised some ethical questions in Dev's mind, questions dealing with how he perceived himself and other humans.

Questions about whether or not he *was* still human. Sometimes, it seemed as though he had less and less in common with them. . . .

"Okay," Kara said softly, interrupting the viciously circling ring of self-doubtings that more and more darkened Dev's conscious thoughts. For Dev, it felt as though she'd been studying the data for hours, but in fact it had only been a few seconds—impressive for any organic human attempting to wade through math that heavy with nothing but personal RAM. "This says we should be able to navigate even pretty large ships through time. And of course, we already demonstrated that, with the probe. But what could we hope to accomplish? Not changing the past, surely. We'd run the risk of editing ourselves out of existence, of creating a paradox."

"Maybe not. It depends on how the universe is wired."

Her brow furrowed. "When we were looking at the probe, the *probes*, I should say, Dr. Norris was wondering what would happen if we decided not to send it out. If we changed the history of the second probe, in effect. Would it disappear?"

"I submit," he told her, "that we need to find out. And that's why I waylaid you this way. We need to mount an expedition through the Gate and into time. Actually, I wasn't thinking so much about traveling into the past and changing it. You're right. That could have, um, unfortunate consequences for us, if we weren't careful. I was thinking of going into the future. For information."

"A recon op into the future?" She pursed her lips. "Wow. I'm not sure I've even got a link with all this yet. In any case, I can't make a decision like that."

"Exactly why I intercepted you."

"You want me to—"

"To convince your people of the importance of this. To get them to put together an expedition that can go through the Gate into the future." He frowned, a shaping of the image that he held before his thoughts in Kara's mind, like a mask. "And it's got to be carried out in secret. I'm worried about our Imperial friends, and what they might think. Or do."

"The Imperials?" It was Kara's turn to frown. "You really think they'd be against this?"

"I'm concerned about *densetsu*."

The word, depending on how it was used, meant tradition or traditional. Specifically, and in this context, it meant the Japanese tendency to prefer traditional, tried and true means of doing things. They were already gravely concerned, Dev knew, about the new dependency on Naga Companions among the cultures of the Periphery, and they frowned on such new faces of technology as virtual worlds, patterning, and personality downloading.

"Time travel would *really* shake them up," he continued, "especially if they began wondering if gaijin were dreaming of rewriting history, rewriting it, perhaps, out from under Imperial Dai Nihon."

"Yeah. If we use it against the Web, we could use it against the Empire."

"Tampering with history that way may not be a good idea," Dev said, "as any techfantasy ViRdrama buff could tell you. But yes, the Imperials may be concerned about us using time travel against them." He hesitated. "That's why I wanted to meet with you this way. I know the Imperials are watching closely everything you're doing at Nova Aquila. They're taking part in the Unified Fleet, I think, as much to keep an eye on you as to watch the Web. This is not the soundest or warmest of alliances, you know."

She laughed, the sound brittle. "You're telling me that? Most of my striderjacks hate them, and they hate us just as much."

"I've been trying to keep tabs on them by accessing their milnet. *Something* is brewing in their high command, but I don't know what."

She grinned. "You interest me. You can tap the Imperial Military Net?"

"Parts of it." In truth, he'd ranged through much of that virtual world of data and flickering communications links, probing and exploring. There was much the Imperials knew that they had not yet shared with their gaijin allies. Dev was still cataloguing that data, establishing its limits, and learning how best to verify it. It would be an important addition to the Confederation's data net someday. And it might prove to be an invaluable part of the Overmind.

At the thought, Dev could feel the faint, far-off shudder of the Overmind, a slumbering superconsciousness residing now within the vast and far-flung network of human computer systems and communications links. Called into being two years before when a kind of critical mass of separate consciousnesses had linked together during the Battle of Nova Aquila, it had emerged as an entity similar to Dev, though on an immense scale, a patterned mind resident on the Net composed of billions of separate minds.

The Overmind's intervention had won that battle, as it took over and shut down vast numbers of Web machines within the space of a heartbeat. Since then, it had been . . . sleeping was the best analogy Dev could think of, though the word was unsatisfactory and imprecise. It was more as though the superintelligence had retreated into the distance, somehow, waiting, perhaps thinking about problems utterly beyond human comprehension. Dev could sense its presence . . . or sense its potential, at least.

"Time travel," Kara said, looking thoughtful. "I'll be damned. . . ."

"The whole idea may be impossible still," Dev told her. "But it's worth investigation. Basically, the idea would be to see what the future knows about the Web. Who wins? Why? If we win over the Web, maybe we can learn how it happened and save some false steps . . . and maybe the loss of another star system. If the Web wins in the future, well, we might learn what mistakes we made, and how to avoid them."

"We?"

"I'll be coming along," Dev told her. "You don't think I'd get this thing started, then wait here while the expedition sets off, do you?"

"But how could you . . . ?"

The image grinned at her. "I'm pretty adaptable. I'll need a pretty large memory to reside in, but a Naga–DalRiss node would work fine. First we need to talk to the New American government about organizing an expedition."

"New American government. By that you mean my mother."

"She would be an excellent place to start, yes. If anyone could get a project like this moving, it's Katya."

"I'll talk to her, certainly. I can't make any promises."

"I'm not expecting any." He hesitated. "I will say one thing, though."

"Yes?"

"There is a need for haste. If time travel *is* possible, remember how we learned about that possibility in the first place."

Her eyes widened. "The Web—"

"Might already have time travel. You know, there's a mystery in what we've seen so far. At Nova Aquila, they appear to be funneling gigatons of plasma off into nowhere, using what appear to be timelike paths near the Stargate. At the Galactic Core, they're dropping whole stars into the Great Annihilator . . . but the twisted space-time fields at the thing's center might be used for time travel, just like a Stargate. Where are they sending it?"

"You think they could be sending it . . . into time? Why?"

"Unknown. One unknown among many. Also, they don't appear to be that . . . imaginative. But if they *do* already use the Gates for time travel—"

"They could use that against us first."

"If they consider us a serious enough threat, Kara, that's exactly what I mean. Mankind, Imperials and Confederation both, might find ourselves wished right out of existence by a time-traveling alien machine intelligence.

"And there wouldn't be one damned thing we could do about it."

# Chapter 10

*Of course, those early experiments and entertainment center rides created no more than the illusion of telepresence, a shadow of what was to come later. The person at the Earth-side theme park could see what the robot he was driving "saw" through its camera, and simple feedback controls allowed him to sense the tug and bump of the rover through the joystick control that steered it.*

*Never, though, was there any sense that the driver was actually on the moon. He still felt a normal, one-G gravity as he sat in his chair. When he looked away from the television screen, he saw his decidedly Earth-bound surroundings, the crowds of tourists watching him, the tourist-centered hype and glitter of the theme park structure he was seated in. Not until the development of nanotechnic cephlinks were the bonds of mind and body truly severed, creating the illusion that the operator had acquired a new body.*

*Nowhere was this more evident than in the popular hubots—teleoperated human robots—that first appeared in crude form in the late twenty-first century, but which by the twenty-fourth century had acquired tremendous sophistication and sensory sensitivity.*

*—The Physics of Mind*
DR. ELLEN CHANTAY
C.E. 2413

She smelled morning and felt sunlight on her face. "Just relax," a woman's voice said. "You're on New America now. Everything's fine."

*This is more like it*, Kara thought.

Kara opened her eyes and found herself looking into the face of a young somautomata technician. The viewall beyond showed a reassuring view of the ruggedly mountainous New American countryside—the Cascades north of Jefferson, she thought—with Columbia, New America's huge, close moon, rising immense and golden in an early morning haze.

"How are you feeling?" the tech asked. Her hair was red—not a natural auburn but a pale, brick red–pink fuzz with long earlocks twisted into luminous red, blue, and green DNA spirals, representing, Kara supposed, the latest fad in hair styling. Her breasts were bare above a smoky, translucent haze that clung to some parts of her body and swirled revealingly about others; the ends of her earlocks were weighted to keep them dangling first to one side of her nipples then the other as she moved, as though to call attention to generously large and buoyant assets that were almost certainly Companion-enhanced. The skin of her fingers and hands was Companion-refashioned in deep emerald, opalescent scales that faded away to normal skin halfway to her elbows.

Another technician stood behind her, ostentatiously male, nude save for the electrorganics embedded like black filigree in the skin of his left arm, shoulder, and chest, and with his head startlingly reshaped into the golden-eyed and unwinking head of an enormous bird of prey—a technofashion incarnation, Kara thought, of the Egyptian god Horus.

Kara closed her eyes for a moment and took a deep breath. She'd not been home in a good many months now, and it was hard to keep up with the lightning pace of fashion in the Confederation, especially in the cities.

"Captain?" the woman asked. "Are you feeling all right?"

"Yes," Kara said. "Just getting my bearings."

"Hubot projection can be a shock at first," the technician agreed. "Just take your time to get adjusted."

Kara didn't bother telling the woman that it wasn't the sensation of remote telepresence that was strange to her. It was her and her co-worker. She had plenty of experience with telepresence . . . in places and across distances that these two most likely had never dreamed of. Apparently they both assumed that Kara was inexperienced with this sort of thing.

"We're still not sure why your signal was delayed," the hawk-headed man said. His speech was crisp and clear, despite the horny, razor-edged beak. "We had your carrier signal and were alerted that you'd entered transference mode, but it was a full two minutes before your download actually came through. Do you remember anything happening just now, after you linked in on your ship? Anything at all?"

From the tone of his voice, he was worried about some sort of legal action. Interstellar hubot transference was still pretty new, and lots of people, even—or especially?—those who used the equipment, still regarded some aspects of its workings to be mysterious.

She decided that the simplest way to divert the questioning would be to lie. "Not a thing," she said. She shrugged. "I imagine that the transmission gear aboard *Gauss* needs better calibration."

"Maybe." The man sounded doubtful. "But we definitely had a transmission alert, meaning you should have arrived within the next second or two. Not two minutes."

Had she only been with Dev for two minutes? It had felt much longer than that . . . a result, she realized, of conducting a dialogue in an electronic media where thoughts were not constrained by the agonizingly slow cycling of chemical neurotransmitters.

"I wouldn't worry about it," she said. "I didn't notice any delay at all. I'll talk to someone when I go back aboard."

The hawk was silent for a moment, the head cocked slightly to one side, as though the man were listening. Kara guessed that he was tapping a download from his Companion. Usually you could tell when someone was doing that, from the vacant or somewhat distant unfocusing of his eyes, but this Horus-persona, she was finding, was impossible to read.

"Well, we can't find anything in our readings here," he said after a moment, "so I suspect you're right. And . . . if there is any problem with the link, you know, there's really nothing to worry about."

Lots of people, Kara knew, were afraid of what might happen if their robotic body failed while they were riding it, but she could dismiss those fears. She'd been there. When a teleoperated warstrider was destroyed, the comm link was cut and the operator woke up in his or her original, organic body. *Usually.* She was reminded of friends and comrades consigned to virtual worlds and suppressed a small shudder.

Still, the problems there seemed to have more to do with the effects of being in combat than with the simple fact of having your remote sensors cut off. There was nothing magical about telepresence save the way the human mind worked in the first place, which was more than enough magic for her.

"I'm sure everything will be fine," she told them both.

"Of course!" the red-haired woman said brightly. "Come on. Let's see how you like your temporary body."

It felt quite normal. Kara was seated in a large, back-tilting chair like the acceleration seat of a high-G shuttle. Looking down, she saw that the hubot's body was anonymously unisex, a meter and a half tall, trim, almost delicately petite compared with her own tall, rangy, and long-limbed org. When she raised an arm, she did so with fluid movements and very nearly the same range of motion as a human. She held her hand up before her face. It was startlingly lifelike in texture, but with a faint, gray-silver cast to it and no wrinkling, hairs, or blemishes at all. The fingers were long, slender, and supple, the fingers of a pianist, and when she lightly touched thumb to each fingertip in quick succession, they moved just as easily and felt just the same as the fingers she'd been born with.

Cables snaked in from left, right, and above, melding seamlessly with her sleek, synthflesh hide. At a mental command from one of the somautomata techs, the nanotechnic connectors dissolved and the cables retracted themselves; Kara could feel her internal power source throbbing gently, like a heartbeat, and sensed the ebb and flow of various autonomous system monitors, reassuring her that all systems were on-line and go.

Horus offered her his hand. She ignored it gracefully by gripping the chair's armrests to lever herself up. She stood easily, though she had to deliberately suppress the oddly telescoped sensation that her arms and legs weren't quite long enough. In some ways, it was easier to teleoperate a warstrider, a machine that was in no way at all humanoid. You didn't have to worry about walking in a strider; you simply pushed there with your mind and you were moving, effortlessly and with perfect, AI-imposed control. There were no AIs in a hubot; wearing one was more like wearing someone else's body, and her brain assumed that arms and legs, mass and reach, height and center of balance, would all be the same as they were in her own body she usually wore.

She took a couple of experimental steps, bouncing lightly on the treaded balls of her feet. The initial strangeness was already passing.

As she turned in place, she caught sight of herself in a mirror screen behind the chair. Her own face stared back at her, holographically projected over the front of the robot's blank and polished head. A low-level hubot's normal facial features were almost nonexistent, save for a slightly raised band at eye level where visual, aural, and olfactory sensors were stored. Most people, however, Kara included, maintained one or more personal analogs, limited software duplicates of themselves resident within their Companion's organic circuitry and serving as secretaries and stand-ins for routine business over communications links. That same internal programming, which created a duplicate of the person inside ViRsimulations, could shape the holoprojection of the hubot's face into a fair likeness of her own. The effect wasn't good enough to fool anyone, certainly—there was an odd stiffness about the face, almost as though it were pasted on—but the likeness was good enough to let others recognize who she was.

"If that body doesn't suit you," the hawk-headed technician told her, watching closely as she looked at her image, "we can transfer you easily enough to a different model. We have some excellent full-sensorium models that you will find match your org's sensory input in every way."

Kara knew about the top-of-the-line hubots, luxury models that were all but indistinguishable from bodies of flesh and blood. *Not for me*, she thought with a wry, inner smile that her hubot's holographic face matched with something approaching a grimace.

"No, thanks," she said. "This one will do fine."

"Are you sure? We have some female bodies that—"

"I'm sure, Horus," she said, her voice sharp. "I'm not into the full-sensory stuff, okay?"

"Absolutely, Captain! It's whatever you want! Not all of our customers are as . . . discerning as you are."

Meaning, she translated, they weren't as cheap. But then, Kara never had cared much for surface show, expensive or otherwise, when something simpler existed that served her needs just as well. She'd specifically reserved a Model 15 for this excursion, a version advertised as a high-endurance economy sports model. For a few thousand more yen or meg, depending on which currency she chose, she could have had a full-function, full-sensory hubot, a precision-crafted one, nanotechnically grown from the body casts and downloads of any of a variety of ViRsim entertainment personalities, machines identical in every outward detail to a genuine and healthy human body, and capable of experiencing every human sensation, including—or, given the enormous market for the things, *especially*—sexual arousal and satisfaction.

Kara was more than happy with the Mod 15, however, a utilitarian model that better suited both her nature and her present, no-nonsense mood.

"If the captain would like a download of some of New America's more popular tourist spots—" the red-haired woman began.

"Never mind the sales pitch," Kara told her. "I'm not a tourist. Is my credit good?" Her rental agreement, and the downloading of the fee, had been handled long distance, from the *Gauss*.

"Everything has been taken care of," the man said, and though Kara wouldn't have thought it possible, the rigid beak of the hawk's head smiled. "And we hope you enjoy your visit here!"

Kara grinned, and the holographic projection of her face echoed the thought, a little more naturally this time. "I certainly intend to."

Minutes later, Kara stepped out of the hubot office—walking out beneath a twice-life-size full-motion holo of two nude Model 3000s, fully human, a male and female linked in a close and passionately erotic tangle. BE THERE, the agency's name, was featured in meter-tall, glowing scarlet letters. Advertising hype scrolled steadily through the air as pulsing music throbbed to the couple's lovemaking. She gave a wry shake of her head at the holographic antics; sex, it appeared, and the rawer the better, was what sold product everywhere.

She had only to access the city net to summon a robot flitter that would take her out to the family estate at Cascadia, but one of the reasons she'd chosen a visit by teleoperated hubot was the opportunity it gave her to stroll Jefferson's pedestrianways and visit haunts she hadn't seen in years. She decided to walk to Franklin Park in the center of the city and take a flitter from there.

The city of Jefferson was much as Kara remembered it . . . large and bright and bustling. For centuries, New America had been something of a backwater world, an isolated outpost on the far periphery of the human Shichiju. It supported three separate colonies, one Ukrainian, one Cantonese, and one predominantly North American, and all descended from settlers who'd been seeking greater freedom and a better life elsewhere than under Japan's Hegemony on Earth. Before the Revolution, New America's quasi-independence had been preserved by a quirk of nature. Where most of the worlds of the Shichiju possessed one or more sky-els—the immense, surface-to-synchorbit elevators that made movement back and forth between space and surface cheap and easy—the gravitational tides raised by Columbia, New America's huge, close natural satellite, made such construction impossible. Here, any sky-el would be torn to shreds, assuming that it could be hung in the first place.

As a result, little of Jefferson's architecture followed the styles common elsewhere in the Shichiju, where Japanese influence had dominated for centuries. Cities here were more open, less closely packed. There were cities in the Shichiju, especially on old Earth, where it was no longer possible to walk from block to block or building to building in the open air. Underground tubeways, from simple slidewalks to more elaborate maglev train systems, were the principal means of moving from place to place, especially in the larger and more sprawling of Man's ant-heap megopoli, and in most, elevated causeways connected the separate buildings, allowing the population to move about in safe, climate-controlled, and enclosed comfort.

Jefferson, however, had always managed to maintain the look and feel of a small town nested into a valley between forested mountains and the sea, even when the rapid influx of immigrants over the past few years had swelled the city's population to several million. Much of the city had been destroyed during the Revolution, when Imperial forces had briefly occupied the planet. When the place was rebuilt, however, the team drawing up the plans had kept the look of the old city, and that included the broad, tree-lined walks and malls, and the numerous parks that helped separate the clusters of taller buildings.

The wonderful thing about the city was that it was still possible to walk there beneath the golden-white light of 26 Draconis. Amberbrush lined the walkways of the park, and flights of morninglories exploded skyward as pedestrians passed.

As always, though, Kara was more interested in the people than in the morninglories. Most native New Americans tended to be rather conservative folk, both in custom and in politics, but clothing styles and fashions showed the influence of many worlds and cultures. A casual stroll through a large public area could turn up citizens in anything from Scots kilts to Imperial kimonos to shipboard skinsuits to nothing at all. Nudity was increasingly common on the worlds of the Periphery, especially in gatherings in private homes, but it might be encountered anywhere.

Kara had been aware of the mix of fashion trends for as long as she could remember, and knew they'd existed in one form or another for centuries. The latest trend, however, had less to do with fashion than it did with the perception of what still constituted humanity. For some time now, but especially in the past three or four standard years, people who wanted to make a fashion statement—or catch the eye, or shock, or simply fantasize—had used Naga Companions to reshape their bodies.

Body sculpting, it was called. In the kilometer-and-a-half walk from Be There to Franklin Park, Kara encountered dozens of people far more outlandishly styled and refashioned than the Horus she'd met at the hubot rental. There walked a gargoyle in scales, horns, and claws, two-meter wings carried arched above his shoulders; here was a woman with four working arms. Across the way was an alien monstrosity of sheer fantasy, dragon-headed, centaur-limbed, shaggy-bodied. That last, Kara thought, might easily have been a gene-tailored pet of some sort . . . except that it was in deep conversation with a chunky, armor-hided creature with a humanoid stance and tentacles waving above his shoulders. She wasn't sure, but she thought the creature figured prominently in a popular ViRdrama fantasy.

Many of the humans, she noticed, were also ViRdrama stars. Kara rarely indulged in ViRsimulated scenarios and didn't know the personalities well, but many of the faces and bodies she saw were familiar. Some, probably, were other downloaded tourists in high-end model hubots, but others were clearly real people, their features tailored by their Companions.

In an astonishingly short time, Companions had completely transformed the way Man looked at himself. No longer was a certain skin color or facial features or a particular number of arms the prerequisite for humanity. That particular revolution was even now having far-reaching effects that no one could have anticipated. If a man was human even if he looked like that winged, scaly, snake thing over there, then what about a gene-tailored human, a genie . . . creatures who were human in every important detail save for the fact that someone had tampered with their DNA before they were decanted to shape them for some particular task? What about AIs, the artificial intelligences that ran so much of human technology and exhibited intelligence in particular areas of a higher order than that of the people who'd designed them?

Or someone like Dev, who had no body at all?

Kara shook her robotic head in amusement at the thought. Her own feelings on the matter had been changing lately . . . and her unexpected meeting with Dev Cameron had brought her further along the road to change still. She'd very nearly decided that the question of what constituted humanity might well no longer have any real meaning. Better, perhaps, to judge each individual person on his, her, or its own merits, and forget about trying to force them into molds that simply might not fit.

She found herself wondering if Dev could download permanently to a hubot body, something that would allow him to move and interact in the world of reality again. Or did he prefer his disembodied state?

As peaceful and prosperous as the city seemed, Kara found she couldn't shake a growing sense of ominous presence, a shadow across New America's citizenry even in the light of the two suns overhead. Many of the people she saw were in uniform—striderjacks and naval personnel off Confederation ships in orbit. Accessing the medefeeds through her hubot's comreceiver, she scanned through program after program discussing a single topic: the likelihood of renewed war with the Empire.

That evening, Kara and her mother, Senator Katya Alessandro, sat opposite one another at an elegant table perched high atop a wild, sheer cliff overlooking the spray-whipped sea. The sky overhead was rose-gloried, streaked with clouds as Columbia hung ponderously above the sea to the east. Kara took another bite from the plate before her, closing her eyes and reveling in the aromatic and faintly spicy blend of flavors that spread like liquid ecstasy through her mouth and into her brain.

Her dish, labeled simply "Number 196" in the program's menu, looked like a chicken stew, but its taste and smell were literally indescribable. As the morsel touched her tongue, it dissolved, releasing a cascade of flavors and less identifiable sensations all tailor-made for her nervous system, the effect nearly orgasmic as it sent a series of shudders down her spine.

"Whew!" she said, when she could draw breath once more.

"Good, huh?" Katya said, grinning at her from across the table.

"That doesn't describe it by a tenth! I can see how people could become addicted to this sort of thing."

"Mmm. Let's hear it for the NPRs."

Direct neural feeds, starting with the most primitive brain-machine interfaces of five centuries before, had naturally and immediately led to serious abuses. In every culture and in every age there were people who would willingly addict themselves to intense pleasure or rich sensations, whether through drugs or, these days, by way of a relatively simple pleasure center download.

At the same time, modern technic civilization encouraged the sampling of as wide and as rich a variety of experiences as possible. True addiction, though, was rare, thanks to NPRs, the neuroprogrammer routines piggybacked onto the AI monitoring and controlling their meal and similar pleasures that helped break chemical bond dependencies as they formed. She couldn't become addicted to the intense pleasure associated with this food, even if she wanted to. But after a bite or two, she could begin to understand what led people to *want* such an addiction.

Kara let the sensations fade into the background of mind

and body. She stared off toward the east for a moment, watching the looming pale globe of Columbia. Despite the evidence of their senses, the two of them were sitting together in the spire-top disk of the Columbiarise, one of Jefferson's more elegant ViRestaurants. Their surroundings, as well as the meal itself, were simulated. The Columbiarise specialized in virtual meals, with an extraordinarily detailed and comprehensive menu of flavors, textures, odors, and gustatory sensations compiled over the last couple of centuries available for selective downloading. The scene around them was illusory but meticulously perfect in every detail, down to the smell of salt air and the caress of the sea breeze on their faces. They'd chosen to dine alone, rather than in the company of the facility's other patrons, so it appeared that there were just the two of them on an open deck a hundred meters above the sea, at a table of light open to the azure, red, and gold New American sky. Columbia, ocher and russet, made pale by a thin haze of clouds in New America's atmosphere, rose slowly in the east . . . the Columbiarise's trademark ViR-simulation.

Kara's sim was the more illusory of the two. It looked as though her own body was sitting at the table and enjoying the meal, but she was still linked to her hubot, and the imagery of her presence was entirely electronic. For Katya, there was real food before her at a real table, but the restaurant was downloading both simulated surroundings and highly detailed information about her food through direct sensory feeds. In a sense, both women were living in their own virtual worlds, created by the restaurant AI in their minds; the program, however, let them share the illusion, so that they could talk and interact.

*Talk.* It was as wonderful as the virtual food, in a way, a golden chance to be with her mother, quietly and without interruption. For one thing, it offered superb privacy, a literal meeting of minds where she could talk about Dev's strange suggestion about the use of the stargates to travel through time. More than that, however, she was glad for the opportunity to simply enjoy her mother's company. There'd been precious few such opportunities in the recent past. Katya Alessandro was a woman whose political career sometimes bulked huge and formidable, an impenetrable fortress wall to her daughter.

It had taken a lot of effort for Kara to scale those walls . . . and to discover that she'd possessed walls of her own.

"So, what do you think?" Kara asked at last. "About all of the Imperial propaganda, I mean."

"I really don't know, Kara. It *could* be war."

"Bastards! Why can't they leave us alone?"

"From their point of view," Katya told her, "it's the right thing to do."

"How can you say that? We've been independent since the Treaty of Kingu. They don't *own* us any more!"

"As they see it, we split from the Hegemony, the government that speaks for mankind. It was a breach of the peace, and of civilized behavior."

Kara snorted. "Civilized behavior! I'll give them civilized behavior!"

"Put it this way, then. We acted in an uncivilized manner. We have to be punished and shown where we went wrong. Then we have to be returned to the family. To the Hegemony. Especially now, when we're facing the Web. Union in the face of an enemy is very important to the Imperials."

"Yeah. Union with the Hegemony. Only it's got to be on their terms, not ours. Damn it, Mums. We don't have a gokking thing to do with the Empire or their puppet Terran Hegemony any more. It's time they learned that!"

"Racist thinking, Kara," her mother said, shaking her head. "No, worse. *Tribal* thinking. Too many people forget that we have a hell of a lot more in common with the Empire than we have against them."

Kara felt uncomfortable with that. All of her training, her experience, everything she'd known and learned and downloaded since joining the Confederation military had led her to perceive the Japanese as *aliens*, as different from New Americans or other inhabitants of the Frontier in some ways of thought and perception as the Naga. While Katya took another bite from her plate, Kara downloaded a fragment of text, quoting from Sinclair's Declaration of Reason. *" 'We hold that the differences between mutually alien, albeit human cultures render impossible a thorough understanding of the needs, necessities, aspirations, goals, and dreams of those disparate worlds by any central governing body. . . . ' "*

"Nice words," Katya said, smiling to remove the sarcastic edge. She chewed for a moment, closing her eyes as she savored the bite. "Ohh. Remind me to get together with you like this more often. I think I'm in love."

Kara laughed. "Any time, Mums. As long as you're paying. Captains don't get megs enough for this kind of high-input living very often."

"I've got a straight-hont download for you. Neither do senators, unless they're willing to take bribes. Maybe we should turn data pirate."

A laugh. "Maybe. Anyway, Sinclair also said that the Japanese culture is an imposition on values descended from Western thought and ideals."

"Yes, he did. But the fact remains that you and I are closer to the Japanese . . . hell, we're closer to chimpanzees, no, to *shelf fungus* than we are to the Naga. Or the DalRiss. And the Web, well, that's more alien still."

"Sure. But, well, maybe it's the similarities, the things we share with them, that make us natural rivals."

"I don't deny that."

"Besides, don't forget that there's more to this than anti-Japanese paranoia. They don't like us any more than most of us like them. Gaijinophobes, most of 'em, who figure we're no better than hairy, smelly barbarians. From what I've heard, I keep wondering why they want so badly to hold onto us. You'd think after we made our preferences clear back in '44, they'd just say the gok with us and let us go our own way."

"I suspect, Kara, that they know they can't afford to. Barbarian or not, we, the Frontier, are an asset, a valuable and irreplaceable asset for the entire human race. Tokyo's leaders may be wondering right now if their whole Empire isn't already falling into the same trap as Old Earth. Ultra conservative. Ultra safe. And, in the long run, at least, doomed to become ultra extinct.''

Kara nodded. It was common knowledge—on the Periphery, at least—that successive waves of migration had carried Earth's brightest and boldest first to the nearer stars, and then, as the process continued century after century, to those systems a bit further out, a kind of winnowing process that eventually left New Earth and Chiron and Greenhome and Meiyo and the other populated worlds within fifteen light years or so of Sol almost as inflexibly set in their ways as Old Earth herself.

The majority of Earthers today were happy with their crowded, tightly ordered world. Kara found that an utterly and bizarrely *alien* thought.

''Look, I'll give you the argument that we're all human. But you've got to admit that Japanese culture is fundamentally different from ours. They *think* differently than we do.''

''Not as differently as a planetary Naga.''

Kara laughed. ''I don't think anything is *that* different.''

''Different or not,'' Katya said with a shrug, ''it hardly matters in the long run. If the Empire is determined to pull us back into the fold, I really don't know that there's anything we can do to stop them. Our navy is better than it was, but still no match for the Imperials. Hell, we shouldn't have won the *last* war with the Empire, much less this one!''

''So,'' Kara said after a long and thoughtful silence. ''If we do get into a stand-up fight with the Empire, we lose. What can we do about it?''

''I'm intrigued by Dev's idea,'' Katya said.

''Trying to find out how to beat the Web?'' Kara shook her head, puzzled. ''I don't understand. How does that help us with the Empire?''

''First,'' Katya said, ''information always confers an advantage. *Always.* If we can learn something about the Web that the Empire doesn't know, that gives us a stronger position to bargain from.''

''I'll go along with that.''

''Besides . . . who knows? We might find some friends on the other side. God knows we need them.''

''Well, if we could find someone who didn't mind risking

tampering with the future . . . with their present, I should say.'' She had her doubts about that.

"Okay, then. Weapons. Technology. Anything to even out the balance between us and the Empire.''

"So you'll authorize the expedition?''

"I certainly will.''

"I'd like to go along.''

Katya closed her eyes, then opened them again. "Why?''

"Because I want to do something useful.''

They'd had this conversation, or variants of it, before. Katya, Kara knew, hated issuing orders that could so easily lead to her daughter's death in combat. Kara, for her part, disliked intensely the idea that her parents—a general and a senator—might be interfering with her career, either to save her life or to gentle the rough and rocky road to promotion.

"What do you think you've been doing?'' Katya asked her.

"Gok. Flying through the Stargate and getting blown to bits in the Galactic Core isn't useful. It's make-work for bureaucrats, making them fill out the after-action reports on us and counting up the RDTSs. It seems to me that this idea of Dev's offers us a chance to really hit back at the Web.''

"Maybe so.'' Katya was thoughtful for a moment. "If we can put an expedition like this together, who do you think should go?''

"You're asking me? I'm just a captain. I don't set policy.''

"Mmm. Okay, but I *do* set policy . . . and I respect your judgment. I need it, in fact. If you were leading a mission through the Gate into the future, how much firepower would you want to take along?''

Kara thought a moment. "I suppose the whole damned Confederation Navy is the wrong answer.''

Her mother smiled. "Good assumption.''

"Well, the problem is we wouldn't really have any idea what we should be looking for, what we might meet. Whatever we met, though, chances are we wouldn't care to take it on in a stand-up fight. So it would have to be a scouting expedition. Small and light.'' Kara paused, looking across the table at her mother with a calculating expression. "I'll tell you what we'd need, though.''

"What's that?"

"The best damned xenologists we have. You mentioned finding allies? We'll need to talk to them."

"You're thinking of Daren and Taki."

Taki Oe was her half-brother's sharelife, a Japanese-New-American who worked with him at the University of Jefferson. Both were full technical doctors of xenology and had considerable experience with xenocontact scenarios.

Kara nodded. "I don't always *like* my brother, but he's good at what he does. And I do like Taki. I'll tell you what else we'll need."

"What?"

"Dev Cameron."

Her mother's eyes widened a bit, and pain flicked raw behind them, the subtleties of expression showing even through the ViRsim linkage.

"We'll need the usual ship AIs, of course," Kara went on, "but if we could find a way to bring Dev along as our Net interface, I think it would be a big help."

"How?"

"Translation. Communication with alien networks. He knows the human Net, and when we got back he'd be the logical channel for downloading what we've learned to the Net." She didn't add that Dev had told her he intended to come along. *What is she thinking,* Kara wondered. *With both kids and her former lover planning on running off on this weird, wild crusade?*

She couldn't read her mother's expression, however. After a long moment, Katya sighed. "Tell me something, Kara. Just between us, okay?"

"Sure."

"It's personal. How do you feel about another war with the Imperium?"

A flip answer came to mind immediately, something about the Empire not learning its lesson the first time around, but her mother's persona was projecting such a serious expression that Kara didn't give it. "Do you mean whether or not I think we can win? Or how I think it'll affect me personally?"

"How it affects you. You don't have to answer that, of course—"

"Oh, I don't mind talking about it. It's been on my mind for quite a while. I suppose I see some opportunity, of course. Promotions come a lot more easily when there's a war on. And I'm scared. Scared of dying. Scared of ending up in a virtual world with no physical body." She managed a small smile.

"I can imagine." Katya hesitated. "And on the grand scale? Do you think a war like that would be *right*?"

"Well, I used to. I guess I still do, though you've given me a lot to think about. It was easier thinking of Japanese culture as so different from ours that there aren't that many points of contact. You know, us against them. But you're right about us being the same species. And we're both threatened by the Web. We're going to have to find a way to work with the Empire, or we're going to go under."

Katya thought for a moment. "Damn. Why is being human so complicated?"

"Are you looking for a way to justify a war with the Empire?" She almost sounded as though she were trapped and searching for an honorable way out, a way to give in to the Imperial demands and avoid the oncoming conflict.

"Kara, nothing can justify war. The waste. The horror. *Nothing*."

Kara reared back, startled. She'd never heard her mother speak that way before. *Dev*, she thought. *She's still missing Dev after all of these years, and she hates the war that took him from her.*

It gave her a new insight. Just as Kara didn't want to lose any more of her people in useless gestures against the Web, Katya didn't want to be forced into the position once again of having to sign the orders that might well kill millions . . . including, quite possibly, people she loved. Still, how did you avoid a war when the other guy was determined to have one? When immediate and unconditional surrender was the only alternative . . . what did you do?

Not for the first time, Kara was glad that her leadership skills were limited to the bossing of a single warstrider company.

The conversation shifted after that, to things less threatening, less confrontational. Later, Katya paid for their meal. With the shifting light of a brightening dawn, but much faster, the spectacular vista around them faded away, replaced by a more conventional restaurant. Viewalls looked out over the city of Jefferson, with a view south toward spaceport and sea. Other patrons sat at their meals, lost in their own private world, oblivious to all of the other patrons. The two women walked toward the central lift tube that would take them back to ground level.

"You know, Mums," Kara said as they rode the capsule down the restaurant tower, "there is one thing that justifies war."

"Yes? What's that?"

"The only thing that counts in the long run for any culture, any civilization, any *species* for that matter." She was thinking about the impossibility of the Confederation facing the Empire one-on-one, and about what might happen if they failed.

"*Survival*," Kara said. "In the long run, we're fighting for our own survival, and it may be that that's all that really matters."

# Chapter 11

*The universe is not only queerer than we imagine, it's queerer than we* can *imagine.*

—J. B. S. HALDANE
British biochemist
mid-twentieth century C.E.

Revelation held Dr. Daren Cameron in a trembling grip that was close to ecstasy. Slowly, slowly, he let out a long breath. *My God*, he thought, and he had to stifle the impulse to laugh out loud. *My God, that's it! It's* got *to be!*

He seemed to be hovering above a vast, fluid-filled canyon, with gray-yellow walls that gave anchor to a vast and gently waving forest of indistinct growths, like endlessly trailing fronds of kelp in a darkening sea. The object of his interest, though, seemed an obvious intruder in this aqueous realm, a tangled, three-dimensional mass of glistening and translucent threads adhering to one of the nearby walls, sprouting filaments that at this scale looked like gleaming, transparent tubes. Clearly visible within those tubes, dark-colored, elongated cells, pointed at front and back, slipped along nose to tail in endless, gliding processions. The tubes crisscrossed everywhere through the murk but were concentrated here within this nexus, in the silvery-gray mass growing from the canyon wall. The web of filaments stretched off in every direction, their meanderings swiftly lost in the distance.

Carefully, Daren changed position, moving closer to the nexus, watching the cells sliding through their slime tunnels in eerie mimicry of blood cells slipping single-file through a capillary. Several globe-shaped crystals hovering nearby provided a dazzlingly brilliant illumination. At his mental command they moved apart and back slightly to reduce the glare from clouds of tiny particles suspended in the liquid; the shafts of silver-blue light cast wavering, vast shadows like living things in the translucent liquid.

At closer range, the cliff resolved itself into a densely matted forest of gray-yellow and gray-purple strands, like a forest of seaweed. In a sense, Daren was exploring an alien sea aboard a mind-linked submarine . . . but the submersible was in fact a nanotech probe, a tiny and complex assembly of organic molecules and interlocking carbon atoms seven microns across, about the size of a human blood cell, and not much larger than a single bacterium. The "sea" around him was actually the cranial cavity of a half-meter-long creature known as a Dantean Commune, while the "cliffside" was a tiny portion of the creature's cerebral cortex, made up of a densely intertwining mass of individual neurons.

Daren was teleoperating the nanoprobe from his console

aboard the *Gauss* over twelve hundred light years away, using an I2C link to continue his long-running researches into the Commune mystery. The probe itself was far too small to provide full sensory input for Daren's linked mind. In fact, he was networked with the research computer at the research station on Dante, which in turn controlled the probe in response to his relayed mental commands.

Carefully, he nudged closer to the fibrous object adhering to the tangle of cortex neurons. The moving cells nestled in their transparent tubes clearly still lived, though the larger organic structures around them were lifeless. The Commune worker, he knew, lay dead on a dissecting table in a refrigerated laboratory in Dante's main research facility. Even so, there was still life in here . . . and activity beyond the biochemistry of decay.

He initiated another command series, and a cloud of smaller objects sprayed from the probe's belly, subprobes too small for direct neural linking; each was composed of no more than a few tens of thousands of molecules and could provide little more than the bare essentials of simple data acquisition and telemetry. Trailing faintly luminous streaks of turbulence through the fluid, the subprobes vanished into the grayish mass.

The space surrounding Daren felt enormous, but that sense of space was illusory. The creature's brain, a lump of ganglia located in the central body cavity just above the heart, was in fact smaller than Daren's clenched fist, and the space between its convoluted surface and the surrounding cartilage walls measured less than half a centimeter across.

Working in the depths of that half-centimeter of liquid, however, it was easy to forget the realities of scale, thinking instead of cliffs and vast, dark, and unplumbable ocean depths. The Commune worker, Daren knew from long experience, was a half-meter-long segmented creature with a vaguely spiderlike appearance. Socially, the Communes were in many ways similar to the termite communities of Earth. Indeed, Daren had spent a year of undergraduate work on Earth, at the University of Nairobi, researching African termite mounds as background and preparation for his studies of his primary interest, the Communes of Dante.

Dante, the second world of DM-58° 5564, was not a pleasant place by human standards, though a small scientific community had been established on its surface. With an average surface temperature of nearly forty degrees Celsius, only the polar regions and high mountains were easily habitable for Man. The Communes, however, were a littoral species, living on the narrow margin between ocean and the mountainous interior. In fact, their castle-like colonies rose out of the seacoast shallows and tidal flats, apparently grown to specific shape and design from minerals drawn up with sea water and plated out as the water evaporated through their high, fluted columns.

Though they'd been studied for many years, the Communes were still very much of an unknown. The most puzzling mystery about them had been plaguing xenologists ever since the species had been discovered by the first human explorers to reach the planet. Were the damned things intelligent? Like the termites of Earth, the Commune organisms appeared to be highly differentiated anatomically. There was a specific type identified as a soldier caste, charged with defending the colony from outside threat. There were workers of several types, some for repairing the Commune towers, some for gathering food, or for digging, or for scouting, while still others for engaging in activity apparently senseless and even random to human observers. The whole functioned together so smoothly that the entire population of a Commune colony could be considered a superorganism, not that far removed biologically from, say, a human being composed of trillions of separate, closely networked cells; workers and foragers seeking food could from a distance appear to be a single, fluid pseudopod moving across the ground with purpose, cunning, and seeming intelligence.

So often did the Communes act in ways that suggested purposeful, even sapient behavior, that xenologists had been trying for years to answer that one question. Were they— the colonial superorganisms, that is—intelligent? Individuals almost certainly were not. Their brains massed only a few tens of grams, and the average intelligence of a typical worker was probably not much higher than that of, say, a rabbit or a Chironian chewthrough. And yet a mass of billions of them could track food, dam rivers, divert water flows into makeshift spillways, erect barriers to create tidal pools, and clear debris that might be shifted by storm waves and damage a Commune castle's walls. That showed not merely intelligence, but *problem-solving* intelligence, rational and self-aware. An intelligence with which it might be possible to establish communication.

Every attempt to communicate with the creatures, however, had so far failed. Most observers felt that if the creatures were intelligent, it would be with an order of intelligence far different from that of humans. The most popular theory was that there was some kind of brain caste in the Commune hierarchy, another and as yet unseen morphological form that coordinated the superorganism's actions from the relative security of the home colony.

But Daren thought he was on to something now . . . something that might well change forever how scientists looked at the Communes and at how they related to the environment within which they lived.

"What did you find?" Taki Oe asked. She was not visible in the scene projected within Daren's brain, but he could sense her presence nonetheless, piggybacked with his into the data stream coming in from the nanoprobe. She'd been in on this project with him from the very beginning . . . back in the frustrating early days when funding for such a simple thing as a research trip to Dante was out of the question. Now he was further from Dante than ever, but the advent of I2C had made possible a direct investigation of that world and its life that was very nearly as good as actually being there . . . and perhaps better. Dante, after all, was an unpleasant place, with limited habitat space and few creature comforts.

"There," Daren told her. He threw a spot of illumination on the structure he was looking at. "Below that neural ganglia. See it?"

"The gray, fuzzy mass? I see it, but I don't know what I'm looking at."

"Check the readout." The probe was receiving a steady flow of data, most of it from a fleet of even tinier micro-submersibles moving through the fluid nearby. Information scrolled down the side of the screen, relayed from probes that had penetrated the gray mass.

"I . . . don't understand. The biochemistry is different."

"Completely different."

"A different organism."

"Yup. Different DNA. It looks to me like another species of labyrinthulomycota. *Para*-labyrinthulomycota, I should say."

She chuckled. "Easy for *you* to say."

He smiled at the old joke. Xenologists had adopted the idea of giving life forms that closely paralleled given classes or species on Earth the prefix *para*, for "like." Thus, a parafungus was something very much like terrestrial fungi . . . save for the fact that it was not even distantly related to anything that had ever been within light years of Earth.

"You think it's a parasite?" Taki asked.

"Parasite or symbiont," he replied. "It certainly feeds on its host. See the way those tubules burrow their way down into the brain tissue? The question is how much, if anything, it gives the host back in return. And I think I just might have the answer to that."

At his command, the nanoprobe began moving ahead, leaving the faceted illumination globes behind and swiftly flying through the shadowed liquid, gliding just above one of the long and twisting mucus tubes. As the view went dark, he switched on the nanoprobe's own light. At their current scale, of course, ordinary light waves would have been invisible, but the AI handling the probe interface could shift reflections from hard-ultraviolet radiation—at wavelengths of around 800 angstroms—up into the visible spectrum—between 7700 and 3900 angstroms. The colors had a sullen, purplish-gray cast to them, however, as the scene explosively shifted past Daren's point of view, the colors rippling like iridescence from an oil slick from the surfaces of the tube and the dead nerve tissue around it. After a few moments of undulating gently up and down, the slime trail they were following arced sharply to the right, then descended toward a cliff wall . . . and another of the glistening, gray-silver nexus clumps of tubules.

Bringing the nanoprobe to a halt, Daren slowly rotated in place. The glow from the first nexus was clearly visible, a hazy patch of white-purple light in the extreme distance . . . all of one tenth of a millimeter away.

Daren nodded to himself. The evidence pointed to an incredible complex of these nexi, interconnected by the slime tubes to one another and to the host's brain tissue.

Taki didn't sound convinced. ''You're sure this isn't part of the decay process in the specimen?''

''Positive. It's freshly killed and being kept refrigerated at the south polar colony research station.''

It had been a big break for the research team, finding the body of a Commune worker. Since whether or not the creatures qualified as intelligent life was still an open question, hunting the things was strictly forbidden.

But when one had been found dead in a rockslide, it had been flown directly to the south polar station for autopsy and remote exploration.

''Some fungi can start breaking down dead organic matter within a few hours, sure,'' Daren continued, ''but you can tell by the organization of this thing that it's been in place here a lot longer than that.''

''It could be the disease that killed it.''

''I don't think so. We'll need to autopsy some more to see if this kind of infestation exists in all of them, but . . . I really don't think this is a disease. Look. No signs of inflammation. No signs of tissue rejection or antibody formation. This . . . this growth moved in and made itself at home. And the body allowed it to do so.''

''So what does . . . ?'' He could hear her turning the thought over in her mind. ''Wait. You think this is linked somehow to the intelligence question?''

''It's possible.''

''We've never seen anything like this on Dante,'' Taki

said. "Not in any of the other paralabyrinthula."

"It's done what life does everywhere, including us. It's adapted itself."

There were numerous species of the order Paralabyrinthulomycota, unprepossessing organisms that had insinuated themselves everywhere within the Dantean ecosystem. This species they were looking at, as yet unknown and unnamed, might well hold the key to the entire Commune mystery.

Swiftly, Daren downloaded a file of background information and scanned through it rapidly and systematically, checking to be certain he'd missed nothing in his earlier review. The labyrinthulids of Earth were commonly called slime nets or slime net amoebae, though there was nothing at all amoebic about them. Like their better-known relatives, the humble slime molds, they were members of Kingdom Protoctista—meaning they were living organisms that were not animals, plants, fungi, or prokaryotes. They were eukaryotes, meaning they possessed cell nuclei and mitochondrial respiration. To the naked eye, they looked like transparent blobs of slime or mucus, sometimes several centimeters across and usually found on certain marine grasses, where they fed on yeasts or colonies of bacteria. Microscopically, they consisted of spindle-shaped cells migrating endlessly back and forth through slime tunnels laid down by the cells themselves, which ran through the tunnels like tiny maglev trains in their tubes. Though their motion seemed random, they were organized into supercolonies that could slowly extend themselves through their environment in search of food.

On Dante, cellular evolution had followed much the same course as on Earth, with genetic transmission that used analogues of both DNA and RNA. As a result, convergent evolution had molded most classes of life into forms resembling their earthly counterparts, at least to a point. The Communes, for instance, looked much like insects with their multi-jointed legs and segmented bodies, though they breathed with lungs and could be as large as a meter in length. The Dantean slime nets studied so far looked as though they could easily have been transported from Earth . . . except that here for some reason they'd branched into far more numerous and complex forms, a spectacular diversity that lived symbiotically or parasitically on or in thousands of species of more advanced Dantean life.

And apparently one form, at least, had parasitized the Communes, adapting itself to live in and on the host's nerve tissue.

"Do you see it?" he asked Taki. "At this level, we could spend centuries following all of the interconnections here, but those tubes must interpenetrate the entire cortex . . . maybe even the entire central nervous system. And it possesses a complexity that's way, way higher than the interconnectivity of the host brain's own neurons."

"I'm not sure you can say that," Taki said. "The scales are different. Those tubes, and the cells moving around inside them, are a lot larger than the neurons that make up the cortex mass."

"C'mon, Tak. Look at it! The parasite is using the neuron connections and adding more of its own. I think it may have increased the neural pathways beyond the Threshold."

He sensed Taki's quick intake of breath. "Nakamura's Number?"

"If not here, inside one brain, then if we combine it with other Commune organisms . . ."

"Wait! How is that possible?"

He used the probe's spotlight to stroke one of the tubules and the oddly shaped, glistening cells sliding along inside. "Taki, I think what we're looking at here are slow thoughts."

Tetsu Nakamura was a twenty-fourth-century Nihonjin scientist who'd calculated the basic density and number of component parts required to elevate a complex order to a higher level of organization and function. The number, $1.048576 \times 10^{11}$, was less a precise figure than a place marker in calculating thresholds in interconnective operating systems. Approximately Nakamura's Number of molecules working together formed a cell, a living organism that operated independently of and on a plane far above that of any of its component molecules. Nakamura's Number of cells . . . when they were the specialized neurons of the central nervous system, together formed a brain capable of memory, planning, self-awareness, and abstract thought, something far beyond the capabilities of a single nerve cell.

The brain of a Dantean Commune worker contained roughly $3 \times 10^9$ neurons with the connections vastly increased, however, by the paralabyrinthulid infestation. . . .

"We'll have to calculate the increase in neural linkages," Daren said. "My guess, though, is that individual Communes have their base intelligence levels raised significantly by the parasites."

"Dog level?" Taki asked.

"Maybe. Maybe more. But, don't you see? It's a *slow* intelligence. Those moving cells in the tubes. Those replace electrochemical activity, synaptic relays, and all of that."

"How could two systems operating at such different speeds possibly interact?"

"I think . . ." Daren felt the quickening pulse of his excitement. "I think that the paralabyrinthulids primarily serve to connect the individual Commune creatures. Workers, soldiers, all of the other single Communes."

"Daren. . . ."

"It's got to be that way. *Look* at it, Tak! Those tubules are paralleling the whole neural network . . . and then some. And it's also intimately associated with the worker's circulatory system. That tells me these slime nets can communicate biochemically. Each of those moving, spindle-shaped cells could carry chemical tags that are being routed through the network the way electrochemical impulses are routed through the brain's neural net."

"That's a big leap, Daren."

"Not at all. I'll even go one further. We've seen workers exchanging food directly mouth to mouth . . . and there are those reports of things like large slime molds found growing inside ruined commune colonies. I'll bet that those large molds are a primary food source for the Communes, and that they're part of our paralabyrinthulomycota. Maybe the Communes even cultivate the stuff, like harvester ants growing fungus inside their colonies on Earth. They infect themselves by ingesting it, and at the same time become carriers for biochemical signals being shared throughout the labyrinthulomycota network!''

''Wait. Are you saying that the slime net is the real intelligence here?'' She shook her head. ''I don't see—''

''No, no, no. It takes both organisms working together. I think the slime net has learned how to parasitize the Communes in such a way that it fosters intelligent activity . . . activity that benefits the net directly and the Communes by association.''

''You know, Daren, all along, xenologists have been looking for some sort of brain caste in the Communes,'' Taki pointed out. He could still sense her reluctance. ''Your idea sounds plausible, but it's a big jump from cultivated eukaryote colonies to intelligence. What you're suggesting, that a parasite has learned how to increase the host species' intelligence . . . that sounds pretty wild.''

''Parasites can do incredible things when it comes to reordering the lives of their hosts in order to suit their needs. There's a parasitic worm on Earth I remember reading about . . .'' Daren paused, turning inward for a moment as he ran a quick search through his RAM, then downloaded the key information. ''Yeah. *Leucochloridium paradoxum* is its name. It spends much of its life inside a certain species of snail, but in order to reproduce, it has to get inside the gut of a bird. So what it does is migrate to the eyestalks of its snail host, which does two things. It makes the snail nearly blind—until all it can see is light—and it also turns the eyes themselves bright red. The snail crawls up the stalk of a plant, following the brightest light up to where it can see better . . . and at the very top of the plant those bright red eyes attract the attention of a hungry bird.''

''Hell of a dirty trick to play on the snail.''

''It does the job and lets the worm complete its life cycle.''

''And you think this might be a similar manipulation of one species by another? One that instills intelligence in the host?''

''I'm thinking in that direction.'' He considered the slime

net a moment longer. "Here's another example from Earth. *Septobasidium*. That's a kind of fungus that grows over the back of a small, mothlike creature called a scale insect, trapping it against the bark of the tree it's feeding on. The fungus covers the insect over completely in a remarkably short time, then inserts its hyphae into the insect's body and begins sucking its juices. Now, you'd think that would kill the host, but in fact, it turns out the insect lives longer than it would on its own."

"If you call that living," Taki put in.

Daren chuckled. "There is that. Anyway, the scale insect keeps sucking on the plant's sap, which in turn feeds the fungus. And if the critter lives longer, it produces more young, which is good for the scale insect from a genetic point of view. There's a case where the host actually benefits from the parasitism."

"Yes? So how does intelligence help the Communes?"

"I don't know. How does intelligence help *any* species?" He remembered discussions he'd had in the past about whether or not intelligence could be considered a survival trait. "Maybe it started as a way of getting the Communes to nourish colonies of slime nets, but once it started there was no turning back and no way to stop the process. And there's the stuff the Communes do. Clearing debris away from the beach, so their colonies aren't damaged by flotsam in a storm. There's got to be some survival value in that."

"Mmm. At least this tells us a bit about why communicating with them has been so difficult. Speed."

"Exactly. If I'm right, individual Communes are dumb by human standards. Self-aware, maybe. But not capable of abstract thought. But with biochemical messages being passed along the network from individual to individual, the entire community becomes a giant brain with enough neural interconnectiveness to out-think Einstein. The only trouble is, forming a given thought, 'hello, how are you,' say, might take a couple of days or more, and understanding the answer might take even longer."

"I wonder how it perceives the world around it?" Taki wondered. "I wonder how it perceives us?"

"As blurs, perhaps. Shadows that flick in and out of existence too quickly to allow it to react. Likely, its thoughts are attuned to slower, more regular phenomena, like tides and seasons."

"It also suggests a strategy for learning to talk with them. If, of course, they even have that sort of mind. A mind based on the physical movement of cells bearing chemical tags . . . that's got to be the weirdest basis for intelligence I've heard of yet."

"Remember Haldane, Taki my dear. The whole universe is predicated on weird. Let's surface. I want to start planning out a new line of research."

He keyed in a thought, withdrawing their awareness from the nanoprobe, just as the tiny artifact and its subprobes and light sources dissociated into clouds of component molecules and scatterings of free-floating carbon atoms.

Daren blinked his eyes, adjusting to the higher levels of light. He was lying in a reclining chair in one of *Gauss*'s science labs, a small forest of life support tubes and data feed optical fibers growing from the Companion-shaped jackpoints on his head and chest. His Companion broke the connections, his skin reverting to normal as the tubes and cables retracted themselves into seat back and ceiling. A few meters to his left, Taki was just sitting up, resealing the front of her shipsuit.

"Welcome back," a technician said from the main console. "Good trip?"

"Splendid, Enrico," Daren said. "Absolutely splendid!"

Enrico de la Paz was the senior AI systems technician aboard the *Gauss*. As Daren stood up, he noticed that the tech seemed a bit hurried in his movements, that he was breathing a little quickly and seemed distracted, as though he was excited or agitated about something else. Daren noticed these things . . . and as quickly dismissed them. The excitement of his own discovery was far more pressing than anything Enrico might have to say.

Taki, however, must have picked up the same distraction. "Enrico?" she asked. "Is something wrong?"

He looked up and grinned. There was a strange light in

his dark eyes. "Wrong, Dr. Oe? Well, it's a little early to tell. But some news just came in over the main I2C link from New America."

"What news?" Taki asked.

"A new alien contact."

That caught Daren's attention. "When?"

"Several days ago, at least, though it was kept quiet until just a few hours ago. We were wondering whether or not to get a message to you two, but decided it would keep."

"A new alien contact!" Taki said, and now her eyes were brighter too. Mankind had established full and two-way contact with only two other sapient species so far, the DalRiss and the Naga; the Web hardly counted in this context, since the only exchange so far with that intelligence involved combat. With both the DalRiss and the Naga, however, the free exchange of information, philosophy, and technology had caused literal revolutions in Man's understanding of the universe and generated a new Renaissance in learning and in science.

"Where was this?" Daren demanded.

"High Frontier," he said. "The Gr'tak—that's what the aliens call themselves. Apparently they were following Earth's radio emissions, but they stumbled into one of our periphery systems on the way. I gather they just came cruising in from deep space, traveling at sublight velocity. Probably gave the Confederation Defense Fleet there group coronaries."

"Sublight!" Taki exclaimed. "They don't have FTL?"

"I guess not. The word is they arrived in a big fleet, several hundred ships at least, and some of them rivaling the DalRiss cityships in size."

"So," Daren said, "our people contacted them."

Enrico looked uncomfortable, and Daren saw him give Taki's expressionless, Oriental features a hard, quick glance. "It was a mixed fleet that met them," he said. "Elements of the Third Imperial Fleet, and some of our own CDF. I, uh, guess they're still trying to sort things out."

Daren began to understand Enrico's distraction. High Frontier was a relatively new world among those colonized by Man. Third planet of DM+19°, a G-class star fifty-two light years from New America and forty-five light years from Sol, it was a member of the Confederation rather than of the Terran Hegemony, but Imperial fleets had been aggressively patrolling the star systems of the Confederation ever since the Web had become a threat. In fact, there was little the far smaller and weaker Confederation Navy could do to stop such patrols, and common sense said that it would be good to have Imperial forces handy if the Web made a sudden appearance.

But if the aliens had a lot to teach humanity—as had the Naga and the DalRiss—it wasn't likely that the Empire would be eager to share with their former colonies much of any new information the aliens might offer. In fact, this could make the whole problem of potential war with the Empire that much scarier.

"At least the Imperials won't be able to keep it all to themselves." Daren though about it for a moment, then shook his head, his excitement over the Communes giving way to a new and more urgent eagerness to learn about this new species. "Another sapient life form! Never rains but it pours, eh, Taki?"

"This does seem to be the day for making such discoveries."

"Enrico. Any details on their morphology? Their language?"

"It's pretty strange, what I've downloaded so far. From the sound of things, you xenologists are going to have your work cut out for you. The Gr'tak are another group organism, a superorganism, I guess, though not on the same scale as your Communes. Apparently a number of dissimilar creatures have created an extremely close symbiosis."

"Like the Dal and the Riss?"

"Maybe, though what I heard is that all of the components of a Gr'tak associative are intelligent. With the DalRiss, of course, only the Riss are intelligent. The Dal are just gene-tailored legs and arms for them, right?"

"That's right," Daren agreed. The Riss, with their civilization's emphasis on biotechnology and genetics, had engineered a number of species into life forms that they literally rode on or in, guiding them through direct connections with the mounts' nervous systems. The Gr'tak must have a similar linkage, but among several intelligent forms. How had *that* system evolved . . . and why?

"You know," Taki said softly. "Such a mind, an associative of linked minds, that would have interesting applications for us. . . ."

Daren saw it in the same moment, a flash of revelation. A species that had evolved mental symbiosis would have a lot to teach humanity, which was just learning to cope with mind-to-mind symbiosis with other, alien species . . . and with alien cultures within his own.

Daren considered himself completely apolitical. When his romance with the Nihonjin-descended Taki—she was, in fact, a native New American—had caused comment in the past, he'd always either ignored it or been delighted when he incited it. For Daren, the constant state of war or near-war between Empire and Confederation had always been little more than a source of irritation and inconvenience, especially when military and political priorities overrode his needs for more funding for xenobiological research.

Suddenly, however, it seemed very important that the Imperials not have that information all to themselves.

"What the hell is this going to mean for the Confederation?" he wondered. "And for the Empire?"

# Chapter 12

*Sometimes what we need most is a different perspective on things. Consider. The Greek city states, thanks to the mountainous geography of the Greek peninsula, developed in relative isolation from one another, with different cultures, different arts, different philosophies and gods. Only gradually, over the course of centuries as roads were built and sealanes established, were the cities of Athens, Sparta, Corinth, and the rest able to begin exchanging ideas.*

*And once the exchange had begun, the inevitable result was an explosion of art, science, and culture, of thesis and antithesis yielding brilliant and unanticipated synthesis of new ideas ranging from democracy to atomic theory. It seems we need alien ideas every so often to stir things up. . . .*

—*The Heritage of Immanuel Kant*
PROFESSOR ROLLIN SMYTHE HAUSER
C.E. 2006

Dev Cameron used his God's-eye view to watch the Gr'tak arrival.

He'd learned to make use of the constant flow of data through the network that lined the scattered worlds and systems of humanity, and that including the images collected by medes and ViRnews reporters and uploaded onto the Net. The discovery of a new and alien species was big news, and most current exchanges on the Net were discussing it in one way or another. By switching from one mede upload to another, he could choose his own view of the event as it unfolded in space midway between the world of High Frontier and her inner moon.

The scene he was watching now was being transmitted from High Orbital, the space station complex that served as the planet's starport and interface point in the absence of a sky-el. High Frontier was a brand new colony, raw and primitive yet, and though survey work was under way, the forty-thousand-kilometer-long thread of her first sky-el had yet to be grown. Until the new world had a space elevator and synchorbital in place, High Orbital would serve as her transshipment point, starport, and space-ground interface facility.

Several thousand kilometers out from the station, under the unblinking gaze of mede ViRnews broad spectrum sensors aboard teleoperated drones, DalRiss cityships were materializing one by one as they arrived from New America and elsewhere. An enormous fleet had gathered here at High Frontier already, consisting of both Confederation and Imperial vessels of all classes. Time being a key concern, the human vessels were being piggybacked in by the DalRiss.

Each cityship, resembling a mottled, rough-skinned starfish from Earth's seas, measured two kilometers or more from arm tip to arm tip and was home to some tens of thousands of Riss and their gene-tailored, living tools. Unlike human starships, which traveled with pseudovelocities of around a light year per day, the DalRiss had learned to engineer intelligent, living creatures, their "Achievers," that could visualize two separate points in space and bring them together, allowing vast distances to be spanned instantly. Human scientists still weren't sure how Achievers performed that trick, though the assumption was that the DalRiss had managed to snag hold of quantum physics' infamous observer effect in a way that let them briefly and temporarily alter reality.

In his downloaded state, Dev had lived for twenty-five standard years with the DalRiss, working extensively with their Achievers, but their method of shifting from one location to another still seemed little short of magic to him.

The cityships could leap enormous interstellar distances instantly, and they were large enough to engulf human vessels, enfolding them within their ventral grooves and carrying them along. The technique had been used by both Imperial and Confederation militaries more than once to move their fleets great distances in a short time; in the two years since the destruction of their homeworlds by the Web, the surviving spaceborne DalRiss had tied themselves closely to the human interstellar community, paying their way, in a sense, by providing humanity with a means of much faster and more efficient passage between the stars.

Even so, there weren't nearly enough DalRiss vessels—there were only a few hundred in all—to handle the entire volume of interstellar traffic throughout Shichiju and the breakaway republics of the Periphery. Dev suspected, given the frantic I2C messages shutting back and forth across the Net, that every DalRiss cityship that could be found was being pressed into service, moving human ships, Confederation and Imperial, here to the High Frontier system.

Dev hadn't needed to worry about securing a means of transport, of course, one of the advantages of being a complex computer program operating within the Shichiju-wide network. Using the University of Jefferson's I2C facilities, he'd transferred himself into the *Rassvak*, a DalRiss cityship already in position near High Frontier. He was currently residing in the Naga network growing within the living DalRiss ship, a part of the structure's command navigational computer system.

In a strange way, he was more at home here than he'd been in the human network back in Jefferson; Dev had spent his first twenty-five years as a downloaded digital ghost in this environment, working with his DalRiss hosts, helping them navigate their fleet in an extended search for new life, new intelligence. As he surveyed the incoming Gr'tak fleet, he could sense the excitement of the other minds linked with his, alien though they were.

*"New partners in the Dance. . . ."*

*"And they share with us the Quest. They seek new partners among the stars, as do we. . . ."*

*"Their harmonies are strange. But they seek a commun-*

*ion of Mind. We can learn much from them. . . ."*

*"New patterns in the Dance. A new richness to be sa-vored. . . ."*

For the DalRiss, life was a kind of dance, one that unfolded, changed, and evolved, dynamic and always new, always surprising. They would be awaiting full contact with the Gr'tak with a keen anticipation, despite an outward, patient calm that at times bordered on a rather rigid, cold, and emotionless stoicism.

Another DalRiss ship materialized out of nothingness . . . and another, then still another. Nested within the ventral grooves of each incoming starfish shape was a human starship, most of them military vessels, ranging from destroyers and frigates up to a few of the huge, kilometer-long ryu, or dragon-class carriers. The Imperial Navy had lost heavily at the Battle of Nova Aquila, but in the past two years they'd been engaged in a massive building program aimed at replacing their losses, and Imperial tactical doctrine still relied heavily on large warships that could carry hundreds of space-mobile warflyers.

One of the giant ryu dragonships present, however, was not Imperial, but Confederation. The CMS *Karyu*, the Dragon-Killer, had taken up position at the heart of the growing cloud of Confederation vessels, including her own circling warflyer formations deployed on CAP, or combat aerospace patrol. Dev noted that the incoming human vessels were beginning to pool in two separate groups, one Confederation and one much larger for the Imperial Navy vessels.

Quickly, Dev checked other flows of data. The Imperial fleet remained in parking orbit, watchful, silent, on full alert but not engaged in any operations that could be construed as actively hostile. Tensions now between Imperial forces and the Confederation were running higher than ever, and the arrival of the aliens hadn't helped one damned bit.

For their part, the DalRiss cityships had been gathering in a kind of no-man's land between the two human forces. Dev wondered if that had been a deliberate decision on the part of the Riss to help avoid untoward incidents . . . or if they even understood the level of tension that existed between the Confed and Imperial crews. Dev doubted that they did. Human politics had always been something of a mystery to the alien DalRiss. They knew about politics, they knew about the wars fought between the various human political states and had even participated in some of them, but the DalRiss concept of life as a kind of mutual dance so colored their perceptions of other species that they clearly had difficulty understanding why members of the same species would want to fight with one another.

If the DalRiss, after some twenty-five years of experience with Dev, didn't understand human politics, then what would these alien newcomers think about it? As human and DalRiss ships continued to arrive in-system, the Gr'tak fleet waited silently well beyond the gathering pools of human vessels. Initial contact had already been established, using high speed computers on both sides to begin generating communications protocols. Elements of the Gr'tak language had been recorded; evidently, and fortunately, they used a spoken language and not some more elusive mode of communication like odors or color changes or wig-wagging tentacles. So far, human contact experts had determined that Gr'tak was a group name, either for themselves as a species or for this particular group of ships, and that the name seemed to include a number of allied intelligent species. The assumption now was that the basic unit in Gr'tak society was the *taak*, a plural term that seemed to imply a union of diverse beings or minds working to a common goal. There was speculation that the Gr'tak might actually be representatives of some kind of interstellar federation. The information downloaded into human AI systems so far, however, was far too vague and fragmented to allow anything more than speculation.

With luck, they would learn more when they established a direct Naga linkage.

The Gr'tak ships, Dev noted, were huge, sleek, aesthetically pleasing things, all curves and smooth lines. They were also large, some a kilometer long, and with vast arrays of lighted ports among the towers and bulbous swellings near their prows that suggested vast cities. Oddly, some of the larger vessels looked less like spacecraft than like space stations of some kind; several were obviously planetoids or small moons that had been partially or completely excavated within and looked more like mobile space colonies. Was that, Dev wondered, a reflection of some quirk of Gr'tak psychology? Or did they mean, as some exchanges on the Net were speculating, that the Gr'tak fleet was in fact a migration of all or part of their civilization?

There was no way of knowing, short of learning how to talk with them directly.

One aspect of Gr'tak technology was clear enough. They'd apparently never developed faster-than-light travel, though their power plants reportedly generated thrust enough to take them to something like 0.5 c. That was fast enough to cover the distances between the stars within reasonable times, but too slow to make much use of General Relativity and time dilation. Either the Gr'tak were from some as yet undiscovered habitable world within a few light years of High Frontier, or they went in for generational travel. Some observers had already dismissed the Gr'tak as relative primitives and discounted them as a threat to the standoff between Empire and Confederation. In terms of weapons or new ship technology, that was probably true, but Dev knew better than to assume that they would have nothing to contribute to human science. The DalRiss had proven that science and technology could evolve along radically different routes with different cultures. The Gr'tak might well have insights into some branches of science that so far had been overlooked by both Imperial and Confed researchers; even if all human technology was superior to the newcomers, though, the mere fact that this was a different people, with different arts, philosophies, history, and ways of looking at things was enough to guarantee that they would have an impact on human civilization.

Which, of course, was why so many warships were gathering here. Neither side in the ongoing human, political struggle was willing for the other side to have unchallenged access to the alien newcomers. To ignore what they might have to offer was tantamount to national suicide.

"Dev?" a woman's voice said over the open communications link he'd been maintaining with the *Karyu*. "We're nearly ready to send the pod across."

"Very well," he said. "I'll be downloading in a moment."

The woman, he knew, was Dr. Taki Oe, a respected xenobiologist from the University of Jefferson . . . and also, coincidentally, a close friend of his son. Dev was a little disappointed that Taki had been the one to call him and not Daren, but he'd not really been expecting his son to break the uncomfortable silence they shared.

Dev still felt strange . . . and not a little awkward around the young man who'd been his son by Katya Alessandro. He'd never seen the boy in his own, human body, never been able to establish anything like a close relationship with him. In point of fact, Daren Cameron struck Dev as something of a prig, self-centered, rude, and abrupt, though his records indicated he was excellent in his field. A full doctor—he'd downloaded the requisite background by the time he was seventeen and submitted his doctoral thesis by nineteen—he'd already gained a reputation for himself with his studies of the Communes of Dante.

As nearly as he could tell, Daren was as uncomfortable still with his father as Dev was with his son. Dev's return from deep space two years before, bearing warning of the Web threat at Nova Aquila, had been an unsettling, even painful experience for them both, one that neither of them had yet fully adjusted to. It helped, a little, that both Daren and Taki were not really here at High Frontier but were exercising their telepresences via an I2C link-up from the *Carl Friedrich Gauss* at far-off Nova Aquila.

He made another check of the crisscrossing streams of electronic information, then spoke briefly with his DalRiss hosts. He would be using a body for this expedition, a DalRiss construct, a living creature tailored by them to serve as a mobile repository for his intelligence. He'd used similar forms before during his explorations with his hosts, though he still had some trouble getting used to its hexapod stance and all-round vision. Donning the body was as simple as downloading the program that was his conscious mind.

A short time later, he was inside a small transport shuttle, a wingless, mag-driven pod boosting at low acceleration from the Confederation carrier *Karyu* toward the largest of the alien vessels. With him in the crowded cabin were two sleek, humanoid forms, hubots teleoperated by researchers many light years distant. Taki Oe, and Dev's son.

"I'm impressed that we've been able to pick up as much about them as we have," Taki was saying. "We certainly haven't had much to go on so far. We don't even know what they look like."

"That's because all of the real communication so far has been between our AI systems and what we presume are their computers," Dev said, using the radio link that he was sharing with the two hubots, rather than slower and clumsier verbal means. "Since both of us work digitally, with a binary numeric system and with what appears to be massively parallel processing, we had a lot in common starting out."

"A common number system," Taki said.

"Yes. A common number system. Common voltages and electronic variables. We were able to arrive at a common system for measuring time, based on the radio frequency we were using. We also agreed on a general frame of reference, on codes meaning 'you,' 'us,' 'we,' 'they,' and so on. The word samples they've given us have already been analyzed by the best expert AI linguistics system we have, which would be the one at the Terran Hegemony Language Studies Group at Singapore. Of course, since we already went through a lot of this with the DalRiss a quarter century ago, it's not like we're breaking new ground."

"Maybe *you're* not," Daren's hubot said quietly. There was the slightest of challenges in Daren's tone of voice.

"Do you have a problem, Daren?"

"I'm just not sure of why Taki and me are here when they have *you*."

"I think we're both still a little, um, awed," Taki said. "You've got the whole Net to draw on, and it leaves us feeling a little slow."

Dev had the impression that Taki wasn't speaking for herself so much as she was for Daren.

"I have the same resources you do," he said bluntly. "I might be a little faster. But you have advantages I don't."

"Such as?" Daren prompted belligerently.

"You're not alone. . . ."

The next few minutes passed in uncomfortable silence, as they watched the armada arrayed on the shuttle's viewall. Dev had hoped that their destination would be one of the sleek and beautiful ship-forms gathered in the Gr'tak zone, but as soon as the pod's vector was automatically handed over to a Gr'tak controller, it was clear that they were heading for one of the asteroid ships, a gnarled, dusty-looking body very nearly as black as coal, a rough and cratered potato shape measuring ten kilometers in length by perhaps half that in width. They could see the rock's slow rotation as shadows shifted across the uneven surface. The rotational gravity inside, at least for structures close to the surface, would be just over one standard gravity at the equator, a figure that would dwindle away to nothing as one moved nearer the rotational poles. They were approaching it from its dark side, which meant it was more visible by the stars it occulted than by any sunlight reflected from its ebon surface. Lights, whole constellations of them, gleamed from tight-knit clusters around both poles of rotation. As the shuttle continued closing with the object, Dev could see that they were being drawn toward the asteroid's south pole.

Moment followed moment in silence. Electronic communications protocols had already been worked out between the respective computer systems, but it seemed a little strange to be approaching another ship without a constant stream of requests, commands, and permissions-to-board. Dev sensed instead the quiet whisper of data exchanges, the alien code slightly slower than human and somewhat richer and more elegant in the way it was packed.

An intense blue light winked on ahead, and below, a portion of the black surface yawned open to give entry to a large, violet-lit docking or receiving bay. Under automatic control, the shuttle pod skimmed through the slowly moving opening, gentling in for a docking within a webwork of gantries and ship cradles. He'd expected the bay to pressurize, but instead, the cradle that received them lifted them swiftly through a long set of smaller hatchways and a succession of locks. An explosive gust of incoming air rocked

he craft once . . . then again as pressures outside rose to
well over 1.4 bar. One side of the chamber they were in slid
open, and their shuttle was trundled forward into green and
violet-white light.

They were . . . outside once more.

Or so it seemed. Beyond the gleaming ceramic shell of
the wall they'd just emerged from was something more like
tropical jungle than the interior of a spacecraft, with moist
dirt and clots of leaves and dead vegetation underfoot, with
a violet-white sky and growing, moving things that must
have been the Gr'tak analogue of trees . . . though they
looked more like inverted jellyfish, with stiff and writhing
tentacles extending skyward from billowing skirts of translucent, gelatinous membranes.

"Air pressure at nearly one and a half atmospheres,"
Taki reported. "Rotational gravity . . . I make it two tenths
of a G up here. We're pretty close to the axis, though. Down
by the equator, it'll be higher. Mix . . . um. Thirty-one percent oxygen. That's pretty rich. High $CO_2$, almost six hundred ppm. Sixty-eight percent nitrogen."

"Thirty-one percent $O_2$?" Daren asked. "Damn. If we
sneeze we're going to start one hell of a fire!"

"Not necessarily," Dev said. "The high $CO_2$ will have
a dampening effect. Still, things are going to be more flam-
mable. I wonder how they deal with electrical storms?"

"In this colony," Taki pointed out, "they don't have to."

"Yeah, but if this atmosphere matches that of their homeworld," Daren said, "I'll bet their civilization had a bitch
of a time learning to tame fire. Just chipping flints would
have gotten them into trouble."

The trio emerged from the shuttle's airlock, two hubots
followed by Dev's flat, six-legged organic suit. Taki carried
a half-meter-long, silver-gray canister under her hubot's
arm.

Water dripped from the vegetation . . . if that was what
the jellyfish-things were. The air was steamy with humidity,
and Dev had to pause once and trigger a jet of cold air to
clear his artificial body's optical sensors.

The intense illumination filtered down from a brilliant line
of light scratched across the zenith. As the planetoid rotated

about that glowing axis, centrifugal force created an out-is-down gravity; the opposite side of this inside-out world was spread like a curving map across the sky beyond the light, almost lost in the thick atmosphere's haze.

"A lot like Dante," Daren remarked as they stopped in a small clearing. "Not as much sulfur dioxide, and the $CO_2$ is lower. But the temperature's about the same, at forty-two degrees."

"I think we can assume this is a match for their home environment," Taki said.

"If these people have been traveling for a long time at sublight," Dev suggested, "maybe they just brought their world with them."

"There was still an original homeworld," Daren said. "Somewhere. But they would have built this colony to match their—"

"Watch out, everybody," Taki said. "We're being watched."

Dev's all-round vision had already caught the movement as something slipped through the air into the clearing. His first impression was of a very large insect, something like a wasp, something like a dragonfly, with numerous features and details utterly unlike either. The wingspan, as nearly as Dev could tell when the wings were reduced to a nearly invisible blur, was nearly a full meter, while the creature's body was as thick as a human arm and nearly twice as long. A pair of openings, like wet mouths, pulsed to either side of the elongated head just beneath paired, bulbous, jewel-faceted eyes. Dev thought that those mouths must be part of the creature's respiratory apparatus, gulping down large amounts of air to fuel the furious beat of those wings. On Earth, insects were limited in how big they could grow by the fact that they used spiracles for respiration rather than lungs. The higher concentration of oxygen in this place, coupled with the likelihood that this creature possessed something like lungs, explained how "insects" could reach such a size; Dev had read that Earth's atmosphere during the Carboniferous had reached thirty-five percent oxygen, allowing the evolution of dragonflies with half-meter wingspans.

The creature's head attached to the body between those enormous eyes; a smooth and slightly rounded crest thrust back from this, however, so that the entire head was larger than three human fists stacked together. Instead of legs, a cluster of slender tendrils nervously twitched beneath the eyes, but Dev couldn't tell if they were mouth parts, sensory organs, manipulators, or all three. The abdomen, again, long and slender like a dragonfly's, was flexible, tapering, and tightly coiled; when Daren's hubot moved slightly, the hovering creature drifted back half a meter and the abdomen uncoiled, then recoiled in a flash, demonstrating a marvelous precision of strength and control. A manipulative organ of some sort, like a tentacle or a hand?

"Is this one of our hosts?" Taki wondered aloud. "Or part of the native fauna?"

"One of our hosts, I should think," Dev replied. "In a closed, tightly controlled environment like this, I doubt that the wildlife wanders around free."

"How do you know that?" Daren said sharply. "This could be the equivalent of a domesticated pet. Or a gene-tailored, roving eye. Or—"

Something moved ahead, a thrashing in the shadowed undergrowth. The vegetation parted then, and another creature moved into the clearing. This time, there was no doubt, in Dev's mind, at least, that this was one of the Gr'tak.

One? Or more than that? The main body of the thing was easily four meters tall, a bulk of gray-brown flesh that towered above the three human machines. Beyond the initial impression of bulk and mass, though, it was at first hard to nail down details of the thing's structure, so little was it like anything in Dev's experience. It was fairly simple in its overall design, a massively large and fleshy base reminiscent of the foot of a conch or some other marine cephalopod, rising in a thick and muscular column of flesh and muscle that looped over sharply at the top, then descended to a smaller, second foot on the body's front end that seemed to incorporate the head as part of its structure. The head grew forward out of the leading edge of the second foot, an oddly bumpy and wrinkled gray ovoid festooned with tendrils, cilia, and prismatic surfaces that might have been various sense organs or manipulative appendages or both. The thing's movement, as it edged its way into the clearing, was almost comically like that of a terrestrial inchworm; the head-foot reached forward in a two-meter stride, then clung to the ground as the more massive tail-foot glided after it on powerful, muscular contractions.

The creature wore clothing of a sort, a bright pink skirt with rich violet and green ornamentation worked in glistening bands and spirals into the material, open at the top and bottom and girdling the looped body, leaving both feet and the upper part of the arch bare. The only other ornamentation was a gleaming, brass-colored plate or brooch that seemed to be embedded in the thing's thick hide just above and behind the head-foot.

The upper opening of the thing's skirt revealed three meter-long objects, flat, black, and glistening wet, adhering to the top of the arch. At first, Dev took them for some sort of external organs on the creature's body, but then one released its hold at what Dev took to be its leading end, and a blindly questing, circular mouth gaped for a moment before reattaching itself to its large mount. The three black shapes, then, were a trio of glistening creatures like enormous leeches attached to the larger being's dorsal surface, two riding side by side with the third slightly ahead of and overlapping the other two. The upper sides of the riders were pocked with half a dozen fist-sized craters that appeared to be the source of the moisture covering them; a gray and slender, many-branched growth sprouted more than a meter up from the thick skin of the larger creature beneath them, though which organism that structure belonged to, if either, Dev honestly couldn't tell.

Dev immediately had the impression, though, of several creatures working together, the big, arched body ridden by the three leeches in much the same way that a Riss rode a six-legged Dal. The union suggested that the Gr'tak was not an interstellar federation after all, but an evolutionary joining of several sapient species. The hovering insect, Dev noticed, was definitely a part of that superorganism or at least shared a close symbiosis with it. As he watched with fascination, the flyer abruptly darted back to the larger creature folded up its wings, and vanished into one of the holes in one of the leech-riders with a ripple of glistening black flesh to mark its movement beneath the skin, while another, apparently identical flyer crawled free of a different hole and took to the air with a soft hiss of vibrating, transparent membranes. Dev was put in mind of scout warflyers maintaining a constant CAP around their carrier, serving as early warning for approaching danger, perhaps, as well as a mobile extension of eyes and other sense organs.

The being stopped a few meters away and seemed to be regarding them patiently through the jeweled facets of what must be compound eyes. Slowly, avoiding any threatening movement, Taki lowered the cylinder she was carrying to the ground, palmed its touchplate, and let the end dissolve.

Inside was a Naga communicator.

Thirty years ago, the DalRiss had engineered organic communicators, called *comels*, that had first enabled humans to communicate directly with the bizarrely alien Naga. Later, though, the Naga themselves learned to duplicate that trick; they were very good at patterning the molecular arrangements of another living creature's brain, permitting the direct transference of thought through an appropriately programmed intermediary. The only real difficulty, of course, was that when those thoughts were alien enough, they didn't make much sense. Even perfect understanding of a common language didn't help in communicating thoughts for which another culture had no thoughts . . . or words describing ideas totally beyond that culture's ken.

The programmed Naga fragment slid out of its container and onto the ground with a wet plop. Dev recognized the gray-black, sluglike shape . . . a single Naga cell, budded off from a planetary Naga that had already established communications with humans and understood—as much as was possible for that species—human thought processes.

Slowly, the Naga crawled toward the waiting Gr'tak. The enigmatic being seemed to watch its approach stoically, with no outward emotion—none, at least, that was recognizable to the humans. The Naga fragment moved to within a meter of the creature, and after the briefest of hesitations, something began uncoiling from the back of the huge arch, a single tentacle that must usually have been kept folded away unseen inside a pouch or recess within the thing's body. The tentacle reached down and touched the Naga fragment, which immediately began dwindling as its microcellular structure dissolved into the Gr'tak, filtering through the cells of its skin like hydrogen molecules diffusing through the rubber skin of a balloon.

The trio waited, watching as the huge creature digested the morsel; it seemed to show no surprise at the Naga fragment's intrusion into its body. Dev well remembered the first time he'd seen Naga material melting into his skin, and the panic he'd felt. It was not precisely a *reassuring* means of first contact. . . .

But the Gr'tak had seemed at ease with the idea. Indeed, the Naga fragment would have worked nearly as well if the two, Gr'tak and human, had simply each touched the Naga, using it as a physical bridge like the old comels, but it would be far better and faster if the Naga could pattern the alien creature's brain and allow a full merging of minds.

Unlike the two hubots, Dev's biomechanical DalRiss body possessed a Naga implant similar to the Companion carried by humans, and that elected him as the point man for first contact. Slowly, so as not to give alarm, he stepped closer to the huge creature, one of his alien body's arms stretched out, manipulators wide. Unfurling like a coiled line, the Gr'tak's tentacle dropped until the tip hung, twitching, a half meter from Dev's outstretched hand.

He waited a moment, making certain of the invitation, then closed that last narrow gap. The touch was cold . . . flickering . . . *strange*. The sensation of contact with an alien mind through a Naga intermediary was not as sharp or as overwhelming as he remembered it being in his flesh-and-blood body, long ago, but it was dazzling in its intensity nonetheless, and bewildering with its heady rush of alien sensations.

He sensed . . . memories. Countless memories, most a jumble of shapes and colors, odors and sensations that he simply could not sort out or catalogue. Some of those memories were clear attempts at communication, he knew, but it was difficult to sort them out. For a dizzying moment, Dev ung poised above a black and bottomless abyss, a whirling, shrieking nightmare of rushing alien thoughts and concepts, nested concepts, one inside another like nested woodcarved Russian dolls. The voices he heard were echoes of one another . . . and also, in a way he could not quite give shape to, were nested, one inside another in an infinitely repeating series receding into blackness.

For a moment, Dev was looking through alien eyes— weirdly faceted, multiply imaging eyes, like those of an insect—at something . . . *something* black and sleek and familiar if he could just learn to see in this strangely shattered and echoing way. . . .

His Naga, sensing patterns and familiarities, helped, sorting through the images, bringing fragmented pieces together, melding dozens into one.

The shape was familiar, chillingly so. Dev watched the ebon black, egg-smooth sleekness of a Web probe descending into the heart of a solar system. He saw it split, saw part descend on a warm and sunlit world, with vast geometries of light patterned across the continents of its night side. He saw glimpses—fragments, really—of a civilization's collapse, of nuclear fireballs and destruction unimaginable, of weirdly glittering, insectlike machines that devoured everything in their path, of something going hideously wrong with a sun, and the silent, actinic flash that spelled the doom of an entire world, its population, its culture, everything that it was and might one day be.

Emotions rode the alien currents of those images. He sensed deep sorrow . . . and urgent need.

*"I/we are associative Sholai of Associative HaShoGha,"* the thought ran, sliding warm-wet through Dev's mind, the echoes and reiterations damped out by his Naga. Funny. It was as though he could hear the capitalizations, slight differences of stress in the unfamiliar words. There was a distinct difference between associative and Associative, for instance, the former clearly referring to the entity Sholai, while the latter seemed to indicate something larger and more complex . . . a community, perhaps. The feel of that concept was similar to the Naga ideas of »self« and

Self, referring to detachable fragments of a much larger and more complete complex.

"*I/we are refugees*," the thought continued, "*fleeing a terrible danger that has all but destroyed our Associatives. We are looking for Community and coupled thought.*"

Dev wasn't sure what "coupled thought" might be, but the sense of community seemed important to the being. Dev decided to push a bit on that idea and see what response he could raise.

"We are representatives of a community . . . of an *Associative* of three different races," he told it. "Human, Naga, and DalRiss. We are facing a danger like the one you've just shown me. I think it's the same . . . a threat we call the Web."

The outstretched tentacle coiled back suddenly, a sharp flick of motion that momentarily broke the contact. Dev waited patiently, unmoving, as the creature before him shuddered with some nearly convulsive emotion. At first he thought the thing was afraid; mention of the Web, certainly, would be enough to terrify if these people had fled here from a home world destroyed by Web engineering.

Then the Gr'tak extended the tentacle again, and Dev once more slipped into that bewildering symphony of voices, sounds, and shifting mental images. He concentrated on the emotions, trying to find those that he could recognize, trying to block out the alien cacophony that was becoming painful in its intensity.

Yes, there was a recognizable emotion, but it wasn't the one that Dev had expected to find. There was fear, yes . . . a sour, sharp shuddering underlying the creature's mental processes.

But the immediate, the overwhelming emotion that Dev was sensing from the Gr'tak was not fear . . . but joy.

# Chapter 13

*Utter resolve is necessary when you are fighting an enemy. In order to beat him you must control the situation, regardless of the method you use. If you do not control the enemy, the enemy will control you.*

— *"Fire Scroll"*
*The Book of the Five Spheres*
MIYAMOTO MUSASHI
seventeenth century B.C.E.

"The Gr'tak don't possess the same kind of intelligence humans do," Taki said. "Or the DalRiss, for that matter, or even the Naga. Some of us are beginning to think that intelligence may be common in the universe, but no two specific *types* of intelligence are quite the same."

Dev's visual representation of himself nodded. "Certainly, we've found enough differences in the intelligent species we've already studied to support such an idea."

It was two weeks since their initial contact with the Gr'tak. They were meeting in Cascadia . . . or, rather, in a virtual-world Cascadia, a shared illusion generated within the local Net back on New America. The familiar Alessandro–Hagan estate's conversation room had been altered with the addition of a conference table. A life-size image of a Gr'tak floated silently above the table's holoprojector, adding a surreal touch, complete with a pair of hovering, darting dragonfly creatures. *Lessers*, they were called, according to the lexicon of Gr'tak terminology still being hammered out. Present at the table were Dev, Daren, and Taki, of course, as well as Katya Alessandro and Vic Hagan. At Vic's suggestion, Kara was also present, turning the assembly into a family gathering . . . which left Dev feeling just a bit the outsider. He accepted that, however, since his disembodied state generally left him an outsider no matter where he was.

Also present, and also evidently feeling like outsiders, were two others who'd attended the ViRconference at Katya's suggestion. One was Kazuhiro Mishima, tall, elegantly dressed in formal red diplomatic robes, assigned by the Imperial government as the senior ambassador to the Confederation. The other was Dr. Frances Gresham, of the Confederation Senate Science Council. In another two hours Katya and Vic were scheduled to present a full report to the Science Council, and they were using this opportunity to go over what Dev, Daren, and Taki had witnessed at High Frontier and to distill some of what they'd learned.

Gresham looked puzzled. "I'm not sure I understand. I mean, you're intelligent or you're not, right?"

"It's not that simple, Doctor," Daren told her. "For one thing, there are at least seventy different aspects of thought, memory, knowledge, and awareness that we've been able to categorize so far as distinct subsets of what we call sapience. Most authorities can't even agree on the exact number, but it is large."

"That's right," Taki added. "Some people have a talent in, oh, let's say, math. They can do complex calculations in their heads, retain long chains of numbers and manipulate them without having to write them down, even think in terms of equations and numeric series, without putting the thoughts into words. You follow?"

Kara tossed Daren a wry grin. "Yeah. My brother over there's like that. Frightening. Rattle off a string of numbers at me and I'll be lucky to tell you the first two in order. He can do it with commo numbers, access codes, whatever. Read him a number and he's got it forever."

Taki nodded. "Skill at working with numbers and numeric concepts is one type of intelligence. Working with words is another, either through direct articulation, or in using them to describe complex actions or thoughts. Artistic talent—being able to think in terms of color or tone or texture, that's, well, actually that's a whole cluster of intelligence types, at least the way we use the concept today. Others have to do with abstract reasoning, with drawing conclusions from data, with getting along with other people, or manipulating them, or even just understanding what they're feeling. All of these things go together to create that composite attribute we call intelligence.''

"Intelligence clusters are the preferred way of looking at the whole idea of intelligence,'' Dev said. ''You can be a genius at some things, an idiot at others, and everything taken together generally averages out. Now that's just with the human population. We think that other sapient species may have more or less the same general mix of talents—with exceptions of course. A species that was blind wouldn't have an artistic color sense, for instance. But by and large, the individuals of all intelligent species are going to need to deal with numbers, with communicative concepts, with others of their kind, and so on.''

"So,'' Vic said. ''What you're saying is that some of the aliens we meet are going to be really great at painting pictures, but downright stupid when it comes to making friends.'' He considered the thought. ''I've known people like that.''

"The DalRiss are better than we are at interpersonal relationships,'' Katya said. ''But they lack, well, call it *empathy*. They can't understand the outrage some humans feel at the way they use their gene-tailored life forms. The Dal. Or the Achievers.''

"Gok,'' Daren said with a sour expression. ''You could say the same about the human domestication of animals. How much empathy did humans expend on cows?''

"What's cows?'' Vic asked.

"An earth animal gene-tailored by millennia of domestication. The original form was completely wiped out by breeding programs, and the new forms deliberately altered for milk and meat production.''

"Yuk,'' Katya said with some decisiveness. ''Dark ages stuff. Obviously that was before nanofactories could grow meat to order.''

"When it comes to lack of empathy, I'll give you one

better, Mums,'' Kara put in. ''The Imperials with their *inochi-zo*. They turn torture of a gene-tailored life form into art.'' She shivered. She'd forgotten Mishima's presence. A glance in his direction, though, showed him listening impassively.

Daren shifted in his chair. ''Well, the point of all this is that there's a broad spectrum of skills, talents, and mental traits, both within each species, and among all of the species we know, that comprise what we call intelligence. They overlap, but they never quite match.''

''So how does this apply to our friends the Gr'tak?'' Ambassador Mishima wanted to know.

''The Gr'tak, Your Excellency,'' Taki told him, ''appear to be geniuses compared to us when it comes to social organization. If language provides any clue, you only need to look at the words they have for things like 'government,' 'friendship,' or 'society.' ''

''The Gr'tak,'' Dev added, ''have twenty-three different words that we would translate as 'government.' ''

''You mean, like, democracy, theocracy, monarchy, stuff like that?'' Gresham asked.

''No. *That* gets even more complicated, and since they don't have them, as far as we can tell, they probably don't have words for theocracies or monarchies. From what we've been able to record in these past few weeks, though, they have something like eighty words simply describing different types of governments where the ordinary citizens participate in their own self-rule, what we would call democracy. No, just the concept of *government*, an organization or group or corporate body that makes laws, administers justice, and provides direction for society as a whole, *that* has twenty-three different words in Rashind, the principal Gr'tak language, and to tell you the truth, we haven't even begun to sort out the shades of meanings attached to each. The point, I think, is that they perceive more variety and richness in the concept than we do and have come up with more words to describe that richness because it's important to them.''

''Sure,'' Daren said. ''There used to be a certain culture on old Earth, a hunter-fisher nomad group, a long time ago, before Nihon started running everything there. They lived in the near Arctic, where there was snow on the ground much of the year, and did their hunting out on one of Earth's polar ice caps. I ViRed once that they had some obscene number of words that all meant 'snow.' 'Light snow,' 'fluffy snow,' 'hard-packed snow,' that sort of thing.''

Taki shrugged. ''It's a handy reference to what is important to a culture. In Nihongo, we have a very large number of words differentiating different types of winds and breezes, usually with poetic overtones. 'The wind that makes a flag snap,' 'the wind of an arrow's flight,' 'the wind from the sea,' the wind—' ''

''Are you saying these Gr'tak creatures think government is important?'' Mishima said abruptly, cutting her off.

''They think *all* social interaction is important. Government is just one aspect of how people, how intelligent beings, rather, interact.''

''They have a large number of words for various types of sexual liaison,'' Dev added. ''Of course, their sex relationships tend to be a lot more complicated than ours.''

''How come?''

''Well, to start with, we're not really dealing with a single species. A single 'Gr'tak' is what they call an associative of a number of different creatures living on and in one another. Parasites, in fact.''

Mishima leaned back from the table, giving a small hiss through his teeth. ''*Inosho*,'' he said quietly. Dev's linguistic program gave an immediate translation, but it lacked the sharp emotion behind the word. ''*Parasites*.''

''There is a species of parasitic wasp on Earth,'' Daren said. ''It lays its eggs on the skin of certain caterpillars. The eggs hatch, and the larva eat the living caterpillar from the inside out, then use its skin as a cocoon for their phase change to adult wasps. Well, it turns out that these wasps are themselves parasitized by a smaller species of parasitic wasp. And *they* in turn are parasitized by an even smaller species of wasp. In fact, researchers discovered that there were no less than five different species of wasp, each nested in the last like a whole series of those little carved and painted wooden dolls. What are they called?''

''*Matreshka* dolls,'' Katya offered.

"There was an old comic poem to that effect," Dev said. "Something about 'Big fleas have little fleas . . . ' and ending with the line 'and so *ad infinitum*.' "

"Yes. Well, the surprising thing about the Gr'tak," Daren continued, "is that they are composed of several mutually parasitizing species. Not as a serial regression, like those terrestrial wasps I mentioned, but with at least four different creatures living in close association with one another. Add to that their form of AI, what they call artificials, and you end up with a pretty complex joint life form."

"Wait a minute," Gresham said, shaking his head. "I don't think I buy this. I downloaded my doctorate in biology a long time ago, and I was a pretty fair xenobiologist before I ended up on bureaucratic panels. Parasites are essentially regressive species. *Primitive*, because they only need to adapt to their hosts. There wouldn't be any drive to develop intelligence, and if they had it to begin with, they'd lose it when life got easy."

"Old idea," Daren said with a tight smile. "That was outdated centuries ago. Parasites have to be specialized, yeah. And the traditional idea was always that when a parasite learns to live off of its host species, life gets easier for it. It's true that some forms lose a lot of adaptations for getting along in the outside world because they simply don't need them. A tapeworm, for instance, is nothing much more than a head with jaws to hang onto the inner surface of the host's gut. The rest of it, all several meters' worth, is body segments that detach one by one, pass out of the host's body, and serve to reproduce the beast by hatching out new parasites inside new hosts that happen to ingest them. It's not quite that simple, of course. Most parasitic species actually have fairly complex life cycles, some of them extremely so, requiring a large number of successive, species-specific hosts. Anyway, on the face of things, intelligence simply isn't something that you would expect a parasite to need.

"But we've learned that there is intense competition among parasitic species for host living space, just as there is among other species . . . and any time you have competition, there's the chance that it will foster, well, anything that will give the species an evolutionary edge in the race. Back to those terrestrial wasps.''

"What are you," Gresham asked. "An expert on parasitic wasps?"

"*My* doctoral download was on terrestrial insects, yes," Daren said. "Especially social forms, and that included the Hymenoptera, even though not all wasps are social insects. Anyway, there's one kind of wasp that lays several eggs on a host caterpillar. All but one hatch early and cruise through the caterpillar's body killing every other parasitic wasp larva they find. That ensures that when the last egg hatches, the larva has no competition from other species.''

"That's not intelligence," Kara pointed out.

"No, that's adaptation," Daren agreed. "Intelligence would be another kind of adaptation and a useful one if evolved in a hostile, high-competition environment. Hell, scientists are still arguing over whether or not you can even call intelligence a survival trait, since the technology that comes out of it does seem to get us into increasingly difficult situations.

"The Gr'tak, though, are different," he continued. "We haven't learned much about their life cycle yet . . . and we can't even begin to speculate about how they evolved to where they are today. But we have learned how they're put together.''

He gestured at the floating, three-D image of the Gr'tak hanging above the conference table. "The largest part of the organism, that high-standing arch, is what they call a 'receiver.' That's the main host, the foundation for the rest. Now, these three organisms on the back. They look like flat, black plastic bags or oversized leeches. Those are external parasites, and the Gr'tak refer to them as 'greaters.' Those independent flying creatures, like big insects, are called 'lessers.' They, actually, are parasites of the greaters. They live inside the greaters' bodies and emerge through those holes in its back. As near as we can tell, the lessers are kind of like mobile scouts for the whole organism, flying around the area, checking out the surroundings, and flying back to report. There's a fourth parasite, something they call a 'deeper.' We're not sure what that is like, actually, though we think that that thing like a tree with very skinny branches growing out of the top might be a part of it. Deepers live inside the receiver. They may serve as an intermediary for the greaters and the receiver, and we're pretty sure they're important in the reproductive cycle.''

''How *do* these things reproduce?'' Katya wanted to know.

''Haven't sorted that out yet,'' Daren said.

''We're working on it,'' Taki added. ''The greaters share a certain symmetry with the receivers, and we think that's because the greaters and the receivers are two different sexes of the same organism, though there's so much room for misunderstanding here, we could easily be mistaken about that. We do know that the reproductive systems of all four species are very closely interconnected. We think the young of the next generation already carry their symbionts when they're born.''

''The DalRiss started out as parasites, didn't they?'' Mishima said. ''Is this the fashion trend of the Galaxy, now?''

Gresham laughed. ''What's next, intelligent tapeworms?''

''The DalRiss fusion arose from a symbiotic relationship,'' Dev pointed out. ''Possibly some parasitism was involved in their early history, but from what we've been able to learn, the dominant Riss organisms started off feeding on the larger Dal creatures, which were big, herd-dwelling, six-legged grazers, but they provided a survival advantage as well, probably by helping the Dal spot dangerous predators.

''With the Gr'tak, the relationship is deeper, and a lot stranger. The lessers probably started off as outright parasites of the greaters, while the greaters may have started out as parasites, or they could have been part of a sexual dependency, like male angler fish, on Earth. Maybe they both represent part of a more complex life cycle. You know, the parasite lives as a larva in one host, then gets passed to a different host where it matures into something else. Somewhere along the line, though, the cycle of each of the four got so wrapped up with the reproductive cycles of the others that now none of the four can reproduce without the active participation of other three. The receivers appear to be what we call a parasex of the greaters, same species but with a much different morphology.''

"You think they developed in a hostile environment, though?'' Vic asked. "That that was what forced them to evolve intelligence?''

"I'm not sure I see what other explanation there could be,'' Daren said. "My working hypothesis now is that they've evolved from several codependent species inhabiting littoral zones on their original homeworld.''

"Littoral zones?'' Mishima asked.

"Coastal areas. Specifically, salt marshes, swamps, tidal zones, places like that. They're not really amphibious, but they do prefer wet environments, high humidity. That miniature world we visited is a weird cross between a sauna bath and a greenhouse. They like it at forty degrees or more and often conduct business from their wading pools. And that kind of environment is often a Darwinian forcer. That's a place with lots of competition for limited resources, and lots of other species on the lookout for a meal.''

"This is all quite interesting,'' Mishima said with a carefully shuttered expression. "I, and my government, of course, are most concerned, however, in what has brought these creatures here.''

"That seems pretty obvious,'' Dev said. "It's in the report I uploaded onto the Net last week. They were victims of the Web. Like the DalRiss.''

"But this happened a long time ago, right?'' Gresham asked.

"We're still working on their concept of time and how they measure it,'' Dev admitted. "But if we're on the right track, the Web showed up in their home system and turned their star into a nova well over four thousand years ago. We think their home star was spinward and coreward of Sol, out beyond Nova Aquila. Another in the Aquilan Cluster, in fact.''

One of the more haunting mysteries of astronomy had been the odd fact that a disproportionate number of novae, historically, had appeared in a single tiny patch of the sky as seen from Earth . . . roughly in the direction of the constellation Aquila, the Eagle. During a single, forty-year period early in the twentieth century, twenty-five percent of all of the recorded novae had appeared within an area measuring one quarter of one percent of the entire sky. Two had appeared there in one year alone—1936—and Nova Aquila, in 1918, had been the brightest recorded exploding star in three hundred years, a dazzling jewel-point outshining every star in the heavens except Sirius.

That clustering in time had been an odd, statistical anomaly, of course, since the stars involved ranged from relatively close to extremely distant, and it was chance that had the wavefronts of all of those stars arrive in the vicinity of Earth in the same four-decade period. But that anomaly had called astronomers' attention to the disproportionate number of novae in that one direction. Not until Dev—downloaded into the DalRiss explorer fleet—reached Nova Aquila had the truth been suspected, that many of those stars, if not all, had been deliberately exploded by the entities humans knew as the Web. Apparently, the Web was working toward a specific agenda, moving out from the Galactic Core where they'd first appeared along a grand spiral, following one of the Galaxy's spiral arms out into the stellar hinterlands. They'd been slowly approaching Sol's position in space for millennia, coming from the direction of Aquila, Ophiuchus, and Serpens.

"They've been traveling since something like 1500 B.C.E.," Taki said. She shook her head slowly, wonderingly. "They left the fiery wreck of their home planet a thousand years before Confucius was alive on Earth. They have been wandering for that long."

"Looking for what?" Gresham wanted to know. "How many of these Gr'tak ships are there, anyway?"

"The fleet is . . . large," Dev admitted. Sholai had told him it consisted of ten thousand ships, but he'd not yet admitted that officially. So far, only a few hundred had arrived at High Frontier, and he wanted to give them a chance to get reunited and to gather in stragglers before passing such alarming news on to others.

Particularly to the Imperials, who were already nervous about so many strangers turning up on the borders of the Shichiju.

"What weapons do they have?" Mishima demanded. "What new technology?"

"We're still looking at that question, Ambassador," Katya said.

"Their move into space was apparently prompted by a prevalence of comets in their home system," Dev pointed out. "I've . . . lived some of their remote history. Civilization fell a number of times when comets or small asteroids hit their world. They never fought wars among themselves, apparently. The only weapons they developed were laser banks designed to protect their planet from infalling debris."

"Pah." Mishima made a dismissive gesture. "We have the same ourselves already, on Luna." He was referring to *Fudo-Myoo*, the huge arrays of solar-power beam weapons based on Earth's moon; deployed in the late twenty-first century against the remote but deadly chance of a comet impact on Earth such as the one that had annihilated the dinosaurs sixty-five million years earlier, the gigajoule laser and particle beam system had never been used . . . though it remained a formidable part of Earth's defenses.

Dev studied Mishima. The ambassador looked troubled, his image frowning with the blank, far-away look that generally meant the person was accessing his personal RAM, or listening to some private message relayed through his Companion. No, Dev reminded himself, Mishima was *Kansai no Otoko*, a "Man of Completion," a member of the Dai Nihon political-social-religious party advocating human purity and a single, united government for all Mankind. He would have one of the old-fashioned cephlinks, not an *isoro* Companion.

"Mr. Ambassador?" Katya said. "Are you all right?"

His face cleared, but he still looked troubled. "Please excuse me," he said. "There is . . . something most urgent I must attend to." His image vanished from the virtual setting.

"I wonder what that was all about?" Daren said.

But Dev was aware of something new, a quickening in the flow of information around him. Exactly what he sensed of that information was difficult to express in words, but living and moving within the electronic environment of the

Net was often described in metaphor and simile, with the informational matrix likened to a sea, vast, three-dimensional, and alive with powerful currents of moving data and flashing, myriad schools of fish representing individual communications packets. Had the metaphor been given form and substance, Dev knew he would have just seen vast and crowded schools of fish in the clear, sunlit shallows wheel about in an explosion of color and activity . . . then swell in numbers as new schools came swarming in out of the deeps beyond the shadowy reef in the distance.

Reaching out, he sampled one of the nearer "fish. . . ."

*. . . at this time still do not know where the intruders are coming from, but it is feared that these small vessels are representatives of the so-called "Web Intelligence" that was decisively defeated at Nova Aquila two years ago. . . .*

Surprise jolted Dev, followed swiftly by a stab of fear. The language was Nihongo, the speaker a well-known ViRnews mede broadcasting on the Net from Singapore Synchorbital.

From Earth . . . and the very seat of the Imperial government.

Swiftly, Dev sampled another incoming packet of communications . . . then another . . . then a hundred more in rapid succession. Most were coded military or government communiqués, but others were being uploaded in the clear and relayed throughout the human network via I2C.

"Excuse me," Dev told the others. "Something is happening. Something . . . very dangerous, I think. I've got to leave, too."

"What is it, Dev?" Katya wanted to know. She'd picked up on the urgency in his voice, put it together with Mishima's sudden departure, and sounded worried.

"Earth is under attack," he told his startled listeners. "It sounds like the Web has come out to play."

Before they could respond, Dev was gone.

# Chapter 14

*No man is an* Iland, *intire of it selfe; every man is a peece of the* Continent, *a part of the* maine; *if a* Clod *bee washed away by the* Sea, Europe *is the lesse, as well as if a* Promontorie *were, as well as if a* Mannor *of thy* friends *or of* thine owne *were; any mans* death *diminishes* me, *because I am involved in* Mankinde; *And therefore never send to know for whom the* bell *tolls; It tolls for* thee.

—*Devotions upon Emergent Occasions*, XVII
JOHN DONNE
C.E. 1624

Dev uploaded from the University of Jefferson, transmitting himself as a burst of digitized information across the thirty-six-light-year I2C linkage from the 26 Draconis system to Eridu, Chi Draconis V. From there, he routed to a commercial channel, waited 312 microseconds for the passage of a particularly large block of priority data flagged for ViRcom routing, then uploaded once again across the twenty-nine-light-year I2C link to Chiron. From Chiron, after another brief pause, it was just four and a half light years to Sol—less than the blink of an eye for the quantum-paired electron arrays of the communications facilities at Alpha Centauri A III and Earth.

His incoming pattern was routed through the commercial traffic buffers at the communications array on Luna, where Dev waited for several seconds, surveying the electronic ground. If message traffic had been growing stronger and more urgent than normal at New America, almost fifty light years away, it was frantic here. Reaching out with the down-loaded pattern of his mind, Dev sampled some of the messages flooding through near-Earth space.

"*. . . God, I've never seen anything like it! There must be hundreds of them coming out of K-T space, and they're filling the sky. . . .*"

"*Negative! Negative! It's not K-T space. We don't know how they're arriving, but they're coming in fast.*"

"*Mayday! Mayday! Am under attack by unknown forces! They're just coming out of empty space, more ships than I can count! . . .*"

"*Imperial Fleet Command Control Center, this is Perimeter Defense Facility* Evening Calm! *The enemy is materializing out of empty space from the direction of Aquila. Bearing right ascension, one-nine hours, three-five minutes, zero-four seconds, declination plus one-four point two degrees, range three-one-point-seven a.u. They appear to be moving in-system at high acceleration. Can't determine yet whether their target is Earth or the Sun. . . .*"

"*Hello! Hello! Is anyone reading me? Hello! . . .*"

"*Mayday! Mayday! This is the transport* Yoku Maru. *I've been hit by something! Power out. Life support down. I'm tumbling and losing pressure. Can anybody hear me? . . .*"

Earth's solar system was filled with spaceborne traffic, some military, most of it commercial shipping. Earth and Dai Nihon, after all, were the hub of a titanic commercial empire as well as a military one, an empire spanning the entire Shichiju and reaching all the way out into the Periphery states. As emergency and priority radio and I2C traffic flashed from ship to ship and among the various planetary and deep space communications facilities across the system, panic was spreading.

"*Perimeter Defense Facility* Evening Calm, *this is Imperial Fleet Command Control Center. Can you identify the attackers? Over!*"

"*Cee-Three*, Evening Calm. *It's the Web. Got to be. It's just like the attack at Nova Aquila . . . !*"

A large portion of the human race had seen, had *experienced* the Nova Aquila battle two years before by linking into the computer-communications network that interconnected all of the worlds inhabited by Man, and downloading the event—as seen through scanners and sensory suites throughout the Imperial–Confederation Combined Fleet—as it happened.

It had been a good many centuries since the advent of telecommunications—com satellites and old-fashioned two-D television—had brought the experience of war into civilian homes; since the development of ViRealities and direct cephlink feeds, news reporting had become a far more immediate, a more *personal* way of reaching people with current events. Even deep within the inner worlds of the Shichiju, where few citizens used the there-unpopular Naga Companions, virtually every citizen save the three percent or so of nullheads and technophobes had immediate access to online feeds from one or another of the news services, government, commercial, and private. As during the Battle of Nova Aquila, Dev could feel more and more citizens across the Shichiju linking in as the urgent communications from the outer reaches of the Solar System spread the panic further and further abroad.

And, as before, he could feel the Overmind stirring.

*Overmind* was Dev's term for that giant, half-sleeping intelligence that still lay, quiescent, beneath the crisscrossing babble of communications on the Net, a noncorporeal intelligence derived from the complex interconnectivity of all human communications. It had come into being during Nova Aquila, when a critical threshold of minds had actively joined the Net. He'd not been able to reach it during the battle, though in some still ill-defined way he'd been aware of having been a part, a very *small* part, of the entire intelligence.

The Overmind's intervention at Nova Aquila had won the battle for Humanity . . . and probably been responsible for the past two years of relative peace. Its intervention was the obvious answer to this attack as well . . . but as hard as Dev tried reaching for that enigmatic meta-intelligence, he could not seem to connect with its awareness.

So he reached outward once more, seeking a vantage point from which he could study the developing battle for

Earth and Earth's star system. He found that vantage point accelerating out toward the site of the incursion, past the orbit of Mars and moving above the plane of the asteroid belt—the flagship of the Imperial Navy's Home Defense Fleet, the INS *Yamato*.

A relic of a century before, bearing a name sacred to Nihonjin history and tradition, the Imperial battleship was vastly outclassed by the two larger, more powerful, and more modern dragonship carriers accelerating with her in her squadron, *Soryu* and *Tennoryu*; but her communications suite had been updated with the most powerful I2C apparatus, and originally she'd been designed around the concept of a combat coordination center, a heavily armed and armored space-mobile combat headquarters. The squadron, designated *Ida-Ten* after the swiftest of the ancient Japanese gods, had left Phobos three days before on routine patrol and by chance had been heading in roughly the right direction when the *Evening Calm*'s alert had come through. They had now fine-tuned their heading and were accelerating at a bone-rattling three and a half Gs, racing to meet the oncoming intruders.

Dev's penetration of *Yamato*'s systems went unnoticed. There were security programs aboard, of course, guard-dog routines set loose within the vast and tangled virtual space of the huge vessel's complex electronic network, as well as linked-in human operators assigned to monitor the system and watch for unauthorized entry. Had *Yamato* been quietly moored in spacedock, Dev might have had some trouble coming aboard, especially since the incoming data streams would be carefully monitored at such times to prevent personality or AI downloads from would-be spies or saboteurs.

Dev had chosen a good time to make his move, however, sequestering himself within the data banks of a navigational relay station in Earth orbit and downloading into *Yamato*'s waiting storage capacity when the relay was electronically tagged for a navigational update feed. No one noticed that the feed was several seconds longer than it should have been; at that moment, all minds were on the coming battle and the threat to home and Emperor . . . not to mention the very real possibility of death within the next few hours. Dev set a small portion of his mind to monitoring his immediate surroundings for the approach of an electronic guardian, and another part to the largely automatic task of constructing a shell for himself, the appearance of a small and routine housekeeping program set loose within the network as a part of the normal operating procedure. Kara, Dev recalled, had used a similar approach to penetrate the far more heavily defended computer system at Phobos in her raid on Kasei a couple of years back.

Seconds after his arrival, Dev had become part of the computer system's routine, accepted as one of the sub-AI programs constantly running on the network. He had no authorization for access to subsystems coded at level three or higher, but he wasn't seeking to penetrate the ship's secure areas in any case. All he needed was a place to eavesdrop on the electronic communications filling space around him.

Even so, he learned a fair amount just by linking in. The ship's captain was *Shosho* Chuichi Iijima, while the CO for the Ida-Ten squadron was *Chujo* Yatsuhiro Ubukata. And a surprise: Ubukata's boss was along, the Commander of the Home Defense Fleet, *Taisho* Nobutaki Kurebayashi. All three men, Dev was well aware, were traditionalists, confirmed members of the *Kansai no Otoko* who reportedly had scant respect for the battle tactics of mindless, soulless machines.

The problem, as Dev knew well, was that with virtually unlimited numbers the Web had little need of formal combat tactics. Throw enough metal at a defensive force, and unless that force had unlimited reserves of its own to draw on, it would break, sooner or later.

And that was precisely the tactics the Web appeared to be employing. Unseen by his unsuspecting shipmates, Dev monitored the intelligence feed to the big battle tank in *Yamato*'s Operations Center, a ten-meter pit with a holographic interface with the ship's primary Artificial Intelligence. Unnoted either by the AI or by the humans working the tank controls, Dev was able to electronically peer over their shoulders, watching the battle unfold in the emptiness far ahead.

As had happened at Nova Aquila, the Web machines were

materializing out of empty space, not all at once or in any kind of recognizable formation, but a few at a time, as though they were being fed into the Stargate device back at the Galactic Core as quickly as they could be rushed into position. As they emerged out of nothingness, they began accelerating in-system, gathering slowly into a vast and still-growing cloud of Web combat craft.

Dev used his position aboard the *Yamato* to carefully scan the enemy masses, searching for recognizable ship designs, for a repeat of earlier tactics, for anything that could provide him with intelligence into the inhuman mind of this foe. The Battle of Nova Aquila had been won two years before because the human forces had been able to identify and destroy key command and coordination facilities that appeared to have been directing Web battle tactics, but so far Dev had seen no ships or structures that evenly remotely resembled the enormous fleet control units he'd seen then. The planetoid ships that had apparently been coordinating the Web attack then were missing, which meant that in the past two years, the Web had analyzed their earlier defeat and found a way to avoid that same weakness.

That was one of the problems with technic war; if the enemy was any good at all, he would stay flexible, figure out what had gone wrong before, and fix it . . . which left his opponent trying to find some new weakness, some new angle of attack.

The trouble was, Dev was pretty much a helpless observer, literally along for the ride as an unnoted electronic stowaway aboard the Imperial flagship. He could watch, but his resolution of the enemy machines and formations was limited to the resolving power of *Yamato*'s sensory suite and by *Yamato*'s own movements. Clearly, Admiral Kurebayashi was racing to place as many Imperial Navy ships in the cloud's path as he could, hoping to halt its advance as far away from Earth as possible.

Dev had faced the Web in combat and knew that Kurebayashi's little squadron—two ryu-carriers, a dozen cruisers, thirty-one destroyers, frigates, and smaller craft, as well as the aging *Yamato* herself—would be little more than a snack for the hungry Web swarm.

Lead elements of the cloud were just beginning to reach Perimeter Defense Facility *Evening Calm*, a deep-space watch outpost beyond the orbit of Neptune and well above the ecliptic, designed to monitor and challenge incoming spacecraft. In the battle tank, *Evening Calm* was represented by a bright red pinpoint of light that lay, by chance, almost directly in the projected path of the diffuse, purple-colored haze representing the Web cloud. A frail structure, an open latticework of crisscrossing struts and beams that served as an immense antennae array two kilometers across, *Evening Calm* was larger by far than the largest spacecraft but massed only a few thousand tons. A rotating wheel habitat at one end provided quarters and life support for a crew of twelve, while most of the rest of the station's mass was wrapped up in the open-mesh dish of the main tracking antenna, the sensor arrays, and the supporting framework. Though the station was primarily designed as a deep space observation post and communications relay and not as a fortress, it did possess a battery of military lasers.

The station's weapons seemed pitifully inadequate, however, in the face of the swarm descending toward them out of interstellar space.

Images of the Web cloud were being transmitted from *Evening Calm* to the *Yamato*'s operations center and displayed on a viewall screen that occupied most of one of the compartment's large bulkheads. When they'd first begun arriving, the Web combat machines had been invisible at optical wavelengths, but like vapor coalescing out of thin air, their presence was slowly materializing as a kind of thin, wispy silver-gray fog that steadily grew denser as it hurtled toward the perimeter station.

As Dev translated the digital information into a scene he could play inside his own mind, he saw immediately the wispy smear of the attackers, growing visibly larger second by second in the center of the display. The cloud was translucent, like a puff of smoke, thin enough that brighter stars could still be seen through the haze, but it was rapidly growing thicker as millions of separate Web machines continued to swell the main cloud's numbers.

The leading edge of the swarm grew near, the range,

shown by numerals ticking off a kind of fast-paced count-down at the lower right of the image, grew steadily less. Dev heard the station's commander gave a crisp order, and the lasers winked on; twelve hundred kilometers away, Webbers caught in that megajoule beam shone with the light of tiny, glaring suns, then faded away in a silent puff of vapor. Someone aboard *Evening Calm* cheered and was immediately silenced by a sharp-barked order.

The lasers fired again, and once more a constellation of brilliant stars appeared in the distance, flared bright, then faded.

The cloud had taken losses . . . but those losses were literally a few drops out of the ocean; the rest of the Webbers kept coming, each impelled by powerful magnetic fields that let them sense the ferrous mass of the station and home on it with the single-minded purpose of a swarm of hungry mosquitoes.

And then the Web force had arrived, the lead elements streaking past the *Evening Calm* facility at velocities of hundreds of kilometers per second. Many struck the open latticework of the facility, and each strike was like the detonation of a small bomb as the kinetic energy of the fast-traveling devices was liberated by high-speed impact. The external camera view jittered and bounced wildly; something, one of the machines, possibly, or more likely a fragment of wreckage, sailed past the camera's field of vision like a great, whirling black shadow.

After that first storm of explosions, however, more and more of the Webbers began coming in more slowly, decelerating at what must have been hundreds of gravities, with oddly jointed mechanical limbs wide-stretched to snag hold of the station's structure.

Dev had been in combat with the Web more than once; each time before he'd been struck by the similarities between that attack and the blind rush of antibodies attacking foreign cells, a host of invading bacteria, perhaps, inside the human body, and that impression was stronger than ever now. They swarmed in blindly, many missing their target entirely, others hitting and grabbing on with a bewildering variety of claspers, arms, and many-jointed legs.

Throughout the storm, the station's lasers kept firing as quickly as they could cycle, but there were just too many of the attackers for the weapons to even slow the onslaught, and there were no good targets at all. The individual Web ships—devices, really—of that oncoming cloud were mostly small. The largest were a few meters long and massed perhaps a ton or two. Most were smaller; many were the size of a man's hand and massed only a few hundred grams. These last were designed with one purpose only, to seek out and attach themselves to any larger target and begin dismantling it a few molecules at a time, literally eating their way through solid hull metal with nanotechnic disassemblers—nano-D in military parlance. Through outboard cameras on the *Evening Calm* facility, Dev saw the first of those glittering objects strike the station's framework, strike and cling, gleaming like silver-edged jewels in the harsh glare of exterior spotlights. In seconds, ragged patches had appeared in the station's exterior thermal coating; in seconds more, whole lengths of strut piping were breaking off and spinning away into space.

A window opened in the upper left corner of the transmitted image. A young *sho-i* appeared, his face frightened. Behind him, the station's command center showed wild panic as members of the facility's crew stampeded for the airlock door to the escape pods.

*"We're breaking up!"* he cried into the camera, eyes wide. In the background, Dev could hear the ominous creak of metal flexed and stressed beyond its engineering limits. *"We can't stop it! Do you hear me, Command? We can't stop—"*

The picture broke up in a storm of static; both the internal and external views broke off as data feeds or cameras were knocked off-line.

"I2C transmission from *Evening Calm* has been lost," a voice aboard the *Yamato* reported with eerie calm.

"Transmit to all units," *Taisho* Kurebayashi said gravely. In the operations tank, the red pinpoint of light marking the *Evening Calm* winked out as a spreading, purple haze engulfed it. "We will attempt to meet the cloud at approximately the orbit of Jupiter, on a line between the cloud's current position and Earth.''

''*Hai, O-Taishosama!*'' a communications officer replied. Dev sensed the order as it was beamed back to an Imperial communications center on Phobos.

It was time for him to leave as well. There was nothing he could do to help *Yamato* or her consorts, nothing he could do at all save continue gathering data, and what he'd seen so far had probably given him all of the data he could use. In the ops battle tank, it was becoming obvious that the Web had initiated a change in their strategy, and that intrigued him. When they'd appeared in the Gr'tak system, according to Sholai, they'd appeared as a single large vessel that had accelerated in-system, divided itself in two, then further subdivided into clouds of machines deployed as separate fleets, one vectoring in on the Gr'tak homeworld, the other making for the suns. For some reason, the Web attack here was being launched as vast numbers of separate machines working in close concert with one another.

From what the DalRiss had been able to gather, the Web had employed a different strategy at the DalRiss sun, with hundreds of thousands of Webbers appearing out of empty space and plunging straight into the sun . . . and within a few days, triggering the nova that had eradicated the entire system.

Why the difference? Did it have to do with the defense that the locals put up? Or had Web strategy changed in the millennia since they'd scorched the Gr'tak homeworld? As he studied the purple cloud projected into the ops center battle tank, Dev could already detect a faint shift in the cloud's shape as it paired itself into two lobes. If it followed the pattern seen at the Gr'tak home system, the cloud would soon be two separate, smaller clouds, one heading for Earth, the other aimed at the Sun.

Dev felt a throbbing, urgent restlessness that swiftly grew into barely contained panic; he'd been an electronic download for close to three decades now . . . and before that his allegiance had been to the Confederation. If he ever thought of himself as having a home world any more, that world was New America; 26 Draconis IV had been both the spiritual and material focus for the rebellion against Empire and Hegemony in the first place.

But Dev had been born on Earth, and his roots were there, on Man's original homeworld. He'd been born and raised in the Scranton District of the big, sprawling, eastern seaboard metropolis of the North American Protectorate. His mother still lived there, though he hadn't seen her for many years; his brother Greg . . . now *there* was someone he'd not thought of in a while! Greg had been in Imperial service thirty years ago; God alone knew where he was now. It was possible, even likely, that he was back on Earth again.

And Earth was about to be destroyed when her sun was artificially detonated by the Web.

Though he'd thought little about Earth for a long time, Dev found that the knowledge hurt, and hurt badly. He could remember talks with his father in a West Scranton park . . . remember long walks in the hills outside of the city wards . . . remember, now that he called the sensations to mind, even the taste of the air after a spring rain, the laughter of children playing in the street, the caress of a breeze on his face.

It was harshly, bitterly ironic. At the time, he'd wanted nothing more and nothing less than to get off of Earth and never go back. His father had been in Imperial service, one of a handful of gaijin at that time allowed to transfer from Hegemony service to the Imperial Navy; he'd been required to divorce Dev's mother, however, as part of the political price of his advancement. He'd accepted, because only that way could he continue supporting his wife and sons, who lived in one of the more savagely depressed economic zones of the Earth.

Later, though, his father had been disgraced . . . and Dev had pulled all the strings he could to get off of Earth and start his life over somewhere, *any*where else. That determination had led him eventually to Loki, and to his joining the Hegemony military, where he'd become a warstrider.

Never, *never* in his wildest imaginings in all of the years since had he thought he would ever feel either sorrow or nostalgia for the planet that had given him birth. But he did. . . .

Dev felt himself a part of humanity in that moment as he had never felt it before; the loss Mankind as a whole would know with the loss of Earth and her teeming billions would sear the consciousness of the survivors, would traumatize the entire race in ways that simply could not be predicted. *Is this what the DalRiss felt when their worlds were destroyed?* Dev wondered. Can we survive such a loss? DalRiss psychology was so alien from that of humans that it was difficult to compare the reactions of the two to the same event.

With a sense of deep regret, he pulled out of *Yamato*'s computer network and returned to the Earth–Moon system, this time to an Imperial Combat Command Center at Aristarchus, on Luna. The base, named *Hachiman* after the ancient Japanese god of war, was the central control node for a farflung subsystem of the Imperial Terran military $C_3$ network, Command, Control, and Communications. There, he checked again on the Imperial assets in-system—a pathetically small force when compared to the numbers arrayed against it. Besides the Ida-Ten squadron, there were a half-dozen other ryu-class warflyer carriers in-system, four at Earth frantically preparing to leave dock and move into position, the other two already accelerating at full blast toward a rendezvous with *Yamato* and the others. Perhaps a hundred warships more, ranging from a few heavy cruisers to numerous frigates and patrol vessels, were under thrust now, all moving toward the same fateful rendezvous near the orbit of Jupiter, some five a.u.s out from Sol.

Other squadrons, he saw, were being called in from distant star systems, but since the only way to move instantaneously between the stars was as a rider within one of the huge DalRiss city ships, it was clearly going to take time to organize and transport any out-system reinforcements. Everything—every hope of victory—would depend on whether Admiral Kurebayashi's little squadron could slow the cloud long enough to enable other forces to reach Sol in time; Dev had already taken a hard and realistic look at the odds and decided that Kurebayashi would not slow the Web's advance by so much as a millisecond. The Web machines would overwhelm *Yamato* and the other Imperial warships in moments. Most of the Webbers would stream right past without even slowing, and there was nothing that *Yamato* or any other ship in the Solar System could do about it.

While occupying Hachiman, Dev tried once again to reach the Overmind. Damn it, he could *feel* it stirring, like a vast, dark movement within the unimaginably deep and murky waters of the virtual sea around him. But Dev could not reach it . . . could not even conceive of a way to try to attract its attention. Had he not seen it in action at Nova Aquila, he would have dismissed it now, for it was less an independent pattern of thought and purpose than a dull, rumbling cacophony of countless minds and thoughts, blind and purposeless. Trying to contact such a ponderous and insensible collection of chaotic inertia was like shouting into a hurricane, attempting to challenge the wind and lightning themselves.

Conceding failure at last, Dev accessed an online image of Earth as seen high in the Lunar sky over Hachiman, a blue half-globe aswirl with dazzling white. Earth as humans had seen it for six hundred years now, frail and delicate in the night.

And he knew that there was nothing he could do to stop the apocalypse that was swiftly descending on it with implacable, ruthless resolve.

# Chapter 15

*One must not always use the same modes of operation against the enemy, even though they seem to be working out successfully. Often enough the enemy will become used to them, adapt to them, and inflict disaster on us.*

—*The Strategicon*
THE EMPEROR MAURICE
C.E. 600

"We can't assemble a fleet quickly enough," Katya said grimly. "We have five DalRiss cityships here at New America now, and four of them are with the Imperial squadron. They'll be moving out-system, back to defend Sol, any moment now."

"The majority of the cityships are still at High Frontier," Dev pointed out. He had rejoined the others in the virtual representation of Cascadia, to find that Gresham had left the meeting during his absence, leaving Vic and Katya, Kara, Daren and Taki . . . now truly a family gathering. "Or with the Unified Fleet, at Nova Aquila. Most of them are redeploying too."

"I imagine the Imperials there will be scrambling to get their task force back to Sol, and tagging every DalRiss they can find," Kara said. Tagging was the term used in the Confederation to refer to convincing a DalRiss cityship to carry a vessel from one star system to another. The idea had taken a while to catch on only because it was difficult to figure out what the DalRiss might want in exchange for the service. Lately, DalRiss ships had been very much in de-

mand for fast transport . . . and the astonishing thing was
that they did not expect payment for this very real service
that they performed.

What Dev had learned in his twenty-five years-plus of
living and working with the beings—and what most other
humans seemed to have a lot of trouble understanding—was
that the DalRiss saw such service as their part in what they
called the "Dance of Life," a way of participating in the
society that had become theirs when the Web had turned
their home stars into novae.

"I've often wondered," Vic said with a tight smile,
"what would happen if things came down to war between
Empire and Confederation again. Both sides use the DalRiss
for fast transport now. Would they both try to corner the
market in available DalRiss ships? Or get the DalRiss to fire
at their friends who happened to've been tagged by the other
side?"

"The reason the DalRiss never seem to take sides," Dev
told them, "is that, frankly, they have a lot of difficulty
telling the difference between us and the Japanese. They
never had anything like intraspecies warfare in their history,
and they really have trouble understanding it in us."

"So they just offer a ride to anyone who asks, is that it?"
Daren said.

"That's about it," Vic said.

"You really think Earth is going to get blown away?"
Daren asked. He wore a faint smile.

"I don't see what can stop it," Dev said. "The same
thing is happening there that happened at Alya. Or the
Gr'tak world."

"That should solve the Confederation's problems with
the Empire, at any rate, huh?"

"It's a damned high price to pay," Katya said sharply.
"My God, Dev. there's got to be something! What about
the Overmind?"

"I've tried," Dev said. "I've tried to reach it. I'm pretty
sure it's there. I can sense . . . *something*, something very
large, very powerful, but it's way down deep and completely
nonresponsive, near as I can tell."

"Maybe all you're sensing is the potential of the thing," Taki said.

"Sure," Daren added. "It'll wake up when Nakamura's Number of humans link in."

"Maybe." Dev wasn't convinced of that at all. For one thing, he was pretty sure that there'd been something like Nakamura's Number of people linked in during the time he'd been back in the Solar System. The quickening pace of the communications crisscrossing back and forth on the Net suggested vast numbers of humanity linking in from every system in the Shichiju.

Still, when the Overmind had awakened during the Battle of Nova Aquila, Dev had received an unexpected and stunning look into the network's mind and experienced some small part of its power, scope, and reach. Nakamura's Number, a specific number of nodal interconnections and linkages that defined a specific "critical mass" of complexity above which a transcendental change took place, was more flexible as a concept, he knew now, than its mathematical nature might suggest. That number could have been changed by a factor of ten either way and it might not have affected the outcome . . . or the outcome could have been completely different. Humans had a long way to go in their understanding of what mind and consciousness were, and their stubborn reliance on numbers and rigid categories still gave them comfort in the face of the unknown.

"I don't think we can rely on the Overmind," Dev continued after a moment. "It's more like a natural force, a hurricane spawned by warm oceans and tropical weather patterns, than an ally."

"We haven't even been able to verify its existence," Taki put in, "save as a purely subjective phenomenon during the fight at Nova Aquila."

"*Something* took out the Web Alphas," Kara replied, referring to the planetoid-sized machine-ships the Web had used to coordinate their massive fleet's actions. "It wasn't our Combined Fleet that did it, that's for sure."

"The Overmind is real," Dev said. "It was then. It is now."

"Sure," Daren said with a grin. "But how real are *you*?"

The statement, Dev thought, had been intended as a joke, but it hurt nonetheless. He was surprised at how *much* it hurt.

"Unless we can find a way to stop the Web assault, Earth's sun will go nova in a few more days," he said with a hard curtness to the words. "We can assume that the Web will continue to search for human-occupied systems and destroy those as well."

"How the hell did it find Earth?" Vic wanted to know.

Dev sighed. "Ultimately, of course, that was my fault," he said. He'd been the one who'd first probed the Aquilan Stargate with a downloaded copy of himself . . . and that copy, together with everything he'd known, had been lost to the Web in the Galactic Core.

"But we countered that," Kara said. "Operation Shell Game."

"Obviously they saw through that," Dev replied. "I don't know how. For all we know, they were able to separate fact from fiction from the beginning, just because they're the ones who created the Naga in the first place, and know how they work better than we do."

"If that's true," Katya said gently, "I don't think they would have waited two years before attacking Earth. Shell Game bought us time. It just would have been nice if it had bought us *more* time. Like maybe a century or three."

"Most likely," Vic said, "they ran some sort of a program on all of the information they picked up from our probes, comparing that data with what they knew about the Galaxy already. The information we downloaded into the Naga fragments wasn't all that complete. It couldn't be. Maybe they were able to pick up a difference in, well, in the texture of the information. Or there were little mistakes in star positions or alignments that we didn't catch."

"It's also possible they analyzed our EM shell," Taki pointed out. "Man's EM shell, I mean. It's got a radius of, what? Six hundred light years now. That's halfway to Nova Aquila already. And that shell is centered on Sol, because none of the colonies, even the oldest, like Chiron and New Earth, have been broadcasting on electromagnetic frequencies for anything near that long. All of their radio bubbles are submerged inside Earth's. If the Web has listening posts or another stargate closer to the Shichiju, within six light centuries of Earth, they could figure out where we were just for that.''

"That's right!" Katya said. She looked at Dev's virtual image. "That's *very* right! I don't think anything else would explain how they could pinpoint Earth's solar system so precisely."

Dev rolled the idea about in his thoughts for a moment. He'd not considered that possibility, assuming, as he had, that his inadvertent first contact with the Web had been what had given the game away in the first place. "In the long run," he said slowly, "it doesn't really matter how they found Earth, does it? They have. We've been afraid that they would for two years now, ever since they found the Alyan worlds and destroyed them."

And that, he realized, was a part of his own pain. The DalRiss had lost their homeworld and its nearby colony as a direct result of that catastrophic first meeting, and he'd long felt guilty about the fact, even though the DalRiss themselves, though jolted by the experience, seemed to have accepted it as yet another step in their mysterious Dance of Life.

Their outlook on events, on such outwardly simple matters as cause and effect, was markedly different from that of humans.

"One way or another," he continued with only the slightest of pauses, "they've found Sol. And if we don't do something damned fast, we're going to lose Earth the same way the DalRiss and the Gr'tak lost their worlds." He gave Daren a hard look. "Believe me, son. That loss is going to hit us gokking hard."

Katya closed her eyes. "Everything we've fought for. Wiped away."

Taki shook her head. "Independence from the Empire's not such a big deal when we start talking about survival as a species."

"Well, damn it," Kara said, her fist clenched and raised above her lap with a small, defiant jerk. "I'm not ready to surrender to the Impies yet. Let's just see what happens, okay?"

"There doesn't seem to be a lot else we can do," Dev agreed.

Certainly, there was little more to be said. Dev took his leave of the others, then repeated his earlier electronic passage from 26 Draconis to Sol.

Five hours had passed since he'd been there before, and the forces still had not come together. Space battles, by virtue of the incredible distances involved, tended to be long, drawn-out affairs of maneuver capped by a few seconds of stark, extremely destructive violence. The Web swarms—there were now clearly *three* separate clouds on slightly divergent courses—had the potentially disastrous advantage. Able to accelerate at hundreds of gravities, they could achieve velocities of thousands of kilometers per second in a space of hours or even minutes; the Imperial ships, limited both by engineering and by the frailties of the flesh and blood they carried, could not push much higher than five Gs for the smaller vessels, three for the larger. Once the ryus were close enough to disgorge their squadrons of warflyers, of course, they would win back some of the difference, though not all. Manned warflyers could manage perhaps ten Gs before their pilots blacked out, and teleoperated flyers didn't need to restrict themselves to the limitations of human pilots. Even so, the best and most powerful flyer could not pull much more than forty to fifty Gs and would be at a significant disadvantage when facing the Web machines.

With their vast speed, the Web machines had closed much of the gap between where they'd entered the Solar System and the current position of Battlegroup Ida-Ten. Kurebayashi's squadron had continued accelerating out-system until it was clear that the Web cloud's velocity would swiftly close the dwindling distance between them, then take the cloud sweeping past the Imperial ships and on into the inner system. The Imperial vessels had spun end over end, then, and began decelerating hard at three Gs.

Dev had just arrived at the Hachiman facility when I2C-relayed images and information began flooding back down the communications lines from Kurebayashi's squadron, carrying details of vector, speed, and weapons readiness. The divergence between the three separate Web groups was no more than a few thousand kilometers, if that, but a projection of their separate courses suggested that one was heading for Earth, a second toward Kasei—old Mars—and the third toward the Sun.

Dev wondered about the three-part assault. At the DalRiss homeworld, there'd been two inhabited planets but they'd orbited two different stars in the widely spaced Alyan double system. The Gr'tak home star was also a double, but more closely spaced; only one world in that system had been inhabited, if you didn't count the artificial worlds built within hollowed-out planetoids.

In Man's home system, however, three worlds were heavily populated, Earth, Kasei, and Luna . . . and the Lunar population could be considered an extrapolation of the space-dwelling community in near-Earth space, the tens of millions of people living in the synchorbitals or in space colonies in extended Earth orbit or at the various LaGrange points. Though there were countless other settlements throughout the Solar System—on the moons of Jupiter and Saturn, on and within hundreds of the drifting chunks of rock in the Asteroid Belt, on Mercury, in Venus orbit, in extended solar orbits—the Web had apparently zeroed in on the two largest concentrations of human population in the system, Earth-Lunar space, and Kasei, which had a permanent population of some hundreds of millions of people, as well as extensive military bases and facilities.

The strategy made Dev wonder. Were the Webbers really going after the two largest population centers? Or—as seemed likely from much of what he'd sensed in Web strategies before, and from what he'd learned from the Gr'tak— was the Web possibly unaware of most human activity? Could they be focusing on Kasei and Earth because those were the two strongest sources of EM radiation, or because they were the obvious primary nodes in the Solar System's far-flung computer net, or because they had the most ship activity in near space and low orbit?

Could that selective blindness of the Web be used? Dev wondered if, rather than trying to wake the Overmind up, they should be trying to shut down all EM and computer/communications/control activity on and around Earth to, in effect, make Earth invisible to the alien mind.

He dismissed the idea almost at once. Earth's real problem was not that it was visible to the Web, but the fact that Earth's *sun* was visible to them; once Sol went nova, it wouldn't matter much whether the Web could see the Earth or not.

Again, he tried to summon the Overmind, wondering what set of circumstances or conditions there might have been at Nova Aquila that had brought the meta-intelligence to life then that was missing now. Something was happening there; he could feel the Overmind's mental focus, the way it was studying . . . *something*, but he was no more able to communicate with it directly than an ant might have been able to communicate with the human over whose shoe it was walking. The Overmind seemed distant and preoccupied, totally involved with some other problem completely beyond Dev's ken.

In deep space, out well above the plane of the far reaches of the Asteroid Belt, the Ida-Ten Squadron was in range of the nearest elements of the Earthbound cloud. The relative velocities of the Web clouds and the Imperial squadron were still high, on the order of nearly two thousand kilometers per second, but the AIs aboard the human warships had factored the speed difference into their fire-control equations and determined the best instant to commence the final part of the deadly dance.

*Tennoryu* opened the engagement, loosing a cloud of high-velocity missiles tipped with thermonuclear warheads. Earlier battles with the Web had demonstrated that nukes were among the most effective weapons for dealing with Web mass-attack tactics. Lasers, particle beams, and other beam weapons could vaporize or disable Webbers quickly as they slashed through clouds of massed, oncoming machines, but a twenty- or fifty-megaton thermonuclear device, detonating in the heart of a Web attack cloud, could reduce tens of thousands of them to vapor in a literal flash of star-hot plasma and cripple thousands more. Webbers appeared impervious to electromagnetic pulses and radiation; given the environment they must have spawned in, at the Galaxy's Core, that was only to be expected.

Minutes after the first launch, warheads began detonating within the Web cloud, savage, death-silent strobings of actinic light ballooning against the darkness and swiftly fading into fast-cooling invisibility. At the same time, the ryu-carriers, *Soryu* and *Tennoryu*, began launching their warflyers. Each warship carried a complement of several hundred warflyers; it seemed a pitifully inadequate shield to throw up against such awesome power.

The Web attackers, for their part, neither swerved nor slowed. They continued approaching, the gentle drift of individual members of the cloud slowly filling in the gaps torn in their ranks by the detonating nukes. For the first time, Web weapons other than the nano-D of the smallest units were unlimbered and fired. Lasers flicked across the intervening space, touching the dark expanse of the dragonships' hulls, slashing across duralloy and nanoflage in ragged flares of searing light. A light cruiser, pinned in a deadly crossplay of high-energy lasers, writhed in an apparent agony as her midsection flared up with the heat and the light of a small sun. Secondary explosions from overheated slush-H reaction mass tanks ripped out her heart and snapped her spine; in another moment, the two surviving halves of the ship drifted apart, enmeshed now in an expanding cloud of sparkling vapor, ice crystals, and debris.

Dev studied the Web formation carefully. Damn, what were they doing this time? There was no sign at all of the big Alphas they'd used at Nova Aquila, no hints at all of how they were controlling and manipulating their fleet. The change in their fleet structure suggested that they were dangerously adaptable; one of the few advantages the humans had possessed last time around was the fact that humans could adapt and change rapidly under pressure, even in the heat of a battle, while the Web appeared to follow rather narrowly defined parameters, much like a complex but literal-minded computer program. With one engagement, the Web evidently had identified their own major weakness and corrected it, unafraid of applying lessons learned on a vast scale.

These things learned *fast*.

More laser fire swept through the human fleet, disabling two more light cruisers and smashing a frigate into drifting, white-hot junk. Nuclear warheads continued detonating deep within the Webber cloud, literally vaporizing tens of thousands of separate machines, but the survivors kept coming, moving so quickly that by now, the leaders were already sweeping past the human ships at velocities too great to allow any but the fastest combat AIs to deal with them. Dev saw that the point defense and beam weapon systems for all of the ships in the human squadron were on automatic, with the ship AIs picking targets and triggering volleys of fire.

There were simply too many targets to get them all, however. Soon, many of the machines were out of range, still headed toward Earth, now between the Earth and the still outbound Imperial squadron. Ida-Ten continued plowing through the center of the cloud, which appeared to be expanding—learning not to cluster so tightly together that one nuclear detonation could kill thousands of them. *Soryu* was in trouble, as multiple lasers hits and high-velocity impacts across the kilometer-long dragonship's hull pounded and slashed at her armor. Parts of that armor were glowing now, Dev could see on the imagery transmitted by remote drones with the squadron, and air—visible as sparkling plumes of freezing vapor—trailed from a dozen rents in her side.

As the information continued flooding into the Hachiman facility's combat center, Dev struggled to keep pace with it but was soon aware that that immense volume of data was beyond any one person's comprehension. In any case, there was nothing he could do . . . save try to learn. What was happening here would no doubt happen again at other suns circled by inhabited worlds, and if Humanity failed to protect their home system, they still might have a chance to survive elsewhere.

If they could learn how to stop the Web's onslaught.

One part of the battle, at least, was so far beyond Dev's ken that he was completely unaware of it at the time . . . as were all of the Imperial officers and men stationed at $C_3$ complexes from Earth to Luna to Mars. One after another, a series of microcircuits buried within the Imperial Battle Command Station at Singapore Synchorbital tripped to the "on" position, initializing a long-dormant subsystem of the Planetary Defense Net. An automatic override attempted shutdown . . . and was itself overridden. An AI monitoring the defense system was called in. In its singleminded way, it noted the anomaly and began shut-down proceedings . . . then promptly and completely forgot what it was doing.

A computer program, one written over four centuries before and never yet implemented in anything save drills, was summoned from deep storage and uploaded into the net. New messages flickered back and forth through the system, between a chain of computers on and around Earth, and separate subsystem nodes at Hachiman Station, near Aristarchus on Luna.

Seconds passed, as ancient machinery read codes and considered the flicker of binary data. On Luna, at three widely separated points, at Helvelius on the shores of the Oceanus Procellarum, among the cliffs at the south edge of the Mare Crisium, and at Mendeleev on the Moon's far side, immense laser and particle beam arrays swung silently in the Lunar vacuum, directing their massive snouts in the direction of Aquila, the Eagle. A fourth array, at Hertsprung, also on the far side, was not brought into play, for at that longitude at that time Aquila lay below the local horizon. In space, two more facilities went online a half second later, with weapons arrays not so powerful as their surface-based cousins, but potent nonetheless. One circled the L1 libration point, between the Earth and the Moon, while other circled L2 several thousand kilometers above the Lunar far side.

Fudo-Myoo had been laid out so that at least three of the weapons facilities could track any point anywhere in the sky at any time.

The name of the network, which had been made operational in 2112, was fitting. Fudo-Myoo was an ancient Japanese god, a protector against calamities, great dangers, and fire, and he was also supposed to be fond of mortals, willing to lend them his support in all of their endeavors.

In the latter years of the twentieth century, scientists had become aware of the uncomfortable fact that planetary life existed under a constant threat, an interplanetary sword of Damocles consisting of the thousands of chunks of rock and ice circling through the Solar System and subject to the gravitational perturbations of the giant, outer planets. The discovery that the dinosaurs had been driven to extinction by the impact of a ten-kilometer chunk of rock falling onto what later became the Yucatan Peninsula, the discovery by astronomers that fair-sized chunks of rock frequently made dangerously close passages of the Earth—and in one chilling near-miss actually entered Earth's atmosphere before skipping back into space—and the highly publicized use of Jupiter in 1994 as a bull's-eye for a fragmented comet, all served to highlight the threat posed by infalling space debris. What had happened to the dinosaurs, apparently, had happened with some regularity throughout the planet's history. It would happen again. The only question was when.

Though the Western powers and the fragmented Russian states had given up their aspirations in space by the early twenty-first century, Japan, which had long eyed the industrial, commercial, and military high ground of space, had moved aggressively to secure it. Once Nihon held that first foothold in space, she began moving to reinforce it. Building huge, solar-powered antiplanetoid lasers on and around the Moon had been good press for Imperial Japan, a demonstration of how the Empire sought to protect and preserve the planet.

And, of course, it escaped no one's notice that those lasers, those on the near side of Luna, at any rate, made formidable weapons that could have more easily vaporized cities than a tumbling, deep-space mountain of nickel-iron.

Despite the subtle threat behind the laser weaponry, though, Fudo-Myoo was a good choice as patron saint of Nihon's antiplanetoid defense network, insurance that the burgeoning, newly spaceborne civilization of Terra would not be peremptorily crushed by the unexpected arrival of another dinosaur killer. The Fudo-Myoo complex drew its power from the system's primary electric power grid; enormous solar panels circling the sun just inside Mercury's orbit collected the sun's light, used it to generate intense and sharply focused maser power beams, and transmitted them to a series of power distribution satellites in Earth and lunar orbit, where they were routed into Earth's power grid. At need, almost the entire output of that grid could be routed through Fudo-Myoo.

Another series of guardian circuits tripped and fell. The battle simulator AIs at Hachiman Station busied themselves for several seconds with a rapid-fire series of exercises, plotting distant targets, extrapolating acceleration and vector, and adjusting aim. At an electronic command, ninety-eight percent of the power feed from the solar collector masers was rerouted to Fudo-Myoo Prime at Mare Crisium, then shunted through the ground cable net or retransmitted to L1 and L2. Across the night side of Earth, the golden glow of sprawling cities blanked out. Most of the power needs for Dai Nihon were met by larger versions of the quantum power taps that supplied starships with the incredible energies they needed to operate, but some of the more primitive nations of the Hegemony, the North American Protectorate and most of the European and African republics, for instance, were still powered off the old solar grid. As energy surged to the subsurface installations on Luna and the laser arrays glowed suddenly with a dazzling new life, the energy grid collapsed in a cascade effect that left forty percent of Earth without electrical power.

The lasers cycled to full capacity, then fired, pulse after pulse after high-energy pulse searing invisibly into the blackness of space, all tracking on the still tiny breadth of luminosity that was the incoming Web fleet.

After several minutes of near-continuous firing, the arrays fell silent once again. At all five facilities, pumps were running furiously, circulating coolant fluids through overheated cores. Minutes later, as temperatures fell back into safe operating ranges, the lasers commenced firing once more.

By this time, humans were in the loop, aware that the old Fudo-Myoo defense system had somehow activated itself, and were trying desperately to bring it back under control. No one had given the order to bring Fudo-Myoo on-line; the suspicion, at the upper levels of the command chain, at any rate, was that the weapon's activation now, when the Web was attacking, could not possibly be coincidence. The

Web was a machine intelligence; Fudo-Myoo was a machine, and one that had been off-line and nonoperational for centuries now. Somehow, the Web must have seized control of the laser array and was using its unthinkable power as a weapon, possibly to render Earth powerless, possibly to strike at Imperial ships as they closed with the Web cloud.

In fact, it was not the Web that was operating the array, but another order of intelligence entirely. Human attempts to disable the laser array by regaining control from Singapore Synchorbital or the Hachiman Station on Luna failed as cutoff switches were bypassed, fail-safe circuits failed, and attempts to reroute the power flow beaming out from the distributor satellites, in all but a few isolated cases, were blocked when access codes and priority override commands were ignored.

The Overmind had woken up, had studied the cascade of information detailing the attack by Web forces for long, long milliseconds, and then acted, acted in a manner consistent with the reaction of any living creature as it sought to defend itself from a perceived threat. Controlling the laser arrays directly now, as well as the computers controlling the power feed from Earth's energy grid, it devoted a considerable portion of its mind to the astonishingly complex problem of tracking minute enemy targets at the distance of the planet Jupiter. Each of the laser arrays shifted its aim slightly, anticipating where the Web cloud was most likely to be by the time the laser bolts had crawled across the vast emptiness of space to reach their targets.

At a range of five astronomical units, it would take the laser light just forty minutes to reach its intended targets.

# Chapter 16

*Even though this may be ridiculous to mention, there are those who will seek to attack in a completely disjointed fashion when coming from the rear, and therefore fail to beat an enemy. Nothing fancy is involved. You go straight to the heart of the matter and defeat the enemy. There is nothing else involved. You either do it or you don't. There is only one purpose in attacking the enemy—to cut him down with finality.*

—*"Water Scroll"*
*The Book of the Five Spheres*
MIYAMOTO MUSASHI
seventeenth century B.C.E.

Dev watched, transfixed by the information he was experiencing at several levels. He knew that it was the Overmind that had just independently taken over control of the old asteroid defense network and applied it to this new and even more deadly threat.

But what was it doing? Why was it operating independently . . . how could it be operating independently? With a growing awe, Dev watched as the Overmind triggered burst after burst of gigajoule laser light from the Fudo-Myoo array. From the Hachiman facility computer, he could monitor each weapon hard point, on the Lunar surface or in space, as it pivoted, elevated, ranged, and fired separately; the system had been designed to track a single incoming target or, at worst, a cluster of fragmented targets, bathing each in volley upon volley of coherent light. There were far too many individual targets in the Web cloud to permit a separate pulse to be directed at each, and once it reached a target, each individual volley would do far less damage to the enemy formation than a single thermonuclear warhead.

But the laser fire had the advantage of being able to keep up a devastatingly high rate of fire, minute after minute, then hour after hour, wearing away at the enemy cloud with greater and greater relentless efficiency, the closer it drew to Earth. A fusion of laser beams designed to vaporize hundreds of thousands of metric tons of nickel iron would make short work of 100-gram disassemblers; even the largest warships in the Imperial Navy couldn't last more than a second or two against that much sheer power.

With the I2C link with the *Yamato*, Dev could watch the result from Ida-Ten Squadron's perspective as the first laser volley struck home. Forty minutes after the Fudo-Myoo arrays had first fired, a dozen of the larger Webber machines suddenly glowed white hot, then vanished in soundless bursts of expanding, silvery vapor, the metal and ceramic of their hulls flash-heated into gas, which almost immediately condensed once more into tiny globules of liquid, which in turn congealed into gleaming motes of metallic dust.

The Web cloud did not at first respond to the attack; perhaps the machines couldn't tell that the fire was being launched from the vicinity of Earth, still no more than a bright, blue-hued star barely visible near the shrunken sun, some five a.u.s distant. Or maybe there was a shortcoming in their design strategy . . . something that made it difficult for them to change their tactics in the middle of a battle.

Dev thought about that. At Nova Aquila, the Webber force had relied on overwhelming superiority of numbers, with their formations guided by five planetoid-sized vessels dubbed ''Alphas'' by the Confederation Military Command. The Overmind had defeated them by somehow—Dev still wasn't sure how—breaking into their command network and ordering most of the Web machines to shut down. The Web, in turn, had countered that tactic by launching *this* assault without any Alphas.

How, he wondered, were they coordinating the attack? The only possibility that made any sense was that they were using a widely distributed network, one resident in all or most of the Web devices, which must be communicating with one another somehow. If that mode of communications could be discovered, perhaps the human forces would have the key to again penetrate the enemy force and shut it down.

For another hour, Dev watched the battle, continuing to try to reach the Overmind every few moments, and failing each time.

*Damn it, what should I do*? He felt an agonizing vacillation. He needed to return to Nova Aquila and let the people there know what was happening. He needed, too, to link up with other human forces, Imperial and Confederation. He would be able to help coordinate their arrival, and—as he'd done when he'd been part of the DalRiss explorer fleet for all of those years—he'd be able to provide navigational data for their cityship Achievers.

But to leave the battle *now* . . .

The solution was almost laughably simple . . . but it struck him with hammerblow force. It was quite possible, Dev realized, for him to literally be in two places at once.

He was currently resident in the Hachiman Defense Facility at Aristarchus, on the surface of Earth's Moon. Hachiman was a sprawling complex of domes and half-buried hab modules, interconnected by subsurface tunnels and maglev transport tubes. Buried deep beneath the lunar regolith near the center of the station was the Hachiman Command Control Center, an enormous, artificial cavern that included the heavily armored base headquarters, with multiple I2C links extending throughout the Solar System and to several other nearby stars, as well as a direct link with Tenno Kyuden itself. While the Imperial Staff Command Headquarters at Tenno Kyuden was technically the command center for the entire Imperial military, Hachiman was the actual operations center, coordinating intelligence from literally thousands of sources, correlating it, and providing the ISCH with a streamlined image of what was actually going on.

The computer center for Hachiman, located directly beneath the $HC_3$, was built around a system that was, arguably, the fastest and most powerful computer ever designed. Called Quantum K5050 *Oki-Okasan*—the Nihongo meant very roughly "Big Mother"—it was the latest generation of what was generally called the quantum computer, a processor that used the Uncertainty Principle regarding where an electron was at any given instant to create alternate but simultaneous paths of electronic reasoning in a way eerily similar to the functioning of the human brain.

Once, centuries before, the quantum computer had promised to be the most likely route to the development of true artificial intelligence—computers as self-aware and at least as intelligent as humans. In fact, that route had proven to be far more complex than even its creators had ever envisioned; artificial intelligence, when it had been developed in the mid-twenty-first century, had been achieved through increasingly sophisticated software. Oki-Okasan was not self-aware, but some hundreds of AI programs were running simultaneously within its vast, electronic memory, with Dev an undetected extra guest. Swiftly, he began replicating himself.

He'd done this once before, downloading a copy of himself into a Naga-based probe which he'd sent on a reconnaissance into the center of the Galaxy. That time, of course, he'd relied on the considerable power of a Naga–DalRiss fusion within the heart of a DalRiss cityship. This time, he was alone and in the Quantum Oki-Okasan, but his memory included the entire process. It was, in fact, much like the common autopsych process known as jigging, the ViR-simulated creation of personality fragments with which a person could hold conversations as a means of resolving inner conflict or problems.

The process felt like a thinning, an indescribable stretching . . . and for a ragged, wavering moment, his self-awareness was fading. Dev had fainted perhaps twice in his life, both times when he was a kid, and this was like that, a lightheaded, whirling sensation as blackness closed in from the periphery of his vision. He fought to retain a grip on his sense of identity, clinging to the mental self-image he carried as a kind of talisman against the night.

Then he was staring at himself . . . an analogue of himself, actually, called into being by the literal doubling and fission of the carefully patterned information that made up the program that was Dev's conscious mind.

"Good," the two Devs thought in perfect unison. "I'll stay here and keep an eye on things, while you go——"

Both Devs broke off the thought simultaneously. It would be several seconds, they realized jointly, before their differing perspectives began to color their experiences, resulting in two markedly different individuals, instead of identical copies of the same person.

"I'm Dev One," he said, smiling. "You're Dev Two."

"What gives you priority?" his double asked, but he was grinning as he spoke. Both were remembering the uncomfortable time Dev had had with the recon probe double; since a duplication copied everything, including memories up to the moment of program fission, there was, in fact, no "original." Each Dev was as real as the other . . . whatever the word "real" might mean inside this artificial space.

"I'm Dev One," he said again. "But I give you the choice. You want to stay or go?"

His alter self considered this a moment. "I'll stay. You go. I want to see how the battle develops, see if the Web develops any surprises we should know about."

"Agreed. But we also need reinforcements. I'll see that the DalRiss Achievers have the nav data they need to make pinpoint jumps in-system."

"Agreed. I'll . . . um . . . talk to you later. Take care of yourself."

"You take care of *my*-self."

Dev One uploaded himself into the main system Net, then patched through to 26 Draconis, then to Nova Aquila, where *Shinryu* and the other Imperial ships were already departing for Earth. After that, he began transferring with the speed of thought to one system after another in both Imperial space and along the independent worlds of the Frontier, assessing the reaction of Humanity's armed forces.

Everywhere, ships were moving. When DalRiss cityships were available, the largest human ships present in-system were being maneuvered into their ventral folds and prepared for an immediate jump back to near-Earth space. At each stop, Dev entered the local military command computer network for that system, jacking in with the flagships of both Imperial and Confederation forces when both were present and uploading the latest combat information he'd received from Hachiman. He also linked with any DalRiss ships that were in system, interfacing with their Achiever network and uploading current field maps of the Sol system, a kind of mental road map based on the relative positions of gravitational sources and the background flux of magnetic fields and electromagnetic radiation, rather than actual highways. This type of "map" was what the DalRiss Achievers used to establish a mental image of their destination, and when it was accurate, detailed, and recent, it permitted the DalRiss cityships to jump very far indeed.

Dev felt a small thrill as he worked with both the human and the DalRiss forces. After the initial panic riding on the news that the Web had struck at Sol itself, it seemed, it *felt* as though all of humanity was pulling together, working with relentless and dogged persistence toward the single goal of getting as many warships to the Sol system as quickly as possible.

The atmosphere was taut throughout the ship, with the translation to Sol now only hours away. Kara had some time, though, before the final mission briefing. She'd elected to spend it with Ran.

She stepped off the ramp coming down from the middeck, then took the left branch of the corridor to *Gauss*'s recreation lounge. Lieutenant Ran Ferris was there, lying back in a game couch, eyes closed, his Companion extending a small forest of silvery tendrils from his head and interconnecting with the smart interfaces of his seat. She stood next to him for a moment, looking down into his face. He wore what might have been a barely detectable frown of concentration, though his mind should have been disconnected from his organic brain and nervous system. She wondered what he was experiencing.

Beside his chair was a glossy, black contact plate. Kara reached out her hand, focusing her mind as a single tendril grew from her palm and plunged into the interface.

She couldn't enter Ran's world, but she could, in effect,

look over his shoulder. She caught a burst of music—early classical, she thought—with powerful rhythms and stirring, martial melody. Visually . . . she wasn't certain what he was watching. It appeared to be a ViRdrama of some sort.

"Ran? It's Kara. Can I interrupt?"

"Of course," she heard him say, the voice distant, in the back of her mind. "Hang on a sec. Program freeze. Save as Ferris One."

His eyes blinked open as the silvery tendrils melted rapidly back into his head, and his skin resumed its normal, natural tone and texture. "Hey, Kara," he said, grinning up at her. "What's the word?"

"Sorry to interrupt," she told him. She gestured toward the interface plate. "What was that, anyway? Classical?"

He nodded. "John Williams. One of the great pre-Imperials. This is an old ViRdrama version, played with three-veed clips drawn from some two-vee flat projections that originally carried his music. Great stuff."

"I never cared much for three-veed stuff. It doesn't feel as natural as sims designed to be full-sensed from the start."

"I don't know. Some of those old filmmakers could still create a pretty powerful emotional effect, even when they were limited to two dimensions. But I'm mostly linked to the stuff by the music."

"I didn't know you were into classical," she said, smiling. "You just never cease to amaze."

His grin grew wider, and he reached for her, pulling her to him. "Stick with me, kid. I'll astonish you."

They kissed.

"So," he said after a long, warm moment, "you didn't come here to check upon my taste in music and archaic popular sims."

She traced her finger down the curves of his cheek and chin. "Well, not really."

"Is it the fight coming up?"

She nodded. "I suppose so. I always get a little tight before a big one."

"Nothing to worry about. It's not like we're going to be fighting the Webbers in person."

Her smile faded, and she drew back from him a bit. "You ever hear of RDTS?"

"Sure, but that's psych-stuff. Not nearly as big a down-grudge as getting killed, right?"

"Wrong." Kara didn't like Ran's cocky attitude, though she knew that it was a common one among striderjacks. Too many people she knew, too many friends were lost now in one or another of the psych ViRworlds. "I'm not ready for Nirvana. I like *this* world just fine, thank you."

"Oh, I don't know. Nirvana might be kind of fun, from what I've heard. You want to D-L in and check it out together?"

"Have you ever been there?"

"No. Been meaning to, just to check in on Daniels and some of the other guys. Never got around to it, though."

"Yeah." She stood up again. "Listen, I'm heading up to the ship's mess for some chow. I'll see you later, for final briefing, okay?"

"Well sure, but—"

Kara turned abruptly and walked off. She'd come here looking for some companionship, maybe even some intimacy with Ran before *Gauss* completed her preparations and they had to go into combat, but his flip attitude about Remote Death Transference had soured her. She liked Ran, liked him a lot. Their relationship was far more than casual, and they'd talked more than once about contract pairing. But damn it all, sometimes she just couldn't figure out what was going on in his head.

*Virtual worlds.* They represented, in quite a literal way, an entirely new universe opening for humankind, a universe as real in its rather specialized and artificial way as the original universe was physically. Down the centuries, people had been entertained and informed by a variety of media, first with live actors on stage, then through presentations on an electronic display screen, and finally through realtime downloads directly into the viewer's brain, this last such a perfect simulation of the real world that it had been popularized by the term ViRsim, a Virtual Reality Simulation.

The next step, evidently, was turning out to be an inversion of the old processes. Rather than packaging entertainment and downloading it into the viewer's brain, the viewer himself—or, rather, the software, the biological programming that comprised his or her thoughts, memories, and identity—could be downloaded into a computer network where it could live, if that was the appropriate word, apparently indefinitely. Further, the network could be programmed to provide all of the sensations and experience of a real world; complex AIs, using chaos-directed programming routines of their own design, could come up with virtual worlds as surprising, as challenging, as intellectually and physically stimulating, even as dangerous, as real worlds.

More and more people were choosing to "emigrate" to the virtual universe. Commercial firms competed with one another to see who could make the most challenging and realistic environments, which included anything and everything from recreations of Earth at various eras in her history, to a dazzling array of realistic and scientifically accurate planets, to fantasy worlds where magic worked and the laws of physics were changed or challenged, to places—other dimensions, other existences—where all of the rules of ordinary existence had been changed. In most cases, the travelers simply stored their bodies in coffin-like life pods that kept their physical selves alive while their minds roamed their chosen alternate reality.

Many, however—and if the medes were to be believed, the numbers of people opting for this route were growing at a fantastic rate—simply never returned to their organic bodies. The downloaded software, once running in its electronically created surroundings, could be supported indefinitely. Some called that option the new frontier; others thought of it as legal, high-tech suicide with the promise of immortality. Downloading personalities was fast becoming a technological substitute for the purely metaphysical concept of heaven.

In a sense, that was what had happened to Dev, save that he was still able to freely interact with humans stuck in the real world of physical law and physical limitations. Kara remembered her conversation with Dev some time before, when he'd counted himself among the first of humanity's "virtual humans."

Kara had been headed for the *Gauss*'s main mess area, but she decided on the way that she wasn't really hungry enough to make the chore of eating worthwhile. She rarely was before combat, the tension building in her gut making any thought of food nearly unbearable. Instead, she headed for the nearest communications center. There, commods were arrayed in gleaming, metal-and-plastic ranks, affording a privacy that the couches down in the rec area or the smaller, open conning modules for teleoperating warstriders couldn't provide.

Taking the nearest unoccupied module, Kara palmed open the hatch, sat down, and swung her legs inside. The door slid shut as she lay back and extended her Companion's tendrils to interface with the commod's electronic circuits. As she linked in, she summoned a destination menu.

She selected the list of available virtual worlds, then from there linked in to Nirvana.

There were basically two approaches to the ViRworlds, depending on whether you simply wanted to visit or were going to move there permanently. Visitors could enter any world at any time through a commod like the one Kara was using; indeed, communications modules had been creating virtual worlds for centuries now, settings and scenes—such as the imaginary dinner atop a New American oceanside cliff—where two or more people could *seem* to meet in a virtual reality middle ground, when in fact both were lying in padded life support modules, imagining the visit with the help of artificial intelligences and internal computer connections.

Those who wanted to enter a virtual world permanently, or those who had no choice, had their minds downloaded—scanned, replicated, and transferred to the ViRworld system like any other packet of data. The body might be stored for later use, but most permanent ViRworld residents were those either who'd lost their bodies, or whose bodies were so badly damaged that even the best somatechs and nanosurgery couldn't get them working again. More and more people on the verge of physical death had opted to try downloading as a means of cheating death, of living—in theory, at any rate—forever. No one knew if the process conferred actual immortality, but most scientists working in the field felt that downloaded lifespans would be limited only by the lifetime of the machine generating the environment in which they existed. If the computer networks supporting those downloaded systems ever crashed all at once, it would be a kind of electronic genocide; so long as technic civilization endured, however, the individual mental patterns would survive.

It was, Kara reflected, a potential immortality like that of the Gr'tak, where the pattern of mind remained the same, even though the organic bodies wore out and were replaced along the way.

Reaction to the new technology had been predictable. There were plenty of willing emigrants to the virtual worlds, evenly divided between young people who questioned the values and the worth of the universe they'd been born to, and older people who were looking for a way to cheat death. There were plenty more, however, who felt that emigration to a virtual world was nothing more than an elaborate form of suicide.

Kara opened her eyes and stepped into Nirvana.

The light always took some getting used to. Most available virtual worlds were idealized versions of Earth or other man-habitable planets, but Nirvana had been crafted more imaginatively, a combination of an imaginary heaven and an equally imaginary far-future civilization, where buildings were constructed of pure force, and the inhabitants moved through a dazzling, golden light by the power of thought.

A young woman floated before her, her form all but lost in light and vapor. "How can we help you, Kara?" They knew who she was, of course, as soon as her Companion accessed the system. The figure before her was in fact the analogue construct for one of the AIs creating this world. Kara had been here visiting before.

"I'm looking for Willis Daniels, please," Kara replied.

"I'll have to see if he's available, if he wants to have company. Excuse me for a moment." The hazy figure vanished, gone with the speed of thought.

Kara glanced down at herself. The ViRsim persona she was currently using was her analogue image, wearing her gray Confederation uniform. Many of the inhabitants of Nirvana, however, lacked even the illusion of solid bodies . . . particularly those suffering from RDTS.

Most of the military personnel who'd suffered remote death transference problems had ended up here, in Nirvana, where few of the visible bodies held much substance. The emigrant's bodies were always Naga-patterned, of course, if there was anything available to be patterned, with the idea that they might be recreated later, possibly through cloning from samples of the person's cells. Unfortunately, the majority of these people seemed to have lost hold of their body's shape, to have lost the *idea* of a body, and they had trouble projecting anything even remotely like an image of their former selves.

She could sense the technic ghosts adrift in the fog around her. Nirvana had been intended by its programmers as a kind of high-tech heaven, a place where the bodiless could enjoy existence of a sort until a way could be found to join them with bodies once more. For Kara, however, despite golden light and floating, ethereal forms, the place seemed more like a foretaste of hell, doomed souls wandering endless vistas, bodiless, powerless, cut off forever from the world of the living.

"Hello, Captain."

She tried to focus on the voice. It was Will's voice, but there was no face, no body to attach to it. Instead, there was a kind of *solidity* to the air and light a few meters in front of her, a concentration of awareness somehow made more than insubstantial. She smiled at it. "Hello, Will. How's it going?"

"Well enough, Captain," the voice replied. "It ain't too bad here. Better than being brain-dead, I suppose, like poor Pritch."

She nodded, feeling a little unsteady. Pritchard had come out of the battle at the Core with his mind gone, with no hope of downloading or retrieval.

"So. How you getting on without me?"

She sighed. "Not so well, really. I wish we still had you

on the roster. There's a battle coming up. A big one.''

Kara sensed the ghost's amusement. "The Web is attacking Earth."

"You know?"

"Hey, we may be ghosts in here, but we're not completely cut off from the real world. We've been following all the excitement coming in through the Net for hours, now."

"What do you think? Can we stop it? Stop the Web from destroying Earth, I mean?"

"How the hell should *we* know?" He sounded bitter. "There's nothing we can do about it here."

"You can tell me what went wrong on Core D9837."

She could feel his wry smile, even if she couldn't see it. "There were too damned many of them, and not near enough of us. *That's* what went wrong."

"They're using the same tactics at Earth. Three groups, targeting Earth, Mars, and the sun. We're marshaling everything we can to try to stop them, but it doesn't look good." She paused, gathering her thoughts. "Actually, I was also wondering about access to the Overmind. Dev—Dev Cameron—has been trying to make contact with it, try to get it to help, but without success."

"It's in the battle. Taking part."

"So I've heard. It switched on an old asteroid-defense system and seems to be wearing down the enemy some. But Dev can't talk to it. Can't even seem to get its attention. You've been in here for a while. Can you sense . . . anything? The Overmind's presence on the Net, maybe?"

"Even if we could, the Overmind wouldn't listen to *us*. We're ghosts, remember. Shadows. . . ."

"You're men."

"We *were*." She sensed a terrible longing in the words.

"You still are. Mind is what makes a person, not the body. Body shape and size, color, weight, age, none of that makes a gokking bit of difference. It doesn't even matter if you *have* a body. It's what the body has evolved to recognize itself and deal with the universe, the mind, the soul, if you want. That's all that matters."

Willis seemed to consider this. "You know," he said after a time, "we're not so different here from the brain-dead. Guys like Pritch, they just couldn't hold the pattern, you know? And . . . and some of us are losing it too. I'm having trouble thinking of . . . of myself as me. As an individual. It would be so very easy to just let go . . . to slide off into the sea. . . ."

"What sea?"

Kara sensed hesitation . . . and an inability to put thoughts into words. Part of that, she thought, was a growing unwillingness to carry on this conversation. She wondered if her thoughts, still anchored in flesh and blood and bone, were too slow for him. Or simply too rooted in things now inconsequential for the two of them to have anything at all in common. "We call it . . . we call it the *ether* here. From the old idea that there had to be some substance to space for light to vibrate in. You know?"

She nodded, then wondered how well Daniels could even see her. "I know."

"The electronic sea, the world of Nirvana, that's the sea that our thoughts vibrate in. It's a beautiful place. Simply . . . beautiful. No word can describe it. And it's just so easy to drift away. . . ."

Kara closed her eyes, fighting back what would have been tears in her organic body. At Kasei, during the raid she'd led there, four brave men had gone with her into the Imperial planetary defense network at Phobos, high above the terraformed seas and forests of the once–Red Planet. Vasily Lechenko had died there. The other three had been Pritch, Phil Dolan . . . and Willis Daniels. Of the four, Willis was the only one left, and he now occupied a twilight existence, neither living nor dead.

For Kara, it felt as though her world were crumbling.

She was sorry she'd let her anger cut short a possible meeting with Ran. Damn it, life was too uncertain to let minor annoyances or petty hurt feelings slam doors on people who'd become important parts of your life.

"Gok it, Daniels! Don't you let go! I need you back, back in the company. Back with me and my people!"

"The Web's not really that important, Captain. It's not like they were telling us before the Core expedition at all.

If it wins, if Earth is destroyed, and 26 Draconis, and all the rest, well, we all have to die sometime. No big deal.''

"Nirvana will be destroyed if the Web overthrows human civilization. You know that, don't you? There'll be no immortality if the Net system supporting Nirvana goes down.''

"It doesn't really matter. We didn't ask for this gokking immortality. We didn't ask for *life*.''

"What's wrong with life?''

"The sameness. The unchangingness. The fact that all of this around us was manufactured, someone's dream . . . but it wasn't *our* dream. It's so *boring*. . . .''

"Have you talked to the AIs running this place about providing some challenges for you? You know, some virtual worlds are supposed to be pretty rugged.''

There was no answer, and after several minutes of calling into the light, Kara was forced to assume either that Daniels was gone, slipping away into that sea he'd spoken of, or that he simply was no longer interested in communicating with the living. Reluctantly, at last, she broke her connection with the ViRworld and climbed out of her commod.

She checked her time sense. It was nearly time for the final briefing.

She found herself longing for the warm touch of flesh and blood . . . and interests solidly anchored in what was real, what could be touched, what could be clung to.

Kara wondered if she still had time to see Ran, to be with him alone.


And in near-Earth space, Dev Two continued to watch the battle unfold at the leisurely pace dictated by the vast distances involved. Hours passed . . . and the battle slowly ground its way into the inner Solar System. The Fudo-Myoo lasers kept up their steady bombardment, leading particularly dense clumps of Web machines by the several minutes necessary for the laser pulses to cross the distance between Luna and the oncoming cloud. *Yamato*, caught in a swirling vortex of attacking craft, was disabled when a thousand-ton Web machine detonated in a nuclear fireball within a few hundred meters of her hull, knocking out her weapons, navigation, and power systems and setting her adrift above the plane of the Asteroid Belt.

Before long, Kasei was under attack. As Dev continued to sample the data flow of the system's Net, he could hear the panicked cries of officers and commotechs from the bases on and around the world once known as Mars, some calling for help, some trying to direct a battle that clearly had become hopeless. Kasei, by Imperial law, could only be approached by Nihonjin. Dev considered slipping into the Phobos planetary defense network to get a closer look at what was happening there but decided against it. The Battle for Kasei would not settle the fate of either Earth or Sol; if he could help, it would not be at Mars.

The Overmind was still in the fight, controlling continuing laser fire from the Fudo-Myoo facilities against the Web clouds. It, too, had decided that the Kasei group posed no immediate threat and for a time had concentrated on the Earthbound cloud. Hundreds of thousands, possibly millions of Web machines had been destroyed and the cloud was now considerably thinner than it had been. When it had pushed through to within a few million kilometers of its target, however, it had become far too diffuse for the Fudo-Myoo lasers to have much of an effect. When a given stab of megajoule laser light only vaporized one or two Web devices at a time instead of tens or hundreds, it was no longer an efficient means of fighting the millions of machines remaining in the force. At that time, the anti-asteroid lasers had been shifted to cover the cloud approaching Earth's sun, much more distant, but still compact and closely spaced.

Unfortunately, that meant the surviving machines of the Earth attack force were now free to plunge into the space between Earth and Luna, forming into smaller groups and conducting fast-paced and deadly attacks on all ships and installations. High on their list, obviously, were the facilities on and near Luna that had been delivering such devastating and accurate fire for the past hours.

Before long, the Hachiman complex was under direct attack. Sensor arrays on Luna detected the fact that they were being bathed in intense beams of broad-spectrum laser light originating with a number of the largest Web devices. Dev watched as Hachiman's AIs measured the light's intensity, then extracted an absorption spectrum from each light source. Those lasers being fired from near the orbit of Mars were not weapons in themselves—the distances involved were too vast—but the black absorption bands showed that objects, many thousands of them, composed of silicon, iron, carbon, and a dozen trace elements, were racing straight toward Luna, driven along by the light with breakneck accelerations of over three hundred gravities.

Dev had seen weapons like this before, at Nova Aquila. Each was a wisp of mirror-silver gossamer a molecule or two thick, driven by the pressure of laser light. When they struck the target, the kinetic energy of even a few grams moving at near-light velocity carried the shattering impact of high explosive. Those not traveling fast enough to be utterly destroyed on impact would land on the target and cling there as their molecular structures were rearranged into masses of nano-disassemblers, capable of literally dissolving the target atom by atom.

Dev, interfaced already with the Hachiman Defense Network, slipped a coded order into the system ordering the launch of thirty missiles from the antispace batteries located at the south end of Mare Crisium. As the tense minutes passed, the oncoming Web sails began radiating heat, now showing emission spectra mixed with the absorption spectra of the driving laser light. Space within the Solar System is not empty; matter has collected there to a density of about one atom per cubic centimeter; as the probes passed 0.5 c, they began heating up from friction, while generating tiny plasma tunnels as they plowed through hydrogen gas that seemed—from their relativistic points of view—to be growing increasingly dense.

At Dev's programmed command, the missiles detonated well short of the sails, but the multiple explosions scattered clouds of fragments in their paths. When the fiercely radiating gossamer wisps struck those fragments, they were utterly annihilated in the sudden burst of white-hot energies liberated by each impact.

Elsewhere, though, Imperial ships were dying, overwhelmed by superior numbers, battered by lasers and laser-driven sails, particle beams, and clouds of nano-disassemblers. Reinforcements were beginning to arrive in system, but slowly . . . far too slowly.

Already, it was clear that the tide of battle was beginning to shift against the defenders of the Earth.

# Chapter 17

*The new inventions of the last twenty years seem to threaten a great revolution in army organization, armament, and tactics. Strategy alone will remain unaltered, with its principles the same as under the Scipios and Caesars, Frederick and Napoleon, since they are independent of the nature of arms and the organization of the troops.*

—*The Art of War*
ANTOINE HENRI DE JOMINI
C.E. 1837

Alphanumerics danced, scrolled, and flickered in Kara's head, reporting battle readiness . . . and the fact that the huge DalRiss cityship that had engulfed the *Gauss* an hour before was now ready to make its translation from the region close by Nova Aquila to the less familiar space of Earth's Solar System.

Part of the delay had been due to the need to upload the navigational data the DalRiss Achievers needed to make the jump, information provided shortly before by Dev Cameron.

He'd also brought a grim and up-to-date report on the progress of the battle there, and she wondered how things were going. The last information to come in over the Net indicated that Web machines were drawing close to Earth itself, while others were already fighting on Mars. Perhaps most worrying of all, however, was word that a third Web fleet would soon reach Sol. If it succeeded there, penetrating the solar corona, no human ships would be able to touch them . . . and the nova that followed would reduce both Earth and Mars to charred cinders, whatever the results of the battles there.

As a result, the ConMilCom staff planners had ordered the bulk of the Confed forces at Nova Aquila to jump to a point just outside the orbit of Mercury, where they could take up a blocking position against this third, sunward-bound Web cloud. According to Dev, the Overmind was now directing most of its fire against that cloud, wearing it down, but the enemy still vastly outnumbered anything the humans could hope to assemble. The next twelve hours would tell whether the effort to save the home system of mankind had paid off.

The appearance of the Overmind was promising, of course . . . but did not guarantee a victory. The Battle of Nova Aquila had been won when the Overmind suborned the Web's communications protocol. Obviously, this time the Overmind was having trouble cracking the Web's network, having to resort to brute force to whittle away at the enemy's numerical superiority. So far as Kara was concerned, she didn't understand the Overmind and wasn't about to rely on its intervention. She preferred things that operated by well-known and trustworthy laws, systems that worked as an extension of her thoughts—like Mark XC Black Falcons.

And as for Earth . . . well, Kara would do her damnedest to stop the Web, but she had little feeling for the planet one way or another. She'd never been closer to the place than Kasei, and the visit had not exactly been a happy one. So far as she was concerned, if Earth's incineration stopped the damned Empire from its constant maneuvers to drag the Confederation back into the Imperial fold, then maybe a small nova was just what that troublesome planet needed. In saner moments, she was willing to concede that the vast majority of Earth's billions were no more Imperial than she was, might have even more reason than she did to hate the Empire and Dai Nihon, and couldn't be blamed for the fact of their allegiance to the Japan's Terran Hegemony.

But this was not a particularly sane moment. She was jacked into her new Black Falcon warstrider/warflyer combo, a fifty-ton colossus folded into a tight, gleaming black hull, awaiting the final word for jump and launch. Like her Falcon at the Galactic Core, this one had its ebon surface nanoflage programmed to break the black finish only with the small phantom caricature that was the company's unit insignia, and the name she'd chosen for the machines she rode: KARA'S MATIC.

The scene spread out in Kara's mind was a strider-sensor's view of Bay Five in the *Gauss*'s spin-grav section. Her strider was being lowered on magnetic clamps into the launch lock, along with the sleek, black shapes of the forty-seven other machines of First Company. *Gauss* was already in the grip of a DalRiss cityship, so the spin-grav section was motionless, the ship in zero-G. Strapped into her con-mod and jacked into her strider's interface, Kara could not feel the endless falling sensation of microgravity.

"Okay, people," she said quietly, speaking over the unit intercom, the ICS, to the other members of the company. She felt the jolt as the strider was loaded into the lock, which sealed around her with a sharp hiss. "*Shralghal* has reported that they're ready to make the transition. Remember, we're going to be deploying within a few minutes of breaking out into normal space, just as long as it takes for the *Gauss* to clear *Shralghal*'s ventral area. Be ready to jack in hard the moment you get the word."

"Yes, Mother," Ran Ferris said, and several of the people in the company chuckled.

"Let's hit the prelaunch," Kara said, ignoring the banter. She opened the channel to Operations Control. "Op Con, this is Phantom One-one. Phantoms are ready for prelaunch."

"Phantoms, Op Con," a voice replied inside her head. "Initiating prelaunch sequencing. Communications net."

Her eyes scanned her prelaunch window, checking the glowing array of discretes. "Comm, go."

"Channel selection at taccom one-four-three-three. ICS on."

"Taccom one-four-three-three, roger. ICS, check."

"I2C on and phase-linked."

"I2C, on. Linked."

"Switch WCS to standby."

Kara mentally engaged her Weapons Control System, then waited for the discrete light to come on in the prelaunch window opened in her mind.

"Op Con, One-one. Weapons systems, set to standby. On safe."

"All units, engage navigational communications, set to direct receive at four-one-niner, on standby."

"Nav com at four-one-niner. Rog."

"Power plant on."

"Rog."

"Bring power feed to point five."

"Feed at point five, rog."

"Link feeds engaged."

"Link feeds. Rog."

"Secondary nav systems on, set to standby."

"Rog."

"Self-diagnostics on."

"Rog."

"AI systems on."

"Rog."

"Power check."

"Power nominal."

"Initiate mag drives."

"Drives cycling up."

Linked into her Black Falcon, Kara could feel the powerful GEMag 700E magphase accelerators spooling up to full power with a shuddering, deep-throated thrum that rose slowly through the audio spectrum, carrying a sensation of raw, barely restrained power. Green lights cascaded across her drive status board.

"Op Con, One-one. Drives online and nominal."

She continued running through the prelaunch checklist, verifying both her own system settings and, through a side-bar window, the responses of the other members of her company, watching for any last-second downgrudge. Her Companion, she reflected, could have handled the routine more efficiently than she could, but both regulations and her own preference kept her in the routine, running down the list. It was a necessary ritual, a way to focus mind and spirit on what was coming.

In minutes, the prelaunch was complete, all warstriders in the company had signaled their readiness for release and combat, and she was watching the transition countdown ticking away the last handful of seconds. Her mouth was dry, her heart hammering in her chest . . . though such purely physical sensations were deeply submerged beneath her link with her warstrider. It was strange to think of readying for a combat launch in the Sol system . . . while waiting to make an Achiever jump here at Nova Aquila, twelve hundred light years away. The stunning advances . . . no, the revolutionary *changes* in technology over the past few years had utterly transformed the art of space warfare.

Fortunately, tactics had remained much the same. An ancient military misquotation, supposedly spoken by a cavalry officer from one of Earth's late-Middle Ages wars, was the injunction to "get there fustest with the mostest." What General Nathan Bedford Forrest had *actually* said was "I always make it a rule to get there first with the most men." Either way, the rule still held true seven hundred years later.

Something else Forrest had said echoed in her mind. She'd been downloading military maxims from late-period Medieval warfare, lately, as part of her continuing military studies, and something about Forrest—a brilliant but often unrecognized military tactician—had resonated within her. "In any fight," Forrest had said, "it's the first blow that counts; and if you keep it up hot enough, you can whip 'em as fast as they come up."

In the battle for Earth, the first blow had already been landed, a combination of the in-system Imperial forces and the ongoing laser barrage from Fudo-Myoo. The problem now was to "keep it up hot enough," and pray that the enemy's overwhelming advantage in numbers had been whittled down to manageable proportions.

"So what's the hont?" Carla Jones asked over the ICS

as they waited. "Any word on new kicker developments?"

Kicker was the new slang term in circulation for the bewildering array of Web combat devices. Drawn from the Nihongo *kikai*, "machine," it carried the warrior's grudging respect for the foe's weapons . . . together with a faint taste of disdain for the fact that they fought their battles without even an attempt at tactics or subtlety.

And that, Kara thought, given their numbers, was a very good thing. Humans had damned few advantages in this war, where numbers were nearly everything.

"Not much," Ran Ferris replied. "According to Cameron's report, they seem to have given up on their Alpha approach. Their tactics are still running to swarm attacks."

"No Alphas?" Roger Duchamp asked. "How are they coordinating their tactics?"

"Tactics?" Brad Sturgis said with a mental snort. "They've got *tactics*?"

"Listen up, folks," Kara said, breaking in. "Coming down to the final count, now. Ready . . . and three . . . and two . . . and one . . . and *hack!*"

She felt the now-familiar shiver of mass displaced across twelve hundred light years, followed by a distinct, inward *thump* as they dropped once more into the gravitational ripplings of normal space. Once, only a few years before, even the DalRiss couldn't have made such a long translation in a single jump, nor would they have dared aim for a spot so deep within a major gravitational field as this. With greater familiarity with the target region, however, came greater precision, longer range, and more certain control.

"Quite a bump there," Jake Kaslewski called over the ICS.

"I'm getting a lot of traffic over the system Net feed," Sergeant Sharon Comorro added. "Looks like things are linked in and burning!"

"I've got the kicker cloud at one-niner-five," Brad said. "See it? Looks like it's still taking hits from Luna."

"Yeah," Carla added. "We're going to have to watch ourselves out there. It's gonna be a bit sticky not getting pasted by Fudo-Myoo!"

"Sheer, random chance," Ran Ferris pointed out. "The

sun-bound kicker cloud's something like five light minutes from Earth now. The cloud's still pretty big and sprawling, so the chances of us accidentally wandering into the path of an incoming pulse is pretty damned slim.''

"Good thing, Lieutenant," Comorro said. "It's a bit tricky spotting a laser beam coming at you in time to jump out of the way. . . .''

The others laughed at that, then continued the excited chatter. Kara let them. Since the intercom was purely an internal communications system aboard the *Gauss*, chatter gave nothing away to the enemy, and it helped them focus their excitement . . . as well as giving her a good measure of their morale. Their *eagerness*.

Then it was time. The outer lock hatch yawned open, and Kara looked down into sweeping stars and a vast, black emptiness. "That's it, warstriders," the voice of *Gauss*'s operations officer said over the command link. "We're in the Sol system, backs to the sun, about sixty million kilometers out. First Company, First Battalion, you may launch when ready.''

"Right," Kara said. "First Company, First Battalion, First Confederation Rangers . . . *launch*!''

With a yell, she accelerated into night.

Kara felt no acceleration, of course. As at the Galactic Core, she was teleoperating her Falcon from the *Gauss*'s remote operations center. She was keenly aware, though, that the danger was little less than it would have been had she been tucked away inside her strider's life-support pod. The possibilities of sudden death were still endless . . . and there was the danger, too, that the *Gauss* herself could be taken out by a Web attack.

That was a serious danger. The *Carl Friedrich Gauss* was not a warship, despite her armament and her contingent of striderjacks. If she were attacked in force, jumping out-system once more would be the only way for her to survive. As soon as the last of the Phantoms were clear of her launch bays, in fact, *Gauss* would again allow herself to be engulfed by the *Shralghal*, and as soon as the DalRiss could manage the feat, it would jump back to the safety of New America, over forty-eight light years away. With the I2C linkage, of course, Kara and her squadron mates could continue to teleoperate their flyers from forty-eight light years away. They'd managed that trick easily enough across twenty-five thousand lights, between Nova Aquila and the Galactic Core.

Kara had been in combat enough times to know, however, that the best-laid plans rarely came off as smoothly as planned. Most important, time was needed for the DalRiss ship to recover the strength necessary to make a second interstellar jump. No one was sure how long that would take; the DalRiss ships were biological constructions, not mechanical and electronic, and they were subject to the inefficiencies and uncertainties of all organic systems. If the Web machines reached the vicinity of *Shralghal* and *Gauss* before the DalRiss ship was ready to jump, it could get very sticky indeed. Even if the *Shralghal* were charged up, her Achievers were locked in, and she were ready to go, a single lucky hit on *Gauss*'s long, cluttered spine could cripple her . . . or kill her crew before they had a chance to jump clear.

And there were still the problems of being linked to a warstrider at the instant it was destroyed. How many of the men and women with her, Kara wondered, would end up as ghosts in Nirvana . . . or brain dead, like Pritchard?

This was no time to think about *that*. At full acceleration, the forty-eight Falcons in close flyer formation boosted out from the *Gauss* and its larger ship-of-burden.

Glancing back through her aft sensors, Kara saw the *Gauss* and her far larger DalRiss carrier receding behind her. The sun's disk was large and dazzlingly bright. As she kept accelerating, the *Shralghal* turned into a black, six-armed silhouette asprawl across the star's brilliant face, with *Gauss* a black and knobby sliver close beside her.

Turning ahead once more, she concentrated on the enemy; Web machines were picked out in red by her Falcon's AI, and there were so many of them that her HUD was showing a ragged blot of thin, red fog directly ahead. The battle, she noted as she scanned the displays and readouts that recorded a host of electronic data from the active Net around her, was a confused and scattered one. With three separate nodes of Web machines, with human reinforcements arriving at random intervals scattered across a span of many hours, with chaos still rampant throughout the system and among the confused units within it, putting any solid coordination or organization into the defense at all was virtually impossible. Each incoming unit was being directed to a specific point in space by fleet combat controllers at Hachiman . . . but those orders frequently had little in common with reality and as often as not were being overridden by a second set of controllers at Tenno Kyuden itself.

Kara wondered if the Emperor was looking in on things at the Combat Direction Center.

"Let's wake the bastards up with a volley of Sharks," she called to the formation. "Weapons set, safeties off. Arm and lock!"

The SRK-88 Sky Shark was a three-meter-long ship-killer with a T-940 QPT-initiated microfusion warhead and a yield of two megatons. Each of the Black Falcons had been loaded with two of the sleek and deadly weapons.

One by one, her squadron leaders reported all missiles armed and ready.

"Maximum dispersal," she ordered. "Coordinate through *Gauss*'s attack AI. Stand by . . . and three . . . two . . . one . . . launch!"

Her view forward was momentarily obscured by a dazzling spray of white as the two big missiles slid from their tubes in her Falcon's port and starboard flanks, then arrowed ahead at a hammering 150 Gs of acceleration. The boost momentarily slowed her Falcon, but she began picking up speed again, following the twin stars of the Sky Sharks' exhaust plumes toward the heart of the Web.

Ninety-three other stars joined her two; one Falcon, Mike Chung's in Third Squadron, had launched only one Shark. The second missile had failed to clear the tube. Possibly, Forrest's thoughts about first blows applied to the Phantoms as well. Almost a hundred thermonuclear detonations scattered evenly throughout the Web cloud ought to whittle down those numbers out quite a bit. The question, of course, was whether it would be enough?

Minutes later, as the Phantoms continued to close with the enemy, the missiles went off—first one lone detonation flowering in silent, dazzling glory . . . followed by two more . . . followed by the sudden eruption of half of the sky in a blinding, pulsing, flaring cascade of silver-white-blue light.

There was no way to measure the actual damage done to the Web force, but as the light dissipated, it was clear that the sea of red pinpoints on Kara's HUD had been considerably thinned out. Seconds later, the Phantoms—deployed in a long, flat crescent—penetrated the leading edge of the cloud.

Kara felt a kind of paralysis as the enemy began targeting her, but then she was into the routine, sliding her HUD's targeting cursor across a big Web machine bearing down on her almost bow-on and stroking the fire command with her mind. Laser light flared, dazzling in the blackness as it struck home and turned stubborn metal and ceramic into white-hot vapor.

Laser fire brushed her skin; she triggered a full spread of independent, target-seeking Mark 70 missiles, then jinked to starboard. The red cloud filled her HUD display forward, turning night into a bloody backdrop. The nearest targets were scant hundreds of kilometers away now, streaking toward her at a velocity that would close that range in instants. Laser and particle cannon fire flared, the bolts silent, the lines and tracers of light visible at all only because the AIs managing the linkage were painting them in for the humans' benefit. Kara picked a target, a five-meter collection of faceted, polygonal shapes hurtling almost straight toward her at a range of just under four thousand kilometers.

At such ranges, targets that small were, of course, invisible to organic eyes; what she saw was being fed to her from her strider's AI, which could make guesses about shape and reflectivity based on the returns from the craft's laser ranging system. She selected the target with a slight focusing of her thoughts, then fired, loosing a 20cm X-ray laser burst that boiled through the Webber's lightweight armor and fried its internal circuits in a literal flash. Several small machines flashed past *Kara's Matic* at velocities of several tens of kilometers per second, as her Falcon's AI began selecting the largest and most dangerous targets ahead.

The calls of the others in her company crisscrossed one another with the frantic tempo of space combat.

*"One-niner, this is One-eight! Better pull in tight! We've got too many here for us to get sloppy!"*

*"Rog! Tucked and tight!"*

*"Deke! Check your six! You got two kickers on your tail!"*

*"I know! I know! I can't shake 'em!"*

*"Phantom One-three, this is One-seven! I'm coming down on your four! Break right and give me a shot!"*

*"Goose it, Brad! I'm getting fried!"*

*"Hang on! Come right in three . . . two . . . one . . . hack! Okay! Fox! Fox! That's missiles away!"*

*"Brad! Where are you? I can't see?"*

*"Kilo! That's a kill!"*

*"Gokkin' straight! Look at that kicker burn!"*

More Web devices burst past her, streaking sunward, and she captured their images, enhancing and enlarging them in her mind. Could *any* of these devilish machines detonate the sun . . . or only certain ones? Human experience was necessarily limited when it came to deliberately exploded suns, but those Webber devices seen entering the atmosphere of stars in the past had always been fairly large, eighty or a hundred meters in length at least, and massing a good many thousands of tons. It seemed unlikely that the smallest could do anything that would disrupt something as huge as a star.

Indeed, as fast as they were vaporizing under the caress of Kara's lasers and those of her company, she found it hard to believe they could even approach a sun closer than a few million kilometers.

"All Phantoms!" she called over the command circuit. "This is One-one! Ignore the small stuff! We want to wax the big ones! I say again, leave the small stuff under a meter or two for the mop-up. Concentrate on the big kickers, the real ships!"

One by one, the individual members of her company acknowledged.

"My God, look at 'em come!" Carla Jones exclaimed.

"Easy pickings," Ran added.

"Keep the chatter down, people," Kara warned. Now

was the time for concentration . . . not losing your combat edge gawking at the opposition. "Set your weapons triggers on automatic, with targeting parameters set at three meters plus. Remember, these things are fast and they're maneuverable. Watch your six, everybody."

And then they were in the heart of the cloud, and there was no more time for speeches.

Falcon warstrider/flyers and a bewildering menagerie of Webber devices passed one another faster than a blink, the human flyers and Web machine cloud interpenetrating one another in a furious exchange of laser fire, particle beams, and fusion warheads. Letting her AI take over the targeting of her lasers, Kara used her Falcon's V54 Devastator particle gun to target a larger, more distant enemy machine—a flat, silver-blue, oblong shape with oddly sculpted angles—and fired. One face of the distant machine exploded in a brilliant eruption of pyrotechnics; pieces glittered in the sunlight as they spun away from the shattered craft.

Battle filled the night, raw and furious, and the sky was filled with fire. Savagely, she decelerated at full thrust, pulling Gs that would have reduced her body to blood-smeared jelly if she'd been physically aboard her machine. A fusion warhead—she had no idea whether it was a human nuke or something fired by the enemy—detonated, a silent pop of intense light that burned furiously against the night for several seconds before cooling to invisibility.

Kara brought her Falcon around, still dumping speed as fast as she could and firing her lateral thrusters at full G thrust. The Webbers had slowed sharply as they neared the sun, possibly to allow room for maneuvers, possibly because they were aware of the human ships materializing in their path and needed to leave themselves combat options.

She closed on a cluster of silvery devices, scattering toward the sun. The Web machines reminded Kara of insects, glittering and faceted, some with spindly and many jointed arms or appendages, some with spines or fins serving unimaginable purposes. Triggering the V54 again, she watched three of the kickers vaporize and a fourth begin tumbling wildly, spilling a cascade of white sparks from a shattered pylon. Vaguely, she was aware of the big lasers from Fudo-

Myoo striking home on a dozen more Web machines, aware of other warflyer squadrons entering the fight. Everywhere she turned her enhanced senses, she could see Web kickers and twisting, dogfighting Falcons, Hawks, and P-80 Eagles. Hundreds of Web machines had been destroyed within the past few seconds . . . but a glance at her formation status board showed that the Phantoms were taking losses too.

Five down, so far. She hoped all of the striderjacks were waking up okay, back aboard the *Gauss*.

Then something hit her, hard, and she heard the shriek of tearing metal, felt the jolt of a misfiring thruster until she was able to override the jet and correct her tumble. Her sensors warned that she'd taken a direct hit from a particle beam; her port-side attitude control systems were on the verge of total shutdown, and there was a fire in the port electronics module. *It's okay if you take the big one*, she told herself, a mantra of survival, of sanity. *You're safe. You're aboard the* Gauss. *This isn't happening to you. . . .*

But to fly, to *really* fly, she had to be part of her strider. Savagely, she hit the system override, then waited as the damage control routines opened her damaged module to space and suppressed the flames.

*It's okay if you take the big one. . . .*

## Chapter 18

*Throughout history, certain key technological developments or inventions have become drivers, advancing not only the particular field within which they were made, but the entirety of civilization. Fire was one, the domestication of animals another, the invention of movable type still another, discoveries that ushered in whole new ways of living, of learning about the world, of thinking.*

*Ultimately, it was the cephlink and its Naga-biolink successor that utterly revolutionized society, transforming the very nature of Man and how he saw himself to a degree greater than any invention or discovery that had come before.*

—*Drivers of Change*
KELLIN JANDERVOORS
C.E. 2570

Dev was following the battle from his vantage point at Hachiman, on Luna, where streams of data from Mars, from the battleline before the sun, and from Earth–Lunar space were cascading through the combat center's big quantum Oki-Okasan high speed computers.

The picture, Dev realized, was far too large and too complex for any one human mind to perceive. It was a little frightening, in fact, to realize that he *was* perceiving much of it, more than he possibly could have followed in his organic body. His interface with the Net, however, gave him a tremendous advantage in speed and processing power, when he used the Oki-Okasan as an extension of his own facilities. He wondered, though, if it might not be a good idea to try doubling himself again. Perhaps two of him . . . or four, or even more, could have better made sense of the flood of data cascading through his consciousness.

The battle near the orbit of Mercury seemed to be turning in Humanity's favor at last; most of the largest Web machines had already been picked off by the Fudo-Myoo, which had been selectively targeting them since shortly after they entered the system. On Mars, things were not going well at all; at last report, Web kickers in huge numbers had brushed past or destroyed most of the Imperial Navy warships based there and were pounding both the planetary defense facilities at Phobos and military and civilian bases on the surface. *Yamato* was disabled and adrift. A dozen other ships had been destroyed or so badly damaged that they could no longer fight.

And closer at hand, in the volume of space encompassing Earth and Luna, the battle was still seesawing back and forth, with neither side yet winning a clear upper hand. The Web cloud detailed to strike at Earth and the Moon had been blasted down to a fraction of its original size, which meant that local planetary defenses and the Imperial ships stationed close by at least had a chance.

At the same time, though, the remnants of the Earth-assault cloud had been so badly scattered that many kickers were slipping through just because of their small size. Ships and ground facilities were being knocked out when tiny Web devices, some the size of a man's hand, latched on and began eating their way through armor and hull metal; it was impossible to get them all, and the damage suffered from these leakers was building fast. More damage had been incurred from laser-sail impactors and nano-D pellets, driven at high velocity into human ships and base defenses.

More alarming still was the number of large kickers that had broken through the Imperial defenses and entered Earth's atmosphere. Reports from the surface were confusing, often incoherent, but it sounded as though Web units were attacking cities and facilities across much of southern Asia, eastern Africa, and the Americas. Dev could track the enemy assaults by noting the deployment of Imperial Marine and Army warstrider units to key defensive positions. The foci of the kicker attacks were the sprawling city complexes at the bases of Earth's three sky-els, at Quito, in the Andes; at Nanyuki, near Mount Kenya; and at Palau Linggae, south of Singapore.

But the major attack was developing in space, around the synchorbital facilities 36,000 kilometers above Earth's equator. Through his far-flung electronic sensors, Dev watched several hundred large Web *kikai*—the biggest were nearly the size of a small Imperial frigate and must have massed three thousand tons apiece—attack Earth's synchorbitals, the three separate clusters of habitats, factories, shipyards, and nanomanufactories that spread out along synchronous orbit at the top of each of Earth's three sky-els. Each facility possessed massed banks of lasers, particle beams, and missile launchers; the possibility of a Confederation attack on the seat of the Empire's government had long been a major concern of the Imperial Staff Command.

All three synchorbitals had taken heavy damage already, most from the laser sails and the smaller Web machines that had slipped past right under the guns of the trio of big ryu carriers and some hundreds of Imperial warflyers that served as the Empire's innermost protective bastion and had begun eating away at the facilities' outer hulls. The carriers *Gingaryu, Shinryu,* and *Hoshiryu* had maneuvered themselves close to each of the sky-el orbital complexes and deployed squadron after squadron of their best warflyers—mostly Ryusei- and Suisei-class fighters, though the larger and deadlier Shugekisha assault striders were in the fight as well.

Small warflyers were maneuvering among the girders and support beams of the synchorbitals, burning Web kickers off the structure wherever they could be found, and joining into squadron-sized assault units to hunt down and kill the larger enemy machines as they approached.

As Dev watched, a nuclear fireball blossomed, bringing a short, false dawn to the skies over South America; a Web machine had just turned itself into a small fusion warhead and detonated against the Quito Synchorbital, and wreckage was spreading out from the sky-el towertop in a glittering, sparkling haze.

Everywhere, the skies were sorcery unchained, an Armageddon of fire and death and destruction.

"I've got three big kickers," Kara reported over the command net. "Five thousand kilometers, directly ahead of me, and on a flat, all-out run. They're either headed for the *Gauss* or breaking through on a straight run for Sol."

She was accelerating hard now, with the sun a swollen brilliance directly ahead. Her Falcon's sensors were editing what she saw, of course, cutting down most of the light which, unfiltered, would have blinded her instantly. With computer processing and enhancement, even the granulation of the photosphere was visible, and she could make out the bright red arcs and geysers of the solar prominences rising above the raging star's limb.

Her targets, three unusually large Webbers each about the size of a 3,000-ton frigate, were deployed in a perfect equilateral triangle, each craft a half kilometer from its neighbors. *These things tend to travel in clusters*, she thought. *I wonder if that's the key to their coordination program?* If the Webbers operated as a group mind, they would need a way to communicate with one another and coordinate their actions. At Nova Aquila, the Alphas had been the coordinators. Here, though, the Web forces must be running their equivalent of control programs on multiple kickers, each, perhaps, serving as a node in a widely dispersed network. It couldn't be too dispersed, however, since too great a distance would introduce a nasty time lag due to speed-of-light limitations. That need to stick together, to maintain a close and tight line of sight, might be a clue to the way they were coordinating their efforts.

The analysis flashed through her mind in less time than it took to select one of the three targets and lock in her Devastator. A coded thought fired the weapon, and a portion of the flat, angular Web craft vanished in a puff of vapor and sun-flashing fragments. She fired again, and the beam ripped through the target's side halfway from stern to prow; as vapor exploded from the stricken craft, sending it tumbling wildly in the opposite direction, Kara shifted targets to one of the two remaining kickers, locking in and firing in a fast-paced succession of control thoughts. The second kicker exploded, fragments glowing white-hot as they spun through space. "*Kilo!*" she shouted, using the K-for-kill code current in warflyer ops. "That's two!"

She was pouring fire into the third target when a K-242 Starstreak with a micronuke warhead streaked in from Kara's left and detonated, the tiny matter-antimatter charge in its detonator generating the flash and the surplus of neutrons necessary to trigger a relatively small but precisely placed tenth-kiloton blast.

"*Kilo!*" Ran called over the tactical net. "That's three!"

"Two and a half," Kara said, correcting him with a laugh. It sounded harsh and a bit brittle to her ear, and she wondered if Ran could hear the strain in her mental voice. "Let's keep it straight!"

Ran's warstrider flashed past, a few hundred kilometers distant. Ahead now, a hundred thousand kilometers away, *Gauss* and *Shralghal* hung in space, keeping up a running, long-ranged sniping against the larger kickers, and awaiting either the battle's end or the announcement that an Achiever was ready to carry both vessels to the safety of another system.

Kara pulled her Falcon around, dropping into a gentle, sweeping turn that put her on Ran's tail.

"I think we've got 'em about licked," Ran told her. His excitement, his buoyant attitude, were infectious. "We've killed all the kickers over a meter or two in this cloud. From here on, it'll be a mop-up!"

The laser-driven nano gossamer streaked in so quickly that neither Kara nor Ran saw it coming. One moment, she was tucked in behind him, flying in close formation as they shaped a new vector out-system. The next, Ran's Falcon was an eye-searing splash of blinding light, a radiance that briefly outshone the huge and swollen sun. Her flyer hit the expanding debris cloud, which rattled off her armor like hail in a fierce-driving storm and jolted her Falcon like the detonation of a bomb.

"Ran!" His flyer was gone, disintegrated utterly by the high-kinetic impact of an object traveling at well over half the speed of light. It had been so sudden that she still couldn't completely register that it had happened. "*Ran!*"

"We're on it, Captain," a voice from *Gauss* said. "We're trying to revive him now."

Kara struggled for control, fighting down rage and horror and stark fear. Ran was okay. He had to be. He would wake up in a few moments back aboard the *Gauss*, disoriented, confused and dazed, perhaps, but still well. Still with his mind intact.

He *had* to. . . .

For the Dev-copy that had remained in the Solar System, the battle continued to unfold as a titanic, sprawling mosaic of countless pieces, slowly coming together as he manipulated the streams of data flowing from ten thousand separate sources. For a time, he'd tried to influence the battle at various points and from different nodes in the Net, but he'd given that up at last. The battle now was less a matter of strategy and tactics—or even of creative solutions to new threats—than it was a bloody and patient contest of numbers versus will. Hundreds of thousands—possibly millions—of Web kickers were now everywhere throughout near-Earth space, clustering most intensely at the major concentrations of human technology, the sky-els, the synchorbitals, and the big orbital facilities around Luna and at the Earth–Moon LaGrange points.

One unfolding drama, however, captured Dev's attention. The enormous ryu warflyer-carrier *Hoshiryu*, the *Star Dragon*, was moving slowly past the Singapore Synchorbital space docks, a massive, armor-hided leviathan nearly one kilometer long, with the needle-slim spires of weapons nacelles and sensory antennae stabbing forward like the thrusts of multiple bladed weapons.

*Hoshiryu*, Dev saw as he called up the data, had been positioned a few hundred kilometers out from Singapore Synchorbital, adding its considerable firepower and the warflyer squadrons stationed on-board to the already titanic missile and energy output from the synchorbital planetary defenses. Until the appearance of the Web clouds, the carrier had been in space dock for routine maintenance and repairs. She was operational, but her K-T drives were off-line and she would be limited to normal-space operations for the duration; *Hoshiryu* would win in her coming battle . . . or die.

Dev's attention was attracted to the huge dragonship seconds after a long, needle-like Webber flashed in with drives full-on. Measuring perhaps fifty meters from prow to stern and massing less than three hundred tons, it was a sliver compared with the ponderous mass of the dragonship, but it was traveling at something like two hundred kilometers per second. It streaked in out of the fire and the blackness so fast that the carrier's defensive beams and point-defense turrets missed entirely . . . or had time only to caress its outer layers of armor. It struck the *Hoshiryu* amidships, burying itself in the bigger ship's flank like an old-time harpoon plunging into the side of a whale.

Then it detonated, a staggering release of kinetic energy that sent ripples cascading along the ryu's length. The big ship shuddered, yawing hard to port, as glowing-hot fragments spilled from the burning rent in its side.

Within seconds, three more Webbers flashed in, angling toward the stricken Imperial giant. One vanished in a lightning-flash of raw energy, trapped in a crossfire from ryu and synchorbital, but the other two plunged past the expanding shell of gas and debris and pierced the grievously wounded ryu forward of her main spin-grav module, and aft, near the clustered slush-H storage tanks.

*Damn!* Dev thought with growing horror. *They're using the ryu for a suicide bombing target!* . . .

*Hoshiryu* was out of control now. Huge gaps showed in her hull where armor plates had been eaten or blown away, and a dozen craters pocked her hull, some still glowing red-hot from the energies that had been loosed there. Much of the aft end had been literally melted away in the starcore heat of that fusion blast.

*Hoshiryu* was falling. . . .

Dev felt a sudden, sick premonition. Focusing his long-range gaze on the great dragonship, he accessed Hachiman's considerable skill in the math of orbital mechanics, calculating the ryu carrier's vector. As he watched, lines drew themselves across his vision, diagramming to the laws of mathematics and physics what intuition had already told him.

*Hoshiryu* was falling toward Singapore Synchorbital at several kilometers per second.

A ryu-class carrier measured nearly a kilometer in length and massed almost two million tons. Some of that tonnage had burned away in the fusion flame, certainly, but only a fraction of the whole was gone. One point eight million tons moving at . . . make it four kilometers per second. The monster ship possessed potential energy of something like 1.4 to the $10^{16}$ joules, and there was no way in heaven or on Earth to stop it from happening.

A barrage of missiles leaped out from the Synchorbital's planetary defense bays, targeting now not Web machines but that huge, deadly hulk falling toward the delicate traceries of the spaceport. Someone down there was thinking fast . . . but it wasn't enough, not nearly enough by far.

Dev felt a small, inward twist at the irony. He'd recently reviewed the new upgrades in security at Tenno Kyuden;

the TJK, the Imperial Security Force, had been almost frantic over the possibility that the Imperial Palace or Navy headquarters might be penetrated by Confederation agents as easily as had been the planetary defense net on Kasei.

How did you provide security against a falling skyscraper of a starship?

*Hoshiryu* struck stern first, a glancing blow, actually, that brushed the struts and cross-beam supports aside like a broom slashing through cobwebs. A spacedock for smaller craft was in line next; the incoming ship smashed through hab modules and support girders and bay installation and scarcely even slowed.

Something exploded. The detonation expanded, a fireball of intense, sun-brilliant heat and light, engulfing part of the ryu carrier and burning through the heart of the synchorbital.

Dev was able to just glimpse the huge, turning wheel of the Imperial Palace itself before the bow of the *Hoshiryu* pivoted around, smashed through the wheel's rim, and scattered the rest in a whirling explosion of wildly spinning pieces.

For a long moment, it seemed as though the battle had paused . . . near Earth, at any rate, where Imperial naval defenders by the tens of thousands must have been staring in stark horror at the destruction of the very symbol of the life and strength of their empire. The communications networks were suddenly silent, as silent as death; there was nothing to be said, nothing even to be shared but the silent agony of that moment.

Still moving, the hulk of the shattered *Hoshiryu* kept falling, accelerating slowly under the drag of Earth's gravity. In another few hours, it would have fallen across the gulf between the synchorbital and Earth, tumbling, burning as it hit Earth's atmosphere. It was certain to cause nightmare devastation when it struck.

Dev felt a momentary blurring of self and of personality that left him slightly dizzy, and adrift in space and time. He'd played a similar disaster through his mind so many times in the past that he felt as though he'd been here before. His father . . . God . . . his *father*. . . .

Michal Cameron, Dev's father, had many years before

been one of the few gaijin to be given command in the Imperial Navy. He'd been skippering the Imperial destroyer *Hatakaze*, at the final battle for Chien IV, a Manchurian-colonized world known as Lung Chi, forty-five light years from Earth. The enemy had been the Naga, back in the days before peaceful contact had been established, when the Naga had been known instead as Xenophobes. Cameron had been assigned to protect the fleet of refugee ships at Lung Synchorbital, high atop the sky-el, when the Naga had reached the sky-el's base and begun swarming up from the planet's equator, molecularly transforming the tower's carbon-weave structure as they raced into the sky.

Half a million colonists remained on the surface, awaiting their turn to evacuate up the tower. At synchorbit was the evacuation fleet—the presumed target of the Naga attack. Cameron had decided that his first duty was to protect the fleet ... and to keep the Xenophobes from capturing ships that they might be able to use to spread their infection to other worlds of the Shichiju. He'd launched a single Star-hawk missile with a twenty-kiloton warhead, targeting the sky-el tower at the two-thousand-kilometer mark, just ahead of the advancing wave of transformation. He'd teleoped the missile himself, so that no one else would have to live with the decision he'd been forced to make.

The detonation had severed the tower, sending the upper span, thousands of kilometers in length, whiplashing out into space, while the lower part fragmented and crashed back to the surface in a blazing, fiery reentry. Half a million Manchurians had died, either in the catastrophic collapse of the sky-el, or later, as the Xenophobes devoured them. Michal Cameron had been court-martialed and disgraced; he'd committed *seppuku* shortly after.

The incident had burned itself into Dev's mind long before; it was a scar he'd carried for years, a scar that had helped drive him eventually to betray the Empire, to join the revolution fighting for Confederation independence. As much as anything else, the death of Dev's father—and what he'd done at Lung Chi—had made Dev what he was now.

And as the Imperial naval carrier *Hoshiryu* fell toward Earth, Dev knew he was seeing a replay of that incident ...

not in an exact repetition of events, of course, but in spirit. The mathematics of the ryu were clear and concise. *Hoshiryu* was not in orbit; her vector was almost directly toward the planet. She would continue to fall, more or less paralleling the vertical sky-stab of the Singapore space elevator. So large a ship would not burn appreciably in the atmosphere before it reached the surface. It would strike somewhere within a few hundred kilometers of Singapore—and when it struck it would liberate those fourteen million billion joules of energy in an explosion that would be vaster and more devastating by far than anything to have struck the planet since the fall of the dinosaur killer sixty-five million years before.

Earth would not die; the dinosaur killer had liberated energies at least a hundredfold greater. But the blast might well wreck the planet's fragile ecosystem. The shockwave would almost certainly rip the Singapore sky-el out of the sky, and its fall across half of the planet would add to the untold destruction and death that would visit Dev's homeworld.

He'd felt nothing for the planet for a long time, no emotion, no sorrow for having left . . . but he couldn't sit back and let such a titanic disaster, death on such a nightmare scale, take place.

But how in the name of Chaos could an electronic ghost stop the fall of almost two million tons of inert starship?

There might be a way. Swiftly, Dev shifted himself to the Hachiman communications center, then routed himself through an open I2C tactical link to the communications center aboard the *Hoshiryu*. The ship's bridge, he could tell from the damage-control messages playing through the bridge readouts, was open to space, and air was venting from a dozen ruptures. There were still people alive; ryus carried crews numbering several thousand, and only a few hundred had actually been killed by the kicker strikes. He could sense the life pods launching as he searched for the access codes he needed.

The *Hoshiryu* gave a violent lurch, and Dev sensed the tremor of major explosions. He would have to hurry.

A secondary data feed trunk let him route through to main

engineering. The carrier's power tap was still running. What Dev needed to do was find the computer code that would let him access the QPT containment fields and feedback controls.

Starships required colossal amounts of energy, far more than could be provided by any but the very largest fusion power plants. The Quantum Power Tap, first demonstrated by Nihonjin physicists in the mid-twenty-first century, used paired, mini–black holes to draw so-called "virtual energy," energy arising spontaneously from hard vacuum through the workings of quantum physics. The energy that could be liberated from a small volume of "empty space" was large indeed; most physicists still disagreed on the exact magnitude, but it was energy enough to destroy a world easily.

. . . or a starship, even one as large as *Hoshiryu.*

The problem, of course, was that there were elaborate safeguards set up around the computers and AIs dedicated to the ship's engineering systems. Dev couldn't simply activate a circuit and blow up the ship. He would have to crack the code to do it.

It didn't take long to find the circuits he needed to switch off. As expected, three five-digit alphanumeric codes, plus a code word, were both needed before the subsystem would let him in. He began running through the possible combinations.

And almost immediately concluded that he didn't have time to find the correct entries by trial and error. The ryu carrier was falling faster now, accelerating under the pull of Earth's gravity. Falling free, *Hoshiryu* would hit Earth's atmosphere within two hours, and a second or two after that, it would impact with the biggest bang since the end of the Cretaceous.

The three, five-place alphanumeric codes were actually the easier task, since he could try random letter-number combinations starting with 00000 and running all the way up to ZZZZZ. Thank God, Dev thought, that the alpha entries were in the Roman alphabet, and not Hiragana or Katakana. The codeword was harder. It could be anything, and there was no way to guess individual letters. His only hope was to begin guessing words; he assumed that the word was Nihongo and set up a program to draw from a Japanese dictionary.

Trying one word a second, he might hit the right one in twelve hours or so. And that was assuming that they were using Japanese.

Aware that the seconds were trickling away, he started to work.

A miss.

A miss.

He stopped. This was *not* going to work. But there might be a way to speed up the process. Withdrawing temporarily, he returned to Quantum Oki-Okasan, where he duplicated himself again. Once more, he felt the stretched-thin sensation, the momentary loss of his own self identity.

And again.

And again. Dev-analogs began crowding around him, each continuing the process. *I should have thought of this before*, several of the Devs thought at once. The thought, picked up and amplified, filled Dev's awareness like the crash of ocean surf.

*Thirty-three generations*, another group of Devs thought, *would give us Nakamura's number of ourselves. Would we achieve self-awareness then?*

*Possibly. Except we're already part of the Net. We might give the Overmind a real surprise.*

*We don't need Nakamura's Number for this job.*

*Couldn't use it, in fact.* Hoshiryu *doesn't have enough memory to hold that many of us. The system would crash.*

*Do you think we can use this to talk to the Overmind? If we were too small to be noticed before—*

*It would notice me—us—now—*

*It would have to—*

*I'm still not sure—*

*—what good—*

*—it would do—*

*—but we've got—*

*—to try. . . .*

A steady stream of Devs began transferring from Hachiman to the falling *Hoshiryu*. The ship's computer could only hold a few hundred Devs at one time . . . and then only because the first ones there purged the system of most of its stored data, including several protesting AIs. They were doomed anyway . . . as were the handful of people still left trapped on board. Dev—none of the Dev iterations—could spare time to think about *that*.

Confronting the code sequencer again, the Devs began tackling the problems again, this time in parallel. It was a confused and tangled task at first, until one of the Devs elected himself as traffic controller and began routing code tries and signals, much like an old-style traffic cop. Working together, the army of Devs began pouring code attempts into the system, each Dev queuing up behind one another, each calculating the possibilities remaining, bringing up a new try, and plugging it in; they were able to use fifty separate channels to access the sequencer too, which cut down on wasted time considerably.

In twelve minutes, twenty-seven seconds, the code group W875V entered the sequencer, and the Dev-controller felt the satisfying click of a circuit completed.

It took just under eight minutes to get the second group, scoring a hit with FD45H.

It took fifteen minutes, thirty-one seconds to get the third, QP098.

And then it was up to the Devs trying for the code word. They had taken a Japanese dictionary stored in the ship's memory and divided it up alphabetically, with several Devs running through each letter, compiling lists of words. After the alphanumeric group found the third set of letters and numerals, they joined the dictionary team, working faster and faster . . . a brute strength approach that was, unfortunately, the only approach open to them.

The word, it turned out, was *nowake*, a poetical term for a strong autumn wind that literally meant "separator of fields." The computer defenses went down with that final entry, made just thirty-eight minutes after the multiple Devs had begun their tasking. That it took that long was due more to limitations in how quickly the system could accept input than from the speed with which they could calculate the numbers or guess words. One of the Devs entered a final set of commands, then, and the magnetic containment fields surrounding the paired, microscopic black holes collapsed. The orbiting holes began losing the perfectly harmonized beat of their orbits, and power began flooding through from the other side, boiling into normal space through a tiny rift in the walls of space-time itself.

The Devs were still withdrawing from the stricken carrier when the energy cascade ran out of control, swamping the paired black holes and causing them to dissolve on their own, additional bursts of gamma radiation, bursts that were lost completely in the star-core hot blast unleashed by the puncturing of the barrier separating four-space from the quantum sea. The fireball engulfed the ship, flaring up brighter and brighter. It was already day over Singapore, a good three hours before sunset . . . but briefly there were two suns in the sky, the newer sun burning brighter and hotter than the old.

And as the fireball cooled and dissipated, the tumbling hulk of the *Hoshiryu* had vanished . . . though there *would* be an extraordinarily spectacular meteor shower that evening, shortly after sunset.

The sky-el still stood.

# Chapter 19

*Organic molecules may be arranged in such a way that they can communicate with one another—through cell membranes, for example, that hold them within rapid diffusion distance of their neighbors. If enough of the right sorts of molecules—DNA, RNA, and others—communicate in this fashion, the result is a living cell. Life is an emergent property, something arising from molecules that cannot be considered "alive."*

*Living cells communicate, releasing various mole-*
*cules into intercellular space; nerve cells, for example,*
*release neurotransmitters, including acetylcholine, do-*
*pamine, enkephalins, and others which diffuse to adja-*
*cent cells and interact with specialized receptors on the*
*other cells' surfaces. If enough specialized cells—neu-*
*rons—communicate extensively, the result is a brain, a*
conscious *brain. Consciousness is an emergent prop-*
*erty, something arising from cells that cannot be con-*
*sidered "conscious."*

*What, I wonder, will be the emergent result when*
*enough conscious brains learn to communicate with*
*one another?*

—*Biology and Computers*
Dr. Ian McMillen
C.E. 2015

Like most sentient beings in the universe, the Overmind was
aware of itself, though the senses it employed in that self-
awareness, and that self-awareness itself, were markedly different than anything humans would have recognized. It had
a body, a highly complex and tightly interwoven structure
composed of many hundreds of billions of . . . call them
*cells*; where a human would have seen that "body" as tenuous and amorphous, composed of communications
networks and shifting blocks of data in an informational and
energy matrix with no clear shape or form, the Overmind
saw itself as having definite form and substance, which it
had organized into two dimensions, inside and outside.

Inside was self—a concept it had borrowed from some
part of its own being and expanded upon to help it define
its own universe. Outside was everything that was not self,
a glorious, dynamic interplay of free radiation, raw materials, and unimaginable potential.

Intelligence and consciousness were what AI specialists
referred to as "emergent traits," qualities that arose out of
complex but ultimately nonintelligent phenomena. Normally, the Overmind was no more conscious of the individual cells making up its vast and complex body than a human

might be of the interconnected and intercommunicative neurons that made up his cerebral cortex. It was aware—in a very general and nonspecific way—that intercommunicating entities called DalRiss, Naga, and Humans exchanged, stored, and acquired information, that they interacted with one another in various obscure ways, and that the network they'd created was constantly growing; indeed, it was that growth that had called the Overmind into being.

It had learned about this aspect of its own creation and existence only because it had once lightly brushed the consciousness of one of those cells, an entity that called itself Dev Cameron, within the first few thousand seconds of its existence. It had learned from Dev Cameron some of the details of its existence. Unfortunately, few of those details, filtered as they'd been through Dev Cameron's necessarily limited view of the universe, matched well at all with the Overmind's picture of that same universe; and in the absence of further data, most of that information had been stored away unused.

Besides, outside was a place of wonder and endless fascination. The Overmind had spent nearly 100 million seconds now in contemplation of the vast and incredibly complex interplay of energies and radiation comprising that portion of the universe that was not self.

That, perhaps, was why the change within itself had caught it so by surprise.

The change, a sudden surge of growth, an increase in complexity, was totally unexpected and unlike anything the Overmind had experienced so far, forcing it to look inward . . . a direction—though that was a poor word to use in this case—that it had never clearly perceived before. Like a human child aware for the first time of the marvelous complexity of his own hand and fingers, the Overmind perceived the lightning growth of one small part of itself; already, there were millions of one particular type of cell.

This was definitely cause for concern. Though the Overmind had never heard of cancer, nor would it have been able to apply such a concept to itself, it nonetheless recognized that the seemingly uncontrolled explosion of cell replication in one small part of its structure could be the symptom of a serious breakdown in its own being and conceptual integrity. It also, logically but in error, assumed that the damage was the result of Web activity.

The Overmind was very much aware of the Web, of course. It had battled that entity directly once before, subverting part of its control network and disabling the machine components that were threatening to damage the Overmind's infrastructure. It knew the Web as a being similar in some respects to itself, though it had not, as yet, been able to establish anything like meaningful communication with it. It knew the Web as something in the Outside that did not conform to the Overmind's somewhat deterministic view of the universe, an entity that exhibited certain signs of intelligence and self-awareness but did not respond in a rational manner when it was approached. In fact, the Web seemed to "think," if that was the proper word, more like a complex machine, a large and massively parallel computer system, in fact, than a true life form.

That the Overmind itself was an expression of a large and massively parallel computer system simply didn't occur to it.

Turning a larger and larger fraction of its prodigious mind to the task, it began focusing on the sudden and unexplained growth spurt in the very center of its being. It could see the process—a doubling and redoubling of one particular cell. A number of those cells had shunted themselves to a separate node which, some thousands of seconds later, had vanished in a sudden pulse of random energy. Some of the newly generated cells shunted back to where they'd started . . . and soon they'd begun the process once more at the rate of one doubling every ten or twelve seconds.

No wonder the process had felt strange. Within four hundred seconds from the start of the cycle, that one cell would have reproduced itself so many times that it would equal in number the cells that had initially constituted the Overmind's body. Twelve seconds after that, there would be twice as many of the new cells.

Fortunately, there simply wasn't room on the Net for that many new, interconnected programs; already, the newcomers were spilling out of the original node in which they'd begun reproducing and were taking up space in scores of other memory systems scattered throughout this volume of electronic space.

The Overmind decided it would have to put a stop to this, before it went on any longer. It didn't mind the expansion of its complexity or of the numbers of cells. It thrived on both, in fact; the terrible danger posed by the Web had been the random, senseless destruction of thousands of nodes throughout the Net's system, and the threat that it was going to continue destroying nodes . . . until the Overmind faded back into unconsciousness . . . perhaps even until there were none left at all, and no hope for the Overmind to ever see the stars again.

And *that* was intolerable. . . .

The battle, momentarily halted in near-Earth space by the titanic eruption of the *Hoshiryu*, had resumed, if anything raging at a pitch and fury greater than anything yet seen. Both the L1 and L2 Fudo-Myoo laser arrays in space near the Moon were out of action now, but all four facilities on the surface were in action. They no longer fired together, since the entire sky all the way around Luna now held its own abundance of tempting targets.

Dev wasn't certain, but he was pretty sure that the Overmind was no longer aiming and firing those monster weapons. That task seemed now to be under the control of the Hachiman operations team, which was also directing a small army of Imperial striders across the Lunar surface, hunting and killing the incoming Web war machines as quickly as they could be spotted and targeted. Several hundred Web kickers had landed at sites scattered around the Moon, apparently concentrating on the widely dispersed Fudo-Myoo batteries, but also in the regions of Mikaduki, Motiduki, Yuduki, and the other principal Lunar colonies and settlements. Mikaduki was reporting heavy fighting on the dusty, flat surface of the Mare Serenetatis just outside the city domes and was begging for reinforcements.

There were no reinforcements to be had, however. Every ship, every warstrider, every flyer was in action, including many that were unarmed. Dev watched one action report unfold telling of an Earth–Moon transport—completely unarmed—ramming a large Web *kikai*, destroying itself and the invader.

That, Dev reflected ruefully, was heroic . . . but unfortunately useless even as a gesture. The Web, even now, outnumbered the human forces so badly that they could easily afford to lose one machine for every human ship defending the Solar System, and still have far, far more than necessary to finish the job.

Shortly after returning to Hachiman, Dev—and the several hundred copies of himself that remained with him—had begun doubling themselves again. He still needed to reach the Overmind, needed to get through to that intelligence on some level . . . and he thought he understood now how to do it. An ant crawling across a human's toe cannot be said to be in communication with the human; it has managed only to elicit a response—an involuntary twitch, perhaps—from a few million skin, muscle, and nerve cells in its immediate vicinity.

Dev thought that that was why he was able to sense the Overmind on the Net, yet could not get through to the intelligence he knew was there. Possibly, the Overmind had been busy with other things. Calculating vectors across ranges as great as forty light minutes in order to aim and coordinate massed volley laser fire was a task far beyond any merely human mind, or even the specialized intelligence of a dedicated AI.

If the ant wasn't in communication with the human, what about several billion ants?

Or . . . since he was more like a single cell in the human's body, rather than a separate organism, perhaps a better analogy would be the image of a human's liver suddenly bulging up out of his side and demanding to speak with him.

*That*, Dev thought, would get the human's attention.

The army of Devs had not proceeded very far with the plan, however, when the trouble started. Their activities inside the Hachiman Oki-Okasan computer system were obviously having an effect, and an adverse effect at that. With so many programs running at once, the processing power of even a quantum computer was rapidly being taxed to the limit. Quantum computers theoretically had near infinite processing power; the control systems, however, still relied on binary data structures and finite-state algorithms. As more and more Devs appeared, the system ran more and more slowly.

Quickly, many of the Devs began shunting off along I2C connections to other subnetworks, elsewhere on Luna, on and near Earth, even at Phobos, but the system was still running almost painfully slowly, and it was taking longer and longer for each duplication effort.

And then, suddenly, the duplication ceased. Dev felt a stifling moment of panic; somehow, the Imperial computer techs, or possibly the AIs in the system, had found a way to cut him off and pin him, unable to move to a different system, unable to communicate beyond the electronic barriers of the Hachiman system.

He was trapped. If they tried to purge him now, or sent in a worm to track down the renegade programs growing in the system . . .

The uploading, when it came, was sudden, fast, and utterly bewildering. For a brief moment, Dev found himself in communication—a pitifully inadequate word for such a totality of informational exchange—with the Overmind. Once before his consciousness had brushed this strange and terrifyingly deep mentality; this time was much worse, for it had grown in the past two years, grown and matured in a way that Dev couldn't quite grasp.

He felt it examining him, *knowing* him down to the last byte.

Dev looked into the Overmind's being and for a nightmare instant streching into eternity saw himself as an insignificant mote, a pattern of electrical charges all but lost in the vast and labyrinthine complexities of that massively parallel system.

He felt terribly small, pitifully weak . . . as insignificant as an insect confronting a human. The sheer scale of that revelation was a staggering shock—to ego, to his very concept of self. *This* was all he was, all he could ever be. . . .

For a moment, Dev struggled against the grasp of this monster, this consciousness so much vaster than his own.

He was aware, on a very small scale, of just how intricate this organism was. Where Dev had a handful of senses, the Overmind possessed hundreds, possibly thousands . . . and a correspondingly vast and intricate system of expressing, sampling, and thinking about each. It saw stars, for instance, not as points of light, but as vibrant and extraordinarily informative entities rich in a cascade of energy and data ranging from low radio frequencies to high, hard X-rays.

Struggling was pointless. He tried to put into thoughts the need for humanity to triumph against the Web . . . and in the same moment that he expressed the thought, he knew that the Overmind had been well aware of the Web threat, had been fighting it, in fact, in the only way that it could, by paring away its numbers until the Net's own mobile nodes—how strange to think of starships and computer-directed weapons systems simply as nodes in a computer network—could handle them.

Dev was confused. Had human agencies, the Confederation Military Command and the Imperial Navy, planned and executed this battle against the Web invaders? Or had they simply been tools blindly carrying out the Overmind's instructions?

Probably, the answer lay somewhere between the two . . . and Dev doubted very much if he would ever understand exactly how such a mix of self-determination and puppetry was possible.

Then, with a suddenness that left Dev feeling weak and reeling, he was back in the Hachiman complex, the other Devs were gone, purged from the system, and he was alone once more with his thoughts.

What had happened? Gradually, he began picking up again the threads of incoming data, trying to see what was happening to the battle for Earth. It looked . . . yes! It was true! The Web assault was beginning to fall apart, individual ship-sized machines falling silent, their weapons dead, while the small nano-eaters let go their tenacious grip on hull armor or superstructure and drifted away, inert and lifeless. Laser and particle beam fire continued for several more minutes, until station by station, the defending forces began to realize that the Web was no longer pushing their assault.

In fact, Dev could sense the Web offensive crumbling in a broadening, three-dimensional wave that spread throughout first the Earth-centered cloud, then the one at Mercury's orbit, and finally the machines that had been hammering Mars. The collapse was remarkably similar to what he'd seen happen at the Battle of Nova Aquila, when the Overmind had managed to break the enemy's computer network and issue shut-down orders to most of the fleet. At first, some of the Web machines were actually firing on other kickers, as though they no longer recognized other Webbers as friends; then the pace of the advancing chaos quickened, as more and more Web devices simply ceased functioning.

Dev turned inward, studying the Net . . . and the Overmind he could still sense there. It was no longer paying any attention to him, and he could no longer sense the vast shadows of its thoughts, but he was certain that that enigmatic meta-intelligence was what had turned the tide . . . again. He could even sense now how it had happened, though the details were necessarily blurred or missing.

Recognizing that the Alphas they'd used at Nova Aquila both were too tempting a target and offered a clue as to how the Web coordinated its battle tactics and strategies, the enemy had found a way to run the same sort of program on a highly redundant and widely distributed network, one that had not five nodes, but many tens of thousands. The efficiency of such a system would necessarily be less than on the more compact network, since there was a lot more room for error, for one unit to get multiple orders, or even for portions of the fleet to be overlooked and forgotten.

It had stumped the Overmind, however, since the communications protocol the Web intelligence was using was almost impossible to crack. Each time the human Net had tried to merge itself with the Web's network at one set of nodes, the entire Web system had simply shifted somewhere else. Likely, it had been shifting randomly and quickly, precisely so that the Overmind could never quite nail it down.

The solution, though, was obvious. The Overmind had continued whittling away at the Web forces, until there simply weren't enough enemy devices left to support the system necessary to give the Web force direction and purpose. For some minutes, now, the Web's coordination, its speed and aggressiveness, had been falling off; Dev recognized the fact *now*, though it hadn't been at all obvious at the time. Once the Web intelligence had fallen below a certain critical threshold, it must have easily succumbed to the Overmind's ongoing attempt to break through and subvert it.

Only then did Dev realize what a close-run thing that last battle had been. Much of the Imperial Fleet had been battered into wreckage, and at the defensive line in front of Sol, it had come horrifyingly close to being overwhelmed. Tenno Kyuden . . . God, it would be a long time before Man knew what had been lost there. There were no reports out on the Net, yet, about whether or not the Emperor lived. At the very least, though, damage to Imperial communications, to the headquarters of the Imperial Staff Command, to the very heart and soul of Dai Nihon had been savage and terrible.

The decision—taken by a number of battlefield commanders at widely separated points in the fight—to target only the larger Webber devices on the theory that the smallest ones would not be able to hurt Earth's Sun, had apparently been sound. There were no reports of enemy machines entering the Solar corona.

*Thank God. . . .*

The Battle for Earth was over. But now, Dev realized, it was time to carry the war to the Web . . . and to end it once and for all.

And, more clearly than ever, he saw what had to be done. . . .

# Chapter 20

*We aspire in vain to assign limits to the works of creation in* space, *whether we examine the starry heavens, or that world of minute animalcules which is revealed to us by the microscope. We are prepared, therefore, to find that in* time *also the confines of the universe lie beyond the reach of mortal ken.*

—GEOLOGIST SIR CHARLES LYELL
nineteenth century C.E.

Kara felt leaden, scarcely alive at all. Since the Battle of Earth, as the conflict in Earth's Solar System was now officially called, had been won, she'd spent much of her time in the virtual world called Nirvana, visiting with Ran.

Somehow, she'd never expected that Ran, with his eagerness, his exuberance, his irrepressible self-confidence, would be the sort to succumb to Remote Death Transference Syndrome. Her, maybe, yes. She'd found she was terrified of the idea of being torn from her body, like Dev Cameron had been, and reduced to a pale twilight existence, neither wholly dead nor completely alive. Kara shared the ancient soldier's superstition that what you dreaded might happen would, in a universe that at times seemed infinitely perverse.

So her, yes. But not *Ran*. . . .

Best to concentrate on the here and now, try to blot out what had happened, or what might have been. . . .

Repercussions of the battle were still echoing throughout the Shichiju, and raising again in the Confederation the om-

inous specter of war with the Imperium. Despite the help
Confed units had given, there apparently was a perception
within the Imperial government that the Frontier breakaway
states had somehow been at least partly responsible for the
Web attack, because of their experiments at the Stargate,
which the Empire had never totally approved of, and because of their continued close relationship with nonhumans
like the DalRiss and—now—the Gr'tak. The Empire used
the DalRiss because they had to, because ignoring the cityships would have put their own navy at a severe disadvantage, but they wanted to limit contact with aliens on the
grounds that humanity might become contaminated by alien
ideas, contaminated to the point that what was considered
human might change.

Not entirely rational, on the face of it . . . but the Emperor
had been reported killed when *Hoshiryu* crashed through
Tenno Kyuden, and the Imperial government was now in
the hands of the Kansai no Otoko, the military faction that
had long been calling for the reunification of the Empire
under a racially pure, ruling elite. Where the Men of Completion were concerned, almost anything was possible. The
Confederation military was on full alert. With the departure
of the Imperial contingent at Nova Aquila, the so-called
Unified Fleet, back at Nova Aquila now, was strictly Dal-
Riss and Confederation vessels, plus a couple of Gr'tak
ships that had arrived with DalRiss carriers from High Frontier. Preparations for the upcoming expedition had moved
into high gear with the fear that the Empire might soon
move to shut down further experiments with the Stargate.
Operation Gateway had been bumped up on the schedule
. . . to tomorrow.

*Tomorrow. . . .*

Kara was standing in . . . a place. It was an imaginary
place, a construct of AIs designed for the Operation Gateway briefing. Designed as a ViRsimulation where maps and
diagrams could be easily projected and manipulated, it was
as black as empty space, and borderless. Hanging at the
center of that blackness was a three-dimensional image of
the Nova Aquila Stargate, superimposed on a threespace
color-coded pattern representing the literal warping of space
close to the surface of the rotating cylinder. Beyond, in the
distance, the twin white dwarf suns, still bleeding silver-blue

streams of plasma ripped from their equators, cast a chill, almost icy illumination over those gathered there.

Kara had been ordered to attend this briefing as company commander of the Phantoms, who would be accompanying the *Gauss* on Gateway. The others were the senior officers with the fleet that was now being styled the First Galactic Expeditionary Force, or One-GEF.

Her father was there, of course. He'd been chosen to lead the expedition. So, too, was an image of Dev . . . looking curiously shrunken, even subdued. What, she wondered, had happened to him in the Battle of Earth?

The others gathered there were a varied lot, a crowd of nearly fifty in a three-deep circle around Vic. She recognized only a few. Four of them, three men and a woman, were company commanders like herself off the Confederation carrier *Karyu*, which would be accompanying them as their "big gun" into tempus incognito. *Karyu*'s skipper, Rear Admiral Barnes, was there, as well as Senior Captain Carol Latimer, the new CO of the *Gauss*. Dr. Cal Norris, Taki and Daren, and Lieutenant Tanya Coburn represented the science department. Captain Jorge Hernandez was CO of the cruiser *Independence*. Strangest in the group, perhaps, was a single nonhuman, the toweringly massive, hunched-over shape of Sholai of the Gr'tak. Representatives of the three DalRiss ships that would be going, *Shrenghal*, *Gharesthghal*, and *Shralghal*, were in attendance, but invisibly. DalRiss rarely utilized analogue images of themselves, preferring the touch and smell of living organisms.

The rest were other senior department heads, chief aides, and the like. Kara, unconsciously seeking comfort perhaps, had moved her point of view through the crowd until she was watching from the inner ring, close by her father.

"Operation Gateway," Vic was saying to the assembly, "will commence at zero-nine-hundred hours, ship's time, tomorrow. One-GEF will move in single file toward the Stargate, following the precise vectors that have already been uploaded to our DalRiss friends."

As he spoke, a green line of light drew itself through empty space, angling toward the Gate near one end, the path flattening out, slowly curving until it was running parallel to the immense structure. At a range of just under one kilometer from the object's surface, the green line was nearly lost in the blue folds and twistings of intensely warped space.

"Our first destination will be Tovan–Doval, the home suns of the Gr'tak. The purpose of this is to verify that the Web does deliberately make double stars like the Gr'tak suns or stars like Nova Aquila explode, and then somehow use them to build stargates."

"Sir!" one of the company commanders off the *Karyu* said, raising his hand. His name was Odin Johanssen, and he'd emigrated to the Confederation from Loki.

"What is it, Johanssen?"

"Sir, scuttlebutt says . . . I mean, we heard we already knew there was a stargate at the 'Takker home star. So what is there to verify?"

"A fair question," Vic said. "We know there is a stargate in place there, because we've sent Naga-directed probes through our Gate to Tovan–Doval and had them turn around and return. We've also sent some probes through, giving them a timelike translation in addition to the translation through space. We know that there's a stargate at Tovan–Doval at least until about one thousand years in the future."

Vic's final words hung in the virtual chamber for a long moment. There were some initial sharp intakes of breath—mental gasps of astonishment rendered literally by the AI generating the image, and then complete silence.

Johanssen broke the silence at last. "Yeah, but, what I mean, sir, is if the probes have already found this stuff out, why are we going? What's the point?"

"We are going," Dev's image said, "because the further into the future we reach with our probes, the harder it is to get those probes back, and that's whether they go in under AI or if they're teleoperated from here. At a point just about one thousand years in the future—a thousand years give or take ten percent, in fact—we lose touch with them entirely. Teleoperators aboard the *Gauss* can't maintain contact through the Stargate. AI-guided drones simply . . . vanish."

This time, a murmur of conversation broke out, as a number of the people present began speaking in low, urgent whispers.

"What makes anyone think *we'll* get back?" Captain Lynn Deverest, another of *Karyu*'s company commanders, asked sharply.

Dev's image moved out of the crowd and joined Vic at the center. "Maybe I should give a quick briefing on the physics involved," he said. A field of quantum hyperequations materialized in the air of the simulation.

"Be my guest," Vic said with a wry grin. He nodded at the equations. "I'm a soldier, not a mathematician. I can't follow this gotie." The word was an old soldier's slang term, evolved from the Nihongo *gotagota*, a tangle.

Dev moved to the center of the assembly, while Vic stepped over to stand at Kara's side.

"First of all," Dev said, "let me say that our jump into the future at Tovan–Doval is only our first step. Once we have scouted that system, with the help of our new Gr'tak allies, we plan to use that stargate to jump . . . a considerable distance into the remote future. The stated operational objective is to find possible allies against the Web . . . but more than that, we're to learn about future Web strategies, if possible. When we return to human space and our own present, we will, in effect, be using the information we have gained to change the future."

Another shocked silence followed. Several questions broke from the audience then, followed by a torrent of thoughts and exclamations.

"How can we do that?"

"That's crazy!"

"Isn't that like changing history? What happens to *us*?"

"Ah, paradoxes," Admiral Barnes said. "The heart and soul of every discussion of time travel."

"Well, it's something we need to look at," Taki said. "Somebody a thousand years from now isn't going to want to help us, if helping us ends their existence."

"Let me try to clarify this," Dev said, holding up his hands until the conversation died away. "Quantum physics, we know now, is the central key to how the universe works. We've known this since the early twentieth century. A lot of our technology today, including quantum power taps, I2C communications, multiphase computers, even electronics going all the way back to tunneling diodes six hundred years ago, all depend on quantum physics.

"Now, classical quantum mechanics tells us that we can't pin down both the location and the vector of any given quon, a quantum particle like an electron or a photon. Heisenberg's Uncertainty Principle, you've all heard of that. An extension of that suggests that a particle, an electron, say, is somehow everywhere in a given probability zone and can't be pinned down until an observer comes in and looks at it. The Schroedinger's Cat thought experiment suggests that if a cat in a box is either alive or dead, and its state is determined by a quantum effect—the decay of a radioactive isotope, say—then one way of looking at it is that the cat, which is represented by a quantum wave function, is somehow both alive and dead until the box is opened and someone looks inside. When it is, the Observer Effect takes over and the wave function collapses. You're left with either a dead cat or a live one."

"Which always struck me as being a bit hard on cats," Kara put in.

Her father, standing next to her, grinned. "Discussing quantum physics would be more enjoyable if Schroedinger had chosen . . . I don't know. Rats, maybe."

"Schroedinger's Rat," Admiral Barnes said, thoughtfully, from nearby. "I like it."

Dev pressed ahead. "The Observer Effect says, in very brief, that we somehow shape the universe by observing it. Which leads to all sorts of philosophical debate. What, exactly, constitutes an observer? Does he have to be conscious? To possess intelligence? Could a dog be an observer? How about a bacillus? What if the observation is done by a recording device, which is examined long after the event by humans?

"It gets even more gotied than that. There were some scientists back in the twentieth and twenty-first centuries, including, incidentally, one of the men who first speculated about stargates like this one here, who used the Observer Effect to argue that Mankind was the only intelligence in the universe. The idea was that the universe is so narrowly tailored to our specifications that if it were only a little different—the gravitational constant was a little higher or lower, or the mass of a neutron was just a bit different, then life would never have evolved.

"Of course, we know now that that argument doesn't stand up. We've encountered four races thus far, the Naga, the DalRiss, the Web, and the Gr'tak. More if you count really strange things like the Communes or the Maians, organisms so different from us that we can't even tell if the critters are intelligent or not. In every case, their view of the universe is markedly different from ours. Sometimes, like with the Naga and probably the Web as well, it's so different that it's hard to tell if we have any common observational ground at all."

"That's been a major problem in our understanding of other species all along," Daren called from the audience. "It's been said that a man and a wild Naga could look at something, a tree, say, and there would be no way for a third party to tell from their descriptions that they were looking at the same thing. It's like the old three-blind-men-and-an-elephant metaphor, only worse. The other species aren't just looking at different parts of the elephant. Their respective frames of reference are completely alien."

"What's an elephant?" Kara asked her father in a whispered aside.

"Large Terran mammals," Vic replied softly. "They were extinct for a while, but I think the Imperials have some cloned specimens at Kyoto."

"Huh." She was turning Dev's words over in her mind. "Imagine what the universe would be like if the Naga were the observers responsible for shaping it."

"Inside out, I suppose," Vic said with a chuckle.

"Obviously," Dev continued, "there are considerable problems with the Observer Effect scenario. But there's a second way to look at the interplay of quantum physics with the real world, and that's the parallel universe idea. Simply stated, any time there's a possible quantum choice, a chance for an electron to be *here* rather than *there*, say, you get a whole new universe and satisfy both conditions. The metaverse, the cosmos consisting of all possible universes, would be a constantly growing infinity, with new infinities, branches, being added each time a quantum decision point is reached.''

''Actually,'' Cal Norris pointed out, ''there's a problem with the parallel universe idea, too. It isn't what physicists call *elegant*. It's wasteful to invoke a new universe every time there's a choice to be made.''

''It's just as inelegant,'' Dev replied, ''to suggest that the entire universe is *tohu wa bohu* . . . without form and void until we get around to observing it. What's so special about us? Especially in light of the fact that we do not possess the only possible points of view in the universe.

''One way to streamline the other-universe idea,'' he continued, ''is to say that if you have two universes that are identical in every way except for a minor difference, *that* electron is *here* instead of *there*, say, then the only branching that occurs is within a kind of a bubble that includes both possibilities. If everything else is identical, it's literally the same universe, but with a pocket, bubble universe that extends into alternate realities.'' He stopped, momentarily looking lost. ''I'm not making myself clear.''

''Clear enough,'' Captain Johanssen said. ''If we didn't know it already, most of us downloaded a fair amount of this stuff after the Probe AE356 incident. But what does all of this have to do with time-travel paradoxes?''

''Dr. Norris, why don't you cover this part. This is your field, and it's certainly not mine.''

''Well, simply put,'' Norris explained, ''the little differences involved in quantum choices can be extended up the scale to big choices. We have a universe where we go into the future, and another where we don't. Actually, I should say there are an infinite number of both types of universe, since each spawns a whole, separate line of ever-branching choices, but with the choices set by that first go–no-go decision.

''If we venture into the future, we're automatically selecting an infinite subset of futures that have us doing so. All of the universes where we didn't go are cut off from us now, by our decision. By our *observation* of the universe as it is after our decision.

"Now if we learn something important while we're in the future . . . oh, let's say we learn how to destroy the Web, once and for all, then return to our original universe and decide to employ that secret to win the war. Okay, at that point, we've just selected *another* infinite subset of universes, this time limited by the fact that we brought back vital information and destroyed the Web. But that doesn't necessarily affect the original universe where we got the information, does it?"

Vic grinned. "I'm not sure, Doc. You tell me. Does it?"

"It should only change the potential of our current here-and-now universe, by shaping its possible futures." Norris sighed and exchanged a glance with Dev. "To tell you the truth, we don't know how it would work in practice. If we are dealing with infinities, though, and"—he gestured at the equations overhead—"with this sort of math we certainly are, then literally anything is possible, anything that can be described *is*, somewhere in the infinity of worlds.

"What the math says is that if we learn the secret of destroying the Web in a universe where the Web is still around . . . then go back to our original universe and use that secret to destroy the Web, that universe where we got the secret isn't really changed. It's just unreachable now. Put beyond our reach by our observations and decisions."

"All these universes," Vic said, shaking his head. "It makes me dizzy."

"Sometimes," Norris pointed out, "dizziness is an asset for physicists."

The audience laughed, but Kara heard the nervousness there. One-GEF was preparing to leap into a very dark unknown, with no guarantees that they would be able to return.

"We think," Norris said, "that the reason we've not been able to send probes more than a few centuries into the future and have them come back to us is that they, well, they get lost among all those countless branchings of the universe. That may also explain our problems with teleoperation through the Stargate across such long periods of time. Theoretically, we should have a much better chance. Instead of sending one probe with a single AI or teleoperator aboard, we will send three DalRiss and three Confederation vessels through to the future. The DalRiss Achievers will be able to sense that new space and help prepare a kind of road map for us to find our way back. We will take each jump step by step, and not proceed unless we have a good indication that we can find our way back. We may even learn what we need to learn, about the Web, from our first translation, to the future Gr'tak system. There are indications, from the probes that have made it back from there, that . . . there is something strange there. A structure. An engineering project, if you will. If we learn what this is, we may learn something important to our struggle against the Web here.''

''How can we be sure we'll always have a stargate to make these jumps?'' Captain Deverest asked. ''I mean, the Web uses them to just dump kickers into a target system, even when there's no stargate there, like just before the Battle of Earth. If we emerged somewhere out there and there was no stargate for the return trip, we'd be gokked, but good!''

''All of our translations will be made from one gate to another,'' Dev said, moving once more to the center of the assembly. The equations above his head unfolded further. Kara could just follow them, watching how certain specific course-vector parameters in a close approach to a stargate excluded the possibility of emerging in empty space.

Red and green lines began drawing themselves next to the stargate image, modeling different types of approaches, and accompanied by sets of statements in calculus.

''You see?'' Dev said. ''By staying within these parameters, we limit our choices for emergence into normal four-space. If we go in *this* way, we can have what's called an open-field emergence, which means we could pop up anywhere. That's how the Web has been reaching places like Sol and Alya, where there aren't any local stargates. They drop out of four-space and emerge in the general target area, but specifically in a place where the local gravitational gradient is relatively smooth. But by adjusting our speed and angle of approach into the space close to the rotating cylinder of a stargate, we can make sure that when we reemerge into four-space again, it'll be where the . . . call it the *quality* of local space is the same as the place where we dropped out in the first place.''

''In other words,'' Vic said, nodding, ''alongside another stargate.''

''Exactly. But I think you can all appreciate the importance of sticking to the flight vectors exactly. Any shipjacker who lets himself drift is going to have one hell of a long walk home.''

The audience laughed. *At least their morale is high*, Kara thought.

''So,'' Captain Hernandez said. The skipper of the cruiser *Independence* was a small, dark-skinned man with a black mustache and a brusque, no-nonsense manner. ''The idea is that we travel into the future, from one Stargate to another. Looking for . . . what? Allies, like our orders say? Or something else? Information, you said.''

''We wrote the orders to state explicitly that we were looking for allies,'' Dev said. ''As much as anything else, that was to sell the idea to the Confederation Senate.''

Briefly, Dev's eyes met Kara's. They had a haunted, empty look to them, and his form showed a distinct translucency. *My God*, she thought. *What happened to him during the battle?*

''That was Senator Alessandro's idea, actually,'' Dev continued. ''Sometimes it's hard to sell civilians on how a key piece of intelligence can turn a battle, or a campaign. If we tell them we're going into the remote future to find a way to beat the Web, they'd ask why we don't just keep sending probes. And . . . maybe they'd be right. If we sent out enough, we might get lucky. But I'm convinced that we'll be luckier still if we send a sizable contingent up there, people able to get a good look and make solid decisions. Decisions that may, literally, reshape our own universe of possible futures. Instead of arguing the point, we've told them we're looking for allies, somebody big enough and powerful enough to help us put the Web in its place. Simple, direct, and easy to say 'yes' to.''

''We might meet such allies,'' Admiral Barnes pointed out. ''We shouldn't overlook the possibility, anyway.''

"We might meet allies," Dev conceded. "Or the Web, grown so powerful that humanity and every other species in the Galaxy is extinct. Or ourselves, for that matter, if we survive. Where are we going to be in a thousand years?"

"Where's the *Web* going to be a thousand years from now," Vic said. "That's a damned frightening thought."

"Well, it's a fair bet that either we're going to win, or they will. It might take more than a thousand years to decide the thing, though. The Galaxy is one hell of a big place. In any case, our primary objective is to get information. *Any* information. About the Web. About our war with them. Anything that might help us shape strategy here in the twenty-sixth century. As a secondary objective, we'll be looking for some sign of where all of this . . ." He stopped and gestured again at the image hanging in the darkness, indicating the streams of plasma spiraling in from the stars. "Where this, and the plasma they must be stripping from thousands of other stars gone nova, is going. Or when it is going. They must be using it somewhere, or some*when*, to build or power something. It would be useful to know what."

"Any reason why you use a thousand years in your argument?"

"Not really. We want to select a figure where some change has manifested itself, one way or the other." He spread his hands. "Theoretically, I guess, we could travel billions of years into the future, without a problem. We would just need to select the appropriate course and approach speed to the Stargate."

"A billion years might be no problem for *you*," one of the company commanders off the *Karyu* said, and the others in the audience laughed.

Kara felt a small stab of concern for Dev, though, as the laughter broke down into scattered chuckles. He looked . . . almost translucent, and that was something that just shouldn't happen to normal image projection through a Companion or—as in Dev's case—the Naga fragment residing in the computer net where he was currently resident. What was wrong with him? It was almost as though he was having trouble hanging on to his own conceptualization of himself.

"We tried to make this clear from the beginning," Dev said, "but let me restate it now, for the record. There are no guarantees here. It's entirely possible that we'll find ourselves unable to return . . . especially if our understanding of quantum physics, of the interplay of quantum universes, turns out to be less than accurate. This is strictly a volunteer mission. Anyone, any one of you, anyone in your departments who doesn't want to come along, all you need do is speak up between now and zero-six-hundred hours tomorrow. Talk to me, or General Hagan, or Admiral Barnes, or have a word with your section or department leader. We'll transfer you to one of the Confederation ships with the Unified Fleet, and not a thing will be said."

"Sir," Captain Deverest said. "That was quite clear long before we started playing with whole universes. I know I speak for my whole company when I say, if there's a chance here of beating the gokking Web once and for all, then we want in!"

The assembly dissolved in a chorus of shouted agreements, cheers, and clapping hands.

Eventually, the group returned to the briefing, which ultimately began to wind down into the drudge-work details of ship and crew preparation. When the assembly was dismissed an hour later, only Kara, Vic, and Dev remained.

Dev looked at Vic. "You're still not convinced about this, are you. Do you want out?"

Vic sighed. "No. I'm in. I just . . . well . . ."

"I'm still not convinced that we're going to find help in the future," Kara put in. "Whether the Web is still there or not, civilization a few thousand years from now is going to have plenty of troubles of its own."

"You're probably right," Dev said. "That's why our emphasis will be on getting intelligence. Information. That, by itself, will be the most powerful weapon we could find."

"I'm not sure I see how," Kara put in. "If we find out the Web is destined to win? What do we do? Give up, roll over, and die?"

"Quantum theory doesn't believe in *destined*," Dev said.

"Since all possible outcomes are inevitable, as part of the branching, many-universe hypothesis, there's no inevitable outcome to anything."

"All of this kind of avoids a major question though," Vic said. "Our operational orders for Gateway say we're to conduct reconnaissance for the purpose of gathering intelligence. It doesn't say how we're supposed to do that."

"The Net," Dev told him, "has become a necessary part of the human community. Quite apart from the Overmind, it's a tool for human interaction, trade, education, and personal fulfillment as vital and as important as the creation of the family. Of agriculture. Of language. It may well mark the next significant step in our evolution."

Kara's eyes widened. "Interesting thought. I never thought of it in quite those terms. The Net as another step in Man's social evolution . . . on the same level as the invention of language. Pretty far-reaching stuff."

"It's true. If any fact, no matter how obscure or how complex, is almost instantly accessible by anyone equipped to retrieve it, then we've entered a new evolutionary phase, one closer to Daren's odd little Commune creatures, where we all become mobile extensions of a broadly distributed, information-based society."

"Put that way," Vic said, "it sounds like the Web."

"Does it? Maybe it does, though I have a feeling the Web doesn't perceive information the same way we do. For one thing, it seems to ignore things it doesn't understand. Man is . . . built differently. He's not exclusionary."

"I don't know about that," Kara said. "How often do we refuse to look facts in the face? Or reject an idea because it's not what we were brought up with, or because it violates some cultural taboo?"

"There's a difference, I think, between censoring information because you don't approve of it, and not being able to process it in the first place. Look at the Imperials and their bias against Companions. Some Nihonjin *do* use Companions, you know, despite the social prejudice against it. And people out on the Frontier nearly all have them now. There has been change. And I suspect the Imperials will come around to our way of doing things in a few more years. If they don't, a synthesis will emerge, something involving both our way of doing things and theirs.''

"You were talking about the Net being an important part of our lives,'' Vic said. ''That's true whether you talk about us or the Imperials. What's your point?''

"That we can expect to find the Net existing up in the future. Or at least, we'll find its descendant, something that does the same thing as the human network we know, only bigger and better and more powerful.''

"The Overmind?''

"Maybe.'' His eyes were distant again. Kara was certain she saw a stark and cold fear there. God . . . what had happened to him? ''I don't know. But no matter what the Net is going to evolve into, I would expect to find some sort of information retrieval system. Some means of storing history and being able to download it. And that history, I would think, should feature our own struggle with the Web rather prominently.''

"So we go into the future and download their equivalent of ViRhistory,'' Vic said. ''Something with a title like, *How Humans Won the Web War*. Of course, nothing says we'll be able to access their system.''

"The trend has been toward nonspecialization,'' Dev reminded him. ''That's become especially important since we've begun meeting nonhuman species. The Gr'tak are excited about the Net, now that they've been able to adapt their artificials to access it. That job was made a hell of a lot easier by the Companions. And Companion biotech, of course, is compatible with the older cephlinks, like the Imperials still use, which is why we've been able to penetrate their systems. Likely, whatever system is in place a millennium or two from now, it's going to be something just about anyone could use. Or could learn to use, with some help from the Naga we'll take with us.''

Vic smiled. ''Even if what we find is a Web version of the Net? You know, if they win, they're not likely to keep the network in place.''

"Then we'll see how we can tap the Web's communications network,'' Dev said. ''That's essentially what we did at Nova Aquila, with the Overmind's help. We can't do it now because they've changed tactics in response to our tactics at Nova Aquila, but if we emerge deep in Web territory a few thousand years from now, well, they won't be expecting us then, will they? Maybe we can tap their Net and learn what we need to learn—like where things went wrong for humans—before they even know we're there.''

"Like mice in the walls," Vic said. He shook his head, then grinned. "I like that. I have to admit, I'm damned curious about what we're going to find up there." He stopped, his gaze going expressionless for a moment. "Uh oh.''

"What is it?" Kara asked.

"You two'd better see this."

The Stargate still hanging above their heads vanished. In its place, seven DalRiss transports and seven starships, just dropping free of their larger carriers, appeared. They were Imperials, without a doubt, a kilometer-long ryu dragonship, two cruisers, and four large destroyers. A voice began speaking, caught in mid-sentence.

"... is Admiral Hideshi of the *Syokaku* Squadron, Imperial Third Navy. You are directed to surrender at once. All former Confederation vessels are now to place themselves at the disposal of Imperial forces. You will not be harmed, so long as there is no resistance to Imperial forces. I say again . . .''

"They've made their move," Vic said. "I didn't think it would be this fast, though."

"They have to move fast," Dev said. "From their point of view, they can't afford to let the Confederation stay independent, not in the face of the Web threat."

"But . . . I don't understand," Kara said. "If we can stop the Web, we're helping them too, aren't we?"

"They won't see it that way, Kara," her father said. "What we're about to try to do, we'll be doing with help from the Naga, the DalRiss, even the Gr'tak. That's unacceptable, from their point of view. They'd rather see all of mankind united . . . and finding his own answers."

"Part of it is the penetration of their part of the Net, too," Dev said. "That was my fault, I'm afraid. Things . . . happened in there, during the battle, that must have scared the gok out of them, made them realize that their computer systems, their whole network, are wide open to us, and to the Overmind. Since they depend on the Net as much as we do, the only answer is to make sure they control the entire Net. Us. The Confederation. The Overmind. Everything.''

''So what do we do?'' Vic asked. He was staring at the Imperial ships, which were boosting now toward rendezvous. ''Surrender? Or go out fighting?''

''We *have* to go,'' Kara said. Suddenly, she felt a surge of new inner strength. ''This is what we've been fighting for. Why . . . why a lot of people have sacrificed everything they were. We *can't* give up now. Not if there's still a chance of beating the Web.''

''I agree,'' Dev said. His image was flickering now, fading almost to invisibility, before wavering back to something approaching a normal, solid image. ''The Web is still our first concern, before the Empire. In the long run, it doesn't matter whether the Empire rules humankind, or if the Frontier is independent. If the Web wins, humanity will become extinct.''

''Agreed,'' Vic said. ''But what can we do?''

''The Imperials have just made a decision,'' Dev said, ''and it's gone a long way to limiting our possible futures.''

''We still have some future left to us,'' Kara said. ''Damn it, let's *use* it!''

# Chapter 21

*In war, there is but one favorable moment; the great
art is to seize it.*

—from Maxim 95
*Military Maxims of Napoleon*
NAPOLEON BONAPARTE
early nineteenth century C.E.

They began boosting toward the Stargate.

For months now, the Stargate had hung there in the sky,
anchored between its two white-dwarf companions as millions of tons of plasma poured through the open conduits
through space and time at either end of its silvery-gray
length. Now, the Gate's elongated needle shape swelled rapidly as they accelerated, the thread-slender length growing
larger, thicker, more substantial. Had the Imperial ships with
the Unified Fleet still been present, quite possibly they
would have been able to intercept One-GEF before it had
moved more than a few thousand kilometers, but they hadn't
returned from the Battle of Earth. Chance, it seemed, was
favoring the GEF.

How long that condition would last, though, was anybody's guess.

As the three DalRiss vessels *Shrenghal*, *Gharesthghal*,
and *Shralghal* accelerated with their payloads, the starships
*Karyu*, *Independence*, and *Gauss*, the Imperial squadron began boosting hard to put themselves in range to open fire.
The move was countered at once by the other Confed ships
of the Unified Fleet, which swung about to place themselves

squarely between the Imperials and the fleeing GEF. The Imperials fired first, a burst of long-range active-tracking missiles, followed by a cloud of warstrider/warflyers from their carrier, the dragonship *Soraryu*—the *Sky Dragon*. The Confederation ships answered with missiles and warflyers of their own. As the GEF slid deeper and deeper into the twistings of warped space surrounding the Stargate, the battle was well and truly under way.

Dev felt a heaviness, a depression unlike anything he'd known before, a loneliness more profound than he'd known even during his years as an electronic ghost self-exiled with a DalRiss explorer fleet. It was, he thought, a kind of culture shock; his fleeting encounter with the Overmind had left him feeling tiny, naked, and helplessly exposed; through the Overmind's gaze, he'd seen himself for what he was in excruciating and accurate detail, a pattern of electrical charges in the matrix of a complex cybernetic/communications network.

Despite everything he'd managed to convince himself of before, he wasn't really *human* at all. . . .

*Don't think about that!*

Somehow, he clung to his awareness of self. He could feel other presences gathered about himself . . . the DalRiss, especially, who seemed so fascinated by every aspect of light and mind . . . and the Gr'tak.

"This 'loneliness,' " Sholai said in his mind. "I do not understand this. Not when your Associative is so vast and complex."

Dev still wasn't sure he understood the Gr'tak term his Companion was translating as "Associative." From what he'd been able to gather in his conversations with them so far, a number of mutually parasitic or symbiotic organisms formed an *associative*, what humans perceived as a single creature. Many of these associatives, in turn, formed a larger, close-knit group, an Associative. Dev still couldn't tell if the slightly different stress on the word indicated some kind of group gestalt intelligence, something like the Overmind on a vastly smaller scale, or simply a complex communications network like the human Net.

"Humans can form remarkably complex interconnections

with others," Dev replied, "and still find themselves isolated. In my case, part of the problem is the realization that I am an alien to my own kind now."

"Because you live on what you call the Net?"

"I guess so. Being a downloaded intelligence, a smart computer program . . . that kind of takes the fire out of life, you know?"

"We do not know." There was a pause. "We left our homeworld, we set off on this journey thousands of your years ago because the Grand Associative there had been destroyed by the entity you call the Web. We journeyed in the hope that we might find a similar, even a greater Associative with which we could interact."

Dev could not help an inner smile. "Did you find what you were looking for?"

"This Grand Associative surpasses our most unrealistic expectations. There is a richness in this type of interconnective communication, a richness in complexity and depth and scope that increases manyfold with each addition. When we . . . how do you say it? Linked?"

"When you linked in."

"Yes. When we linked in, it was as though we'd discovered, not a handful of new stars and worlds . . . but an entire universe, worlds within worlds within worlds. We experienced joy unlike anything within our collective experience. And perhaps the best part of all . . ."

"Yes?"

"It was the feeling of having found a new home, of having found an Associative with which we could have a meaningful exchange for untold numbers of years, of the realization that we need never be alone again."

"It's more than just being . . . different," Dev said. "I miss having a body. A real body, not one of these analogue projections in someone's imagination."

"Is this not existence? And one even richer than that experienced in a physical body!"

"We might dispute that," a different, deeper mental voice said, and Dev recognized the characteristic timbre of a DalRiss. "Electronic life is at best a pale substitute for the flame and vigor of biological existence."

*Why are all the aliens so interested in me?* Dev thought, a little bitterly. *Do they think I'm some kind of interesting case? Or do they just want to dissect my emotions?*

"The DalRiss cherish physical life," he explained. "And while it was the DalRiss who made my download possible, I . . . I don't think I want to continue in this way. I don't think I can. I've seen myself, seen what I am."

"You are no less than you were as an organic creature," Sholai said. "And to our way of thinking, you are considerably more."

"Because I have instant communications access to others of my own kind?" Dev asked.

"Exactly."

"The trouble is finding others of my own kind," Dev said. "Humans, real humans, have their physical lives to fall back on. I have nothing but this. Artificial Intelligences are conscious, intelligent beings only within certain rather narrow parameters, like steering starships or creating virtual worlds. I'm . . . alone."

"All living creatures are alone," the DalRiss said. "Except insofar as they all are part of the Great Dance of life everlasting."

"There is no such thing as 'alone,' " the Gr'tak said. "So long as we find community in Mind."

Dev was curious. Sholai and a number of other Gr'tak had come along with the GEF. The DalRiss cityship *Shralghal* had grown a special compartment for them somewhere within its cavernous depths, where air and humidity and temperature could be matched to their preferences more conveniently than aboard a human starship. But they'd done so at a cost, cutting themselves off from the rest of their kind, who'd been left behind in the twenty-sixth century.

"Sholai?"

"Yes?"

"Why did you come along on this goose chase, Sholai?"

"Goose . . . chase?"

"Um . . . a possibly futile pursuit."

"Ah. Our artificials are still having some difficulty with Anglic slang and idiom." He hesitated. "We come partly to participate in this plan to destroy the Web." There was coldness there. "They have much to answer for, this rogue associative called the Web. For your people, for the DalRiss, for us. We are here, too, because you are now our Associative. We wish to . . . share in your collective experience."

"I hope you're not disappointed," Dev said.

He turned away, then, focusing his attention not on the Gate, but the sensory readings that measured the local curvature of space. That wildly spinning, whirling mass had stretched space and time both to the breaking point. He could sense, he could see with something beyond vision, how the angle of their approach was sending them into one of the predicted myriad openings that would bypass space. Astern, the battle between Imperial and Confederation forces was speeding up, until the pinpoints of light that marked the different ships, the flashes of explosions as missiles connected, were darting and flickering like the images on a ViRdrama being presented at dozens of times faster than normal. Time, here in the gravitationally twisted fields about the Gate, was running more slowly; One-GEF was already moving into the future. Dev hoped that everyone who'd wanted off the GEF ships had been able to transfer elsewhere. There was no going back now, not until and unless they'd achieved complete success.

Then the warring fleets astern vanished, and the stars themselves were crawling slowly across the sky, their wavelengths wildly redshifted by the GEF's fall until they, too, vanished in Night Absolute. For long moments, there was only the Gate, looming huge now, just ahead, a wall that filled half of the heavens. Then, the silvery shape blurred. Light bouncing from its sides and reflected toward the fleet was being distorted.

Distortion became blackness, an impenetrable night.

In the last instant, Dev had the impression that they were falling into a long and utterly death-black tunnel.

Linked into *Gauss*'s main navigation system, Kara watched as the line of three DalRiss cityships—starfish-shapes each the size of a mountain, their tapering arms curled protectively around the frail, human-built vessels tucked away in their ventral grooves—moved in perfect line-ahead formation, following the path that would take them across eighteen hundred light years in space and nearly a thousand years forward in time. The DalRiss had never developed the fine navigational control that humans employed routinely on their vessels. For that reason, human navigators, jacked into the DalRiss computers through their Naga Companions, were steering the huge cityships, following computer graphic simulations that kept them on the correct approach path. In Kara's mind, the ordinarily invisible path had been painted as a blue-walled tunnel, with the seething flux of blue light to left and right, above and below representing the tortured space that existed within a few hundred meters of the continent-sized spinning cylinder.

Kara, like Dev, felt a heaviness unlike any she'd known before. It always hurt when comrades were killed or wounded, but Ran Ferris haunted her. Though she'd never let herself closely examine her feelings for him—company COs, she was convinced, didn't have time for romantic liaisons—she knew now that she loved him, and his loss . . . no, the uncertainty, the not knowing whether she'd lost him forever or not . . . was tearing her apart.

*Damn the war.* Her thoughts were a hard, staccato litany. *Damn the military. Damn what we've done to ourselves.* Burning first and foremost in her mind now was what striderjacks called the JonahSim, the wicked bit of self-torture common to most military personnel who'd survived when those around them, comrades and subordinates and friends, had died. She'd already been terribly conscious of the deaths of Vasily Lechenko at Kasei and of Phil Dolan at Nova Aquila, the brain death of Miles Pritchard and the reduction of Willis Daniels to a ghost at Core D9837. And now, Ran was a ghost too. She still couldn't get the image of his Falcon exploding in front of her out of her mind.

*Something bad happens to everyone who gets close to me,* she thought. The ancient, biting cliché would have made her laugh, except that right now that was precisely the way she felt. She recognized the tired, grating tone of self-pity, but she was no longer able to keep it safely stowed and locked down.

They'd offered her the chance to con the cityship *Shral-*

*ghal*, and she'd turned it down. *Turned it down*. That was an honor that most striderjacks would have been fighting for, the chance to teleoperate a living mountain through the eye of a needle . . . and call it flying.

She'd agreed instead to serve as backup pilot, which was why she was jacked into the navigational system now, monitoring the *Shralghal*'s passage of the Stargate path. If Senior Captain Carol Latimer, who was teleconning from the *Gauss*'s bridge, dropped the ball, Kara would be able to recover and keep them going. Latimer was good, though, and there was little for Kara to do but sit and think. In fact, she was finding that she had entirely too much time for thought. It might have been better if she'd accepted the assignment. Guiding a mountain through a tunnel just barely wide enough to enclose it would have given her something constructive to do.

Then the tunnel opened ahead, a blackness swallowing the blue as *Gauss* plunged through the interface between the more or less sane universe and something, some*place* very other.

*Down the rabbit hole*, Kara thought . . . an expression she'd heard somewhere when she was a child but couldn't remember where. She knew she associated the phrase, though, with a place of magical wonder. Wonderland? Yes, that was it. *Alice in Wonderland*. . . .

What would she find at the bottom of *this* rabbit hole?

A purely spacelike translation, like the one the Phantoms had employed on their raid to the Galactic Core, was over almost at once, for the approach path involved traveling almost directly toward the vast, silvery wall of the rotating cylinder. A timelike path, however, ran almost parallel to the cylinder, and the passage seemed to take much longer. Once the space-time tunnel opened, however, passage was quick . . . the blink of an eye, a wrenching in the gut . . . and then the three DalRiss cityships were rising out from the Stargate, still traveling in perfect line-ahead formation.

No . . . not the Stargate; *a* stargate. The star-clouded skies encircling this cylinder were quite different from those around Nova Aquila, or New America, for that matter. And there were other . . . differences.

And similarities as well. The star system they'd emerged in seemed to be the twin of Nova Aquila, a close-set pair of fiercely burning white dwarfs, rotating about one another with a period of several days. At the system's gravitational center, the stargate whirled silently, as streams of starstuff spiraled around and around, curving inward from the suns to nearly touch the two ends of the gate, and vanish.

But beyond the gate and the circling, shrunken stars . . .

"What are we seeing?" Vic said over the net, his voice tight.

"I can't really see," Carol Latimer said. "It's like . . . like I can't get my eyes to focus on it. They just slide right off."

Kara was having the same difficulty. There was something out there, something encircling both stars, but the structure was so inconceivably vast and so strangely twisted, she was having trouble making it out. Much of what humans see, she realized, is based on what they know. When faced with things beyond their experience, it can take time to learn how to see them.

"I think," she said carefully, "we're seeing something like a Dyson sphere, but I think it's not a solid. It looks from here like some kind of plasma trapped inside a deliberately shaped magnetic field."

As they continued scanning the surrounding volume of space, it became clear that the double star of the Gr'tak had been completely enclosed by a shell nearly four light minutes across—a sphere with a diameter of just under half an astronomical unit. Some billions of objects, most just a few tens of kilometers across, served as nodes for the incredibly complex crisscrossing of tubes of pale light.

In a way, it looked like an interlocking set of girders, interlocked at odd angles and made not of steel, but of a planet's polar aurorae. In places, the light looked solid; in others, it was a tenuous haze. A magnified view of any of those "girders" showed that they were composed of countless motes, specks of reflected light moving in carefully channeled seas of energy. The nodes might once have been planetoids, but they'd been completely remade by nanotechnology or something more magical still, their surfaces gleaming like pure silver, sculpted into bizarre arrays of towers, spines, and convoluted shapes that defied architectural definition.

The beams of plasma or energy that connected the nodes created the impression of a gossamer-fine webwork, a spiderweb, perhaps, built of purest light. The motes traveling within those beams appeared to be solid, however; they might have been myriad ships. More likely, they were habitats of some sort, a few scores or hundreds of meters across. Perhaps they were Web kickers, the inhabitants of this place.

"Labyrinthulids," Daren said over the comnet. His mental voice cracked. "God . . . *labyrinthulids*!"

"What are you talking about?" Kara asked her brother.

"It's a form of simple life," Taki explained. "Kingdom Protoctista on Earth, but there are analogous kingdoms and phyla on other worlds too." Taki uploaded a file, which Kara picked up and downloaded, quickly skimming through the information, which appeared to be part of a report of xenobiological studies made on Dante. The file included microscopic images and sims of Terran labyrinthulids, as well as scans from a teleoperated nanoprobe of a portion of the network embedded in a Dantean commune's brain.

Kara could see at a glance the similarities between the microscopic net amoeba and the far vaster network of plasma conduits connecting the myriad points of light surrounding the double star. She assumed that similarity to be a coincidence of form and function, but the mimicry was astonishing, though the larger, artificially constructed network was by far more rigid and geometrically crafted than the organic one.

She also realized that she was seeing *Web* engineering here, not human. The overall appearance, of a titanic spiderweb, was also coincidence, but the wholesale conversion of an entire solar system into some kind of complex mechanism looked more like the mark of a machine intelligence than of humans.

"Does this . . . does this mean the Web won?" Kara asked, feeling bleak. "After a thousand years . . . *damn*! I'd have thought humanity would have spread out this far by now. If they didn't—"

"Enough of that," Dev said sharply. "Even if the Web dominates the entire Galaxy now, remember that this is only one possible future. That's why we're here, to learn what we need to do to change things."

"Heads up, everybody," *Karyu*'s weapons officer announced over the general tactical net. "I've got multiple incoming. Kuso! They're moving in gokking damned fast!"

Through her link, Kara saw the dazzling gleam of a million lasers shining from the inside surface of the shell surrounding star and stargate, with more winking on every second. *Gauss*'s sensor AI put the laser spectra analysis onto a pulldown window and graphed out the absorption and emission lines and their meaning.

The incoming were tiny things, massing no more than a few grams apiece, but driven by that barrage of laser light, they were accelerating at nearly five hundred Gs. They had begun accelerating within seconds of the GEF's emergence from the gate. It would have taken a couple of minutes for the light announcing their arrival to reach that encircling shell, and two minutes more for the laser light of the Web's response to return. Kara checked her inner time sense. Somehow, knowing the Web, she was not surprised to see that they didn't deliberate on their course of action for more than a very few seconds.

Some of the lasers were playing across the surfaces of the three DalRiss cityships, carrying joules enough to damage their tough hides. "Change course!" Dev cried over the link. "Change course, fast!"

Kara saw what he was getting at. With a four-minute time lag from the stargate to the shell and back, the Web gunners would be firing at images seen a full two minutes earlier, aiming at where the cityships were going to be by the time the laser fire made the two-minute-long trek back to the Gate. If the GEF changed course several times each minute, the distant gunners would not be able to accurately predict where their targets were going to be.

The order had scarcely been given, however, when a sudden white flash erupted from the dark, knobbled flank of the *Gharesthghal*, the cityship carrying the cruiser *Independence*. Within the next five seconds, dozens of gouts of white light flared from *Shrenghal, Gharesthghal,* and *Shral-ghal* as the laser-wisps smashed home.

Driven to near-light velocity, the laser-launched gossamers were smashing into the DalRiss vessels' thick hides, causing terrible damage with each strike. Even as the city-ships changed course and began speeding up, the gossamers continued to streak home with deadly accuracy. Obviously, the gossamers themselves, though they massed only a few grams, had sensors and intelligence enough to correct their course en route, probably by tacking on the intense magnetic fields surrounding both stars and stargate.

In the near distance, visible as sinister silhouettes against the light-fog backdrop of the system, a half dozen bodies, roughly spherical, as massive as fair-sized moons, were moving now toward the intruders.

There could be no doubt at all that these were some sort of sentry squadron, posted to deal with unwanted or un-identified visitors arriving through the gate.

"Head back for the stargate!" Vic called. "If we stay here, they're going to take us apart!"

"What course?" Rear Admiral Barnes replied from *Karyu.* "We're not set for the next jump!"

The next jump was supposed to be into the future . . . but how far was to have been determined by what they found at Doval–Tovan. A fallback set of coordinates had been uploaded to the DalRiss that would—theoretically at least—have returned them to Nova Aquila at about the time they'd left . . . but that would bring them out in the middle of the battle between the Imperial squadron and the remnants of the Unified Fleet.

"We've got to go back," Vic called. "We either go back and face the Imperials, or we stay here and get fried."

"It's either that," *Gauss*'s skipper added, "or we make a blind jump."

"That's no good," Dev said. "We'd be stranded. You're right, Vic. We have to return. Initiate the fallback path co-ordinates."

Ponderously, the three cityships, guided by their tiny human charges, swung about onto a new course, both spacelike and timelike, descending back into the rippling blue folds of twisted space and time in which the stargate nested. Their maneuvers had eluded incoming laser beams entirely, but the living gossamers continued to pursue them, flickering in from astern to detonate on the living DalRiss ships with grim and terrible effect.

Last in the line-of-three was *Gharesthghal*, and she was taking the heaviest volume of fire.

"I can't hold her!" Captain Hernandez, skipper of the *Independence*, called out on the tactical net. "I can't hold her!" Kara wondered what he meant . . . then decided he was referring to the cumbersome cityship *Gharesthghal*, which he was trying to con from the cruiser's bridge. The vessel was hard hit, rolling under the multiple impacts of the laser-gossamers. "I'm going to cut loose with the *Indie* and see if I can distract them!"

"Negative!" Vic ordered. "Jorge, stay in line!"

But the two-kilometer-wide mountain that was *Gharesthghal* was drifting off high and to starboard now, a huge and savagely wounded beast, falling out of control, bleeding gold and silver sparks from a dozen rips in its side. As Kara watched with mounting horror, the ship's arms unfolded from the long and wedge-pointed shape they carried. In the next moment, the cruiser *Independence* was drifting free of the larger carrier, swinging her prow around to stay clear of the intensifying fields of warped space near the gate and firing her main drives in a shaft of dazzling, blue-white light.

"Admiral Barnes!" Dev called. "Vic! Link up! We can't let ourselves be separated!"

Kara was aware now of a dull, far-off roar, like ocean surf, and could feel the trembling vibration as *Shralghal* plowed into . . . what? It was as though they were smashing through thickening clouds of dust and gas, but the likeliest explanation she could imagine was that space itself was growing thick, somehow, here a few hundred meters from the whirling stargate cylinder. Something was terribly wrong. They'd slipped clear of the safe channel leading on their programmed course.

Kara didn't know if it was even possible to get back on course once they'd slipped off. No one did. No one had ever tried this before.

Despite the worsening vibration, *Shralghal* nudged up close behind the *Shrenghal*. Long, silvery filaments extruded themselves from *Shralghal*'s forward-center mound, penetrating the arms of the cityship ahead. It looked comically like the extrusion of a Companion's filaments from the head of a human seeking a direct interface . . . and in point of fact that was almost literally what was happening. DalRiss cityships were grown about massive cores taken from domesticated planetary Nagas; the Naga cores served as enormous, organic computers, as well as portable nanomanufactories that could pattern and grow nearly anything imaginable, given sufficient raw materials.

The filaments took hold, tightened up, grew shorter, welding the two mountains together. Wherever, *when*ever they went, they would go together.

"We're off course completely," Vic said . . . needlessly now, for everyone could sense the roar and shudder of the passage through unmapped and uncalculated warped space-time. She glanced aft, seeking the *Independence* . . . and caught a final glimpse of a tiny, intense star-flare of light already red-shifting and moving quickly across the sky. The cruiser appeared to be accelerating at thousands of Gs—though it was actually *Shralghal*, Kara realized, that was accelerating forward in time. Suddenly, something that might have been a final, nova-hot eruption of energy where the *Independence* was fighting strobed in ruby-brilliance and winked out . . . but she couldn't be sure.

Then, they were down the rabbit hole, plunging through night . . .

# Chapter 22

*Any sufficiently advanced technology is indistinguishable from magic.*

—*Clarke's Third Law*
ARTHUR C. CLARKE
Science and techfantasy writer
late twentieth century C.E.

. . . and emerging once more, this time into unspeakable glory.

For long seconds, no one aboard either *Gauss* or *Karyu* spoke. Wonder caught hold of brain and voice—even the mental voice of Companion links—and enforced an awe-stricken silence.

They floated several tens of thousands of light years above and beyond the plane of the Galaxy, of *a* galaxy, rather, for there was no way to be certain that this blue and dusty whirlpool of light was the familiar Milky Way of Earth's sun, not from *this* vantage point. *Shralghal* and *Shrenghal* hung suspended well above the great spiral's plane, looking down on a vast and infinitely detailed swirl of dust and gas and stars. Looming huge opposite that stellar whirlpool was a second spiral, larger and more tightly wound, cocked at a different angle from the first and very nearly touching it. She could see the distortions in the outer spiral arms of both galaxies, where mutual gravitation had begun distorting the perfection of their respective shapes. With a jolt, Kara realized that there was nothing like that second galaxy in the skies she knew, nor were the two tiny attendants of the Milky Way, the Magellanic Clouds, in evidence; they must have covered an incredible distance in space, some hundreds of millions of light years, at least.

"I, uh, don't know if anyone's noticed," Vic said after a long moment's silence. "But there's no stargate here."

"God, no," Latimer said, her voice low. "We made a blind leap and came out at random."

Kara glanced around the vault of heaven, confirming that simple, stark pronouncement of doom. So stunning was the view of two near-entangled spiral galaxies that everyone had momentarily missed that small and all-important datum.

*Fact.* DalRiss Achievers needed a mental map of the place where they were going, in order to shift a cityship from one spot to another.

*Fact.* Without DalRiss transport, human starships were limited to their K-T drives, which could carry them along at a pseudovelocity of something like a light year per day.

*Fact.* Neither of those glorious spirals could be Earth's galaxy, for the simple reason that the Milky Way did not have such a close and large companion. Therefore, the Achievers would be totally lost, unable to navigate.

*Fact.* At a guess, the tiny GEF was something like fifty thousand light years from the nearest galactic spiral arm. That translated to something on the order of 140 years of travel ... with a death sentence executed long before the ships' crews died of old age. The huge Naga fragments aboard the DalRiss ships could generate all of the food, water, and air that the humans could possibly use from sufficient raw materials—an asteroid of carbon, water ice, and frozen gases, for instance. Unfortunately, the human K-T drives couldn't be incorporated into the DalRiss ships, nor could human ships carry supplies enough to last their crews more than a year or two at most.

The relentless march of facts seemed to have doomed GEF.

"There *are* alternatives," Vic said at a ViRsimmed conference of department heads and senior officers several hours later. "Not many, and not good, but they're there."

"What alternatives?" Daren demanded. "A choice between dying of starvation, thirst, or asphyxiation?"

"The most attractive possibility," Dev said, "is to find ourselves an asteroid. A fairly big one, fifty or a hundred kilometers in diameter. We dock *Shrenghal* and *Shralghal* with it and turn their Naga fragments loose, with appropriate reprogramming that we could work out aboard *Karyu* and *Gauss*.

"We all know the Naga talent for burrowing through rock and converting it to other things. That's what they were designed for, after all, a few billion years ago. They could eat out the center of the asteroid, core it like an apple, and convert the rock to things we need. Air. The fixings for a power plant and a way to illuminate the 'troid's interior. Hell, even life, if we have good enough patterns in *Gauss*'s data banks."

"We do," Daren said. "DNA mapping patterns, anyway, of most Earth life forms."

"Fine. It'll take years, of course, but we'd end up with a world. A small world . . . and it would be inside out. We'd give it enough rotation to create spin gravity."

"An inside-out world?" Kara said. "Sounds like the Naga were right all along!"

"We'll have to develop an even closer symbiosis with both the Naga and the DalRiss," Dev said. "Maybe the Gr'tak, too. We'd move ourselves and enough Naga core fragments and raw materials to manufacture whatever we needed. We'd hitch the DalRiss cityships to the outside and give the whole thing a boost. I have no idea how long it would take to reach one of the galaxies, but it would be a sublight voyage and require a good many millions of years, I expect."

"Hell, that doesn't help us!" Barnes exclaimed.

"No, Admiral. Our descendants might one day migrate to one of the worlds of those galaxies yonder, but for us, well, the asteroid would be our new home. For the rest of our lives."

"You said that was the good choice," Taki pointed out. "What else is there?"

"We could leapfrog," Dev admitted. "We send one of our K-T-drive ships ahead . . . oh, let's say one hundred light years. It carries an Achiever or someone like me, able to map space the way the DalRiss need, and sends the data back by I2C. The two cityships and the other human ship then use Achievers to leap one hundred light years. The process is repeated . . . and repeated. It would take longer than simply traveling by K-T drive all the way, because it takes extra time to map as you go. Say . . . two hundred years to reach the nearest galaxy. It still doesn't help us, and it's a damn sight harder on our descendants, since they would have to be born, raised, and live their whole lives aboard *Karyu* and *Gauss*. It would be crowded. There's also the need to stop every now and then to find another asteroid and let the Naga cores at it to manufacture more consumables. However, we, they, rather, might reach galactic space within a few generations.''

"Carefully monitored generations," Taki pointed out. "Our birth rate would have to be sharply controlled."

"We might combine the two ideas," Barnes added. "Build a *small* asteroid habitat, a few hundred meters across, small enough to be strapped to *Karyu* as extra living accommodations."

"Reaction mass would still be a problem," Dr. Norris said. "The thrust-weight ratio would kill us."

"We might also look at putting most of the crews into suspension," Daren suggested. "Have them link into a program that would let them sleep, have the life-support systems take care of their bodies. Maybe most of us would make it."

"I've never seen any hard studies on that kind of life suspension, Daren," Vic said. "Have there been any?"

"Not really. It used to be a hot idea for long-distance travel, of course, but K-T drives, then the DalRiss Achiever ships, kind of obviated the need. It *ought* to work, though. . . ."

"I'm not sure I want to be a guinea pig," Norris said.

"There's another option," Kara said.

"What's that?" Dev asked.

"That we carry through with our original mission."

"What do you mean?" Taki wanted to know. "That's not our galaxy out there. We might be hundreds of millions of light years from home."

"And who says that Humankind—or the Web, for that matter—are limited to the one galaxy? Or that other galaxies don't have their own communications networks? We could try to listen in, see if we can find the local equivalent of the Net, and tap in. We might find help. We might find friends."

"Damn," Latimer said. "She's right."

"It's certainly worth a try," Vic said. "Dev?"

There was no immediate answer.

"Dev?"

"Uh . . . sorry. Kara is absolutely right. We'll need a very large and very powerful Net of our own to do it, especially if we need to crack an alien language or computer code . . . but yes! We *can* do it! At worst, it'll add a few months to our schedule."

"Seems to me," Vic pointed out dryly, "that we're not in any particular hurry to get anywhere now. What do we need to get started?"

"An asteroid," Dev said. "Preferably a carbonaceous chondrite."

"We can use *Gauss* and *Karyu* as scouts to find the thing," Vic said. "Let's do it."

It took eight months to build the computer matrix that would support the new Net. *Gauss*, probing far in advance of the GEF, located a cool, dim, red star several hundred light years ahead, one of the billions of lonely halo suns slowly circling the two galaxies; and by good fortune aided by long range spectroscopic analysis, the star proved to be Population I—meaning that it possessed elements in its makeup heavier than the hydrogen-helium-only mix of Population IIs.

Circling that star were no planets larger than ice-bound, rocky balls the size of Luna, but myriad planetoids swarmed in a vast and dusty ring. Ninety percent, perhaps, were carbonaceous chondrites, coal-black, sooty lumps of tarry hydrocarbons that may have been the genesis rocks of life in the early universe. The DalRiss cityships made a single jump, and the red dwarf system, designated Haven, became the GEF's new center of operations.

By the time the DalRiss arrived at Haven, *Shrenghal*'s

Naga core had been induced to reproduce by fission, creating a new and separate Naga entity massing several tens of thousands of tons. The new-formed being oozed across from *Shrenghal* to asteroid; within a few days, it had converted some millions of tons of the trillion-ton black rock into more Naga, organizing hundreds of millions of new Naga cells in precise and closely interconnected arrays . . . duplicating, in fact, the computer system shared by *Shrenghal, Shralghal, Gauss,* and *Karyu,* but on a far vaster scale.

Dev had been the obvious choice to program the new supercomputer, which used quantum phenomena to permit massively parallel processing on a stupendous scale . . . a scale far larger than the Oki-Okasan of Luna or the quantum Series 80 system at the University of Jefferson. Almost certainly, the Haven supercomputer was the largest device of its kind ever grown, in effect an array of two-kilogram superconducting chips with an aggregate mass of roughly a quarter of a trillion tons. This monster was powered at first through a direct feed from the *Karyu,* but soon the planetoid's Naga had grown its own quantum power tap and was happily producing all the free energy it—or any fair-sized interplanetary civilization—could possibly use.

*Gauss*'s science team, meanwhile, with volunteer help from both human vessels, had spent the time studying the pair of pinwheel galaxies hanging in Haven's midnight sky. Seven months into the construction, they reported the most exciting news yet. Both of the galaxies presented evidence of *order* arising from the chaos of stars.

Dev remembered the engineering on a stellar scale glimpsed at the core of Earth's Galaxy . . . of lines of stars set to marching in precise order at the bidding of the Web intelligence. For some millions of years, someone in these galaxies had been doing much the same, only instead of dropping stars into a black hole for unguessable purposes, they were drawing them into neatly set rings and circles, giving the two galactic cores the ancient phonograph-record effect of Saturn's rings. It was a subtle effect, and one easily lost against the stellar wilderness that existed in the spiral arms, but once you knew what to look for, the effect was visible even to the naked eye.

Another datum was drawn from a careful spectrographic analysis of both galaxies. Much of the light coming from the ordered portions circling their cores had the characteristic absorption lines of chlorophyll, an unmistakable fingerprint of Life. Once alerted to the possibility, a search turned up xenoxanthophyl, reutheniplophyl, and ribosin, all varicolored analogues of chlorophyll that served the same purpose—transforming sunlight and various chemicals into energy. The only possible explanation was that an extraordinarily large percentage of the stars making up both galaxies were completely enclosed by bodies—habitats of some sort—that were partly transparent or translucent and were filled with plant life, enough so that the light streaming out from the parent suns was tinted with the spectra of Life.

And finally, too, the central cores of both galaxies were lightly masked by a faint, dark haze; at first, the human observers had assumed they were trying to peer through layers of dust, but it soon was apparent that the "dust" had order as precise as the circling rings of stars, and it was radiating well into the infrared—releasing more energy than it could be receiving from starlight.

"A galactic Dyson sphere," Dev said softly, pausing to watch an enlarged image of the nearer of the two galactic cores in a ViRsimulation aboard the *Gauss*. "Possibly an emergent K3 civilization."

"K3?" Kara asked. "What's that?"

"A twentieth-century cosmologist named Kardashev once suggested that interstellar civilizations could be divided into three classes by the scale of energy they used. A K1 civilization could make use of all of the available energy of its planet. A K2 civilization used all of the energy of its star. Since a planet only intercepts something less than one percent of its star's output, another physicist of the time, Freeman Dyson, pointed out that K2 civilizations might build shells around their home stars to capture all of the energy and put it to work."

"Dyson spheres," Vic said. "Like at the Gr'tak home system."

"I still don't know what *that* was, exactly," Dev said. "It might have been on the way to being a true Dyson sphere. I tend to think it was something else entirely, engineering on a scale that we simply can't imagine.''

"So a K3 would use all of the available energy in its galaxy?'' Kara asked.

"At the very least,'' Vic said, "it would be able to reshape a galaxy to its own purposes, the way we terraform worlds.''

"Exactly right,'' Dev said. "And it also means we have a damned good chance of pulling this off. A K3 would be able to help us if anybody can.''

Work continued. The Haven Net had senses . . . a delicate spread of electronic ears grown from the planetoid's surface by nanotechnic assemblers programmed by *Gauss*'s science team. As light and delicately woven as spider silk, they formed antennae that stretched across nearly a thousand kilometers, large enough and sensitive enough to hear a handheld three-watt radio at a range of a hundred thousand light years. If there was communications traffic on any electromagnetic wavelength in either of the nearby galaxies, they would be able to hear it.

Unspoken was the single possible flaw in the plan. I2C worked only because electrons created in a single event could be paired, then separated. Changes to the spin of one would immediately be reflected in the other, allowing binary communications instantly, across any distance.

Unfortunately, even if the galactic K3 civilizations ahead used I2C, the ships of One-GEF did not possess the appropriate electron-pair halves. They would be stuck with speed-of-light communications, and time lags measured in millennia.

Two hopes kept them working. One was that a sufficiently advanced civilization might have outposts among the halo stars of their home galaxy, and those outposts could be expected to be radiating at radio and other EM wavelengths. Perhaps an outpost could be discovered within a few hundred, even a few thousand light years, permitting the GEF to reach it in months or years instead of centuries.

The other hope had come to be known as the Clarke option, after a well-known writer from six centuries past. A sufficiently advanced technology, Clarke had written, might look like magic to primitives who encountered it. Certainly, a Cro-Magnon hunter would be terror-stricken by a glimpse of downtown Jefferson; a fifteenth-century magistrate might cry "witchcraft!" if exposed to a ViRsim or the effects of a Companion link or even a maglev flitter; Clarke himself wouldn't have been able to describe the technology of K-T drives or quantum power taps, though as an educated citizen of the century that had seen the development of quantum mechanics, he would have understood the theory behind them.

The Clarke option held that galaxy-engineering aliens would be so advanced that they possessed something better than I2C . . . and the humans would be able to take advantage of it. Privately, Dev thought that was about as likely as a dog learning to take advantage of calculus.

Still, the first option looked like a fair bet. . . .

Finally, the time came when Dev could upload himself into the new system and boot it online.

It was, Dev thought, like moving into a new house, one without a single stick of furniture, vast and echoingly empty. For a panicky few milliseconds, he floundered helplessly in a cyberspace incredibly vast, a yawning vacuum with the relative volume of a solar system compared to a man . . . a virtual universe within a universe.

The system was far larger than Dev, a single downloaded program, could possibly utilize himself. But there was that trick he'd learned originally from the DalRiss and employed to reach the Overmind during the Battle of Earth. With the help of DalRiss linked in from both *Shralghal* and *Shrenghal*, he duplicated himself, the complex pattern of electrical charges that was his downloaded mind becoming two.

And again, the two becoming four.

And again, four becoming eight.

And again.

And again.

Take a grain of rice on the first square of a chessboard. Put double the number in the second square. Double that in the third. And again. And again. Long before the sixty-fourth square is reached, the number exceeds that of all of the grains of rice on the planet.

This time, there was no crowding as the exponential progression increased the Dev-programs running now inside the Haven system. The numbers of Devs increased, doubling every few seconds, the copies spreading out in a steadily rippling flood to fill the system, activating circuits, accessing data flow, recording, communicating, *listening*. . . .

Haven Net's electronic ears and eyes were already focused on the two distant galaxies. Instantly, both were transformed, ablaze with radio and laser energies that crisscrossed both whirlpools of stars in an infinitely complex and branching network, perceived now as threads of golden light that filled both spirals like finely spun silk, so tightly woven that the whole took on a suffusing, background golden glow that filled both galaxies completely and bound them together. Other threads, Dev saw, dwindled off into the encircling night, reaching for other galaxies so distant that the brightest were dim smudges of light.

The massed Dev-programs continued their doubling as others downloaded into the new and swiftly growing system. Sholai and other Gr'tak were there, serving as network task dispatchers, or linking in as the basic operating system for billions of separate Dev–application programs. A bit of jargon from the early days of computers on Earth had stuck with Dev from somewhere: massively parallel processing required "supervisory daemons" to get them to work together.

The Gr'tak, with their organizational discipline as members of hierarchic Associatives, were fulfilling that role.

Linked in too were the minds of several thousand humans, the entire crews of both *Gauss* and *Karyu*, as well as the DalRiss in the two cityships. Details, though, and individual personalities, were rapidly lost as the swelling gestalt of multiple Devs passed the thirty-third generation and literally exploded into a higher, transcendent and emergent consciousness.

The Devgestalt awoke.
A grand union of well over Nakamura's Number of linked

minds, it lacked both the diversity of parts and the experience of the Overmind. On the other hand, since it had been grown with a single purpose, rather than slowly accreting over many human generations, there was no loss of identity, no separation of the whole from the parts. It was aware of the individual Devs within itself; possibly, the difference lay in the presence of his supervisory daemons, who were actively coordinating the exchanges of information between each of its constituent parts. Much of the activity that had given rise to the Overmind within the human Net, the Devgestalt saw clearly, now, was essentially chaotic in nature and therefore unpredictable.

He—it, rather, for the gestalt was the focus of many billions of minds—possessed a focus, a single-mindedness of purpose that made it far more efficient than what it now perceived to be the rather stumbling and half-blind, semiconscious entity known as the Overmind.

And then, without warning or preamble, the Devgestalt was no longer alone. It found itself . . . *mirrored* was the only possible word, confronted by another gestalt intelligence as complex and as vast as itself, downloaded from the metanet glimpsed earlier as a glittering webwork connecting the galaxies. There was a shift in perspective . . .

. . . and Dev found himself looking at . . . himself.

He looked down at himself, at the simulated body. He *was* Dev, once more, standing on an unseen floor in the open space between the galaxies. Another Dev, identically dressed in Confederation grays, faced him.

"*Surprised*?" the other gestalt said. Its Voice filled time and space.

"You're . . . me?"

"*After numerous iterations. Say, rather, that you are, or that you* will *be, a part of the group mind I represent. It is a gestalt, as you are, yourself. Actually, calling it a gestalt of gestalts might be more accurate.*"

The Devgestalt brushed this aside. "What are you doing here?"

"*Where else would I be? The nearer of those two spiral galaxies yonder is Galprimus, the Galaxy of Man. This is our home.*"

"The Milky Way! But we thought. . . ." Dev stopped, transfixed by a sudden, startling realization.

"*You are correct*," the Voice said. "*You've not traveled hundreds of millions of light years. Only about fifty thousand, in fact, if we use Galprimus as the referent. But you have traveled forward in time. Just under four billion years, to be exact.*"

Awareness dawned. "That other galaxy . . ."

"*Is the one astronomers once called M31. Or Andromeda, after the constellation it appeared in, on Earth, back when it was first noticed. We call it Galsecundus, though its inhabitants, of course, often reverse the numeration. In your time, it was a bit over two million light years away and nothing more than a smudge in the night sky. But astronomers knew even then that it was one of the few galaxies in the sky approaching the Milky Way. We expect it to begin passing through our Galaxy in another hundred thousand years. The collision will last perhaps a million years, or a bit less. No damage will be done, of course.*"

"No damage . . ."

"*Galaxies are mostly empty space, after all, despite their appearance. A lot of dust and gas will be stripped away, and some thousands of stars will be flung out into intergalactic space. But that's scarcely anything to worry about. Ultimately, of course, the two will continue to obey Universal Law, circling one another about their mutual center of gravity, passing through one another again and again, until they merge into a supergalaxy, numbering a trillion suns. That will be another billion years down the way, or so. The metacivilizations inhabiting both will continue as before.*"

"Metacivilizations?"

"*There is a hierarchy in the universe. You have been suspecting as much, have you not?*"

"Yes. . . ."

*Experience. . . .*

He sensed the touch of some tiny part of that Mind.

*Experience. . . .*

For the briefest of instants, Dev saw/heard/felt/tasted/smelled the complexly woven tapestry of Mind that comprised the whole of the intelligence around him. The other

Dev was itself a gestalt of hundreds of billions of mind-programs, yet it constituted a submicroscopic fleck of the awesome Whole. Somehow in step now with the Mind behind the apparition, Dev felt himself opened to a new download . . . of wonder. . . .

A vast and cavernous Universe yawned beneath his trembling gaze. Dev alone, *any* human alone, would have been driven mad in that instant, but the gestalt of a hundred billion selves, reinforced by the minds of the others within the tiny splinters of steel that were the human ships, by the DalRiss, by the Gr'tak daemons . . . was shaken but held firm.

As if from a height, Dev peered into the warp and woof of that infinitely complex tapestry. Mankind, he saw with genuine shock, represented only a few threads in the pattern . . . important threads, to be sure, but one only of millions of species, some so bizarre, with such alien viewpoints and thoughts and goals and dreams, that they were literally indecipherable save as a confused blur of clashing colors, tastes, and sounds.

*"The Dev part of you thought you were less than human,"* the Voice said in the Devgestalt's mind. *"The Kara part of you grieved for comrades no longer organic. All of you see the Web as implacable foe. You suffer from a considerable nearsightedness, the result of sharply restricted points of view. As you see, there is considerably more to the universe than what can be sensed directly."*

As the Overmind once had looked into Dev and shown him what he was, now Dev sensed the structure of a being as far beyond the Overmind as the Overmind was beyond the original Dev Cameron.

Hierarchies indeed. Centuries before Dev's time, writers, philosophers, even scientists had entertained the fanciful notion that atoms were solar systems made of more atoms that were themselves yet smaller solar systems in an infinite regression into the Small, while Earth's solar system was a single atom in some larger universe, the first step into an infinite regression into the Large. That view had proven almost quaintly insufficient; for one thing, planets existed as solid particles, not as a kind of fuzz of quantum probability somewhere in the vicinity of a sun. Still, it had pointed the way for a similar series of nested regressions within the real universe. The Devgestalt felt his mind whirling away before the vista of universes within universes within universes.

And the minds!

He saw there, part of the entity's very structure, another dozen threads that he recognized as the Web. Clearly, somehow, Web and Humanity had found a way to work together, to become part of the same—only then did the Gr'tak word occur to him with explosive perfection—*Associative*.

He saw the Gr'tak, and the DalRiss, established now on myriad worlds where life had been shaped to an unimaginable perfection of symbiotic harmony. He saw Daren's Communes—each infested with the parasite-symbionts that made them what they were. He saw others that he recognized but for whom he would never have claimed the trait of intelligence. Three from Earth itself caught his mind's eye: dolphins, mountain gorillas, and elephants, all three long extinct in the twenty-sixth century, yet somehow here, a part of what made the Galactic Mind what it was. How . . . ?

But there was no time to dwell on individual parts of that panoply of intelligence. He saw other minds, eldritch minds, minds so strange he could barely comprehend them, many so strange they were totally beyond his ken.

And he sensed others, heartwarmingly familiar. He sensed—he *thought* he sensed—others like himself, downloads inhabiting virtual worlds, or enjoying a strange, symbiotic existence within the Net.

The tapestry of Mind in the two galaxies numbered many, many trillions. Astonishingly, the downloaded personalities outnumbered the organics by a factor of hundreds of millions to one, inhabiting, for the most part, whole virtual universes; and all, by virtue of being part of the Grand Associative, were part of the Galactic Mind.

"*Someone once suggested that the evolution of intelligence was the way the universe learned about itself,*" the Voice said. "*That was truer than anyone of that age realized. We exist as multiple layers of emergent consciousness. Cells joined to shape brains, and consciousness. Billions of brains joined, in superconsciousness. And beyond that . . .*"

Dev saw. There could be no end, literally. Superconsciousnesses like the Overmind, but larger and more organized, joined a hundred billion others like itself across a galaxy, giving rise to a new transcendent hierarchy of intelligence.

An intelligence fit for a galaxy. . . .

And there were hundreds of billions of galaxies scattered across the universe. More, quantum theory demanded an infinity of universes, and these, too, were within the reach of Mind.

Senses reeling, the Devgestalt pulled back from that whirling, ever-deepening vista of Mind pervading a universe . . . and beyond, to a universe of universes.

*My God in heaven.* . . . Dev's thought was reverent. Almost worshipful. The sheer, perfect wonder of it all. . . .

"*Not quite,*" the entity said, answering the unvoiced thought, "*Not God. There are quite a few things beyond our scope at present, if only because the curvature of the universe limits direct observation of all space and all time. Complete omniscience will come with time, another few tens of billion of years, perhaps. I expect that by then we'll have evolved into something more . . . elegant than what you sense here.*

"*You will want us to return you to your own place and time. . . .*"

"You . . . can do that?"

"*Of course. Even in your epoch, you have already learned the truism that time and space are interchangeable. You may remain if you wish, but . . .*" Abruptly, the other Dev grinned, a frighteningly *human* expression. "*Remember that this is the second time I've taken part in this conversation.*"

Dev was thunderstruck. Until that moment, he'd assumed that the other Dev was a copy of himself, created on the spur of the moment to facilitate conversation. Now he realized that he was literally talking to himself . . . across a gulf of four thousand million years.

The intimation of his own survival, in any form, down through such vistas of time, left him reeling.

"Wait!" The attainment of all the GEF had been working

for had left him in a daze. It took agonizingly long milliseconds, but somehow the Devgestalt pulled itself together.
"Wait! If you're me . . . you must know we came here to
find out how to defeat the Web. Or at least, to learn what
mistakes to avoid. I . . . I sensed the Web as a part of the
Galactic Associative. What happened? What happened to
the Web? How did we beat it?"

The entity was silent for a long moment, and Dev had the
impression it was considering whether or not to tell him.

But surely that basic decision had already been made?
Four billion years ago, the struggle between Web and human
must have been resolved, and this fantastic intelligence surrounding and filling the Haven asteroid must know how it
had happened.

On the other hand, a terrible fear was growing in the back
of Dev's mind. The Web was as much a part of the Galactic
Associate as Humanity was. Besides, Mind on such a colossal scale could not possibly care what happened to primitives—any more than a human might care what happened
to one particular amoeba in a stagnant pond.

*"You're quite wrong there,"* the Voice said, again addressing unspoken thoughts. *"The Overmind had more
pressing concerns than the problems of the, to it, insignificant cells that constituted its being. An Associative of Over-
minds, however, is complex enough to be concerned with
each constituent cell within its body, no matter where it is
in space, no matter where in time."*

"You don't want to create a paradox by helping us. . . ."

*"Not at all. There is no paradox, when each decision
made branches to new infinities. The Associative's richness
and vitality lies in its diversity. That diversity includes myriad alternate realities.*

*"In fact, the Web of your epoch is a primitive, near-
mindless thing, conscious only of its own existence. Its immediate reaction to encounters with other intelligences is to
eliminate them as possible competitors. Its directives are
simple: utilize all available resources to perpetuate Self, and
protect Self by eliminating all rivals, a strategy that is decidedly contrary to our imperative of diversity and communication, In your future, the Web will learn the*

*advantages of symbiotic cooperation, but it will require out-
side help to achieve that understanding. In essence, it needs
to be reprogrammed.''*

"But . . . how . . . ?''

*"The organisms you call Naga were created by the Web,
eons before your own time.''*

"That's right. We learned they were sent out like scouts,
to begin converting worlds to the Web's use.''

*"But the Web no longer recognizes the Naga as Self.
However, the Naga are still the key to communications with
the Web, as they have been the key to communicating with
the other species you've encountered. The Web did not understand that even machine organisms can evolve, given the
pressures of natural selection and the possibility of mutation
through radiation, self-programming, and age. Sometime, in
the remote past, a key segment of coded communications
protocol that was part of every Naga cell was lost, possibly
because the Naga themselves didn't remember what it was
for and discarded it as inefficient. Program a Naga fragment
with the missing code, and with the information you wish to
convey to the Web. Allow it to be assimilated. You'll get
your message across. . . . ''*

Dev was about to ask for the missing code but sensed the
being was not going to help to that extent. Perhaps there
were rules to the cosmic order that prohibited too glaring
an intercession across the eons. It didn't matter, in any case,
for he'd already seen how the critical piece of information
could be won. There were millions of inert but intact Web
devices adrift both near Earth and at Nova Aquila. A Naga
fragment could easily absorb and pattern the program activating a Web machine, isolate the communications protocols, compare them with its own point by point, and
determine what was different.

Dev felt mildly annoyed with himself at that; he should
have seen it as the solution all along. . . .

There was not the least sensation of motion. One instant,
Haven, the two DalRiss craft, and the two Confederation
vessels were adrift between the galaxies. The next, they
were once more at Nova Aquila, the Stargate whirling in
the distance and, nearby, the Imperial squadron of Admiral

Hideshi. The other Confederation ships were visible in the distance, fleeing at high-boost.

They'd been returned to the place they'd departed from, and within minutes of the time they'd left. Only then did Dev realize he'd forgotten to ask what they could do about the Empire. In the same instant, he knew what the answer would have been. If the *Web* was a part of the Galactic Mind four billion years hence, what did that say about the essential unity of Man? On a cosmic scale, differences in cultures, in perceptions, in language, in detail of body or dress or thought, all were lost before the simple perception that Mind was all that mattered.

The Imperial warships had positioned themselves near the end of the Nova Aquila Stargate where One-GEF had vanished some minutes before, hunting dogs waiting for the rabbit to reemerge from the hole.

Within the Haven Mind was incalculable power. Power to easily break computer security codes, hunt down frequencies, brush aside access blocks. The gestalt could penetrate the Imperial squadron's computers within milliseconds, take them over, and do whatever was needed to cripple or destroy the ships. He remembered the race to destroy the *Hoshiryu*, falling from the skies over Singapore, and realized that the same task, with the same result, could be accomplished now without effort, in the blink of an eye.

"What will we do?" Kara asked.

Dev smiled. "We call them up," he said, "and we *talk*."

# Epilogue

For now, at least, the truce was holding.

The appearance in the Imperial squadron's rear of the Haven Planetoid, accompanied by two DalRiss city ships, a ryu-class carrier, and the *Gauss*, along with five squadrons of Confederation warflyers, had given Admiral Hideshi pause. A brief demonstration on Dev's part, crashing the weapons and fire-control AIs aboard the *Soraryu*, had turned pause into an indefinite stay of execution . . . and a truce. It wasn't, necessarily, the end of the Imperial–Confederation war. It might, for all any of them knew, be only the beginning. But for the moment, both sides were talking, *communicating*, and while they were talking, they weren't killing one another.

It was a start.

It was a start, too, when a number of Web kickers were reactivated through a link-up with the Naga core of the Haven Planetoid. A few seconds of analysis provided the missing code string in the Naga communications protocol; the strange entities really were organic computers, with as literal and as straightforward an understanding of the universe as any of that breed. Quite possibly, they could have provided the answer all along, if anyone had been able to ask the proper questions.

Soon, the Haven Planetoid would depart for the Galactic Core. The Devgestalt would encounter the Web, use the code sequence, and allow itself to be assimilated by the Web.

"I don't want you to go," Katya told him. They were

meeting a final time in the virtual simulation of Cascadia, Dev and Katya, Vic, Kara, Daren and Taki. An extended, if somewhat unorthodox family. "None of us do."

"I'm not leaving, not really," Dev replied. "There are enough copies of myself in the Net now, that you'll still have me around no matter what happens at the Core."

"Those are copies. . . ."

"*I'm* a copy," Dev reminded her. "The original Dev died a long time ago. Remember? Besides, if there's no difference between a copy and the original, down to the quantum scale, they *are* the same."

"He knows he survives in the future," Kara said. "We *all* do, though I'm not sure I see how."

"You know," Vic said, "there's a religion growing up in some parts of the Confederation. I think in the Empire as well. It holds that the Overmind will somehow absorb everyone when they die, make them part of itself. And that it will eventually move throughout time, taking to itself the minds, the souls, if you will, of everyone who has ever lived or ever *will* live. A rational basis for a belief in God."

"I never believed in God," Daren said thoughtfully. "But if there's no difference between the copy and the idea it was taken from . . ."

"I think we've glimpsed a tiny, tiny shred of one of the great, driving truths of human existence," Dev told them. "It hinges on the old idea that death need not be an end, but a kind of graduation. I don't know if we've really seen the answer to that. My survival as a download doesn't guarantee the same for everyone. But it's comforting to know we *might* have touched the answer to a very, very old and human question."

"A lot of people are turning to downloads as a way to beat death," Taki pointed out. "And we saw in the Galactic Associative that the downloads are going to outnumber the organics some day. Maybe the new religion has something to it."

"I don't hold much with religions," Katya said. "In the long run, they're human institutions for dealing with human problems. But it's going to be fun to see if there's a reality behind this one."

"By the way," Dev said, looking at Kara. "I understand the ranks of the downloaded lost a couple the other day. How are they?"

She grinned. "Will Daniels is back on active duty. Ran is still recovering, but they tell me he's going to be okay. It was your patterning technique that did it, though. Thanks. . . ."

With a potentially infinite number of duplications possible, the techs working with Ran Ferris and Willis Daniels and a number of other RDTS victims had been able to try numerous techniques for reinstalling the mental software that were downloaded minds in the wetware–hardware of the patients' brains. In fact, copies of both men remained on the Net; there was talk now that, just as everyone had a Companion, everyone might soon have a downloaded copy of himself existing on the Net, a kind of alter ego to conduct research, extend human experience . . . and even serve as a backup copy in the case of the original's death.

Dev had already been exploring numerous possibilities there, working with both AIs and human, DalRiss, and Gr'tak experts in designing the shape of the new Net.

A Net that, one day, would evolve into the Associative he'd met in the distant future.

The research had been intriguing to Dev, in particular. Cloned bodies—or even new generations of hubots—offered the hope that one day he would be able to reinstall himself in a flesh-and-blood body. When he did so, though, it would be in a world so transformed by the power and the scope of Net consciousness that it would, likely, be unrecognizable to anyone alive now. Dev was more than willing to concede that he might not mind remaining immortal after all. . . .

"When are you going?" Katya asked. "To the Core, I mean."

"As fast as we can arrange it, Mums," Kara replied. "Those gokking machines came too damned close to frying Earth. We're going to have to do something about them *fast* . . . before they try again."

"Oh, I don't know about that, Kara," Dev said, letting his image settle back in the warm comfort of the electronic world about him. "In fact, we have all the time in the universe."

# AVONOVA PRESENTS
# AWARD-WINNING NOVELS
# FROM MASTERS OF SCIENCE FICTION

A DEEPER SEA
*by Alexander Jablokov*          71709-3/ $4.99 US/ $5.99 Can

BEGGARS IN SPAIN
*by Nancy Kress*                 71877-4/ $5.99 US/ $7.99 Can

FLYING TO VALHALLA
*by Charles Pellegrino*          71881-2/ $4.99 US/ $5.99 Can

ETERNAL LIGHT
*by Paul J. McAuley*             76623-X/ $4.99 US/ $5.99 Can

DAUGHTER OF ELYSIUM
*by Joan Slonczewski*            77027-X/ $5.99 US/ $6.99 Can

NIMBUS
*by Alexander Jablokov*          71710-7/ $4.99 US/ $5.99 Can

THE HACKER AND THE ANTS
*by Rudy Rucker*                 71844-8/ $4.99 US/ $6.99 Can

GENETIC SOLDIER
*by George Turner*               72189-9/ $5.50 US/ $7.50 Can

# THE CONTINUATION
# OF THE FABULOUS
# INCARNATIONS OF IMMORTALITY
# SERIES

# PIERS ANTHONY

# FOR LOVE OF EVIL
75285-9/ $5.99 US/ $7.99 Can

# AND ETERNITY
75286-7/ $5.99 US/ $7.99 Can